CRITICAL RAVES FOR
FOREIGNER

"Close-grained and carefully constructed . . . a book that will stick in your mind . . . ." —*Locus*

"Ms. Cherryh develops her fascinating premise with immense subtlety and stunning perception."
—*Rave Reviews*

"A large new Cherryh novel is always welcome . . . a return to the anthropological science fiction in which she has made such a name is a double pleasure . . . superlatively drawn aliens and characterization."
—*Chicago Sun-Times*

"Cherryh plays her strongest suit in this exploration of human/alien contact, producing an incisive study-in-contrast of what it means to be human in a world where trust is non-existent."
—*Library Journal*

DAW TITLES BY C.J. CHERRYH

C.J. CHERRYH
FOREIGNER

A novel of first contact.

DAW BOOKS, INC.

DONALD A. WOLLHEIM, FOUNDER

375 Hudson Street, New York, NY 10014

ELIZABETH R. WOLLHEIM

SHEILA E. GILBERT

PUBLISHERS

DAW Book Collectors No. 941.

DAW Books are distributed by Penguin U.S.A.

First Printing, November 1994
4 5 6 7 8 9

DAW TRADEMARK REGISTERED
U.S. PAT OFF. AND FOREIGN COUNTRIES
—MARCA REGISTRADA.
HECHO EN U.S.A.

PRINTED IN THE U.S.A.

BOOK ONE

I

I t was the deep dark, unexplored except for robotic visitors. The mass that existed here was Earth's second stepping-stone toward a strand of promising stars; and, for the first manned ship to drop into its influence, the mass point was a lonely place, void of the electromagnetic chaff that filled human space, the gossip and chatter of trade, the instructions of human control to ships and crews, the fast, sporadic communication of machine talking to machine. Here, only the radiation of the mass, the distant stars, and the background whisper of existence itself rubbed up against the sensors with force enough to attract attention.

Here, human beings had to remember that the universe was far wider than their little nest of stars—that, in the universe at large, silence was always more than the noisiest shout of life. Humans explored and intruded against it, and built their stations and lived their lives, a biological contamination of the infinite, a local and temporary condition.

And not the sole inhabitants of the universe: that was no longer possible for humans to doubt. So wherever the probes said life might exist, wherever stars looked friendly to living creatures, humans ventured with some caution, and unfolded their mechanical ears and listened into the dark—as *Phoenix* listened intently during her hundred hours traverse of realspace.

She heard nothing at any range—which pleased her captains and the staff aboard. *Phoenix* wanted to find no prior claims to what she wanted, which was a bridge to a new, resources-rich territory, most particularly and immediately a G5 star designated T-230 in the Defense codebooks, 89020 on the charts, and mission objective, in the plans *Phoenix* carried in her data banks.

Reach the star, unlimber the heavy equipment . . . create a station that would welcome traders and expand human presence into a new and profitable area of space.

So *Phoenix* carried the bootstrap components for that construction, the algaes and the cultures for a station's life-sustaining tanks, the plans and the circuit maps, the diagrams and the processes and the programs, the data and the detail; she carried as well the miner-pilots and the mechanics and the builders and processors and the technical staff that would be, for their principal reward, earliest shareholders in the first-built trading station to develop down this chain of stars—Earth's latest and most confident colonial commitment, with all the expertise of past successes.

Optics told Mother Earth where the rich stars were. Robots probed the way without any risk of human life . . . probed and returned with their navigational data and their first-hand observations: T-230 was a system so rich *Phoenix* ran mass-loaded to the limit, streaking along at a rate a ship dared carry when she expected no other traffic, and when she had no doubt of refuel capabilities at her destination. She shoved the gas and dust around her into a brief, bright disturbance, while her crew ran its hundred-hour routine of maintenance, recalibrations, and navigational checks. The captains shared coffee on the last watch before re-entry, took the general reports, and approved the schedule the way the navigator, McDonough, keyed it.

But what the pilot received of that discussion was a blinking green dot on the edge of his display and a vague sense that things were proceeding comfortably on schedule, aboard a ship in good order. Taylor was On, which meant Taylor had input coming at him at rates it took a computer interface to sort, and, insulated from the tendencies of an unassisted human mind to process laterally and distract itself from the rush of data, Taylor had his ears devoted to computer signals and his eyes and his perceptions chemically adjusted to the computer-filtered velocity of the ship's passage.

The green dot had to be there before he hyped out. The dot had showed up, and what other human beings did about it was not in any sense Taylor's business or realization. When that exit point came at him, and time folded up in his face, he reached confidently ahead and through space, toward T-230.

He was a master pilot. The drugs in his blood made him highly specific in his concentration, and highly abstract in his understandings of the data that flashed in front of his eyes and screamed into his ears. He would have targeted *Phoenix* into the heart of hell if those had been the coordinates the computer handed him. But it was to T-230 he was looking.

For that reason, he was the only one aboard aware when the ship kept going, and time stayed folded.

And stayed.

His heart began to pound in realtime, his eyes were fixed on screens flashing red, lines, and then dots, as those lines became hypothetical, and last of all a black screen, where POINT ERROR glowed in red letters like the irretrievable judgment of God.

Heartbeat kept accelerating. He reached for the ABORT and felt the cap under his fingers. He had no vision now. It was all POINT ERROR. He scarcely felt the latch: and time was still folding as he uncapped the ABORT, for a reason he no longer remembered. Unlike the computer, he had no object but that single, difficult necessity.

Program termination.

Blank screen.

POINT ERROR.

God had no more data.

II

The ship dropped and the alarm sounded: This is not a drill. Computer failure. This is not a drill. . . .

McDonough's heart was thumping and the sweat was running from exertion as he pressed the button to query Taylor. Every screen was blank.

This is not a drill. . . .

The hard-wired Abort was in action. *Phoenix* was saving herself. She blew off *v* with no consideration of fragile human bodies inside her.

Phoenix then attempted to re-boot her computers from inflowing information. She queried her captain, her navigator, and her pilot and co-pilot, with painful shocks to the Q-patch. Two more such jolts, before McDonough found data taking shape on his screens at the navigation station.

Video displayed the star.

No, two stars, one glaring blue-white, one faint red. McDonough sat frozen at his post, seeing in *Phoenix'* future-line a coasting drift to white, nuclear hell.

"Where are we?" someone asked. "Where are we?"

It was a question the navigator took for accusation. McDonough felt it like a blow to his already abused gut, and looked toward the pilot for an answer. But Taylor was just staring at his screens, doing nothing, not moving.

"Inoki," McDonough said. But the co-pilot was slumped unconscious or worse.

"Get Greene up here. Greene and Goldberg, to the bridge." That was LaFarge on the staff channel, senior captain, hard-nosed and uncompromising, calling up the two back-up pilots.

McDonough felt the shakes set in, wondered if LaFarge was going to call up all the backups, and oh, one part of him wanted that, wanted to go to his bunk and lie there inert and not have to deal with reality, but he had to learn what that binary star was and where they were and what mistake he might conceivably have committed to put them here. The nutrients the med-plug was shooting into him were making him sick. The sight in front of him was insane. Optics couldn't be wrong. The robots couldn't be wrong. Their instruments couldn't be wrong.

"Sir?" Karly McEwan was sitting beside him, as stunned as he was—his own immediate number two: she was shaken, but she was punching buttons, trying, clamp-jawed as she was, to get sense out of chaos. "Sir? Go to default? Sir?"

"Default for now," he muttered, or some higher brain function did, while his conscious intelligence was operating on some lower floor. The 'for now' that had bubbled up as a caution hit his faltering intelligence like a pronouncement of doom, because he didn't see any quick way to get a baseline for this system. "Spectrum analysis, station two and three. Chart comparison, station four. Station five, rerun the initiation and target coordinates." The forebrain was still giving orders. The rest was functioning like Taylor, which was not at all. "We need a medic up here. Is Kiyoshi on the bridge? Taylor and Inoki are in trouble."

"Are we stable?" Kiyoshi Tanaka's voice, asking if it was safe to unbelt and go after the pilots, but every question seemed to echo with double meanings, every question trailed off into unknowns and unknowables. "Stable as we can be," LaFarge said, and meanwhile the spectral analysis program was turning up a flood of data and running comparisons on every star system on file, a steady crawl of non-matches on McDonough's number one screen, while the bottom of it reported NOT A MATCH, 3298 ITEMS EXAMINED.

"We're getting questions from channel B," came from Communications. "Specials are requesting to leave quarters. Requesting screen output."

Taylor's routine. Taylor had always given the passengers a view, leaving Earth system, entering the mass points, and leaving them. . . .

"No," LaFarge said harshly. "No image." A blind man could see it was trouble. "Say it's a medical on the bridge. Say we're busy."

Tanaka had reached Taylor and Inoki, and was injecting something into Taylor, McDonough was aware of that. The passengers were feeling the variance in routine, and the NOT A MATCH hadn't changed.

SEARCH FURTHER?

The computer had run out of local stars.

"Karly, you prioritized search from default one?"

"From default," Navigation Two answered. The search for matching stars had started with Sol and the near neighborhood. "Our vector, plus and minus ten lights."

The sick feeling in McDonough's gut increased.

Nothing made sense. The backup pilots showed up, asking distracting questions nobody could answer, the same questions every navigator was asking the instruments and the records. The captain told the medic to get Taylor and Inoki off the bridge—the captain swore when he said it, and McDonough distractedly started running checks of his own while Tanaka got the two pilots on their feet—Taylor could walk, but Taylor looked blind to what was going on. Inoki was moving, but just scarcely: one of the com techs had to haul him up and carry him, once Tanaka unbuckled him and unplugged the tube from his implant. Neither of them looked at Greene or Goldberg as they passed. Taylor's eyes were set on infinity. Inoki's were shut.

SEARCH FURTHER? the computer asked, having searched all the stars within thirty lights of Earth.

"We stand at 5% on fuel," the captain reported calmly—a potential death sentence. "Any com pickup at all?"

At this star? McDonough asked himself, and: "Dead silent," Communications said. "The star's noisy enough to mask God-knows-what."

"Go long range, back up our vector. Assume we over-shot the star."

"Aye, sir."

A moment later, hydraulics whined up on the hull. The big dish was unpacking and unfolding, preparing to listen. *V* was down to a crawl safe for its deployment—safe, if it was Earth's own Sun, but it wasn't. There was no data on this system. They were gathering it, drinking it in every sensor, but nothing gave them even minimal certainty there wasn't a rock in their path. Nobody had ever come in at a close binary, or a mass as large. God only knew what had happened to the field.

McDonough's hands were shaking as he punched up the scope of both search sequences, approaching a hundred lights distant in all directions, search negative, past their objective. They still didn't know where they were, but with 5% fuel in reserve, they weren't leaving soon, either. They had the miner-craft: thank God they had the miner-craft and the station components. They might gather system ice and refuel. . . .

Except that was a radiation hell out there, except the solar wind that blue-white sun threw out was a killing wind. This was not a star where flesh and blood could live, and if the miners did go out to work in that, they had to limit their time outside.

Or if the ship was, as it might well be, infalling, on a massive star's gravity slope . . . they'd meet that radiation close-up before they went down.

"We've rerun the initiation sequence," Greene said, from Taylor's seat. "We don't find any flaw in the com-mands."

Meaning Taylor had keyed in on what navigation had given him. A cold apprehension gnawed at McDonough's stomach.

"Any answer, Mr. McDonough?"

"Not yet, sir." He kept his voice calm. He didn't feel that way. He hadn't made a mistake. But he couldn't prove it by anything they had from the instruments.

A ship couldn't come out of hyperspace aimed differently than it had on entry. It didn't. It couldn't.

But if some hyperspace particle had screwed the redundant storage, if the computer had lost its destination point and POINT ERROR was the answer, they couldn't run far enough on their fuel mass to be out of sight of stars they knew.

Two stars, in any degree near each other, both with spectra matching the charts, were all they needed. Any two-star match against their charts could start to locate them, and they couldn't be more than five lights off their second mass point, if they'd run out all the fuel they were carrying—couldn't be. Not farther than twenty lights from Earth total at most.

But there wasn't a massive blue-white within twenty lights of the Sun, except Sirius, and this wasn't Sirius. Spectra of those paired suns were a no-match. It wasn't making sense. Nothing was.

He started looking for pulsars. When you were out of short yardsticks you looked for the long ones, the ones that wouldn't lie, and you started thinking about half-baked theories, like cosmic macrostructures, folded interfaces, or any straw of reason that might give a mind something to work on or suggest a direction they'd gone or offer a hint which of a hundred improbables was the truth.

III

Something's wrong, was the word running the outer corridors from the minute that the station staff and construction workers had permission to move about. The rumor moved into the lounges, where staffers and pusher pilots and mechanics all stood shoulder to shoulder in front of video displays that said, on every damned channel, STAND BY.

"Why don't they tell us something?" someone asked, a breach of the peace. "They ought to tell us something."

Another tech said, "Why don't we get the vid? We always got the vid before."

"We can go to hell," a pusher pilot said. "We can all go to hell. They're too good to bother."

"It's probably all right," somebody else said, and there was an uneasy silence—because it didn't feel like the other times. That had been a hell of a jolt the ship had dealt when she braked, coming in, and the techs who knew anything about deep space were as long-faced and nervous as the Sol-space miners and construction jocks, who had no prior voyages at all to draw on.

It wasn't Probably All Right in Neill Cameron's thinking, either—even a pusher mechanic like him could feel the difference between this system entry and the last. Friends and couples like himself and Miyume Little were generally just standing close and waiting. Miyume's hand was cold and still. His was sweating.

Possibly—he'd said it to Miyume—the techs up topside were working up some big show for their arrival in their new home.

Maybe there was just a routine lot to do because they were shutting down and staying here—the crew might be figuring their insystem course or their local resources, and they'd get a take-hold call any time now, so that *Phoenix* could do course corrections. He'd heard that speculation offered by someone in the lounge. It was what he sincerely hoped.

Or *Phoenix* was in some sort of trouble. That was implicit in all the questions . . . but it was much too soon to panic. The ship's crew was up there doing their job and a one-sun spacer brat at least knew better than to borrow trouble or start rumors—either with hopeful lies or the speculations on the worst case that had to be in everybody's thoughts, like infall, an entry too near the star itself.

Foolish fear. Robots had been here and fixed T-230's position with absolute certainty. *Phoenix'* crew was an experienced, hand-picked lot—*Phoenix* herself had run trade for five years before they diverted her to the stations start-up at T-230, and the U.N. didn't commit billions to any second-rate equipment or any crew that was going to drop a ship into a star.

God, infall couldn't be the trouble up there. That was too remote a chance.

He could take pusher and miner-craft apart and put them together again. Most that went wrong with an insystem miner ship, a mechanic could fix with a good guess and a screwdriver; but what could go wrong with a stardrive—what could go amiss in the massive engines that generated effects into hyperspace—fell entirely outside his competency and his understanding.

The STAND BY flasher suddenly went off. A starview came on-screen and a collective breath of relief went up from the room, chilled by a murmur of consternation from a handful of techs, all standing together in the center of the room. Miyume's hand tightened on his, his on hers, while the tech staff were saying things like, That's not right and Where in hell *are* we?

The white glare looked like a star to him. Maybe it did to Miyume. But techs were shaking their heads. And there was a red glow in the view he didn't understand.

"That's not a G5," one of them said. "It's a damn binary." And when ordinary worker-types started asking what he meant, the tech snapped, "We're not where we're supposed to be, you stupid ass!"

What are they talking about? Neill asked himself. What they were hearing wasn't making sense, and Miyume was looking scared. The techs were saying calm down and not to start rumors, but the tech who had claimed they were wrong shouted over the other voices,

"We're not at any damned G5!"

"So where are we?" Miyume asked, the first words she'd said. She was asking him, or anyone, and Neill didn't know how to answer that—he didn't see how they could miss T-230 if they had gotten to any star at all . . . by what he knew, by the education he'd had, ships just kept going in the directions they were going, that was a basic law of physics . . . wasn't it? You aimed and you built your field and you went, and if you had fuel enough you got there.

And meanwhile his hardware-biased brain was thinking, Could we have overshot? How far off could we be, on the fuel we've got?

"This is Capt. LaFarge . . ."

That was the general address, and people shouted urgently for quiet.

". . . unfortunate circumstance," was all that got through, that Neill could hear, and he was desperate to hear what the captain said. Miyume's nails bit deeply into his hand, people were talking again, and Miyume shouted, "Shut up!" at the top of her lungs, at the same time others did.

". . . positional problem," was the next clear phrase. Then: *"which does not pose the ship any imminent danger . . ."*

"That's a blue-white star!" a tech shouted. "What's he think it is?"

Someone got the fool shut down. Others hushed the ones that wanted to ask questions.

". . . ask everyone to go about business as usual," LaFarge was saying. *"And assist the technical crew while we try to establish position. We'll be looking into our resources in this system for refueling. We're very well equipped for dealing with this situation. That's all. Stand easy."*

'Establish position' sounded comforting. 'Refueling' sounded even more hopeful. 'Well equipped for dealing with this,' sounded as if the crew already had a plan. Neill clung to that part of it, while a frantic part of him was thinking: This can't be happening to us, not to us. . . .

Things can't go wrong with this ship, there were too many precautions, everything taken care of . . .

They'd been screened, their skills had been tested, they'd had to have recommendations atop recommendations even to come close to this job. They didn't send foul-ups on a ship that carried Earth's whole damned colonial program, and disasters didn't happen to a mission as important as this one. People had planned too long. People had been too careful. Everything had been going so right.

"Establish position," a tech said. "I don't like that 'Establish position.' Are we talking about infall?"

"No," a senior tech said. "We're talking about where we are. Which is clearly not where we're supposed to be."

"Refuel, hell," another tech said. "That's a radiation bath out there."

The pusher-craft aren't shielded to work out there, Neill thought, with a sudden sick feeling, as the dynamics came clear to him. Jupiter was a radiation hazard. This thing . . . this double sun, with light that made the cameras flare and distort . . .

The miner-pilots couldn't survive it. Not for any long operation. The miners couldn't deploy here, not without an inevitable cost, as the exposure tags went dark, and the hours of running time added up. Pusher-craft were shielded for the environment they had to deal with, and their designated environment had been a mild, friendly G5.

He didn't say that. Miyume looked scared. Probably he did. The numbers started adding up, that was what the pilots said when things started going wrong: the company might lie, and the captain the company hired might refuse you answers, but the numbers wouldn't deceive you, no matter what.

They added, and the result didn't, wouldn't, couldn't change from what it was. Wishes didn't count.

IV

McDonough's shadow arrived, hovered over Taylor's chair, saying there hadn't been a mistake. Taylor processed that datum in the informational void. Things came painstakingly slowly or not at all. Other inputs in his surroundings were irrelevant. His mind refused distraction to trivia. But the navigator he paid close attention to ... and tried to ask him, although one had to slow the brain down incredibly to frame a single complex sound:

"What?"

Babble, then, unauthorized people touching him and talking to him. Taylor tuned the voices out until McDonough's voice came back, telling him in its infinite slowness that they were fueled up.

That was something to process: they'd been at this star some months of realtime, then. Major datum.

The navigator said next that Greene was sick, something about an accident, about miner-pilots and crews dead or dying of radiation, pilots training pilots to do their job once they were dead ... something about the star they hoped to go to. The navigator had one for him, and they were fueled and going now, away from this hellish vicinity, this double monster that sang to him constantly in his slow-moving dark. For the first time in a recent, lonely eternity, new data came in.

"Point," Taylor managed to say, needing destination, and McDonough fed him coordinates that didn't make sense off the baseline, or with where they had to be.

"Wrong," Taylor said. But McDonough said then that they'd taken a new zero point, at this star, that they'd spotted a possible mass point by optics and targeted a G5 beyond it.

McDonough reeled off more numbers—Taylor grew drunk with them, the relief he felt was so great, but he didn't process forward, he was still listening to McDonough with painful, slow attention. McDonough said the crew and the captain wanted him to know they were going to move. Said—McDonough wasn't precise on the matter—they thought he might have some awareness of the ship's motion.

Hell, yes, he did. Things were moving faster and faster. There were actual data-points in sight, more than one at a time. Taylor said, laboriously, at McDonough's speed, "Bridge. Now."

McDonough went away. The data stopped. Taylor waited. And waited. Sometimes it seemed to be years, and there was no sanity but to wait for that next point, that next, authorized contact.

But McDonough's voice came back, after a long, long time, saying the captain wanted him to sit as pilot on the bridge. Goldberg would back him up. Greene, McDonough reminded him, was sick. Inoki was dead. Three years ago. Earth time.

Datum. He had to factor in Goldberg as backup. His mind wanted to race. He held it down. There would be numbers. At long last there would be data at speed, mission resumed.

He sat down. He felt the chair around him. Somebody said—it was an authorized voice, Tanaka, he thought—that he didn't need the drug. That his brain manufactured it on its own now.

Interesting datum. It accounted for things. Goldberg talked, then, saying how they were clear to hell and gone from Earth and Sol, that they still didn't know how they'd gotten there, but they'd gone through something they hoped wasn't attached permanently to this star.

Watch it, Goldberg said. Are you hearing me?

"Yes," Taylor said, with slow patience. But numbers had begun to proliferate.

He saw the destination mass. He had it. He couldn't lose it this time.

Goldberg was with him. And the universe was talking

to him again, at a rate he could understand. He skipped into the mass well and out again with a blithe disregard of gravity. He had a G5 in sight. Goldberg stopped talking to him, or had just gotten too slow to hear. He had the star and he reached for it, calm and sure now that those numbers were true.

He brought his ship in.

He shut down, system by system, in the light of a yellow sun.

Then he knew he could sleep.

BOOK TWO

I

The foreign star was up, riding with the moon above the sandstone hills, in the last of the sunlight, and Manadgi, squatting above strange, regular tracks in the clay of a stream-bank, and seeing in them the scars of a machine on the sandstone, tucked his coat between his knees and listened to all quarters of the sky, the auspicious and the inauspicious alike. He heard only the small chirps and the *o'o'o'click* of a small creature somewhere in the brush.

There were more unfixed stars now, tiny specks of light in irregular motion about the first. Sometimes the very sharp-eyed could count them, two and three motes at a time, shining before dawn or before the dusk, in proximity to the foreign star.

Their numbers changed. They combined and uncombined. Should one count the foreign star in their number or reckon only the attendant stars, and from what date? How could one reckon whether such activities were auspicious or not?

Neither had the astronomers been able to say, when, a hundred and twenty-two years ago, the foreign star had first begun to grow in the heavens, a star so faint at first that only the strongest eyes could see it, so the story was—a star that rose and set with the moon, in its ancient dance with the sun.

Then the astronomers had been embarrassed, because with their lenses and their orreries they still could not define that apparition as a moon or a star, since in appearance and behavior it was both, and they could not swear to its influence. Some thought it good, some thought it bad and, as many events as proponents could bring up on one side to prove it good, opponents could prove as many of bad issue. Only nand' Jadishesi had been unequivocal, insisting, cleverly, that it portended change.

But so, also and finally, most astronomers swore, while the star grew in magnitude year by year, and gathered companions to itself: continual instability.

Now dared one call it fortunate?

The tracks yonder, the marks of the machines, were, beyond dispute, real, and bore out the story of repeated excursions from the landing-site—even at dusk, even to the eyes of a city-dweller. The Tachi, who herded in these hills and knew them as well as a city-dweller knew his own street, said that the machines had fallen from the sky, suspended from flowers, and drifted down and down and down by this means until they landed.

So was it indeed from the clouds that the visitations had come, and with those descending flowers, came machines that ran about the land ripping up trees and frightening Tachi children.

Manadgi had doubted that origin in the clouds the same way he doubted that autumn moon-shadow was curative of rheumatism. People nowadays knew that the earth circled the sun, that in the axial tilt they had their seasons confirmed. All such things they had come to understand in this age of reason, and understood them better once the astronomers of the aiji's court had taken to the problem of the misbehaving star and commissioned better and better lenses.

The moon, as all educated people knew now, was a sphere of planetary nature, traveling through the ether, the same as the earth—their smaller cousin, as it were, measuring its year by the earth as the earth measured its time by the sun.

So the falling of machines out of the heavens was astounding, but not incredible. In considering this awesome track which no farmer's cart had ever made in the clay, one could easily suppose people lived on the moon. One could imagine them falling down to earth on great white petals, or on canvas sails, which Manadgi hoped to witness for himself tomorrow, that being the full of the moon, the likeliest source of visitors.

Or, for an alternative source of flower-sails, there was the unfixed star, the persistent oddness of which argued at least that it had something to do with this manifestation of machines, since it was a newcomer to the skies, and since it had been, in the last forty years, acquiring a plethora of what might be unfixed moonlets, mere sparks, yet.

But again, Manadgi thought,—the sparks themselves might grow—or come nearer to the earth and deal with men.

Perhaps moon-folk had drawn the foreign star to the position it presently occupied, sailing their created world across the winds of the ether, in the way that ocean-faring ships used the worldly winds.

There had thus far seemed no correspondence between the appearance of the star or the stage of the moon phases when the flower-sails came down.

But one could wonder about the Tachi's records-keeping as well as their grasp of the situation, when, simple herders that they were, they insisted on flowers instead of ordinary canvas and, in the clear evidence of people falling from the clouds, had endured this event for a quarter of a year debating what to do—until now, now that the machines were well-established and ravaging the land as they pleased, the Tachi aiji demanded immediate and severe action from the aiji of the Mospheiran Association to halt this destruction of their western range and the frightening of their children.

Manadgi stood up, dusted his hands, and found, in the last of the sunlight, a flat stone to take him dry-shod across the brook—a slab of sandstone the wheeled machine had crushed from the bank as it was gouging a track up the hill. It was a curiously made track, a pattern in its wheels repeating a design, its weight making deep trenches where the ground was wet. And not bogging down, evidencing the power of its engine ... again, not at all astonishing: if the moon-folk could catch the winds of the ether and ride enormous sails down to earth, they were formidable engineers. And might prove formidable in other ways, one could suspect.

He certainly had no difficulty following the machine, by the trail of uprooted trees and mud-stained grass. Dusk was deepening, and he only hoped for the moon-folk not to find him in the dark, before he could find them and determine the nature and extent of their activity.

Not far, the Tachi aiji had said. In the middle of the valley, beyond the grandmother stone.

Almost he failed to recognize the stone when he climbed up to it. It lay on its side.

Distressing. But one would already suppose by the felling of trees and the devastation of the stream down below, that moon-folk were a high-handed lot, lacking fear of judgment on themselves, or perhaps simply lacking any realization that the Tachi were civilized people, who ought to be respected.

He intended to find out, at least, what was the strength of the intruders, or whether they could be dealt with. That was ahead of other questions, such as where they did come from, or what the unfixed star might be and what it meant.

All these things Manadgi hoped to find out.

Until he crested the next rise in the barren clay track of the wheeled machine, and saw, in the twilight, the huge buildings, white, and square, and starkly unadorned.

He sank down on his heels. There was no other way to hide in the barrenness the moon-folk had made, this bare-earth, lifeless sameness that extended the width of the valley around cold, square buildings painted the color of death, their corners in no auspicious alignment with the hills. He put his hands in front of his mouth to warm them, because the sinking of the sun chilled the air.

Or perhaps because the strangeness suddenly seemed overwhelming, and because he doubted he could go alive into that place so ominously painted and so glaringly, perhaps defiantly, misaligned to the earth—he began to be in dread of what he might find as their purpose, these folk who fell to Earth on petal sails.

II

The sun eclipsed by the planetary rim was a glorious sight from space, but a station-dweller saw it only from cameras and stored tape—while a planet-dweller saw it once a day, if he cared to go outside, or stop on his way back from work. And Ian Bretano still did care to, because it was still that new to him.

New and disorienting, if he fell to thinking about where he was on the planet ... or where home was, or what it was or would be, for the rest of his life.

And sometimes, at night when the stars swung above the valley, sometimes when the moon was above the horizon line and all of space was over their heads, he missed the station desperately and asked himself for a wild, panicked moment why he had ever wanted to be down here at the bottom of a planetary well, why he'd ever left his family and his friends and why he couldn't have contributed to the cause from the clean, safe laboratories upstairs—Upstairs, they all called it, now, having taken up the word from the first team down.

Upstairs—as if the station and safety and families and friends were still all as attainable as a ride in a lift.

But family and friends weren't in their reach—wouldn't be soon, nor might ever be, for all they could know. That was the gamble they had all taken, coming down here and subjecting themselves to unregulated

weather and air so thin that just walking across the compound was strenuous exercise.

They'd acclimate to thinner air with no trouble, the
medics claimed, they'd adjust—although a botanist who'd
previously had mostly to do with algaes in convenient
tanks and taxonomy in recorded text wasn't sure that he
was adequate to be a discoverer or a pioneer.

Still, for all of the discomforts there were compensa-
tions. Every specimen in the lab was a new species, the
chemistry and the genetics was all to discover.

And for those of them who'd grown used to the day
sky, and all that glowing, dust-diffracted blue space overhead, for those of them who had convinced their stomachs that they weren't going to fall off the planet when
they looked outward to the horizon—thank God for the
hills around them, that gave the illusion of a positive, not
a negative curvature—they could take deliberate chances
with their stomachs, walk with their eyes on an opaque
sky and watch the colors change behind the hills as the
world turned its face to deep space.

Every evening and every morning brought new varia-
tions of weather and different shadows on the hills.

Weather and hills ... words they'd learned in Earth
Science, from photos that had never hinted at the trans-
parencies of a worldly sky, or the coolth of a storm wind
and the rushing sound it made in the grasses. He still
found it unnerving that windows dared be so thin that
thunder rattled them. He'd never realized that a cloud
passing over the sun would cool the air so quickly. He'd
never have guessed that storms had a smell. He'd never
imagined the complexity of sound traveling across a landscape, or the smells, both pleasant and unpleasant—
smells that might be more acute once his nose quit
bleeding and his lungs quit aching.

He still found it hard to make the mental conversion
from being on the station looking at tape of a planet he
couldn't touch, and being on the ground looking at a
point of light he might never reach again.

It had been a hard good-bye, Upstairs. Parents, grandparents, friends ... what could one say? He'd hugged them for what he knew might be the last time, in the lounge where the cameras weren't allowed—and he'd been fine right down to the moment he'd seen his father's expression, at which point his doubts had made a sudden lump in his throat and stayed there for the duration of the capsule ride, even after they had felt the parachute deploy.

"See you," he'd said to them when he was leaving. "Five years. In five years, you'll ride down."

That was the plan—set up the base, and start taking selected colonists down—force the building of the reusable lander, once they'd found something the Guild wanted badly enough; and priority on that safer transport would go to family and friends of the team members on the initial phase of the on-world mission. That was a privilege he won for them by being here and taking the risk ... not quite among the first down, but still on the list, dropped in early enough to be counted a pioneer.

God, he'd been scared when he'd walked out of that room and into the suiting area, with the ten other team members. If there'd been a way to turn around, run back, beg to wait for another year of capsule-drops, to prove to him that that chute was going to open.

If that was being a hero, he didn't want to do it twice, and God, the freefall descent ... and the landing ...

The first astronauts had done planetfall in such capsules, by parachute. The history files said so. All old Earth's tech was in the data banks. They'd known that that first capsule would work, the same way they knew the recoverable lander was going to work—when the Guild turned loose enough resources to see it built.

But come what might, they were down. The Guild might have refused to fly them down, but the Guild hadn't had the right to stop the launch of what they'd built—and what they'd built, by its unpowered nature, hadn't needed Guild pilots; what they'd built had come all of spare parts and plans from history files the Guild in its wisdom had called irrelevant to where they were.

The Guild could have applied force to stop them, hauled the capsules back after launch—of course, the Guild could still do that, and the division was potentially that bitter.

But so had the station its own force to use, if the Guild wanted to play by those rules—and the Guild evidently didn't. The Guild hadn't reached consensus, maybe, or hadn't expected the first cargo lander to make it, or had a crisis of, God help them, conscience—no station-dweller knew what passed in Guild councils, but the almighty Guild hadn't made a move yet. And the Guild couldn't starve them out once they were down here without bringing about a confrontation with the station that they'd already and repeatedly declined. The food and equipment drops, so far, kept coming.

Food and equipment drops that might not be absolutely critical by this time next year. And then let the Guild order what they liked. If they could eat what grew here— they could live here. The first close look *Phoenix* had had at the planet, had seen cities and dams and the clear evidence of agriculture and mining and every other attribute of a reasonably advanced civilization ... natives, with rights, to be sure. But not rights that outweighed their own rights.

The sun sank in reds and yellows and golds. A planet shone above the hills. That was Mirage, second from the sun they called just ... the sun, having no better name for it, the way they called the third planet the world, or sometimes ... Down, in the way the Guild-born didn't use the word.

Stupid way to name the planet, Ian thought; he personally wished the first generation had come up with some definite name they could use for the world ... Earth, some of them had wanted to call it, arguing that was what anyone called their home planet, and this was, in all senses that mattered, home. The Guild had immediately rejected that reasoning.

And others, notably the hydroponics biologist, Renaud Lenoir, had argued passionately and eloquently that, no, it wasn't Earth. It mustn't be. It wasn't the Sun. And it wasn't the star they'd been targeting—when whatever had happened in hyperspace, had happened, and Taylor had saved the ship.

Taylor might be the Guild's saint—Taylor and Mc-Donough and the miner-pilots that, God save them, every one alive owed their lives to—but Lenoir, who'd argued so convincingly not to confound the names of Earth with this place, was due a sainthood, too, no matter that what would soon become the Guild had voted with him for reasons totally opposed to what Lenoir believed in; and that the construction workers and the station technicians, whose sons and daughters would carry out Lenoir's vision and go down to the surface, had mostly voted against him in that meeting.

Not Earth, Lenoir had argued, and not their target star. The planet had undergone its own evolution, all the way to high intelligence, and by that process made up its own biological rules, through its own initially successful experiment at life, and its own unique demands of environment on those ancestral organisms.

The biochemistry, the taxonomies and the relationships of species down to microbes and up to Earth's major ecosystems—whole branches of human science sat in *Phoenix'* library: the systematic knowledge of the one life-affected, human-impacted biosphere humans had thoroughly understood, thousands of years of accumulated understanding about Earth's natural systems and their evolution and interrelationships.

Pinning Earthly names on mere surface resemblances, Lenoir had argued, would confuse subsequent generations about where they were and who they were. It could create a mindset that thought of the world in a way connected with their own evolutionary history, a proprietary mindset, which Lenoir argued was not good; and more, a mindset that would repeatedly lead to mistaken connections throughout the life sciences and, by those mistaken connections, to expensively wrong decisions. Corrupting the language to identify what they didn't wholly understand could on the one hand prove fatal to their own culture and their humanity, and on the other, prove damaging to the very ecosystems they looked to for survival.

So, Earth it was not. The council had deadlocked on the other choices; and what could Lenoir's great-great-grandson find now to call it but the world, this blue, cloud-swirled home they had, that Taylor had found for them?

So now that they had mined the solar system, built the station, built an economy that could, with difficulty, build the lander to reach the planetary surface, the Pilots' Guild wanted them to leave—asked them, after nearly a hundred fifty years of orbiting the world, to shut down the station and transfer everything to the airless, waterless planetary base the Guild would gladly give them on Maudette, fourth from the sun . . . far from interference in a world the Guild adamantly maintained should stay sacrosanct, untouched by human influence, uncontaminated by human presence.

Meaning that the Guild wanted them all to live under the Guild's thumb—because that was also the price of Maudette.

The sun touched only the top of the buildings now. The western face of the hill was all in shadow, and Ian leaned his back against lab 4 and watched the colors flare, gazing past the red clay scar of the safe-tracks toward the hills of sighing grass.

Grasses was definitely what they were, the department had ruled so officially, and they could officially, scientifically, use that word as of two weeks ago—confirming the theories and the guesses of a century and a half of orbital survey. They were exact in their criteria, the ones of them that believed such things were important—the ones of them who had spent their careers memorizing the names for things they saw only in pictures and teaching them to generation after generation—a hundred fifty years of studying taxonomies and ecosystems of an ancestral world they'd never known—

No damned use, the Guild said, of course. The Guild's sons and daughters didn't enter Earth Studies, oh, no. The Guild's sons and daughters had been learning physics and ship maintenance and starflight in all those long years before *Phoenix* had flown again—and was *that* practical, to launch a starship when they were struggling for basic necessities?

But, Fools, the Guild brats called the station kids fools and worse. . . .

For what? Fools for endangering a planet the Guild didn't give an honest damn about? Fools for wanting the world they could see offered abundantly everything they had so precariously, most of what they mined reserved for the Guild's list of priorities?

Fools for challenging Guild authority—when you couldn't *be* Guild if you weren't born a descendant of *Phoenix* crew? Wasn't that the real reason the Guild-born called them fools? Because no station-builder brat could ever cross that line and train as Guild, and the Guild had every good reason for keeping it that way.

Of course the name-calling had stung with particular force, the way the Guild kids had meant it to. Never mind that if the older generations caught the Guild brats at it, they put them on rations for a week . . . it didn't break a Guild brat's pride, and it didn't admit a station kid to what he wasn't born to reach, or make the science of their lost Earth and lost destination either relevant or important to the Guild.

So now the Guild said, Leave this world? Go colonize barren Maudette, while they searched the stars for other planetary systems free of claimants—oh, and, by the way, mine and build stations at those stars to refuel the Guild's ships, and live there and die there and do it all over again, all the lost lives and the sweat and the danger—be the worker-drones while Guild ships voyaged to places that would need more worker-drones to build, endlessly across space, all the while the Guild maintained its priorities and its perks that took most of every resource they had.

Better here, in a cold wind and under a fading sky. *Their* sky, in which Mirage was setting now and Maudette had yet to rise, that curious interface between the day-glow and the true night.

They could die here. Things might still go wrong. A microbe could wipe them out faster than they could figure what hit them. They could do terrible damage to the world and every living creature on it.

The fears still came back, in the middle of the dark, or in the whispering silence of an alien hillside. The home-sickness did, when he thought of something he wanted to say to his family, or his lifelong friends—then, like re-membering a recent death, recalled that the phone link was not all that easy from here, and that there was no ab-solute guarantee that the reusable lander they had bet their futures on would ever be built.

Estevez had come Down with him, God help Julio and his sneezes. Estevez and he just didn't talk about Up-stairs, didn't talk about the doubts . . . they'd gone through Studies together, been in training together—known each other all their lives . . . how not, in the lim-ited world of the station? He and Julio had hashed over doubts aplenty before they'd made the cut, but not dwelled on them once they knew they were on the team, and most of all hadn't rehashed them once they were down here. Here everything was fine and they weren't scared, and Estevez wouldn't worry if he was late for din-ner, no, of course not. Julio would just be standing by the window by now, wondering if he'd gotten sick on the way or gotten bitten by some flying creature they hadn't cata-logued yet.

Ian shoved his hands into his pockets and began to walk back to the barracks—Estevez probably had supper in the microwave, timed to the last of sunset—they had no general mealtime, with all of them on lab schedules, and supper, such as it was, fell whenever the work was done. No amenities, no variety in the menu, no reliance on freezers or fancy equipment: every priority was for lab equipment, everything was freeze-dried, dried, or add-water-and-boil, and damned disgusting as a lifelong prospect. Probably the Guild looked for the cuisine to bring them to their knees ... to have them begging the Guild for rescue and a good stationside dinner.

Meanwhile he had discovered a sudden, unusual preference for sweets, which, with the coppery taste he had almost constantly, was the only thing that tasted good. And mostly those came out of the labs he'd worked in, so he named them what they were, in all their chemical parts.

There was, in their reliance on food from orbit, a most pressing reason to identify grasses, and dissect seeds, and figure out their processes and their chemistry, where it was like Earth's and where it was different: ecologically different, the Guild had said, probably full of toxins, not to meddle with.

But the Guild was going to be wrong on that one, if the results held—God, the tests were looking good, down to the chemical level where it really counted: there were starches and sugars they recognized, no toxins in the seeds that, the *Phoenix* histories informed them, could be processed and cooked in ways human beings had done for a staple food for thousands of years.

That again, for the Guild's insistence they needed no understanding about natural systems—the Guild said they had no use precisely because in the Guild's opinion planets had no use, and, the unspoken part, stations and station-dwellers had no use except for the services they provided. The Guild talked about ecological disasters—about native rights, about all manner of rights including the local fauna that had more rights than the workers on the station ... the Guild, that adamantly refused understanding of any natural system.

But contrary to predictions, the microbes they collected and the ones that necessarily attended human beings showed no dispensation to run amok with each other or with them or the planet—that had been their greatest fear, viruses getting a hold in human bodies or human-vectored bacteria wreaking havoc faster than the genetics people could patch the problems. They'd prepared for it, they'd taken precautions—but it hadn't happened catastrophically; they weren't seeing the problems they'd prepared for, even in lab cultures. The very fact they were finding biological correspondences was a hazard, of course, but so far and with fingers crossed, the immunologists were beginning to argue that the mere fact there *were* correspondences might mean some effective defenses. Talk around the lab began to speculate on microbial-level evolution more intimately related to geology and planetary formation than theory had previously held to be the case, wild stuff, the geneticists and the geologists and the botanists putting their heads together on one spectacular drunk the night they'd gotten the supply drop with the unscheduled Gift from Upstairs—

God, the irreverent insanity down here, after a lifetime of the solemn Cause, and the politics, and the Movement. But discoveries were pouring in on them after a century and a half of stagnant study of taxonomies. They were drunk with invention. They were understanding the natural systems they were seeing. They'd formed a comparative framework with its essential questions foremost, worked out on Lenoir's principles, for a hundred fifty years of information trickling up through optics and hands-off observation of the planet; they'd held on to planetary science—and they'd done it in the face of the Guild's ridicule and the Guild's absorption of resources, and the Guild's ship-building, and every Guild-blessed project that drank up station time and materials.

And if the Guild profoundly repented anything it had let pass council, it had to be the decision that had begun station construction here, in orbit about a blue, living planet, instead of barren, virtually airless Maudette.

Safer, the scientists of that day had argued. Within reach of resources, if something went wrong.

It certainly *was* within reach of resources, resources and the intelligent civilization they had already detected on the planet. Oh, yes, the Guild raised ethical arguments from the start, but say the truth—the Guild with its talk of moral choices, the right of the planet to develop on its own—they had such a deep concern for the planet-dwellers, papa was wont to say. So why is life down there so sacred to the Guild, and why do they count *our* lives so cheap?

So he was here, because papa couldn't be, and mama wouldn't, without papa: the station and the Movement needed them where they were, if that lander was going to pass a council vote.

What the Guild reasoned now, he didn't know. Or care. Thank God, hereafter the politics of the Movement, and who was in charge, and who led and who followed (being an administrator's son, he'd heard all the arguments for and against his being down here, and suffered personally from some of them) and what steps were first and what their policy would be in dealing with the Guild—none of that was his problem anymore. He was down here to practice the science he'd become fascinated with at age eight ... and realized when the Guild brats ridiculed him that he'd have no real chance of doing anything with it as a job.

But papa's dream had been an of-course to him, even at eight ... that was why he'd spoken out without thinking, *of course* they'd go to the world, *of course* they'd walk down there someday.

And now he did walk the planetary surface, now he did Lenoir's work, *he* did it, and for Lenoir's reasons: all the collections, the taxonomies, the equivalencies that might let them extrapolate from the natural system in the data storage to deal with a living one. He was laying the foundation for a natural science of this world and a means of dealing with this world and protecting it from their own mistakes—because, dammit, they had to; sooner or later they had to be here. Lenoir was right—the world might have a higher life form already, and the world already and for thousands of years had surely had a name, in someone or something's language—but humanity had come to this solar system without a choice, and it was equally inevitable that they deal with the world, before it was space-faring or after, because Maudette was not their choice, and they knew Maudette was not even the Guild's choice—just a way to get the Guild's worker-drones away from the only planet that gave them options. The world had become their hope and their way of securing their freedom and their identity, before they had ever set foot on it.

Until here he was, in a place generations had worked to reach, and, one way or the other, he wouldn't be admitting defeat. He wouldn't be going back Upstairs, rescued from starvation by some Guild ship.

And he damned sure wouldn't be gathered up and transported to airless Maudette, on Guild terms.

Too late for that now, everlastingly too late.

Speaking of late . . .

It was Julio in the window, shadow against the light.

Shadow that ducked its head in a sudden sneeze.

III

Perhaps it was cowardice, Manadgi thought, that held him from going down to the valley. Perhaps it was prudence that argued, in the quiet he saw settle about the buildings as the sun set, that watching and thinking through the night might grant him some useful understanding.

One building had windows. Most did not. The size and the height of the windows was ambiguous with distance. He saw the isolated movements of living beings between the buildings, toward twilight, and occasionally after.

He saw the predating machines, prowling about the desolation they had made. None came near him, perhaps because he had settled himself well away from such tracks, which evidently it was the purpose of such machines to make, all about the area, a net of them, as if there were less intent to reach any specific place than to have as many routes as possible within the immediate sight of these buildings.

But did they need devastation on which to walk?

Or was there some purpose to this stripping of the land that made sense to moon-folk? They feared the approach of enemies, perhaps. Perhaps they wished to afford no cover to spies.

Perhaps they wished to demonstrate the devastation, or—one hated to imagine—found such destruction aesthetic.

He might walk up to the buildings as he had purposed and present himself to some authority. But aesthetic destruction . . . that thought gave him considerable pause.

A machine passed below his hiding-place, casting light as bright as the vanished sun along the rutted ground and over the grass along the edge of the devastation. It had no wheels, but linked plates on which it crawled. Its forepart was a claw, which it held rigid. It might be for digging or for stripping the ground. It might be a weapon.

Certainly one did not want to walk up to *that* and ask its inclinations.

A beam of light hit the rocks and ran along the hill, and Manadgi held his breath, not daring to move. *Someone* surely sat in mastery of that machine, he told himself, but there was something so disturbingly clockwork about the swing of those lights that watching it made his flesh crawl.

What, he asked himself, if they *were* clockwork, such machines? What if the owners simply turned them loose to destroy, committing them to fortune and not caring what or whom they laid waste?

A spear of light stabbed backward from the clanking machine. Too close, Manadgi said to himself, and drew back from his position—then stopped cold as he saw the sheen of glass and smooth metal among the brush and the grass of the slope just below him.

An eye, he thought, a machine's single eye thrust up through the grass, as yet not moving, perhaps not cognizant of him.

He had come here to make considerate approach. But not to this. *Not* to this. He held his breath, wondering if he dared move, or if it would move, or how long this eye had been there until the light from the machine showed it to him.

The area of brush where the clawed machine had disappeared was dark, now, and he sat in an awkward crouch, half ready to move away, doubting whether he dared, wondering if there was another such machine lurking with mechanical patience, or if such eyes might be threaded all through the grass and the rocks, and he had somehow blundered through them unseen. He trembled to think, considering that it was himself on whom the fortunes of greater people leaned, and that on his auspicious or inauspicious choice, on a sum of strange participants whose number he could not at all reckon, chance was delicately balanced, awaiting his decision one way or the other to tip events into motion, for good or for ill to the aiji, whose interests bound up many, many lives.

Clearly the moon-folk had no right intruding on Tachi land, within the aiji's power. They had done damage in their arrogance and their power and challenged the people of the whole Earth—and it was on *him* to decide what to do, whether to risk this eye developing legs and running to report, or a voice, to alert other eyes, and to call the clawed machine back to this slope.

It had done neither, so far. Perhaps it was shut down. Perhaps it was not a whole machine, in itself, only a part from a damaged one. If they fell from the sky, perhaps a petal-sail had failed, and one had smashed itself on the rocks.

He could scarcely get his next breath, as he moved himself ever so silently backward and backward, straining his mortal eyes into the dark toward the eye and asking himself if the eye might have ears to hear the whisper of cloth or the drawing of his breaths or—it seemed possible to him—the hammering of his heart. But the eye sat in darkness, perhaps blind, perhaps asleep—or feigning it. *Did* clockwork things hear, or smell, or think?

Or how did they know to move? Did they turn on and off their own switches? That seemed impossible.

It stayed inert, at least. He gained his feet, moving with what stealth he could, uphill, encountering, at least, no other eyes in the grass.

He settled into a nook higher on the hill, there to tuck up among the yet unravaged rocks, to catch his breath and regain his composure.

The aiji, he told himself, should have sent one of his assassins, not a speaker—should have sent some one of his guard accustomed to hazardous actions, who would know how to move silently and how to judge the hazards of this situation.

And perhaps having seen clearly that it was a matter outside his judgment, his wisest course would be to withdraw with what he had seen, and to advise the aiji and the hasdrawad to send someone with the skill to penetrate this devastation. He saw no safe approach.

Yet had any machine attacked him? Had the machines harmed the children, or could the Tachi prove such wandering machines had killed any of their herds?

He had to admit fear had swayed his judgment a moment ago. The clockwork machines had wreaked havoc on the land, but not, though given opportunity, attacked people or livestock. The children that had reported machines had escaped unharmed, and nothing had tracked them to their village. The herdsmen that had spied on the landing places of the petal-sails had escaped, alive and well, without the machines of the moon-folk following them.

So perhaps the machines were deaf and even witless things, and he had been foolish to run, just now.

He was certainly glad no one was here to witness his dilemma, huddled in a hole in the dark, shivering, and not with the cold.

Was that the story he wanted to tell the aiji and his court, how he had fled, without any closer observation? He had confidence in his skills as an observer and as a negotiator. And could he fail to gather at least an assessment of numbers and position, which would be useful as the hasdrawad debated and the aiji arranged another, more aggressive, mission?

He dared not carry back a mistaken report, or ask for assassins, and perhaps, in an assassin's too-quick reaction to threat, push the whole situation to hostilities that might not be anyone's intention. He had come here plainly to ask the moon-folk what they were doing, and to have an answer from them for the aiji. He had always realized the chance of dying by error or by hostile action. It was a risk he had been willing to run, when the aiji asked him the question in the safety of the aiji's apartments.

Could he retreat now, claiming the machines had threatened him—his only excuse but cowardice—knowing that report would be taken as a reasoned conclusion, and that it would loose irremediable consequences?

No. He could not. He could not remotely justify it. The aiji had seen applicability in his skills to make him the aiji's considered choice for this mission.

He hoped the aiji had also seen intelligence, and judgment, and resourcefulness, not alone for the honor of the aiji's opinion, but because his personal resources seemed very scant just now, and the night was very cold, and nothing in his life had prepared him for this.

IV

The morning came as milky pale as the first morning Ian had wakened on the planet, with a scattering of improbably pink clouds. Pink ... and gold, and pearl white, with a little mist in the low places. Condensation due to the air being saturated with moisture and the ambient temperature reaching the critical point: weather. The moisture came from previous precipitation and from evaporation from the ground and from respiration from the plants. One could generate the same effect in the herbarium, up on the station, by a combination of natural and mechanical processes.

It was a pretty effect there. But they'd never thought of pink clouds. A shame, Ian thought. They should put gels on the spots and arrange tours. See the planetary effects.

It's pretty, Julio had said from the barracks door. —It's pretty, it's cold, have fun.

Estevez with his regulated temperatures and filtered air: a life systems engineer with an allergy to the environment was not a happy experimental specimen for the medics.

Estevez flinched from the day sky. And Estevez admit to his fear? Retreat from it? Not if he had to go back in and throw up, after his glance at the weather. Allergies, Estevez said.

And it was funny, but it wasn't, since Estevez couldn't leave this world. Steroids weren't the long-term answer, and they hadn't had an immune response problem in a hundred years and more on-station. Gene-patching wasn't an option for their little earth-sciences/chemistry lab down on the planet, they couldn't send specimens Up-stairs, they hadn't anybody trained to run the equipment if they could get it down here, they weren't a hundred per-cent sure a gene-patch was what they ought to try under exotic circumstances, anyway, and, meanwhile, Archive had come up with an older, simpler idea: find the sub-stance. Try desensitization.

Fine, Estevez said, sleepless with steroids, stuck with needles, patched with tape, experimented on by botanists and zoologists. He'd try anything. Meanwhile Estevez stayed under filtration and stayed comfortable and main-tained his sense of humor—except it was scary to react to something after two months down here. The medics thought it should take longer. They weren't sure. There'd never been a hundred-fifty-year-old genetically isolated, radiation-stressed human population exposed to an alien world. Not in their records.

Wonderful, said Estevez.

Meanwhile all of them who went out on Survey, laying down their little grids of tape and counting grass species, took careful specimens of anything new, bushes, grasses, seeding and sporing plants and fungi and the like. The medics waved a part of that sample past Estevez' nose and taped other samples to his skin. They hung simple ad-hesive strips in the wind, and counted what impacted them, and analyzed snips of the filters, figuring at first that whatever Estevez was reacting to had to be airborne. But they were working on a new theory now, and ana-lyzed samples of soil and dead grasses, looking for molds.

So they added the soil punch to the regular test, and ex-tended the grid of samples beyond the sterilized ground. Ian took a soil sample every hundred meters, a punch of a plastic tube down past the root-line, and left his blue plastic tube inserts in a row down the hillside, to pick up on the way back. The old hands down here could walk briskly. He ambled, stopped often, lungs aching, on the long easterly climb uphill, into the rising sun.

He'd spotted different color on the east hill yesterday. It looked like a blooming plant, and if it did bloom, in the economy of nature, one could guess it did that to put forth genetic material for sexual combination to produce seed, as the grasses did, a likely and advantageous system according to their own Earthly prejudice.

That indicated, then, that it was shedding something into the air, and if it was shedding something, one might well argue it was pollen. The committee was still arguing the matter—quasi-pollen or quasi-spores from quasi-flowers, but ask Estevez if *he* cared. The reproduction of the broadleaf grasses might need debate, and possibly a new nomenclature, but those looked to him like flowers of the sort they grew in the herbarium from Earth seed, red-violet, specifically, different than anything they had yet seen in the landscape.

And sweet-smelling, deliciously sweet, once he'd climbed far enough up the hill to catch the scent, and to take his whole-plant sample.

Stowing that, with best hopes for Estevez, he drew his square, pegging one-meter lines on a plastic grid, took up his handheld recorder, and began counting ordinary grasses—there was a type, Lawton argued, that, with 136 grains per ear on average, showed evidence of artificial selection, probably had drifted from cultivated fields, and that that might let them, at safe distance, gather information on the edibility for humans of what the natives cultivated.

Which would tell them—

A siren blasted out abruptly, down among the base buildings. Ian froze, sitting as he was, looked downhill and looked about him, thinking some surveyor across the valley must have misjudged his position and triggered the perimeter alarm.

Grass near him whispered out of time with the breeze.

Startled, he spun on one knee and found himself staring at a pair of brown, dusty boots, and the hem of a brown, knee-length, many-buttoned coat, and the tall perspective of an ebon-skinned giant.

He couldn't move. He heard the alarm sounding in the distance, and realized in shock that he was the emergency, and this was the cause of it, this . . . *man,* this creature that had picked his approach and his moment and chosen *him* . . .

The native beckoned to him, once, twice, unmistakably, to get up. Impossible not to recognize the intelligence, the purpose, the civilized nature of the native, who was black as night, with a face not by any remotest kinship human, but sternly handsome in its planes and angles.

A third time it beckoned. He saw no imminent threat as he rose. It was imposingly tall—more than a head taller—and broad-shouldered. He saw no weapons about its person—in which thought he suddenly realized that it might take some of his equipment for weaponlike. He was afraid to reach even for the probe he'd used, afraid to make a move in any direction, recalling all Earth's history of war-making mistakes and missed chances for reason.

But he moved a cautious hand to his breast pocket, thumbed the switch on the pocket radio to the open position, all the while watching for the least alarmed reaction.

He said quietly, "Base, I've made contact," and watched the native's face. "Base." He kept his voice low, his eyes constantly on the intruder, as if he were speaking to him. "Base, this is Ian. I've made contact. I've got company out here."

The native still offered no objection, but in sudden fear of an imprudent answer from Base blasting out, he thumbed the volume control in the direction he devoutly hoped was down.

"Nil li sat-ha," the intruder said to him—it sounded like that, at least, a low and, thank God, reasonable-sounding voice. He indicated the downward course toward the base, making his own invitation.

It motioned again up the hill.

"Base," he said, trying not to let his voice shake, "that

was him talking. I think it's a he. It looks to be. Tall fellow. Well-dressed. No weapons. Don't come up here. He seems civilized. I'm going to do what he wants, I'm going out of perimeter, I don't want to alarm him. Stay back. And don't talk to me."

A hard, strong grip closed on his arm. He looked around in startlement at the intruder—no one in his life had ever laid hands on him with that intimation of force and strength. But the situation was suddenly sliding into confusion: a glance downhill showed him his friends running upslope toward them, the intruder was clearly alarmed—and their lives and everything they had worked for were at risk if someone miscalculated now.

Come, the intruder wanted. And a part of him wanted more than anything to run back to safety, back to things he knew, things he could deal with on his own terms.

But the hand that pulled at his arm was too strong to fight to any advantage, and he went where it wanted, still trying to think what to do—he left the communications switch open, hoping no one would chase them or corner the alien,—panted, "Base, it's all right, I'm safe, it's wanting to talk, for God's sake, base, tell them pull back. . . ."

But he had no idea why they were coming headlong after him, whether they knew something he didn't or whether base was talking at all. They couldn't fight. They had a handful of weapons against the chance of animal intrusions, but they were a very few humans on a world they knew wasn't theirs, they couldn't get off the planet, nobody could get down to them, not even the Guild, until the lander was built, and there was no way they could hold out against a native population that decided to attack them.

Someone downslope shouted, he didn't know what, but the intruder began to run and he found himself compelled by a grip on his arm that hauled him along at a breathless, stumbling pace.

"Stay back!" he said to whoever was listening. "Dammit, he's not hurting me, don't chase him!"

Breath failed him. He wasn't acclimated to the air, he couldn't run and talk, he struggled to keep his feet under him as the intruder dodged around brush and rocks and pulled him along.

Then his ankles did go, and pitched him onto his knees on the stony hill, the intruder still holding his arm with a grip that cut off the blood to his hand.

He looked up at the native, then, scared, trying to get his breath, trying to get up, and it snatched him up, wrenching his arm as it looked back the way they had come, as afraid as he was, he thought, despite the pain.

"I'm all right," he said for the radio. "I've turned the volume off. I can't hear you. I don't want to scare the man, don't come after me!"

The native jerked him along, and he cooperated at the best pace he could manage, his lungs burning, his breath coming on a knife's edge. His head spun, then, and he had the intruder half-carrying him, while he gasped after air and saw the world in shades of gray.

At last it dragged him into a dark place and smothered him with its body and his coat. He made no protest, except to try to breathe, and, getting his face clear, lay in the shelter of the native's panting body, wanting only to stay alive, and not to provoke any craziness out of anyone.

V

"Left with the creature," Patton Bretano said, with a sinking heart, and Pardino, down on the surface, went on about how they'd gotten radio transmission, they were still getting it, and they wanted a decision from the station.

Patton Bretano sat with the receiver in his hand, listening to it, asking himself why it was *his* son, and what kind of craziness had sent Ian out by himself, or why Ian hadn't run for the base instead of away from it, but he feared he knew that answer already.

Ian wouldn't risk the project, *wouldn't* risk it. Working near the perimeter, Pardino said. In an area where they thought they had years yet to find the answers.

But the answers had found them. Found Ian, on the edges and unprotected. Pardino talked about how the radio was still open, and if it stayed that way they had a chance to track them.

But, How can I tell Joy? was the thought chasing through Patton's mind, scattering saner notions. The father's instincts were to mount a search party, to curse Ian for doing what he'd done, the father's instincts didn't damn care what risks the search would run.

The father didn't give a damn how a rescue attempt would play politically with the Guild. The politician was thinking of the risks they knew they'd run, where they'd put the base ... God, of course there were dangers, and there were procedures for avoiding them. They'd created an electronic perimeter. The natives weren't advanced enough to bypass it. They'd been down there for months without an incident. They'd never let their precautions lapse, and Ian hadn't been in the first team down, he'd pulled every string he had and absolutely made sure that Ian wasn't in the first team....

"Pat," Pardino said, *"Pat, are you there?"*

"Yes," he said, thinking, God help us, it's happened, hasn't it? Contact's made. Irrevocable from this point. But my son ...

"We can't go after him," Pardino said. *"The staff's in consensus, we can't go after him, we aren't in that kind of position here ..."*

"I want the transmissions." He was trembling. The

shock was still richocheting through his nerves, saying nothing was real. But that open radio was the only fragile link to Ian, and he wanted to be hearing that, not Pardino; he wanted to hear for himself that Ian was all right, never mind what the Guild was going to make of it, never mind that the news was going to be all over the station with the speed of the phone system, and somehow he had to break the news to Joy and get some kind of official news release out.

Had to take a position before the Guild released the story on its own.

He wasn't a bad man. He told himself he wasn't a bad man. He was walking a narrow line between a Pilots' Guild that wouldn't scruple to use the story against everything their hopes rested on, and a council skittish of opposing them too radically . . . and now Ian had gone and put himself in the middle of what, God help him, *he'd* planned.

Because he knew and the committee knew there were inhabitants in that area of the island, non-technological as they needed, as they'd wanted the first contact to be, not to bring them face-to-face with the savviest politicians and the most advanced technology on the planet . . . but he hadn't on any terms wanted Ian in the middle of that encounter.

Pardino was saying something about the patch on channel B, and he couldn't but think how the Guild was going to be monitoring their transmissions the instant they realized there was something happening. Everything they said, everything Ian said, was going to the Guild the same as it went to them, bet on it.

"*Pat,*" Pardino said, obscuring what he wanted to hear, Ian's voice, "*Pat, the boy's resourceful, he's being clever, he's not hurt, they're not threatening him, whatever's happened. He talks, but they can't suspect there's a pickup, they haven't got radio. He said he's got the volume down so they can't hear, but he's not that far away. The batteries are good for at least four days solid, he says don't come after the guy, they're not threatening him. You copy, Pat?"*

"Yeah. Yes, I understand you. I want the transmissions, dammit."

"You've got everything we have."

Pardino signed off with that, as if it made anything better than it was; but, He's resourceful, Pardino had said, too, and Patton clutched that thought to himself when Pardino went out and left him a quiet, static-ridden breathing.

Then Ian's voice, saying, out of breath, *"It's still all right, don't worry, he's just afraid someone's following us. We're in a cave in the rocks. He keeps touching my arm, very gentle, like he's trying to get me to be quiet, he talks to me and I act like I'm answering him."*

The other voice came back then, a low, quiet burr.

"He's at least a head taller than me," Ian's voice said, *"mostly like us, but incredibly strong. His skin is black as space, his eyes are narrow and his nose is kind of arched, flat to the face, he frowns, you can tell that. . . ."*

The other voice again. A pause, then:

"He's talking to me, I guess you can hear that, real quiet, like he's trying to tell me everything's all right."

Ian's voice was shaking. Patton felt the fear in his son, felt the strain telling on him, and Ian's breaths were short and desperate. He knotted his hands together and knew the Guild was recording by now, every desperate minute, to play back to the council and the station at large.

Ian wasn't the type to crack, he knew his son. Ian was doing all right emotionally. It was the physical stress or a physical constraint that was putting that quaver into Ian's voice, but others might not think so.

He punched in his wife's office number, before the news could go out. He said it the way Pardino had said it, just, "Joy, Ian's in a little trouble, don't panic, but they've got a contact down there and Ian's met it."

"A contact," Joy said, on the other end of the line.

"What do you mean, they've got a contact? Is he all right? Pat? Is he all right?"

"So far he's fine," Patton said. "We can hear him, he's got his radio open, I've got him on the other channel. Turn on your B."

"I've got it," Joy said, *"I've got it."*

"—a little out of breath," Ian was saying, and coughed. *"My legs are wobbly. I'm not acclimated down here. I'd say we're a couple klicks from the base, don't know how to judge it. There's like trees around here, kind of soft-trunked, big flat leaves, there's like a lot of moss, there's got to be water near here, I'd think, it's all soft-leaved stuff. . . ."*

God, Patton thought, the boy was still observing, still was sending back his damn botany notes, but it was the native he wanted to know about.

He heard the creature talking again, he heard Joy ask, *"Is that one of them?"* and he muttered, "So far there's just one of them. Walked right through the perimeter alarm and accosted Ian. Ian ordered the rescue party back. He apparently wasn't feeling threatened."

"Sir," his secretary's voice broke in, on override. *"Vordict's calling in, says it's urgent, about your son, sir."*

The Guild *had* heard. The Guild was going to raise bloody hell about the situation and play hard politics with the electorate. He wasn't ready for this. He had a son in trouble down there and Vordict, damn him, wanted to make an issue of what they all sensibly knew had been inevitable from the hour they reached this star, all to read him might-have-beens.

"He wants to keep moving," Ian's faint voice said. *"He wants us to walk again. I'm cold, I'm out of breath, excuse the shakes. . . ."*

"Put him on," he told his secretary, regarding Vordict, and told Joy, "It's Vordict. I've got to talk to him. Ian can't hear us. But whatever he's found down there, it's not hostile, it's all right. . . ."

Ian gasped, a short, small intake of breath, and Patton's heart froze.

Ian said, long-distance, *"I lost my balance, is all. It's all right, it's all right, don't anybody do anything stupid."*

Patton wished the Guild would take that to heart.

"Patton," came the voice from the other channel. *"Patton, you've forced this, this is on your head, it's your son in danger, and you knew damned well there was a settlement close to the base. I have the documents. I have the witness. You knew before you made the drop there, tell me otherwise, and be advised I intend to take this before the council."*

VI

There was no offer of resistance, no threat, no weapon, and thus far the luck had been with the effort. Perhaps the moon-man sensed so and made no resistance to his kidnapping. Or perhaps malicious chance was running otherwise and everything only seemed this easy.

Manadgi did not reckon himself a superstitious man, nor a gullible one, or he tried not to be. Anything that proceeded this easily with so much force available to the other side, he greatly distrusted.

But the moon-man, at least a head shorter than he, seemed a fragile creature, easily out of breath, quickly winded on the mildest climb. The creature's pale complexion turned paler still, and at times it staggered, but it never ceased to try to walk with him.

It might be he had put it in fear of its life. It might be it was simply the disposition of moon-folk to be acquiescent, for reasons such folk understood, but he could not persuade himself to trust that chance, no more than he could entirely persuade himself that the clockwork machines were harmless to intruders.

He walked and walked, and the moon-man stumbled along beside him, muttering to himself so constantly he began to wonder if the creature was habitually that addled or somehow injured in its wits. He had found it sitting in front of a square of grass, plucking stems and talking to itself, while poking at a black box full of buttons that perhaps made sense, but about what business he could not determine.

Perhaps it was mad. Perhaps all moon-folk were—along with those furious early pursuers that had given chase and then given up.

Or perhaps they were, after all, frail and gentle folk who could not even resist the kidnapping of one of their number—

But who then loosed the clockwork machines to destroy the valley?

The moon-man was lagging farther and farther off the pace he wanted, was staggering in his steps and then fell to his knees, holding his side. "Get up!" Manadgi told it sternly, and waved his hand.

The moon-man wiped his face and there was blood, most evidently blood, red as any man's, running from its nose—a flood of life, broken forth by the running and the climbing he had forced it to.

He was sorry for it, then—he had not meant to do it harm and still it was trying to do what he asked it, with the blood pouring down its face.

He gestured with a push at its arm for it to sit down again, and it seemed glad and relieved, bent over and pinched its nostrils shut, then began to cough, which, with the bleeding, made him worry that it might choke itself.

Manadgi tucked his hands between his knees and squatted, waiting, hoping the creature knew what best to do to help itself. It was far from threatening anyone at the moment, rather, it seemed choked, so imminently in peril of its life that he took his water-flask and offered it, hoping it would help.

The moon-man looked at him with suffering eyes, then unstopped the flask and poured a little water out on his hand, to be sure it was water, he thought, before he wiped his face with it. Then he poured a little more into his bloody hand and had a mouthful, which seemed to help the coughing.

And the moment he stopped choking, the moon-man began muttering again, the odd creature . . .

Not an ugly or a fearsome being, Manadgi decided, except the blood smeared on its pale face. Its strangeness made him queasy about touching it, certainly about ever using the flask, but he greatly regretted hurting it, not having known how delicate it was.

Still, for all he knew, its associates had set one of the clockwork monsters on their trail.

"Get up," he said to it, exactly the words he had used before. "Get up."

The moon-man immediately tried to do what he asked, without a gesture, so the creature *had* understood a word or two. He gained his feet with the flask tucked under his arm as if he meant to keep it, and kept talking to himself as he went, a thin, uncertain voice, now, lacking all affirmation.

They were past the stricken grandmother stone. They had left the scarring of the land and they went in tangle-grass that clung to the trousers and about the ankles. There was a stream down the hill, he remembered it at the other side of a steep bank and a stand of fern, a slab of rock. That was what he intended—a cold, clean stream and a moment to rest in a more sheltered place, difficult for the clockwork machines to negotiate.

"Be careful," he cautioned the creature, with a tug at the blue sleeve, and it looked around at him, pale, bloody-faced, with a startled expression, after which the moon-man slipped and slid away from him in a rattle of rock and a crashing of fern.

The creature never cried out. It landed at the bottom half in the water and half on the bank and never moved as he came skidding down to it in fear and fright.

He thought it might have broken bones in that fall. It lay still, and he could only think that if there had been any niche for ill fortune in their meeting he must just have destroyed himself and the aiji at once—he dreaded even to touch it, but what was he to do, or where else could he find help?

So he pulled its arm and its shoulder out of the water— and it looked at him with dazed strange eyes and went on looking at him as if its bewilderment was as great, as if its understanding of its universe was devastated and disordered as his own.

He let it go, then, and it crouched there and bathed its face and washed its neck, while blood ran away in the clean water, an omen of things, he feared as much.

But he saw clearly that he had driven it beyond any sane or reasonable limit, and how desperate and spent it was, and yet not protesting.

Overall it seemed a brave creature, and never violent, never anything but willing to comply with everything he asked of it. He found himself glad when it seemed to recover its breath, and not to be badly hurt from its fall. It looked at him then as if expecting to have to go on, crazed as their course had been, and able only to ask with its eyes who he was and what he wanted and where they were going, all the things a sane creature would want to know—would he not? Would not any man ask what he wanted and why should he go?

Why indeed should he go, when he had every advantage of defense in the strange buildings, and why should he have been alone on the hill, and why should he have run from his own people, this strange moon-man who sat and counted grass stems?

Perhaps fortune was tending that way and the moon-man had felt it, and given himself up to it.

And if that was so, if that was so, dared he lose what

the auspicious moment had put in his hands, or risk its safety by driving it beyond its strength?

He spoke to it quietly, he ventured to touch it gently on the knee as he knelt by it on the stream bank, and kept his voice low and calming. "Rest, rest here, catch your breath. It's all right. Drink." One supposed it regularly drank ordinary water and not substances of the ether. He shaped a cup with his hand and had a drink from the stream himself, said again, "Drink," to make the word sure, and the moon-man said it back to him, faint and weak as he was.

More, the man's eyes were for a moment clear and unafraid, if he could judge expression on such a face, eloquent of curiosity about him, and even gratitude. "Ian," the man said, indicating himself, and said it a second time, so he became reasonably sure it was a name. He said his own name, "Manadgi," in the same way.

"Ian," the man said, and put out his hand, as if he was to do the same.

"Manadgi." He put forth his own hand, willing to be a fool, and the creature seized on it and shook it vigorously.

"Ian, Manadgi," the creature said, and seemed delighted by the discovery. They sat there shaking each other by the hand, fools together, mutually afraid, mutually relieved, mutually bewildered by their differences.

He had no idea what its native customs or expectations must be. It could have very little idea about his. But it was possible to be civilized, all the same, and he found it possible to be gracious with such a creature, odd as it was—possible, the dizzy concept came to him, to establish associate relations with what was certainly a powerful association of unknown scope, of beings skilled in a most marvelous craft.

"We shall walk," he said slowly, miming with his fingers. "We shall walk to the village, Ian and Manadgi, together."

BOOK THREE

I

The air moved sluggishly through the open garden lattice, heavy with the perfume of the night-blooming vines outside the bedroom. An o'oi-ana went *click-click*, and called again, the harbinger of rain, while Bren lay awake, thinking that if he were wise, he would get up and close the lattice and the doors before he fell asleep. The wind would shift. The sea air would come and cool the room. The vents were enough to let it in. But it was a lethargic, muggy night, and he waited for that nightly reverse of the wind from the east to the west, waited as the first flickers of lightning cast the shadow of the lattice on the stirring gauze of the curtain.

The lattice panels had the shapes of Fortune and Chance, *baji* and *naji*. The shadow of the vines outside moved with the breeze that, finally, finally, flared the curtain with the promise of relief from the heat.

The next flicker lit an atevi shadow, like a statue suddenly transplanted to the terrace outside. Bren's heart skipped a beat as he saw it on that pale billowing of gauze, on a terrace where no one properly belonged. He froze an instant, then slithered over the side of the bed.

The next flash showed him the lattice folding further back, and the intruder entering his room.

He slid a hand beneath the mattress and drew out the pistol he had hidden there—braced his arms across the mattress in the way the aiji had taught him, and pulled the trigger, to a shock that numbed his hands and a flash that blinded him to the night and the intruder. He fired a

second time, for sheer terror, into the blind dark and ringing silence.

He couldn't move after that. He couldn't get his breath.
He hadn't heard anyone fall. He thought he had missed.
The white, flimsy draperies blew in the cooling wind that
scoured through his bedroom.

His hands were numb, bracing the gun on the mattress.
His ears were deaf to sounds fainter than the thunder,
fainter than the rattle of the latch of his bedroom door—
the guards using their key, he thought.

But it might not be. He rolled his back to the bedside
and braced his straight arms between his knees, barrel
trained on the middle of the doorway as the inner door
banged open and light and shadow struck him in the face.

The aiji's guards spared not a word for questions. One
ran to the lattice doors, and out into the courtyard and the
beginning rain. The other, a faceless metal-sparked darkness, loomed over him and pried the gun from his fingers.

Other guards came; while Banichi—it was Banichi's
voice from above him—Banichi had taken the gun.

"Search the premises!" Banichi ordered them. "See to
the aiji!"

"Is Tabini all right?" Bren asked, overwhelmed, and
shaking. "Is he all right, Banichi?"

But Banichi was talking on the pocket-com, giving
other orders, deaf to his question. The aiji must be all
right, Bren told himself, or Banichi would not be standing
here, talking so calmly, so assuredly to the guards outside.
He heard Banichi give orders, and heard the answering
voice say nothing had gotten to the roof.

He was scared. He knew the gun was contraband.
Banichi knew it, and Banichi could arrest him—he feared
he might; but when Banichi was through with the radio,
Banichi seized him by the bare arms and set him on the
side of the bed.

The other guard came back through the garden
doors—it was Jago. She always worked with Banichi.
"There's blood. I've alerted the gates."

So he'd shot someone. He began to shiver as Jago ducked out again. Banichi turned the lights on and came back, atevi, black, smooth-skinned, his yellow eyes narrowed and his heavy jaw set in a thunderous scowl.

"The aiji gave me the gun," Bren said before Banichi could accuse him. Banichi stood there staring at him and finally said,

"This is *my* gun."

He was confused. He sat there with his skin gone to gooseflesh and finally moved to pull a blanket into his lap. He heard commotion in the garden, Jago yelling at other guards.

"This is *my* gun," Banichi said forcefully. "Can there be any question this is my gun? A noise waked you. I lay in wait for the assassin. *I* fired. What did you see?"

"A shadow. A shadow coming in through the curtains." Another shiver took him. He knew how foolish he had been, firing straight across and through the doors. The bullet might have kept going across the garden, into the kitchens. It could have ricocheted off a wall and hit someone asleep in another apartment. The shock persisted in his hands and in his ears, strong as the smell of gunpowder in the air, that didn't belong with him, in his room. . . .

The rain started with a vengeance. Banichi used his pocket-com to talk to the searchers, and to headquarters, lying to them, saying he'd fired the shot, seeing the intruder headed for the paidhi's room, and, no, the paidhi hadn't been hurt, only frightened, and the aiji shouldn't be wakened, if he hadn't heard the shots. But the guard should be doubled, and the search taken to the south gates, before, Banichi said, the rain wiped out the tracks.

Banichi signed off.

"Why did they come *here?*" Bren asked. Assassins, he understood; but that any ordinary assassin should come into the residential compound, where there were guards throughout, where the aiji slept surrounded by hundreds of willing defenders—nobody in their right mind would do that.

And to assassinate *him*, Bren Cameron, with the aiji at the height of all power and with the nai'aijiin all confirmed in their houses and supportive—where was the sense in it? Where was the gain to anyone at all sane?

"Nadi Bren." Banichi stood over him with his huge arms folded, looking down at him as if he were dealing with some feckless child. "*What* did you see?"

"I told you. Just a shadow, coming through the curtain." The emphasis of the question scared him. He might have been dreaming. He might have roused the whole household and alarmed the guards all for a nightmare. In the way of things at the edge of sleep, he no longer knew for sure what he had seen.

But there had been blood. Jago said so. He *had* shot someone.

"*I* discharged the gun," Banichi said. "Get up and wash your hands, nadi. Wash them twice and three times. And keep the garden doors locked."

"They're only glass," he protested. He had felt safe until now. The aiji had given him the gun two weeks ago. The aiji had taught him to use it, the aiji's doing alone, in the country-house at Taiben, and no one could have known about it, not even Banichi, least of all, surely, the assassin—if he had not dreamed the intrusion through the curtains, if he had not just shot some innocent neighbor, out for air on a stifling night.

"Nadi," Banichi said, "go wash your hands."

He couldn't move, couldn't deal with mundane things, or comprehend what had happened—or why, for the gods' sake, *why* the aiji had given him such an unprecedented and disturbing present, except a general foreboding, and the guards taking stricter account of passes and rules . . .

Except Tabini-aiji had said—'Keep it close.' And he had been afraid of his servants finding it in his room.

"Nadi."

Banichi was angry with him. He got up, naked and

shaky as he was, and went across the carpet to the bath, with a queasier and queasier stomach.

The last steps were a desperate, calculated rush for the toilet, scarcely in time to lose everything in his stomach, humiliating himself, but there was nothing he could do—it was three painful spasms before he could get a breath and flush the toilet.

He was ashamed, disgusted with himself. He ran water in the sink and washed and scrubbed and washed, until he no longer smelled the gunpowder on his hands, only the pungency of the soap and astringents. He thought Banichi must have left, or maybe called the night-servants to clean the bath.

But as he straightened and reached for the towel, he found Banichi's reflection in the mirror.

"Nadi Bren," Banichi said solemnly. "We failed you tonight."

That stung, it truly stung, coming from Banichi, who would never humiliate himself as he had just done. He dried his face and rubbed his dripping hair, then had to look at Banichi face on, Banichi's black, yellow-eyed visage as impassive and powerful as a graven god's.

"You were brave," Banichi said, again, and Bren Cameron, the descendant of spacefarers, the representative of six generations forcibly earthbound on the world of the atevi, felt it like a slap of Banichi's massive hand.

"I didn't get him. Somebody's loose out there, with a gun or—"

"*We* didn't get him, nadi. It's not your business, to 'get him.' Have you been approached by anyone unusual? Have you seen anything out of order before tonight?"

"No."

"Where did you *get* the gun, nadi-ji?"

Did Banichi think he was lying? "Tabini gave it . . ."

"From what *place* did you get the gun? Was this person moving very slowly?"

He saw what Banichi was asking. He wrapped the towel about his shoulders, cold, with the storm wind blowing into the room. He heard the boom of thunder above the city. "From under the mattress. Tabini said keep it close. And I don't know how fast he was moving, the assassin, I mean. I just saw the shadow and slid off the bed and grabbed the gun."

Banichi's brow lifted ever so slightly. "Too much television," Banichi said with a straight face, and took him by the shoulder. "Go back to bed, nadi."

"Banichi, what's happening? *Why* did Tabini give me a gun? Why did he tell me—?"

The grip tightened. "Go to bed, nadi. No one will disturb you after this. You saw a shadow. You called me. I fired two shots."

"I could have hit the kitchen!"

"Most probably one shot did. Kindly remember bullets travel, nadi-ji. Was it not you who taught *us?* Here."

To his stunned surprise, Banichi drew his own gun from the holster and handed it to him.

"Put that under your mattress," Banichi said, and left him—walked on out of the bedroom and into the hall, pulling the door to behind him.

He heard the lock click as he stood there stark naked, with Banichi's gun in his hand and wet hair trailing about his shoulders and dripping on the floor.

He went and shoved the gun under the mattress where he had hidden the other one, and, hoping Jago would choose another way in, shut the lattice doors and the glass, stopping the cold wind and the spatter of rain onto the curtains and the carpet.

Thunder rumbled. He was chilled through. He made a desultory attempt to straighten the bedclothes, then dragged a heavy robe out of the armoire to wrap about himself before he turned off the room lights and struggled, wrapped in the bulky robe, under the tangled sheets. He drew himself into a ball, spasmed with shivers.

Why me? he asked himself over and over, and asked himself whether he could conceivably have posed so extreme a problem to anyone that that individual would risk his life to be rid of him. He couldn't believe he had put himself in a position like that and never once caught a clue of such a complete professional failure.

Perhaps the assassin had thought him the most defense-less dweller in the garden apartments, and his open door had seemed the most convenient way to some other person, perhaps to the inner hallways and Tabini-aiji himself.

But there were so many guards. That was an insane plan, and assassins were, if hired, not mad and not prone to take such risks.

An assassin might simply have mistaken the room. Someone of importance might be lodged in the guest quarters in the upper terrace of the garden. He hadn't heard that that was the case, but otherwise the garden court held just the guards, and the secretaries and the chief cook and the master of accounts—and himself—none of whom were controversial in the least.

But Banichi had left him his gun in place of the aiji's, which he had fired. He understood, clearer-witted now, why Banichi had taken it with him, and why Banichi had had him wash his hands, in case the chief of general security might not believe the account Banichi would give, and in case the chief of security wanted to question the paidhi and have him through police lab procedures.

He most sincerely hoped to be spared that. And the chief of security had no cause against him that *he* knew of—had no motive to investigate *him,* when he was the victim of the crime, and had no reason that he knew of to challenge Banichi's account, Banichi being in some ways higher than the chief of security himself.

But then ... who would want to break into his room? His reasoning looped constantly back to that, and to the chilling fact that Banichi had left him another gun. That was dangerous to do. Someone could decide to question him. Someone could search his room and find the gun, which they could surely then trace to Banichi, with all manner of public uproar. Was it prudent for Banichi to have done that? Was Banichi somehow sacrificing himself, in a way he didn't want, and for something he might have caused?

It even occurred to him to question Banichi's integrity—but Banichi and his younger partner Jago were his favorites among Tabini's personal guards, the ones that took special care of him, while they stood every day next to Tabini, capable of any mischief, if they intended any, to Tabini himself—let alone to a far more replaceable human.

Gods, no, suspecting them was stupid. Banichi wouldn't see him harmed. Banichi would directly lie for him. So would Jago, for Tabini's sake—he was the paidhi, the Interpreter, and the aiji needed him, and that was reason enough for either of them. Tabini-aiji would take it very seriously, what had happened, Tabini would immediately start inquiries, make all kinds of disturbance—

And, dammit, he didn't want the whole citadel set on its ear over this. He didn't want notoriety, or to be the center of an atevi feud. Publicity harmed his position among atevi. It completely destroyed his effectiveness, the moment politics crept into his personal influence, and politics would creep into the matter—politics would *leap* into it, the minute it hit the television news. Everybody would have an opinion, everybody would have a theory, and it could only be destructive to his work.

He huddled under chill covers, trying to get his wits about him, but his empty stomach distracted him and the smell of gunpowder made him queasy. If he called for something to settle his nerves, the night-staff would bring him whatever he asked, or rouse his own servants at his request, but poor Moni and Taigi had probably been roused out of bed to bewildering questions—Did you shoot at the paidhi? Did you leave his door unlatched?

Security was probably going down the list of employees, calling in the whole night-staff and everyone he dealt with—as if anyone in this whole wing could be sleeping now. The shots had probably echoed clear downhill and into the city, the phone lines were probably jammed, the rail station would be under tight restrictions, clear into tomorrow's morning commuter traffic ... no flattery to him: he'd seen what resulted when someone set off alarms inside Tabini's security.

He wanted hot tea and crackers. But he could only make security's job more difficult by asking for personal errands to be run up and down through halls they were trying to search.

Meanwhile the rain spatted against the glass. And it was less and less likely that they would catch the assassin at all.

Moni and Taigi arrived in the morning with his breakfast cart—and the advisement from staff central that Tabini-aiji wanted him in early audience.

Small surprise, that was. In anticipation of a call, he had showered and shaved and dressed himself unaided before dawn, as far as his accustomed soft trousers and shirt, at least, and braided his hair back himself. He had had the television on before they arrived, listening to the morning news: he feared the case might be notorious by now, but to his perplexity he heard not so much as a passing mention of any incident, only a report on the storm last night, which had generated hail in Shigi township, and damaged roof tiles in Wingin before it had gone roaring over the open plains.

He was strangely disappointed, even insulted, by the silence. One had assassins invading one's room and, on one level, despite his earnest desire for obscurity to the outside world, he did hope to hear confirmed that there had been an intruder in the aiji's estates, the filtered sort of news they might have released—or, better yet, that the intruder was securely in the aiji's hands, undergoing questioning.

Nothing of the sort—at least by the television news; and Moni and Taigi laid out breakfast with not a question nor a comment about what had happened in the garden court last night, or why there were towels all over the bathroom floor. They simply delivered the message they had had from the staff central office, absorbed every disarrangement of the premises without seeming to notice, and offered not a hint of anything wrong, or any taste of rumors that might be running the halls.

The lord second heir of Talidi province had assassinated a remote relative in the water garden last spring in an argument over an antique firearm, and the halls of the complex had buzzed with it for days.

Not this morning. Good morning, nand' paidhi, how are you feeling, nand' paidhi? More berries? Tea?

Then, finally, with a downcast glance, from Moni, who seldom had much to say, "We're very glad you're all right, nand' paidhi."

He swallowed his bite of fruit. Gratified.

Appeased. "Did you hear the commotion last night?"

"The guard waked us," Taigi said. "That was the first we knew of anything wrong."

"You didn't hear anything?"

"No, nand' paidhi."

With the lightning and the thunder and the rain coming down, he supposed that the sharp report of the gunshot could have echoed strangely, with the wind swirling about the hill, and with the gun being set off inside the room, rather than outside. The figure in the doorway last night had completely assumed the character of dream to him, a nightmare occurrence in which details both changed and diminished. His servants' utter silence surrounding the incident had unnerved him, even cast his memory into doubt ... not to mention his understanding and expectation of atevi closest to him.

He was glad to hear a reasonable explanation. So the echo of it hadn't carried to the lower-floor servants' court, down on the side of the hill and next the ancient walls. Probably the thunder had covered the echoes. Perhaps there'd been a great peal of it as the storm onset and as the assassin made his try—he'd had his own ears full of the gunshot, which to him had sounded like doom, but it didn't mean the rest of the world had been that close.

But Moni and Taigi were at least duly concerned, and, perhaps perplexed by his human behaviors, or their expectation of them, they didn't know quite what else to say, he supposed. It was different, trying to pick up gossip when one was in the center of the trouble. All information, especially in a life-and-death crisis, became significant; appearing to know something meant someone official could come asking, and no one close to him reasonably wanted to let rumors loose—as he, personally, didn't want any speculation going on about him from servants who might be expected to have information.

No more would Moni and Taigi want to hear another knock on their doors, and endure a second round of questions in the night. Classically speaking—treachery and servants were a cliche in atevi dramas. It was too ridiculous—but it didn't mean they wouldn't feel the onus of suspicion, or feel the fear he very well understood, of unspecified accusations they had no witnesses to refute.

"I do hope it's the end of it," he said to them. "I'm very sorry, nadiin. I trust there won't be more police. I *know* you're honest."

"We greatly appreciate your confidence," Moni said, and both of them bowed. "Please be careful."

"Banichi and Jago are on the case."

"That's very good," Taigi said, and set scrambled eggs in front of him.

So he had his breakfast and put on his best summer coat, the one with the leather collar and leather down the front edges to the knee.

"Please don't delay in the halls," Taigi said.

"I assure you," he said.

"Isn't there security?" Moni asked. "Let us call security."

"To walk to the audience hall?" They *were* worried, he decided, now that the verbal dam had broken. He was further gratified. "I assure you there's no need. It was probably some complete lunatic, probably hiding in a storage barrel somewhere. They might go after lord Murida in the water garden at high noon—not me. I assure you. With the aiji's own guards swarming about . . . not highly likely." He took his key and slipped it into his trousers. "Just be careful of the locks. The garden side, especially, for the next few days."

"Nadi," they said, and bowed again—anxious, he decided, as they'd truly been when they'd arrived, just not advertising their state of mind, which atevi didn't. Which reminded him that he shouldn't let his worry reach his face either. He went cheerfully out the door—

Straight into a black uniform and, well above eye-level, a scowling atevi face.

"Nand' paidhi," the guard officer said. "I'm to escort you to the hall."

"Hardly necessary," he said. His heart had skipped a dozen beats. He didn't personally know the man. But the uniform wasn't one an assassin would dare counterfeit, not on his subsequent life, and he walked with the officer, out into the corridors of the complex, past the ordinary residential guard desk and into the main areas of the building—along the crowded colonnade, where wind gusted, fresh with rain and morning chill.

Ancient stonework took sunlight and shadow, the fortress walls of the Bu-javid, the citadel and governmental complex, sprawled over its high hill, aloof and separate from the urban sprawl of Shejidan—and down below those walls the hotels and the hostelries would be full to overflowing. The triennial public audience, beginning this morning, brought hundreds of provincial lords and city and township and district officials into town—by subway, by train—all of them trekking the last mile on foot from the hotels that ringed the ancient Bu-javid, crowds bearing petitions climbing the terraced stone ceremonial road, passing beneath the fortified Gate of the Promise of Justice, and trekking finally up the last broad, flower-bordered courses to the renowned Ninefold

Doors, a steady stream of tall, broad-shouldered atevi, with their night-black skins and glossy black braids, some in rich coats bordered in gilt and satin, some in plain, serviceable cloth, but clearly their courtly best. Professional politicians rubbed shoulder to shoulder with ordinary trade folk, lords of the Associations with anxious, unpracticed petitioners, bringing their colorfully ribboned petitions, rolled and bound, and with them, their small bouquets of flowers to lay on the foyer tables, an old custom of the season.

The hall at the end of the open colonnade smelled of recent rain and flowers, and rang with voices—atevi meeting one another, or falling into line to register with the secretaries, on whose desks, set up in the vast lower foyer, the stacks of documents and petitions were growing.

For the courtiers, a human on his way to court business through this milling chaos was an ordinary sight—a pale, smallish figure head and shoulders shorter than the crowds through which he passed, a presence conservative in his simple, unribboned braid and leather trim—the police escort was uncommon, but no one stared, except the country folk and private petitioners.

"Look!" a child cried, and pointed at him.

A mortified parent batted the offending hand down while the echoes rang, high and clear, in the vaulted ceilings. Atevi looked. And pretended not to have seen either him or his guard.

A lord of the provinces went through the halls attended by his own aides and by his own guards and the aiji's as well, and provoked no rude stares. Bren went with his police escort, in the same pretense of invisibility, a little anxious, since the child's shout, but confident in the visible presence of the aiji's guards at every doorway and every turn, ordinary precaution on audience day.

In that near presence, he bade a courteous farewell to his police escort at the small Whispering Port, which, a small section of one of the great ceremonial doors, led discreetly and without official recognition into the back of the audience hall. He slipped through it and softly closed it again, so as not to disturb the advance meetings in progress.

Late, he feared. Moni and Taigi hadn't advanced the hour of his wake-up at all, simply shown up at their usual time, lacking other orders and perhaps fearing to do anything unusual, with a police guard standing at his door. He hoped Tabini hadn't wanted otherwise, and started over to the reception desk to see where he fitted in the hearings.

Banichi was there. Banichi, in the metal-studded black of the aiji's personal guard, intercepted him with a touch on his arm.

"Nadi Bren. Did you sleep last night?"

"No," he confessed. And hoping: "Did you catch him?"

"No, nadi. There was the storm. We were not so fortunate."

"Does Tabini know what happened?" He cast a glance toward the dais, where Tabini-aiji was talking to governor Brominandi, one of the invitational private hearings. "I think I'm on the agenda. Does he want to talk with me? What shall I tell him?"

"The truth, only in private. It *was* his gun—was it not?"

He threw Banichi a worried look. If Banichi doubted his story, he hadn't left him with that impression last night. "I told you the truth, Banichi."

"I'm sure you did," Banichi said, and when he would have gone on to the reception desk, as he had purposed, to give his name to the secretary, Banichi caught his sleeve and held him back. "Nothing official." Banichi nodded toward the dais, still holding his sleeve, and brought him to the foot of the dais instead.

Brominandi of Entaillan province was finishing his business. Brominandi, whose black hair was shot through with white, whose hands sparkled with rings both ornamental and official, would lull a stone to boredom, and the bystanding guards had as yet found no gracious way to edge the governor off.

Tabini nodded to what Brominandi was saying, nodded a second time, and finally said, "I'll take it before council." It sounded dreadfully like the Alujis river rights business again, two upstream provinces against three downstream which relied on its water for irrigation. For fifty years, that pot had been boiling, with suit and counter-suit. Bren folded his hands in front of him and stood with Banichi, head ducked, making himself as inconspicuous as a human possibly could in the court.

Finally Tabini-aiji accepted the inevitable petition (or was it counter-petition?) from Brominandi, a weighty thing of many seals and ribbons, and passed it to his legislative aides.

At which time Bren slid a glance up to Tabini, and received one back, which was the summons to him and to Banichi, up the several steps to the side of the aiji's chair, in the lull in which the favored early petitioners could mill about and gossip, a dull, echoing murmur in the vaulted, white and gilt hall.

Tabini said, right off, "Do you know who it was, Bren? Do you have any idea?"

"None, aiji-ma, nothing. I shot at him. I missed. Banichi said I should say he fired the shot."

A look went past him, to Banichi. Tabini's yellow eyes were very pale, ghostly in certain lights—frightening, when he was angry. But he didn't seem to be angry, or assigning blame to either of them.

Banichi said, "It removed questions."

"No idea the nature of the intrusion."

"A burglar would be a fool. Assignations . . ."

"No," Bren said, uncomfortable in the suggestion, but Tabini knew him, knew that atevi women had a certain curiosity about him, and it was a joke at his expense.

"Not a feminine admirer."

"No, aiji-ma." He certainly hoped not, recalling the

blood Jago had found in the first of the rain, out on the terrace.

Tabini-aiji reached out and touched his arm, apology for the levity. "No one has filed. It's a serious matter. I take it seriously. Be careful with your locks."

"The garden door is only glass," Banichi said. "Alterations would be conspicuous."

"A wire isn't," Tabini said.

Bren was dismayed. The aiji's doors and windows might have such lethal protections. He had extreme reservations about the matter.

"I'll see to it," Banichi said.

"I might walk into it," Bren said.

"You won't," Tabini said. And to Banichi: "See to it. This morning. One on either door. His key to disarm. Change the locks."

"Aiji," Bren began to say.

"I have a long list today," Tabini said, meaning shut up and sit down, and when Tabini-aiji took that tone about a matter, there was no quarrel with it. They left the top of the dais. Bren stopped at the fourth step, which was his ordinary post.

"You *stay* here," Banichi said. "I'll bring you the new key."

"Banichi, is anybody after me?"

"It would seem so, wouldn't it? I do doubt it was a lover."

"Do you know anything I don't?"

"Many things. Which interests you?"

"My *life*."

"Watch the wire. The garden side will activate with a key, too. I'm moving your bed from in front of the door."

"It's summer. It's hot."

"We all have our inconveniences."

"I wish someone would tell me what's going on!"

"You shouldn't turn down the ladies. Some take it badly."

"You're not serious."

No, Banichi wasn't. Banichi was evading the question again. Banichi damned well knew something. He stood in frustration as Banichi went cheerfully to turn his room into a death-trap, mats in front of doors, lethal wires to complete the circuit if a foolish, sleepy human forgot and hurried to shut his own garden door in a sudden rainstorm.

He had been scared of the events last night. Now he was mad, furiously angry at the disruption of his life, his quarters, his freedom to come and go in the city—he foresaw guards, restrictions, threats . . . without a damned reason, except some lunatic who possibly, for whatever reason, didn't like humans. That was the only conclusion he could come to.

He sat down on the step where the paidhi-aiji was entitled to sit, and listened through the last pre-audience audience with the notion that he might hear something to give him a clue, at least, whether there was some wider, more political reason to worry, but the way Banichi seemed to be holding information from him, and Tabini's silence, when Tabini himself probably knew something he wasn't saying, all began to add up to him to an atevi with a grudge.

No licensed assassin was going to file on a human who was an essential, treated presence in the aiji's household—a presence without the right to carry arms, but all the same, a court official and a personal intimate of the aiji of the Western Association. No professional in his right mind would take *that* on.

Which left some random fool attacking him as a symbol, perhaps, or someone mad at technology or at some equally remote grievance, who could know? Who could track such a thing?

The only comforting thought was that, if it wasn't a licensed assassin, it was the lunatic himself or an amateur who couldn't get a license—the sort that might mow down bystanders by mistake, true, dangerous in that regard.

But Banichi, unlike the majority of the aiji's guards, had a license. You didn't take him on. You didn't take on Jago, either. The rain last night had been a piece of luck for the intruder—who had either counted on the rain wiping out his tracks on the gravel and cement of the garden walkways, or he'd been stupid, and lucky.

Now the assassin wasn't lucky. Banichi was looking for him. And if he'd left a footprint in a flower bed or a fingerprint anywhere, that man—assuming it was a man—was in trouble.

He daren't go to a licensed doctor, for one thing. There had been blood on the terrace. Bren personally hoped he'd made life uncomfortable for the assassin, who clearly hadn't expected the reception he'd met. Most of all he hoped, considering Banichi's taking on the case, that life would become uncomfortable for the assassin's employer, if any, enough for the employer to withdraw the contract.

The doors opened. The guards and marshals let the crowd in, and the secretary accepted from the Day Marshal the towering stack of ribboned, sealed petitions and affidavits and filings.

There were some odd interfaces in the dealings of atevi and humans. One *couldn't* blame the atevi for clinging to traditional procedures, clumsy as the stacks were, and there *was* a computer record. The secretaries in the foyer created it.

But ask the atevi to use citizen numbers or case numbers? Convince them first that their computer-assigned personal numbers were auspicious in concert with their other numerologies. Convince them that changing those numbers caused chaos and lost records—because if things started going wrong, an ateva faulted his number and wanted it changed, immediately.

Create codes for the provinces, simply to facilitate computer sorting? Were *those* numbers auspicious, or was it some malevolent attempt of the aiji's court in Shejidan to diminish their importance and their power?

Then, of course, there was the dire rumor that typing the names in *still* produced numbers in the computers, numbers of devious and doubtless malevolent intent on the part of the aiji, conspiring, of course, with the humans who had brought the insidious device to earth.

Not all that humans brought to earth was anathema, of course. Television was an addiction. Flight was an increasingly essential convenience, practiced as see-and-avoid by frighteningly determined provincials, although the aiji had laid down the law within his domains, requiring flight plans, after the famous Weinathi Bridge crash.

Thank the atevi gods Tabini-aiji was a completely irreligious man.

The matters before the aiji had one turn of the glass apiece—a summation, by the petitioner. Most were rural matters, some involved trade, a few regarded public works projects—highways and dams and bridges, harbors and hunting and fishing rights which involved the rights of the Associations united under the aiji's influence. Originating projects and specific details of allocation and budget involved the two houses of the legislature, the hasdrawad and the tashrid—such bills were not the aiji's to initiate, only to approve or disapprove. But so much, so incredibly much, still needed the aiji's personal seal and personal hearing.

For chief example, there were the feuds to register, two in number, one a wife against an ex-husband, over illegal conversion of her property.

"It's better to go to court," Tabini said plainly. "You could get the money back, in installments, from his income."

"I'd rather kill him," the wife said, and Tabini said, "Record it," waved his hand and went on to the next case.

That was *why* humans preferred their enclave on Mospheira. Mospheira was an island, it was under human administration, computers had undisputed numbers, and laws didn't have bloodfeud as an alternative.

It did, however, mean that for all the sixty so-called provinces and conservatively three hundred million people under the aiji's hand, there was a single jail, which generally held less than fifty individuals awaiting trial or hearing, who could not be released on their own recognizance. There were a number of mental hospitals for those who needed them. There were four labor-prisons, for the incorrigibly antisocial—the sort, for instance, who took the assassins' function into their own hands, after refusal by a guild who did truly refuse unwarranted solicitation.

Sane, law-abiding atevi simply avoided argumentative people. One tried to have polite divorces. One tried not to antagonize or embarrass one's natural opponents. Thank God atevi generally did prefer negotiation or, as a last reasonable resort before filing feud, a physical, unarmed confrontation—equally to be avoided. Tall, strong humans still stood more than a head shorter and massed a third less than the average atevi, male or female—the other reason humans preferred their own jurisdiction.

He'd clearly annoyed somebody who hadn't followed the rules. His mind kept going back to that. No one had filed a feud. They had to notify him, that was one of the stringent requirements of the filing, but no one had even indicated casual irritation with him—and now Tabini was putting lethal defenses into his quarters.

The shock of the incident last night was still reverberating through his thinking, readjusting everything, until he had suddenly to realize he really wasn't entirely safe walking the halls out there. Professional assassins avoided publicity and preferred their faces not to become famous—but there were instances of the knife appearing out of the faceless crowd, the push on the stairs.

And in no few of the lords' staffs there were licensed assassins he daily rubbed shoulders with and never thought about it—until now.

An elderly gentleman brought the forty-sixth case, which regarded, in sum, a request for the aiji's attendance at a regional conference on urban development. That went onto the stack, for archive.

One day, he'd told the aiji himself, and he knew his predecessors had said it, one day the archives would collapse under the weight of seals, ribbons, and paper, all ten stories of the block-long building going down in a billow of dust. But this had to be the last petition for the session. The secretary called no more names. The reception table looked empty.

But, no, not the last one. Tabini called the secretary, who brought an uncommonly elaborate paper, burdened with the red and black ribbons of high nobility.

"A filing of Intent," Tabini said, rising, and startling the aides and assembled witnesses, and the secretary held up the document and read: "Tabini-aiji against persons unknown, who, without filing Intent, invaded the peace of my house and brought a threat of harm against the person of the paidhi-aiji, Bren Cameron. If harm results henceforth to any guest or person of my household by this agency or by any other agency intending harm to the paidhi-aiji, I personally declare Intent to file feud, because of the offense to the safety of my roof, with Banichi of Dajoshu township of Talidi province as my registered and licensed agent. I publish it and cause it to be published, and place it in public records with its seals and its signatures and sigils."

Bren was thoroughly shocked. He felt altogether conspicuous in the turning heads and the murmur of comment and question that followed as Tabini-aiji left the dais and walked past him, with:

"Be prudent, nadi Bren."

"Aiji-ma," he murmured, and bowed a profound bow, to cover his confusion. The audience was over. Jago was quick to fall in with Tabini, along with a detachment of the household and personal guard, as Tabini cut a swath through the crowd on his way to the side doors and the inner halls.

Bren started away on his own, dreading the course

through the halls, wondering if the attempted assassin or his employer was in the room and whether the police escort would still be waiting out there.

But Banichi turned up in his path, and fell in with him, escorting him through the Whispering Port and into the public halls.

"Tabini declared Intent," he said to Banichi, wondering if Banichi had known in advance what Tabini had drafted.

"I'm not surprised," Banichi said.

"I ought to take the next plane to Mospheira."

"Highly foolish."

"We have different laws. And on Mospheira an ateva stands out. Find me the assassin in this crowd."

"You don't even know it was one of us."

"Then it was the broadest damn human I ever saw. —Forgive me." One didn't swear, if one was the paidhi-aiji, not, at least, in the public hall. "It wasn't a human. I know that."

"You know who came to your room. You don't know, however, who might have hired him. There is some smuggling on Mospheira, as the paidhi is aware. Connections we don't know exist are a very dangerous possibility."

The language had common pronouns that didn't specify gender. Him or her, that meant. And politicians and the aiji's staff used that pronoun habitually.

"I know where I'm safer."

"Tabini needs you here."

"For *what?*" That the aiji was undertaking anything but routine business was news to him. He hadn't heard. Banichi was telling him something no one else had.

And a handful of weeks ago Tabini had found unprecedented whimsy in arming him and giving him two hours of personal instruction at his personal retreat. They had joked, and shot melons on poles, and had supper together, and Tabini had had all the time he could possibly want to warn him if something was coming up besides the routine councils and committee meetings that involved the paidhi.

They turned the corner. Banichi, he did not fail to note, hadn't noticed his question. They walked out onto the colonnade, with the walls of the ancient Bu-javid pale and regular beyond them, the traffic flow on the steps reversed, now, downward bound. Atevi who had filed for hearing had their numbers, and the aiji would receive them in their established order.

But when they walked into the untrafficked hall that led toward the garden apartments, Banichi gave him two keys. "These are the only valid ones," Banichi said. "Kindly don't mix them up with your old ones. The old ones work. They just don't turn off the wires."

He gave Banichi a disturbed stare—which, also, Banichi didn't seem to notice. "Can't you just shock the bastard? Scare him? He's not a professional. There's been no notice. . . ."

"I'm within my license," Banichi said. "The Intent is filed. Didn't you say so? The intruder would be very foolish to try again."

A queasy feeling was in his stomach. "Banichi, damn it. . . ."

"I've advised the servants. Honest and wise servants, capable of serving in this house, will request admission henceforth. Your apartment is no different than mine, now. Or Jago's. I change my own sheets."

As well as he knew Jago and Banichi, he had had no idea of such hazards in their quarters. It made sense in their case or in Tabini's. It didn't, in his.

"I trust," Banichi said, "you've no duplicate keys circulating. No ladies. No—hem—other connections. You've not been gambling, have you?"

"No!" Banichi knew him, too, knew he had female connections on Mospheira, one and two not averse to what Banichi would call a one-candle night. The paidhi-aiji hadn't time for a social life, otherwise. Or for long romantic maneuverings or hurt feelings, lingering hellos or good-byes—most of all, not for the peddling of influence or attempts to push this or that point on him. His friends didn't ask questions. Or want more than a bouquet of flowers, a phone call, and a night at the theater.

"Just mind, if you've given any keys away."

"I'm not such a fool."

"Fools of that kind abound in the Bu-javid. I've spoken severely to the aiji."

Give atevi a piece of tech and sometimes they put it together in ways humans hadn't, in their own history—inventors, out of their own social framework, connected ideas in ways you didn't expect, and never intended, either in social consequence, or in technical ramifications. The wire was one. Figure that atevi had a propensity for inventions regarding personal protection, figure that atevi law didn't forbid lethal devices, and ask how far they'd taken other items and to what uses they didn't advertise.

The paidhi tried to keep ahead of it. The paidhi tried to keep abreast of every technology and every piece of vocabulary in the known universe, but bits and tags perpetually got away and it was accelerating—the escape of knowledge, the recombination of items into things utterly out of human control.

Most of all, atevi weren't incapable of making technological discoveries completely on their own ... and had no trouble keeping them prudently under wraps. They were not a communicative people.

They reached the door. He used the key Banichi had given him. The door opened. Neither the mat nor the wire was in evidence.

"Ankle high and black," Banichi said. "But it's down and disarmed. You did use the right key."

"*Your* key." He didn't favor Banichi's jokes. "I don't see the mat."

"Under the carpet. *Don't* walk on it barefoot. You'd bleed. The wire is an easy step in. You can walk on it while it's off. Just don't do that barefoot, either."

He could scarcely see it. He walked across the mat. Banichi stayed the other side of it.

"It cuts its own way through insulation," Banichi said.

"And through boot leather, paidhi-ji, if it's live. Don't touch it, even when it's dead. Lock the door and don't wander the halls."

"I have an energy council meeting this afternoon."

"You'll want to change coats, nadi. Wait here for Jago. She'll escort you."

"What is this? I'm to have an escort everywhere I go? I'm to be leapt upon by the minister of Works? Assaulted by the head of Water Management?"

"Prudence, prudence, nadi Bren. Jago's witty company. She's fascinated by your brown hair."

He was outraged. "You're enjoying this. It's not funny, Banichi."

"Forgive me." Banichi was unfailingly solemn. "But humor her. Escort is so damned boring."

II

It was the old argument, highway transport versus rail, bringing intense lobbying pressure from the highway transport operators, who wanted road expansion into the hill towns, versus the rail industry, who wanted the high-speed research money and the eventual extensions into the highlands. Versus commercial air freight, and versus the general taxpayers who didn't want their taxes raised. The provincial governor wanted a highway instead of a rail spur, and advanced arguments, putting considerable influence to bear on the minister of Works.

Computer at his elbow, the screen long since gone to rest, Bren listened through the argument he'd heard in various guises—this was a repainted, replastered version—and on a notepad on the table in front of him, sketched interlocked circles that might be psychologically significant.

Far more interesting a pastime than listening to the minister's delivery. Jago was outside, probably enjoying a soft drink, while the paidhi-aiji was running out of ice water.

The Minister of Works had a numbing, sing-song rhythm in his voice. But the paidhi-aiji was obliged to listen, in case of action on the proposal. The paidhi-aiji had no vote, of course, if the highway came to a vote today at all, which didn't look likely. He had no right even to speak uninvited, unless he decided to impose his one real power, his outright veto over a council recommendation to the upper house, the tashrid—a veto which was good until the tashrid met to consider it. He had used his veto twice in the research and development council, never with this minister of Works, although his predecessor had done it a record eighteen times on the never-completed Transmontane Highway, which was now, since the rail link, a moot point.

One hoped.

There was the whole of human history in the library on Mospheira, all the records of their predecessors, or all that they could still access—records which suggested, with the wisdom of hindsight, that consuming the planet's petrochemicals in a vast orgy of private transport wasn't the best long-range choice for the environment or the quality of life. The paidhi's advice might go counter to local ambitions. In the case of the highway system, the advice had gone counter, indeed it had. But atevi had made enormous advances, and the air above the Bergid range still sparkled. The paidhi took a certain pride in that—in the name of nearly two hundred years of paidhiin before him.

The atevi hadn't quite mastered steam when humans had arrived on their planet uninvited and unwilling.

Atevi had seen the tech, atevi had been, like humans, eager for profit and progress—but unlike humans, they tended to see profit much more in terms of power accruing to their interlocked relationships. It was something about their hardwiring, human theorists said; since the inclination seemed to transcend cultural lines; a scholarly speculation useful for the theorists sitting safe on Mospheira, not for the paidhi-aiji, who had to make practical sense to the aiji of the Ragi atevi in the city of Shejidan, in Mospheira's nearest neighboring Association and long-term ally—

Without which, there might be a second ugly test of human technology versus atevi *haroniin*, a concept for which there was no human word or even complete translation. Say that atevi patience had its limits, that assassination was essential to the way atevi kept their social balance, and *haroniin* meant something like 'accumulated stresses on the system, justifying adjustment.' Like all the other approximations: aiji wasn't quite 'duke,' it certainly wasn't 'king,' and the atevi concept of countries, borders and boundaries of authority had things in common with their concept of flight plans.

No, it wasn't a good idea to develop highways and independent transport, decentralizing what was an effective tax-supported system of public works, which supported the various aijiin throughout the continent in their offices, which in turn supported Tabini-aiji and the system at Shejidan.

No, it wasn't a good idea to encourage systems in which entrepreneurs might start making a lot of money, spreading other entrepreneurial settlement along roadways and forming human-style corporations.

Not in a system where assassination was an ordinary and legal social adjustment.

Damn, it was disturbing, that attempt on his apartment, more so the more time distanced him from the physical fear. In the convolutions of thinking one necessarily was drawn into, *being* the paidhi—studying and competing for years to be the paidhi, and becoming, in sum, fluent in a language in which human words and human thought didn't neatly translate ... bits and pieces of connections had started bobbing to the surface of the very dark waters of atevi mentality as he understood it. Bits and pieces had been doing that since last night, just random bits of worrisome thought drifting up out of that interface between atevi ideas and human ones.

Worrisome thoughts that said that attacking the paidhiaiji, the supposedly inoffensive, neutral and discreetly silent paidhi-aiji ... was, if not a product of lunacy, a premeditated attack on some sort of system, meaning any point of what *was*.

He tried to make himself the most apolitical, quiet presence in Tabini's court. He pursued *no* contact with the political process except sitting silently in court or in the corner of some technological or sociological impact council—and occasionally, very occasionally presenting a paper. Having public attention called to him as Tabini had just done ... was contrary to all the established policy of his office.

He wished Tabini hadn't made his filing of Intent— but clearly Tabini had had to do something severe about the invasion of the Bu-javid, most particularly the employer of the assassin's failure to file feud before doing it.

No matter that assassination was legal and accepted— you didn't, in atevi terms, proceed without filing, you didn't proceed without license, and you didn't order wholesale bloodbaths. You removed the minimal individual that would solve a problem. *Biichi-gi,* the atevi called it. Humans translated it ... 'finesse.'

Finesse was certainly what the attempt lacked—give or take the would-be assassin hadn't expected the paidhi to have a gun that humans weren't supposed to have, this side of the Mospheira straits.

A gun that Tabini had given him very recently.

And Banichi and Jago insisted they couldn't find a clue.

Damned disturbing.

Attack on some system? The paidhi-aiji might find himself identified as belonging to any number of systems ... like being human, like being the paidhi-aiji at all, like advising the aiji that the rail system was, for long-range ecological considerations, better than highway transport ... but who ever absolutely knew the reason or the offense, but the party who'd decided to 'finesse' a matter?

The paidhi-aiji hadn't historically been a target. Personally, his whole tenure had been the collection of words, the maintenance of the dictionary, the observation and reporting of social change. The advice he gave Tabini was far from solely *his* idea: everything he did and said came from hundreds of experts and advisers on Mospheira, telling him in detail what to say, what to offer, what to admit to—so finessing *him* out of the picture might send a certain message of displeasure with humans, but it would hardly hasten highways into existence.

Tabini had felt something in the wind, and armed him.

And he hadn't reported that fact to Mospheira, second point to consider: Tabini had asked him not to tell anyone about the gun, he had always respected certain few private exchanges between himself and the aiji, and he had extended that discretion to keeping it out of his official reports. He'd worried about it, but Tabini's confidences had flattered him, personally and professionally—there at the hunting lodge, in Taiben, where all kinds of court rules were suspended and everyone was on holiday. Marksmanship was an atevi sport, an atevi passion—and Tabini, a champion marksman with a pistol, had, apparently on whim, violated a specific Treaty provision to provide the paidhi, as had seemed then, a rare week of personal closeness with him, a rare gesture of—if not friendship, at least as close as atevi came, an abrogation of all the formalities that surrounded and constrained him and Tabini alike.

It had immensely increased his status in the eyes of certain staff. Tabini had seemed pleased that he took to the lessons, and giving him the gun as a present had seemed a moment of extravagant rebellion. Tabini had insisted he 'keep it close,' while his mind racketed wildly between the absolute, unprecedented, and possibly policy-changing warmth of Tabini's gesture toward a human, and an immediate guilty panic considering his official position and his obligation to report to his own superiors.

He'd immediately worried what he was going to do with it on the plane home, and how or if he was going to dispose of it—or report it, when it might be a test Tabini posed him, to see if he had a personal dimension, or personal discretion, in the rules his superiors imposed on him.

And then, after he was safely on the plane home, the gun and the ammunition a terrifying secret in the personal bag at his feet, he had sat watching the landscape pass and adding up how tight security had gotten around Tabini in the last few weeks.

Then he'd gotten scared. Then he'd known he had gotten himself into something he didn't know how to get out of—that he ought to report, and didn't, because nobody on Mospheira could *read* the situation in Tabini's court the way he could on a realtime basis. He knew that some danger might be in the offing, but his assessment of the situation might not have critical bits of data, and he didn't *want* orders from his superiors until he could figure out what the undercurrents were in the capital.

That was why he had put the gun under the mattress, which his servants didn't ordinarily disturb, rather than hiding it in the drawers, which they sometimes did rearrange.

That was why, when a shadow came through his bedroom door, he hadn't wasted a second going after it and not a second more in firing. He'd lived in the Bu-javid long enough to know at a very basic level that atevi didn't walk through people's doors uninvited, not in a society where everyone was armed and assassination was legal. The assassin had surely been confident the paidhi wouldn't have a weapon—and gotten the surprise of his life.

If it hadn't been a trial designed to catch him with the gun. Which didn't say why—

He was woolgathering. They were proposing a vote next meeting. He had lost the minister's last remarks. If the paidhi let something slip unchallenged through the council, he could end up losing a point two hundred years of his predecessors had battled to hold on to. There were points past which even Tabini couldn't undo a council recommendation—points past which Tabini *wouldn't* undertake a fight that might not be in Tabini's interest, once he'd set Tabini in a convenient position to deny his advice, Tabini being, understandably, on the atevi side of any questionable call.

"I'll want a transcript," he said, as the meeting broke up, and gathered a roomful of shocked stares.

Which probably alarmed everyone unnecessarily—they might take his glum mood for anger and the postponement and request for a transcript as a forewarning that the paidhi was disposed to veto.

And against what interest? He saw the frown gather on the minister's face, wondering if the paidhi was taking a position they didn't understand—and confusion wasn't a good thing to generate in an ateva. Action bred action. He had enough troubles without scaring anyone needlessly.

The Minister of Works could even conclude he blamed someone in his office for an attack that was surely reported coast to coast of the continent by now, in which case the minister and his interests might think they should protect themselves, or secure themselves allies they believed he would fear.

Say, I wasn't listening during the speech? Insult the gentle and long-winded Minister of Works directly in the sorest point of his vanity? Insult the entire council, as if their business bored him?

Damn, damn, a little disturbance in atevi affairs led to so much consequence. Moving at all was so cursed delicate. And they *didn't* understand people who let every passing emotion show on their faces.

He took his computer. He walked out into the hall, re-

membering to bow and be polite to the atevi he might
have distressed.

Jago was at his elbow instantly, prim Jago, not so tall
as the atevi around her, but purposeful, deliberate, dangerous in a degree that had to make everyone around him
reassess the position he held and the resources he had.

Resources the aiji had, more to the point, if, a moment
ago, they had entertained any uneasiness about him.

There was another turn of atevi thinking—that said that
if a person had power like that, and hadn't used it, he
wouldn't do so as long as the status quo maintained itself
intact.

"Any findings?" he asked Jago, when they had a space
of the hall to themselves.

"We're watching," Jago said. "That's all. The trail's
cold." "Mospheira would be safer for me."

"But Tabini needs you."

"Banichi said so. For what? I've no advisements to
give him. I've been handed no inquiry that I've heard of,
unless something turns up in the energy transcript. I'm
sorry. My mind hasn't been on business."

"Get some sleep tonight."

With death-traps at both doors. He had nothing to say
to that suggestion. He took the turn toward the post office
to pick up his mail, hoping for something pleasant. A letter from home. Magazines, pictures to look at that had
human faces, articles that depended on human language
and human logic, for a few hours after supper to let go of
thoughts that were going to haunt his sleep a second
night. It was one of those days he wanted to tell Barb to
get on the plane, fly in here, just twenty-four human
hours. . . .

With lethal wires on his bedroom doors?

He took out his mail-slot key, he reached for the door,
and Jago caught his arm. "The attendant can get it."

From behind the wall, she meant—because someone
was trying to kill him, and Jago didn't want him reaching
into the box after the mail.

"That's extreme," he said.

"So might your enemies be."

"I thought the word was finesse. Blowing up a mail slot?"

"Or inserting a needle in a piece of mail." She took his key and pocketed it. "The paidhi's mail, nadi-ji."

The attendant went. And came back.

"Nothing," the attendant said.

"There's always something," Bren said. "Forgive my persistence, nadi, but my mailbox is never empty. It's never in my tenure here been empty. Please be sure."

"I couldn't mistake you, nand' paidhi." The attendant spread his hands. "I've never seen the box empty either. Perhaps there's holiday."

"Not on any recent date."

"Perhaps someone picked it up for you."

"Not by my authorization."

"I'm sorry, nand' paidhi. There's just nothing there."

"Thank you." He bowed, there being nothing else to say, and nowhere else to look. "Thank you for your trouble." And quietly to Jago, in perplexity and distress: "Someone's been at my mail."

"Banichi probably picked it up."

"It's very kind of him to take the trouble, Jago, but I can pick up my mail."

"Perhaps he thought to save you bother."

He sighed and shook his head, and walked away, Jago right with him, from the first step down the hall. "His office, do you think?"

"I don't think he's there. He said something about a meeting."

"He's taken my mail to a meeting."

"Possibly, nadi Bren."

Maybe Banichi would bring it to the room. Then he could read himself to sleep, or write letters, before he forgot human language. Failing that, maybe there'd be a machimi play on television. A little revenge, a little humor, light entertainment.

They took the back halls to reach the main lower corridor, walked to his room. He used his key—opened the door and saw his bed relocated to the other end of the room. The television was sitting where his bed had been. Everything felt wrong-handed.

He avoided the downed wire, dead though it was supposed to be. Jago stepped over it too, and went into his bathroom without a please or may I? and went all around the room with a bug-finder.

He picked up the remote and turned on the television. Changed channels. The news channel was off the air. All the general channels were off the air. The weather channel worked. One entertainment channel did.

"Half the channels are off."

Jago looked at him, bent over, examining the box that held one end of the wire. "The storm last night, perhaps."

"They were working this morning."

"I don't know, nadi Bren. Maybe they're doing repairs."

He flung the remote down on the bed. "We have a saying. One of those days."

"What, one of those days?"

"When nothing works."

"A day now or a day to come?" Jago was rightside up now. Atevi verbs had necessary time-distinctions. Banichi spoke a little Mosphei'. Jago was a little more language-bound.

"Nadi Jago. *What* are you looking for?"

"The entry counter."

"It counts entries."

"In a very special way, nadi Bren. If it should be a professional, one can't suppose there aren't countermeasures."

"It won't be any professional. They're required to file. Aren't they?"

"People are required to behave well. Do they always? We have to assume the extreme."

One could expect the aiji's assassins to be thorough,

and to take precautions no one else would take—simply because they knew the utmost possibilities of their trade. He should be glad, he told himself, that he had them looking out for him.

God, he *hoped* nobody broke in tonight. He didn't want to wake up and find some body burning on his carpet.

He didn't want to find himself shot or knifed in his bed, either. An ateva who'd made one attempt undetected might lose his nerve and desist. If he was a professional, his employer, losing his nerve, might recall him.

Might.

You didn't count on it. You didn't ever quite count on it—you could just get a little easier as the days passed and hope the bastard wasn't just awaiting a better window of opportunity.

"A professional would have made it good," he said to Jago.

"We don't lose many that we track," Jago said.

"It was raining."

"All the same," Jago said.

He wished she hadn't said that.

Banichi came back at supper, arrived with two new servants, and a cart with three suppers. Algini and Tano, Banichi called the pair, in introduction. Algini and Tano bowed with that degree of coolness that said they were high hall servants, thank you, and accustomed to fancier apartments.

"I trusted Taigi and Moni," Bren muttered, after the servants had left the cart.

"Algini and Tano have clearances," Banichi said.

"Clearances. —Did you get my mail? Someone got my mail."

"I left it at the office. Forgive me."

He could ask Banichi to go back after it. He could insist that Banichi go back after it. But Banichi's supper would be cold—Banichi having invited himself and Jago to supper in his apartment.

He sighed and fetched an extra chair. Jago brought another from the side of the room. Banichi set up the leaves of the serving table and set out the dishes, mostly cooked fruit, heavily spiced, game from the reserve at Nanjiran. Atevi didn't keep animals for slaughter, not the Ragi atevi, at any rate. Mospheira traded with the tropics, with the Nisebi, down south, for processed meat, preserved meat, which didn't have to be sliced thin enough to admit daylight—a commerce which Tabini-aiji called disgraceful, and which Bren had reluctantly promised to try to discourage, the paidhi being obliged to exert bidirectional influence, although without any veto power over human habits.

So even on Mospheira it wasn't politic for the paidhi to eat anything but game, and that in appropriate season. To preserve meat was commercial, and commercialism regarding an animal life taken was not *kabiu,* not 'in the spirit of good example.' The aiji's household had to be *kabiu. Very kabiu.*

And observing this point of refinement was, Tabini had pointed out to him with particular satisfaction in turning the tables, *ecologically* sound harvesting practice. Which the paidhi must, of course, support with the same enthusiasm when it came from atevi.

Down in the city market you could get a choice of meats. Frozen, canned, and air-dried.

"Aren't you hungry, nadi?"

"Not my favorite season." He was graceless this evening. And unhappy. "Nobody knows anything. Nobody tells me anything. I appreciate the aiji's concern. And yours. But is there some particular reason I can't fly home for a day or two?"

"The aiji—"

"Needs me. But no one knows why. You wouldn't mislead me, would you, Jago?"

"It's my profession, nadi Bren."

"To lie to me."

There was an awkward silence at the table. He'd intended his bluntness as bitter humor. It had come out at the wrong moment, into the wrong mood, into their honest and probably frustrated efforts to find answers. Of all humans, he was educated not to make mistakes with them.

"Forgive me," he said.

"His culture will lie," Banichi said plainly to Jago. "But admitting one has done so insults the victim."

Jago took on a puzzled look.

"Forgive me," Bren said again. "It was a joke, nadi Jago."

Jago still looked puzzled, and frowned, but not angrily. "We take this threat very seriously."

"I didn't. I'm beginning to." He thought: Where's my mail, Banichi? But he had a mouthful of soup instead. Making too much haste with atevi was not, *not* productive. "I'm grateful. I'm sure you had other plans this evening."

"No," said Jago.

"Still," he said, wondering if they'd fixed the television outage yet, and what he was going to say to Banichi and Jago for small talk for the rest of the evening. Maybe there was a play on the entertainment channel. It seemed they might stay the night.

And in whose bed would they sleep, he asked himself. —Or would they sleep? They didn't show the effects of last night at all.

"Do you play cards?"

"Cards?" Jago asked, and Banichi shoved his chair back and said he should teach her.

"What are cards?" Jago asked, when what Bren wanted to ask Banichi involved his mail. But Banichi probably had far more important things on his mind—like checking with security, and being sure surveillance items were working.

"It's a numerical game," Bren said, wishing Banichi wasn't deserting him to Jago—he hoped not for the night. When are you leaving? wasn't a politic question. He was still trying to figure how to ask it of Banichi, or what he should say if Banichi said Jago was staying ... when Banichi went out the door, with,

"Mind the wire, nadi Bren."

"Gin," Jago said.

Bren sighed, laid his cards down, glad there wasn't money involved.

"Forgive me," Jago said. "You said I should say that. Unseemly gloating was far from—"

"No, no, no. It's entirely the custom."

"One isn't sure," Jago said. "Am I to be sure?"

He had embarrassed Jago. He had been *mishidi*— awkward. He held out his palm, the gesture of conciliation. "You're to be sure." God, one couldn't walk without tripping over sensitivities. "It's actually courteous to tell me you've won."

"You don't count the cards?"

Atevi memory was, especially regarding numbers, hard to shake, no matter that Jago was not the fanatic number-adder you found in the surrounding city. And no, he hadn't adequately counted the cards. *Never* play numbers with an atevi.

"I would perhaps have done better, nadi Jago, if I weren't distracted by the situation. I'm afraid it's a little more personal to me."

"I assure you we've staked our personal reputations on your safety. We'd never be less than committed to our effort."

He had the impulse to rest his head on his hand and re-sign the whole conversation. Jago would take that as evidence of offense, too.

"I wouldn't expect otherwise, nadi Jago, and it's not your capacity I doubt, not in the least. I could only wish my own faculties were operating at their fullest, or I should not have embarrassed myself just now, by seeming to doubt you."

"I'm very sorry."

"I'll be far brighter when I've slept. Please regard my mistakes as confusion."

Jago's flat black face and vivid yellow eyes held more intense expression than they were wont—not offense, he thought, but curiosity.

"I confess myself uneasy," she said, brow furrowed. "You declare absolutely you aren't offended."

"No." One rarely touched atevi. But her manner invited it. He patted her hand where it rested on the table. "I understand you." It seemed not quite to carry the point, and, looking her in the eyes, he flung his honest thoughts after it. "I wish you understood me on this. It's a human thought."

"Are you able to explain?"

She wasn't asking Bren Cameron: she didn't know Bren Cameron. She was asking the paidhi, the interpreter to her people. That was all she *could* do, Bren thought, regarding the individual she was assigned by the aiji to protect, since the incident last night—an individual who didn't seem in her eyes to take the threat seriously enough, or to take her seriously ... and how was she to know anything about him? How was she to guess, with the paidhi giving her erratic clues? Will you explain? she asked, when he wished aloud that she understood him.

"If it were easy," he said, trying with all his wits to make sense of it to her—or to divert her thinking away from it, "there wouldn't need to be a paidhi at all. —But I wouldn't be human, then, and you wouldn't be atevi, and nobody would need me anyway, would they?"

It didn't explain anything at all. He only tried to make the confusion less important than it was. Jago could surely read that much. She worried about it and thought about it. He could see it in her eyes.

"Where's Banichi gone?" he asked, feeling things between them slipping further and further from his control. "Is he planning to come back here tonight?"

"I don't know," she said, still frowning. Then he decided, in the convolutions of his exhausted and increasingly disjointed thoughts, that even *that* might have sounded as if he wanted Banichi instead of her.

Which he did. But not for any reason of her incompetency. Dealing with a shopkeeper with a distrust of computers was one thing. He was not faring well at all in dealing with Jago, he could not put out of his mind Banichi's advisement that she liked his hair, and he decided on distraction.

"I want my mail."

"I can call him and ask him to bring it."

He had forgotten about the pocket-com. "Please do that," he said, and Jago tried.

And tried. "I can't reach him," Jago said.

"Is he all right?" The matter of the mail diminished in importance, but not, he feared, in significance. Too much had gone on that wasn't ordinary.

"I'm sure he is." Jago gathered up the cards. "Do you want to play again?"

"What if someone broke in here and you needed help? Where do you suppose he is?"

Jago's broad nostrils flared. "I have resources, nadi Bren."

He couldn't *keep* from offending her.

"Or what if *he* was in trouble? What if they ambushed him in the halls? We might not know."

"You're very full of worries tonight."

He was. He was drowning in what was atevi; and that failure to understand, in a sudden moment of panic, led him to doubt his own fitness to be where he was. It made him wonder whether the lack of perception he had shown with Jago had been far more general, all along—if it had not, with some person, led to the threat he was under.

Or, on the other hand, whether he was letting himself be spooked by his guards' zealousness because of some threat of a threat that would never, ever rematerialize.

"Worries about what, paidhi?"

He blinked, and looked by accident up into Jago's yellow, unflinching gaze. Don't you know? he thought. Is it a challenge, that question? Is it distrust of me? Why these questions?

But you couldn't quite say 'trust' in Jago's language, either, not in the terms a human understood. Every house, every province, belonged to a dozen associations, that made webs of association all through the country, whose border provinces made associations across the putative borders into the neighbor associations, an endless fuzzy interlink of boundaries that weren't boundaries, both geographical and interest-defined—'trust,' would you say? Say *man'chi*—'central association,' the one association that defined a specific individual.

"Man'china aijiia nai'am," he said, to which Jago blinked a third time. I'm the aiji's associate, foremost. *"Nai'danei man'chini somai Banichi?"* Whose associate are you and Banichi, foremost of all?

"Tabini-aijiia, hei." But atevi would lie to anyone but their central associate.

"Not each other's?" he asked. "I thought you were very close, you and Banichi."

"We have the same *man'chi*."

"And to each other?"

He saw what might be truth leap through her expression—and the inevitable frown followed.

"The paidhi knows the harm in such a question," Jago said.

"The paidhi-aiji," he said, "knows what he asks. He finds it his duty to ask, nadi."

Jago got up from the table, walked across the room and said nothing for a while. She went to look out the garden doors, near the armed wire—it made him nervous, but he thought he ought not to warn her, just be ready to remind her. Jago was touchy enough. He hadn't quite insulted her. But he'd asked into a matter intensely personal and private.

"The Interpreter should know he won't get an honest answer," she'd implied, and he'd said, plain as plain to her politically sensitive ears, "The Interpreter serves the aiji by questioning the true hierarchy of your intimate alignments."

Freely translated—Faced with betraying someone, the aiji or Banichi, . . . which one would you betray, Jago?

Which *have* you?

Fool to ask such a question, when he was alone in a room with her?

But he was alone in the whole country, for that matter, one human alone with three hundred million atevi, and billions around the world, and he was obliged to ask questions—with more intelligence and cleverness than he had just used, granted; but he was tired enough now, and crazed enough, to want to be sure of at least three of them, of Tabini, Banichi, and Jago, before he went any further down the paved and pleasant road of belief. There was too much harm he could do to his own species, believing a lie, going too far down a false path, granting too much truth to the wrong people—

Because he *wasn't* just the aiji's interpreter. *He* had a primary association that outranked it, an association that was stamped on his skin and his face—and that was the one atevi couldn't help seeing, every time they looked at him.

He waited for Jago to think his question through— perhaps even to ask herself the questions about her own loyalties that atevi might prefer not to ask. Perhaps atevi minds, like human ones, held hundreds of contradictory compartments, the doors of which one dared not open wholesale and look into. He didn't know. It *was,* perhaps, too much to ask, too personal and too dangerous. Perhaps questioning the loyalty atevi felt as a group inherently questioned a tenet of belief—and perhaps their *man'chi* concept was, at bottom, as false as humans had always wished it was, longing at an emotional level for atevi to be and think and hold individual, interpersonal values like themselves.

The paidhi couldn't believe that. The paidhi daren't believe that deadliest and most dangerous of illusions. He was off the emotional edge.

And, perhaps recognizing that the paidhi was off the edge, Jago declined to answer him. She used the pocket-com again, asking Banichi if he was receiving—and still didn't look at him.

Banichi still didn't answer.

Frowning, then, perhaps for a different reason, Jago called headquarters, asking where Banichi was, or if anyone knew where he was—and, no, headquarters didn't know.

Maybe Banichi was with some woman, Bren thought, although he decided he should keep that idea to himself, figuring Jago was capable of thinking of it for herself if it was at all likely. He wasn't sure whether Banichi and Jago slept with each other. He had never been completely certain what the relationship was between them, except a close, years-long professional partnership.

He saw the frown deepen on Jago's face. "Someone find out where he is," she said into the com.

There were verbal codes; he knew that and he couldn't tell whether the answer he overheard was one: *"Lab-work,"* HQ said, but Jago didn't seem to like the answer. "Tell him contact me when he's through," Jago said to HQ, not seeming pleased, and shut the contact off on the affirmative.

"You had no sleep last night," she said, in her smoother, professional tones, and, evading the wire, she slid the glass garden doors open on the lattice. "Please rest, nadi Bren."

He was exhausted. But he had rather plain answers. And he was far from sure he wanted his garden doors open. Maybe *they* were setting up a trap. He was in no mood tonight to be the sleeping bait.

"Nadi," he said, "have you forgotten my question?"

"No, paidhi-ji."

"But you don't intend to answer."

Jago fixed him with a yellow, lucent stare. "Do they ask such questions on Mospheira?"

"Always."

"Not among us," Jago said, and crossed the room to the door.

"Jago, say you're not angry."

Again that stare. She had stopped just short of the deadly square on the carpet, turned it off, and looked back at him. "Why ask such a futile question? You wouldn't believe either answer."

It set him back. And made him foreign and deliberate in his own reply.

"But I'm human, nadi."

"So your *man'chi* isn't with Tabini, after all."

Dangerous question. Deadly question. "Of course it is. —But what if you had two ... two very strong *man'chiin?*"

"We call it a test of character." Jago said, and opened the door.

"So do *we,* nadi Jago."

He had caught her attention. Black, wide, imposing, she stood against that bar of whiter hall light. She stood there as if she wanted to say something.

But the pocket-com beeped, demanding attention. She spoke briefly with headquarters, regarding Banichi's whereabouts, and HQ said that he was out of the lab, but in conference, asking not to be disturbed.

"Thank you," she said to the com. "Relay my message." And to him: "The wires will both be live. Go to bed, paidhi Bren. I'll be outside if you need me."

"All night?"

There was a moment of silence. "Don't walk in the garden, nand' paidhi. Don't stand in front of the doors. Be prudent and go to bed."

She shut the door then. The wire rearmed itself—he supposed. It came up when the door locked.

And did it need all of that—Jago *and* the wire, to secure his sleep?

Or where was Banichi and what was that exchange of questions, this talk about loyalties? He couldn't remember who'd started it.

Jago could have forgone an argument with him, at the edge of sleep, when he most wanted a tranquil mind—but he wasn't even certain now who'd started it and who'd pressed it, or with what intention. He hadn't done well. The whole evening with Banichi and then Jago had had a stressed, on the edge quality, as if—

In retrospect, it seemed that Jago had been fishing as hard as he had been to find out something, all along—pressing every opportunity, challenging him, or ready to take offense and put the worst construction on matters. It might be Jago's inexperience with him—he'd dealt mostly with Banichi and relied on Banichi to interpret to her. But he couldn't figure out why Banichi had deserted him tonight—except the obvious answer, that Banichi as the senior of the pair had had matters on his mind more important to the aiji than the paidhi was.

And so far as he could tell, neither he nor Jago had completely gotten the advantage, neither of them had come away with anything useful that he could figure out—only a mutual reminder how profound the differences were and how dangerous the interface between atevi and human could still turn, on a moment's notice.

He couldn't even get his points across to one well-educated and unsuperstitious woman with every reason to listen to him. How could he transmit anything, via his prepared statements to the various councils, make any headway with the population at large, who, after two centuries of peace, agreed it was a very good thing for humans to stay on Mospheira and grudgingly conceded that computers might have numbers, the way tables might have definite sizes and objects definite height, but, God, even arranging the furniture in a room meant considering ratios and measurements, and felicitous and infelicitous combinations that the atevi called *agingi'ai,* 'felicitous numerical harmony.'

Beauty flowed from that, in atevi thinking. The infelicitous could not be beautiful. The infelicitous could not be reasoned with. Right numbers had to add up, and an even division in a simple flower arrangement was a communication of hostility.

God knew what he had communicated to Jago that he hadn't meant to say.

He undressed, he turned out the light and cast an apprehensive look at the curtains, which showed no hint of the deadly wire and no shadow of any lurking assassin. He put himself to bed—at the wrong end of the room—where the ventilation was not directly from the lattice doors.

Where the breeze was too weak to reach.

He was not going to sleep until the wind shifted. He could watch television. If it worked. He doubted it would. The outages usually stayed through the shift, when they happened. He watched the curtain, he tried to think about the council business . . . but his mind kept circling back to the hall this morning, Tabini making that damnable announcement of feud, which he didn't want—certainly didn't want public.

And the damned gun—had they transferred that, when they moved his bed?

He couldn't bear wondering if anyone had found it. He got up and felt under the mattress.

It was there. He let go a slow breath, put a knee on the mattress and slid back under the sheets, to stare at the darkened ceiling.

Many a moment in the small hours of the morning he doubted what he knew. Close as he was to Tabini in certain functions, he doubted he had ever made Tabini understand anything Tabini hadn't learned from his predecessor in office. He did his linguistic research. The paper that had gotten him on the track to the paidhi's office was a respectable work: an analysis of set-plurals in the Ragi atevi dialect, of which he was proud, but it was no breakthrough, just a conclusion to which he'd been able to add, since, thanks to Tabini's patient and irreligious analysis.

But at times he didn't understand, not Tabini, not Taigi and Moni, God knew what he would figure about the glum-faced servants Banichi and Jago foisted off on him, but that was going to be another long effort. He was in a damned mess, was what he'd made for himself—he didn't catch the nuances, he'd gotten involved in something he didn't understand. He was in danger of failing. He'd imagined once he had the talent to have done what the first paidhi had done: breach the linguistic gap from conceptual dead zero and in the heart of war ...

In the years when humans had first come down here, few at first, then in greater and greater numbers as it seemed so easy ... they'd been equally confident they understood the atevi—until one spring day, twenty-one years into the landings, with humans venturing peacefully onto the continent, when that illusion had—suddenly and for reasons candidates for his job still argued among themselves—blown up in their faces.

Short and nasty, what atevi called the War of the Landing—all the advanced technology on the human side, and vast numbers and an uncanny determination on the the part of the atevi, who had, in that one year, driven humans from Ragi coastal land and back onto Mospheira, attacked them even in the valley the bewildered survivors held as their secure territory. Humanity on this world had come that close to extinction, until Tabini-aiji's fourth-removed predecessor had agreed, having met face-to-face with the man who would be the first paidhi, to cede Mospheira and let humans separate themselves from atevi completely, on an island where they'd be safe and isolated.

Mospheira and a cease-fire, in exchange for the technology the atevi wanted. Tabini's fourth-removed predecessor, being no fool, had seen a clear choice staring him in the face: either strike a deal with humanity and become indispensable to them, or see his own allies make his lands a battlefield over the technology his rivals hoped to lay their hands on, killing every last human and potentially destroying the source of the knowledge in the process.

Hence the Treaty which meant the creation of the paidhi's office, and the orderly surrender of human technology to the atevi Western Association, at a rate—neither Tabini's ancestor nor the first paidhi had been fools—that would maintain the atevi economy and the relative power of the aijiin of various Associations in the existing balance.

Meaning, all of the rivals, the humans *and* the technology securely in the hands of Tabini's ancestor. The War had stopped ... Mospheira's atevi had resettled on the Ragi aiji's coastal estate-lands, richer than their own fields by far, a sacrifice of vast wealth for the Ragi aiji, but a wise, wise maneuver that secured the peace—and every damned thing the Mospheira atevi and the Ragi atevi wanted.

Humans weren't under this sun by choice. And (the constant and unmentioned truth) humans to this day didn't deal with the atevi by choice or at advantage. Humans had lost the War: few in numbers, stranded, their station soon in decay, their numbers dwindling above and below ... descent to the planet was their final, desperate choice.

Impossible to conceal their foreignness, impossible to trust a species that couldn't translate *friendship,* impossible to admit what humans really wanted out of the agreement, because atevi in general didn't—that foreign word—*trust* people foolish enough to land without a by-your-leave and possessing secrets they hadn't yet turned over.

The paidhi didn't tell everything he knew—but he was treaty-bound to the slow surrender of everything humans owned, to pay the rent on Mospheira—and to empower the only human-friendly government on the planet to keep humanity's most implacable enemies under his thumb. The aiji of that day had wanted high-powered guns—the atevi had had muzzle-loading rifles and cumbersome cannon, and took to high-velocity bullets with—terrible turn of speech—an absolute vengeance.

Fastest piece of talking a paidhi had ever done, pressed with the aiji's request for designs that would put a terrifying arsenal in Ragi hands, Bretano had pointed out that such weapons would surely reach Ragi rivals as well, and that the Ragi already had the upper hand. Did they want to tip the balance?

Pressed for advanced industrial techniques, Bretano had objected the ecological cost to the planet, and the whole committee behind him, and his successors, had begun the slow, centuries-long business of steering atevi science steadily into ecological awareness—

And toward material production resources that would serve human needs.

The one tactic, the ecological philosophy . . . hoped to get war out of the atevi mindset, to build experimental rockets instead of missiles, rails instead of cannon, to consider what happened to a river downstream when a little garbage went in upstream, to consider what happened when toxic chemicals blew through forests or poisons got into the groundwater—thank God, the atevi had taken to the idea, which had touched some cultural bent already in the Ragi mentality, at least. It had locked onto successive generations so firmly that little children in this half-century learned rhymes about clean rivers—while human tacticians on Mospheira—safe on Mospheira, unlike the paidhi—deliberated what industry they dared promote, and what humans needed the atevi to develop in order for humans to get launch facilities and the vehicle they needed.

The unspoken, two hundred-year-agenda, the one every human knew and the paidhi walked about scared out of his mind because he knew—because even if atevi guessed by now that getting themselves a space program meant developing materials as useful to humans as to themselves, even if he could sit in the space council meetings and surmise that every atevi in the room knew what they developed had that potential, it was a question he never brought up, not with them, not with atevi he knew the best—because it was one of those impenetrable thickets in atevi mindset, how they'd take the knowledge if it became impossible to ignore it. He'd certainly no idea at all how it would play outside Tabini's court, out across the country—when popular novels still cast human villains, and they appeared in shadow, in *nebai,* in the machimi plays—*nebai,* because they couldn't get human actors. . . .

Humans were the monsters in the closet, the creatures under the bed . . . in a culture constantly on its guard against real dangers from real assassins, in a culture where children learned from television a paranoid fear of strangers.

What were humans really up to on Mospheira? What dark technological secrets was Tabini-aiji keeping for himself? What *was* in the telemetry that flowed between the station in space and the island an hour by air off Tabini's shores?

And why did some loon want to kill the paidhi?

He had a space council meeting tomorrow—nothing he considered controversial, a small paper with technical information the council had asked and he'd translated out of the library on Mospheira.

No controversy in that. None in the satellite launch upcoming, either. Communications weren't controversial. Weather forecast wasn't controversial.

There *was* the finance question, whether to add or subtract a million from the appropriation to make the unmanned launch budget add up to an auspicious number—but a million didn't seem, against six billion already committed to the program, to be a critical or acerbic issue, over which assassins would swarm to his bedroom.

There was, occasionally smoldering, the whole, sensitive manned versus unmanned debate—whether atevi should attempt to recover the human space station, which was in increasing disrepair, with its tanks empty now, in its slow drift out of stable orbit.

The human policy wasn't to scare anyone by bringing up the remote possibility of infall in a populated area. Officially, statistically, the station debris would come down in the vast open oceans, in, oh, another five hundred years, give or take a solar storm or so—he couldn't personally swear to any of it, since astrophysics wasn't his forte, but the experts said that was what he should say, and he'd said it.

He'd advanced his modest paper on the topic of mission goals at his inaugural meeting with the space council, proposing the far from astonishing concept that lifting metal to orbit was expensive, and that letting what was already orbiting burn up was not economical, and that they should do something with the dead, abandoned station before they sank large resources into unmanned missions.

Manned space advocates of course agreed immediately, with celebration. Astronomers and certain anti-human lobbies disagreed passionately. Which put the question into the background, while council members consulted numerologists on truly important issues such as (the currently raging question) whether the launch dates were auspicious or not, and how many dates it was auspicious to approve in reserve—which got into another debate between several competing (and ethnically significant) schools of numerology, on whether the current date should be in the calculation or whether one counted the birthdate of the whole program or of the project or of the date the launch table was devised.

Never mind the debate over whether the fuel chamber baffle in the heavy lift booster could be four-partitioned without affecting the carefully chosen harmonious numbers of the tank design.

The truly dangerous issues that he could think of, lying here flat on his back, waiting for assassins, were all the quiet ones—the utilization of the station as an atevi mission goal was one item of some controversy he'd strenuously advocated, now that he began to add up the supporters, some of them less reasonable, behind the genteel voices of the council.

And always factor into any space debate the continual exchange of telemetry and instructions between Mospheira and the station, which had gone on for two hundred years and was still going.

A certain radical element among atevi maintained there were weapons hidden aboard the abandoned station. The devoted lunatics of the radical fringe were convinced the station's slow infall was no accident of physics, but a carefully calculated approach, perhaps in the hands of humans secretly left aboard, or instructions secretly relayed from Mospheira, now that they knew about computer controls, which would end with the station descending in a blazing course across the skies, 'disturbing the ethers to disharmony and violence,' and creating hurricanes and tidal waves, as its weapons rained fire down on atevi civilization and placed atevi forever under human domination.

Forgive them, Tabini was wont to say dryly. They also anticipate the moon to influence their financial ventures and the space launches to disturb the weather.

Foreign aijiin from outside Tabini's Association actually funded offices in Shejidan to analyze those telemetry transcripts on which Shejidan eavesdropped—the numerologists these foreign aijiin employed suspecting secret assignments of infelicitous codes, affecting the weather, or agriculture, or the fortunes of Tabini's rivals ... and one daren't call such beliefs silly.

Actually Tabini did call them exactly that, to his intimates, but in public he was very *kabiu*, very observant, and employed batteries of number-counters and geometricians of various persuasions to study every utterance and every bit of intercepted transmission, just as seriously—to refute what the conservatives came up with, to be sure.

From time to time—it was worth a grin, even in the

dark—Tabini would come to the paidhi and say, Transmit this. And he would phone Mospheira with a segment of code that, transmitted to the station, would be complete nonsense to the computers, so the technicians assured him—they just dropped it into some Remark string, and transmitted it solely for the benefit of the eavesdroppers, and that fixed that, as Barb would say. Numbers would then turn up in the transmission sequences that burst some doomsayer's bubble before he could go public with his theory.

That, God help them all, was the space program. And that was not worth a grin. That was *every* program they promoted. That was the operation of the council and the hasdrawad and the tashrid and the special interests that operated in the shadows—radical groups among those special interests, groups that called the Treaty of Mospheira a mistake, that called for those things the most radical humans—and God knew there were those—suspected as existing in extensive plans and Tabini dismissed as stupid, like another attack on Mospheira.

Humans might have no illusion of welcome in the world—but there were certainly the serious and the non-serious threats. Serious, were the human-haters who focussed on the highway dispute as a human plot to keep the economy under Tabini's thumb—which cut much too close to the truth neither the paidhi nor the aiji wanted in public awareness.

There was, thank God, the moonbeam fringe—with a slippery grip on history, the laws of physics, and reality. The fringe went straight for the space program (one supposed because it was the highest and least conceivable technology) as the focus of all dire possibility, ideas ranging from the notion that rocket launches let the atmosphere leak out into the ether . . . to his personal favorite, the space station cruising at ground level causing hurricanes and blasting cities with death rays. Atevi could laugh at it. Humans could. Humor at the most outrageous hate-mongering did everyone good, and poked holes in assumptions that otherwise would lie unventilated.

The fringe had done more good, in fact, for human-atevi understanding than all his speeches to the councils.

But if you ever wanted a source from which a lunatic, unlicensed assassin could arise, it was possible that one of the fringe had quite, quite gone over the edge.

Maybe the numbers had said, to one of the lunatics, one fine day, Go assassinate the paidhi and the atmosphere will stop leaking.

Thus far ... Tabini and his own predecessors at least juggled well. They'd dispensed technology at a rate that didn't overwhelm the economy or the environment, they'd kept ethnic differences among atevi and political opinions among humans well to the rear of the decision-making process—with the Ragi atevi and the Western Association they led profiting hand over fist, all the while, of course, by reason of their proximity to and special relationship with Mospheira; and, oh, well aware what that relationship was worth, economically. Tabini had probably had far more than an inkling for years where human advice and human techonology was leading him.

But Tabini's association also enjoyed the highest standard of living in the world, was very fond of its comforts and its television. And Ragi planes didn't crash into bridges any more.

Somebody after Tabini's hide was the likeliest scenario that kept bobbing up—a plausible scenario, in which the paidhi could remotely figure, if whoever was after Tabini, knowing how difficult a target Tabini was, would be content to take out Tabini's contact with humans and make that relationship more difficult for a season.

A new paidhi, a state of destabilization in which no paidhi was safe. Somebody might even be after a renegotiation of the Mospheira Treaty to spread out the benefits to other associations, which had been proposed, and which the Western Association had adamantly refused.

In that case the paidhi-aiji might well become a critical

flash-point. He got along with Tabini. He liked Tabini. Tabini didn't reciprocate the liking part, of course—being atevi. But Tabini and he did get along with all too much levity and good humor, perhaps—as some might see it, like that business at the retreat at Taiben, far too cozy.

Some might think it, even among the Ragi themselves, or among the outlying allies, each of whom, in the nebulous fashion of atevi associations, had at least one foot in other associations.

Maybe the better, special relationship he thought he and Tabini had—had brought this on, transgressing some boundary too rapidly, too inexpertly, in blind, too-confident enthusiasm.

Frightening thought. Appalling thought. Succeed too well and fail completely?

If Tabini's government went unstable, and the network of atevi Associations shifted its center of gravity, say, eastward and deeply inland, where there was never that easy familiarity with humans, where ethnic and historical differences between Ragi and Nisebi and Meduriin could find only humans more different and more suspect than they found each other.

Atevi had been, with the exception of the tribals in the remotest hinterlands and the islands in the Edi Archipelago, a global civilization, at a stage when humans hadn't been. Atevi explorers had gone out in wooden ships, done all those things that humans had, by the records, done on lost Earth—except that atevi hadn't found a New World, they'd found the Edi, and damned little else but a volcanic, troubled chain of islands, not advanced, not culturally up to the double assault of the explorers from the East and the explorers from the West, who'd immediately laid claim to everything in sight and still—still, for reasons the ethnographers were still arguing—the same explorers met each other in those foreign isles and found enough in common and enough difficult about the intervening geography—the continental divide in the principal continent topped 30,000 feet—to trade not overland, but by sea routes that largely, after the advent of full-rigged ships, excluded the Isles where the two principal branches of atevi had met.

Atevi had, historically, cooperated together damned well, compared to humans. Hence the difficulty of getting atevi to comprehend correctly that humans had been very willing to be let alone on Mospheira, and not included in an association—an attitude which the atevi turned out not to trust. Shejidan had thrown itself into the breach, sacrificed its fear of outsiders for the foreign concept of 'treaty,' which it marginally understood as the sought-after association with humans. Which was one of the most critical conceptual breakthroughs the first paidhi had made.

To this day Tabini professed not to comprehend the human word 'treaty,' or the word 'border,' which he denied had real validity even among humans. An artificial concept, Tabini called it. A human delusion. People belonged to many associations. Boundaries might exist as an arbitrary approximate line defining provinces—but they were meaningless to individuals whose houses or kinships might lie both sides of the line.

He lay in the dark, watching the moonlit curtains begin to blow in a generous cool breeze—the weather had greatly moderated since the front had come through last night. He hadn't been in the garden this afternoon to enjoy it. Someone could shoot him from the rooftop, Jago said. He should stay out of the garden. He shouldn't go here, he shouldn't go there, he shouldn't walk through crowds.

Damned if Banichi had forgotten his mail. Not Banichi. Things regarding the person Banichi was watching just weren't trivial enough to Banichi that they completely left his mind. This was a man that, in the human expression, dotted his i's and crossed his t's.

Second frightening thought.

Why would *Banichi* steal his mail—except to rob him

of information like ads for toothpaste, video tapes, and ski vacations on Mt. Allan Thomas?

And if it weren't Banichi that had gotten it, why would Banichi lie to him? To protect a thief who stole advertising?

Stupid thought. Probably Banichi hadn't lied at all, probably Banichi was just busy and he was, ever since the nightmare flash of that shadow across the curtain last night, suffering from jangled nerves and an overactive imagination.

He lay there, imagining sounds in the garden, smelling the perfume of the blooms outside the door, wondering what it sounded like when someone hit the wire and fried, and what he should do about the situation he was working on—

Or what the odds were that he could get Deana Hanks out of the Mospheira office to take up temporary duty in the aiji's household, for, say, a month or so vacation— God, just time to see Barb, go diving on the coast, take reasonable chances with a hostile environment instead of a pricklish atevi court.

Cowardice, that was. It was nothing to toss in Hanks' lap—oh, by the way, Deana, someone's trying to kill me, give it your best, just do what you can and I'll be back when it blows over.

He couldn't escape that way. He didn't know whether he should call his office and try to hint what was going on—he ran a high risk of injecting misinformation or misinterpretation into an already uneasy situation, if he did that. There were code phrases for trouble and for assassination—and maybe he ought to take the chance and let the office know that much.

But if Tabini for some reason closed off communications tighter than they were, the last information his office might have to work with was an advisement that someone had tried to kill him—leaving Hanks de facto in charge. And Hanks was a take charge and go ahead type, a damned hothead, was the sorry truth, *apt* to take measures to breach Tabini's silence, which might not be the wisest course in a delicate atevi political situation. He had confidence in Tabini—Hanks under those circumstances wouldn't, and might do something to undermine Tabini ... or play right into the hands of Tabini's enemies.

Damned if he did and damned if he didn't. Tabini's silence was uncharacteristic. The situation had too many variables. He was on-site and *he* didn't have enough information to act on—Hanks would have far less if she had to come in here, and she would feel more pressed, in the total absence of information, to do something to get him back if there was no corpse ... a very real fear from the first days, that some aiji in Shejidan or elsewhere might get tired of having the paidhi dole out technological information bit at a time.

Something about the mythical goose and the source of golden eggs—a parable the first paidhiin had been very forward to inject into atevi culture, so that now atevi were certain there was such a thing as a goose, although there was not a bona fide bird in the world, and that it was a foreign but surely atevi fable.

That was the way the game went. Given patience—given time—given small moves instead of wide ones, humans got what they wanted, and Tabini-aiji did.

Goseniin and golden eggs.

III

Banichi arrived with breakfast, with an armload of mail, the predictable ads for vacations, new products, and ordinary goods. It was quite as boring as he'd expected it to be, and a chilly, unseasonal morning made him glad of the hot tea the two substitute servants brought. He had his light breakfast—now he wanted his television.

"Are the channels out all over the city, or what?" he asked Banichi, and Banichi shrugged. "I couldn't say."

At least there was the weather channel, reporting rain in the mountains east, and unseasonal cool weather along the western seaboard. No swimming on the Mospheira beaches. He kept thinking of home—kept thinking of the white beaches of Mospheira, and tall mountains, still patched with snow in the shadowy spots, kept thinking of human faces, and human crowds.

He'd dreamed of home last night, in the two hours of sleep he seemed to have gotten—he'd dreamed of the kitchen at home, and early mornings, and his mother and Toby at breakfast, the way it had been. His mother wrote to him regularly. Toby wasn't inclined to write, but Toby got the news, when his letters did get home, and Toby sent word back through their mother, what he was up to, how he was faring.

His mother had taken the community allotment he'd left when he'd won the paidhi's place and had no more need for his birthright: she'd combined it with her savings from her teaching job, and lent his family-bound and utterly respectable brother the funds to start a medical practice on the north shore.

Toby had the thoroughly ordinary and prosperous life their mother had wanted for herself or her children, with the appropriately adorable and available grandchildren. She was happy. Bren *didn't* write her with things like, Hello, Mother, someone tried to shoot me in my bed. Hello, Mother, they won't let me fly out of here. It was always, Hello, Mother, things are fine. How are you? They keep me busy. It's very interesting. I wish I could say more than that . . .

"Not that coat," Banichi said, as he took his plain one from the armoire. Banichi reached past him, and took the audience coat from the hanger.

"For the space council?" he protested, but he knew, he

knew, then, without Banichi saying a word, that Tabini had called him.

"The council's been postponed." Banichi shook the coat out and held it for him, preempting the new servants' offices. "The ratios in the slosh baffles will have to wait at least a few days."

He slipped his arms into the coat, flipped his braid over the collar and settled it on with a deep breath. The weight wasn't uncomfortable this crisp morning.

"So what does Tabini want?" he muttered. But both the servants were in the room, and he didn't expect Banichi to answer. Jago hadn't been there when he waked. Just Tano and his glum partner, bringing in his breakfast. He hadn't had enough sleep, for two nights now. His eyes stung with exhaustion. And he had to look presentable and have his wits about him.

"Tabini is concerned," Banichi said. "Hence the postponement. He wishes you to travel to the country this afternoon. A security team is going over the premises."

"What, at the estate?"

"Stone by stone. Tano and Algini will pack for you, if necessary."

What could he ask, when he knew Banichi wouldn't answer—couldn't answer a question Tabini hadn't authorized him to answer? He took a deep breath, adjusted his collar, and looked in the mirror. His eyes showed the want of sleep—showed a modicum of panic, truth be known, because the decision not to call Mospheira was fast becoming an irrevocable one, with decreasing opportunities to change his mind on that score without making a major, noisy opposition to people whose polite maneuvering—if that was what he perceived around him—might not be profitable to challenge.

Maybe it was paralysis of will. Maybe it was instinct saying Be still—*don't* defy the only friend humanity has on this planet.

Paidhiin are expendable. Mospheira isn't. We can't

stand against the whole world. This time they have air-craft. And radar. And all the technological resources.

They're very close to not needing us any more.

In the room behind him the door opened and Jago came in, he assumed to supervise the two servants, whose words to him had consisted in controversies like: "Pre-serves, nadi?" and "Sugar in the tea?"

Moni and Taigi had known answers like that without asking him at every turn. He missed them already. He feared they wouldn't be back, that they'd already been reassigned—he hoped to a stable, influential, thoroughly normal atevi. He *hoped* they weren't in the hands of the police, undergoing close questions about him, and hu-mans in general.

Banichi opened the door a second time, for them to leave for the audience, and he went out with Banichi, feeling more like a prisoner than the object of so much official concern.

"Aiji-ma." Bren made the courteous bow, hands on knees. Tabini was in shirt and trousers, not yet at his formal best, sitting in the sunlight in front of the open doors—Tabini's doors, high in the great mass of the Bu-javid, faced not the garden, but the open sky, the descend-ing terraces of the ancient walls, and the City that was the fortress' skirt, a geometry of tile roofs, hazed and soft-ened by the morning mist to faintest reds, roofs auspi-ciously aligned in their relationship to each other and in the city's accommodation to the river. Beyond that, the Bergid range, riding above a haze of distance, far across the plains—a glorious view, a cool, breathless dawn.

The table was set in the light, half onto the balcony, against that prospect. And Tabini was having breakfast.

Tabini made a hand-sign to his servants, who instantly procured two more cups, and drew out from the table the two other chairs.

So they were completely informal. He and Banichi sat down at the offered places, with the Bergid range a misty blue and the City spread out in faint tile reds below the balcony railing.

"I trust there's been no repetition of the incident," Tabini said.

"No, aiji-ma," Banichi answered, adding sugar.

"I'm very distressed by this incident," Tabini said. A sip of tea. "Distressed also that you should be the object of public speculation, Bren-paidhi. I was obliged to take a position. I could *not* let that pass. —Has anyone approached you in the meetings?"

"No," Bren said. "But I do fear I was less than observant yesterday. I'm not used to this idea."

"Are you afraid?"

"Disturbed." He wasn't sure, himself, what he felt. "Disturbed that I've been the cause of so much disarrangement, when I'm here for your convenience."

"That's the politic answer."

"—And I'm very angry, aiji-ma."

"Angry?"

"That I can't go where I like and do what I like."

"But can the paidhi ever do that? You never go to the City without an escort. You don't travel, you don't hold entertainments, which, surely, accounts for what Banichi would counsel you as habits of the greatest hazard."

"This is my *home*, aiji-ma. I'm not accustomed to slinking past my own doors or wondering if some poor servant's going to walk through the door on my old key. . . . I do hope someone's warned them."

"Someone has," Banichi said.

"I worry," he said, across the teacup. "Forgive me, aiji-ma."

"No, no, no, I did ask. These are legitimate concerns and legitimate complaints. And no need for you to suffer them. I think it would be a good thing for you to go to Malguri for a little while."

"Malguri?" That was the lake estate, at Lake Maidingi—Tabini's retreat in early autumn, when the legislature was out of session, when he was regularly on vacation himself. He had never been so far into the interior of the continent. When he thought of it—no human had. "Are *you* going, aiji-ma?"

"No." Tabini's cup was empty. A servant poured another. Tabini studiously dropped in two sugar lumps and stirred. "My grandmother is in residence. You've not encountered her, personally, have you? I don't recall you've had that adventure."

"No." He held the prospect of the aiji-dowager more unnerving than assassins. Ilisidi hadn't won election in the successions. Thank God. "Aren't you—forgive me—sending me to a zone of somewhat more hazard?"

Tabini laughed, a wrinkling of his nose. "She does enjoy an argument. But she's quite retiring now. She says she's dying."

"She's said so for five years," Banichi muttered. "Aiji-ma."

"You'll do fine," Tabini said. "You're a diplomat. You can deal with it."

"I could just as easily go to Mospheira and absent myself from the situation, if that's what's useful. A great deal more useful, actually, to me. There's a load of personal business I've had waiting. My mother has a cabin on the north coast. . . ."

Tabini's yellow stare was completely void, completely implacable. "But I can't guarantee her security. I'd be extremely remiss to bring danger on your relatives."

"No ateva can get onto Mospheira without a visa."

"An old man in a rowboat can get onto Mospheira," Banichi muttered. "And ask *me* if I could find your mother's cabin."

The old man in a rowboat would *not* get onto Mospheira unnoticed. He was willing to challenge Banichi on that. But he wasn't willing to own that fact to Tabini or Banichi for free.

"You'll be far better off," Banichi said, "at Malguri."

"A fool tried my bedroom door! For all I know it was my next door neighbor coming home drunk through the garden, probably terrified he could be named an attempted assassin, and now we have wires on my doors!" One didn't shout in Tabini's presence. And Tabini had supported Banichi in the matter of the wires. He remembered his place and hid his consternation behind his teacup.

Tabini sipped his own and set the cup down as Banichi set his aside. "Still," Tabini said. "The investigation is making progress which doesn't need your help. Rely on my judgment in this. Have I ever done anything to your harm?"

"No, aiji-ma."

Tabini rose and reached out his hand, not an atevi custom. Tabini had done it the first time ever they met, and at rare moments since. He stood up and took it, and shook it solemnly.

"I hold you as a major asset to my administration," Tabini said. "Please believe that what I do is out of that estimation, even this exile."

"What have I done?" he asked, his hand still prisoner in Tabini's larger one. "Have I, personally, done something I should have done differently? How can I do better, if no one advises me?"

"We're pursuing the investigation," Tabini said quietly. "My private plane is fueling at this moment. *Please* don't cross my grandmother."

"How can I escape it? I don't know what I did to bring this about, Tabini-aiji. How can I behave any more wisely than I have?"

A pressure of Tabini's fingers, and a release of his hand. "Did one say it was your fault, Bren-paidhi? Give my respects to my grandmother."

"Aiji-ma." Surrender was all Tabini left him. He only dared the most indirect rebellion. "May I have my mail routed there?"

"There should be no difficulty," Banichi said, "if it's sent through the security office."

"We don't want to announce your destination," Tabini

said. "But, yes, security does have to know. Take care. Take every precaution. You'll go straight to the airport. Is it taken care of, Banichi?"

"No difficulty," Banichi said. What 'it' was, Bren had no idea. But there was nothing left him but to take his formal leave.

'Straight to the airport,' meant exactly that, evidently, straight downstairs, in the Bu-javid, to the lowest, inner level, where a rail station connected with the rail systems all over the continent.

It was a well-securitied place, this station deep in the Bu-javid's heart, a station which only the mai'aijiin and the aiji himself and his staff might use—there was another for common traffic, a little down the hill.

Guards were everywhere, nothing unusual in any time he'd been down here. He supposed they maintained a constant watch over the tracks and the cars that rested here—the authorities in charge could have no idea when someone might take the notion to use them, or when someone else might take the notion to compromise them.

What looked like a freight car was waiting. The inbound tram would sweep it up on its way below—and it would travel looking exactly like a freight car, mixed in with the ordinary traffic, down to its painted and, one understood, constantly changed, numbers.

It was Tabini's—cushioned luxury inside, a councilroom on wheels. That was where Banichi took him.

"Someone *has* checked it out," he said to Banichi. He'd used this particular car himself—but only once annually on his own business, on his regular departure to the airport, and never when there was any active feud in question. The whole proceedings had a surreal feeling.

"Destined for the airport," Banichi said, checking papers, "no question. Don't be nervous, nadi Bren. I assure you we won't misplace you with the luggage."

Banichi was joking with him. *He* was scared. He'd been nervous walking down here, was nervous on the platform, but he walked to the back of the windowless car and sat down on the soft cushions of a chair, unable to see anything but the luxury around him, and a single televised image of the stationside with its hurrying workers. He was overwhelmed with the feeling of being swallowed alive, swept away to where no one human would ever hear of him. He hadn't advised anyone where he was going, he hadn't gotten off that phone call to Hanks or a letter home—he had no absolute confidence now that Banichi would deliver it if he wrote it this instant and entrusted it to him to take outside.

"Are you going with me?" he asked Banichi.

"Of course." Banichi was standing, looking at the monitor. "Ah. There she is."

A cart had appeared from a lift, a cart piled high with white plastic boxes. Jago was behind it, pushing it toward the car. It arrived, real and stuck on the uneven threshold, and Jago shoved and swore as Banichi moved to lend a hand. Bren got up to offer his efforts, but at that moment it came across, as Tano turned up, shoving from the other side, bound inside, too.

The cart and the baggage had to mass everything he had had in the apartment, Bren thought in dismay, unless three-quarters of that was Banichi's and Jago's luggage. They didn't take the luggage from the cart: they secured the whole cart against the forward wall, with webbing belts.

Protests did no good. Questions at this point only annoyed those trying to launch them with critical things they needed. Bren sat down and stayed still while Banichi and Jago went outside, never entirely leaving the threshold, and signed something or talked with other guards.

In a little while, they both came back into the car, saying that the train was on its way, and would couple them on in a few minutes. Tano meanwhile offered him a soft drink, which he took listlessly, and Algini arrived with a final paper for Banichi to sign.

What? Bren asked himself. Concerning what? His commitment to Malguri, might it be?

To the aiji-dowager's prison, where she was dying— this notorious, bitter woman, twice passed over for aiji.

One wondered if *she* had had a choice in lodgings, or whether the rumors about her were true ... that, having offended Tabini, she had very little choice left.

The jet made a quick rise above the urban sprawl of Shejidan—one could pick out the three or four major central buildings among the tiled roofs, the public Registry, the Agricultural Association, the long complex of Shejidan Steel, the spire of Western Mining and Industry, the administrative offices of Patanadi Aerospace. A final turn onto their course swept the Bu-javid past the aircraft's wing-tip, a sweep of fortified hill, interlocked squares of terraces and gardens—Bren imagined he could see the very court where he had lived ... and wondered in a moment of panic if he would ever see his apartment again.

They reached cruising altitude—above the likely capability of random private operators. A drink appeared. Tano's efficiency. Tano's proper concern. Bren sulked, not wanting to like Tano, who'd replaced the servants he very much liked, who had had their jobs with him since he'd taken up residence in Shejidan, and who probably had been transferred by a faceless bureaucracy without so much as an explanation. It wasn't fair to them. It wasn't fair to him. He liked them, even if they probably wouldn't understand that idea. He was used to them and they were gone.

But sulking at Tano and Algini wasn't a fair treatment of the new servants, either: he knew it and, in proper atevi courtesy, tried not to show his resentment toward them, or his feelings at all, toward two strangers. He sat back instead with as placid a face as he could manage and watched the land and the clouds pass under the wing, wishing he was flying instead toward Mospheira, and safety.

And wishing Banichi and Jago were culturally or biologically wired to understand the word 'friend' or 'ally' the way he wanted to mean it. That, too. But that was as likely as his walking the Mospheira straits barefoot.

His stomach was upset. He was all but convinced now that he had made a very serious mistake in not calling Deana Hanks directly after the incident, while the attempt on his bedroom was still a matter of hot pursuit, and before Banichi and Jago might have received specific orders to prevent him calling.

But he hadn't even thought of it then—he couldn't remember what he *had* been thinking, and decided he must have gone into mental shock, trying first to dismiss the whole matter and to look brave in front of Banichi; then he'd launched himself into 'handling it,' even to a fear of Hanks' seizing control over the situation—meaning he was losing his grip on matters, and knew it, and was still denying things were out of control.

Now he was well past the end of his options for action, so far as he could see, unless he wanted to contemplate outright rebellion against Tabini's invitation to an estate hours away from the City—unless he was willing to break away in that remote airport screaming kidnap and murder, and appealing to the casual citizen for rescue from the aiji.

Foolish notion. Foolish as the notion of refusing Tabini in the invitation, under the terms he had had—and now that he began to think about phones and the lake estate, and getting any call out to Mospheira, from where he was going—the request to transfer a call to the Mospheira phone system would have to go back through the Bujavid for authorization, so it was the same damned thing.

Eventually his office on Mospheira would wonder why he hadn't called . . . in, say, a week or two of silence. It wasn't unusual, that lapse of time between his calls and consultations.

And, after that two weeks of silence, his office might be worried enough to think about contacting Foreign Affairs, over them, who would tell them to wait while they went through channels.

In another week, Foreign Affairs on Mospheira might have exhausted the approved channels it had at its disposal, and decided to send a memo to the President, who might, might, after consulting the Departments in Council, make personal inquiries of his own and finally lay the inquiry on Tabini's doorstep.

Count it the better part of a month before Mospheira decided for certain that Shejidan had somehow misplaced the paidhi.

Disturbing, to discover that individual atevi he had personally thought he understood and an atevi society he had thought he intellectually understood suddenly weren't acting in any predictable way. He felt it as an offense to his pride that he found nothing now wiser or more resourceful to do than to pretend he was utterly naive and that he wasn't actually being kidnapped across the country— where, face it, he could disappear for good and all. Nobody from Mospheira, not even Hanks, was going to fracture the Treaty looking for a paidhi who just might have made some unforgivable mistake.

Hell, no, they wouldn't demand him back. They'd just send a new one, with as good a briefing as they could manage and instructions to pull in a bit and not to be so stupid.

He'd trusted so implicitly . . . never expected Tabini to be other than a hundred percent for atevi and his own personal interests, but he'd always believed he knew what those interests were. Tabini hadn't resisted his suggestions: not in the rail system, not the space program, not medical research, not the computerization of the supply system. Tabini wasn't opposed to anything he'd put forward, or, for God's sake, Tabini could have said something, and they could have talked about it—but, no, Tabini had listened with intelligent interest, asking lively questions—Tabini's predecessors had all listened to reason, and invested themselves to the hilt in the interlocking of ecology and technological advance, a concept that atevi were quick to understand.

Reciprocally, there'd never been anything an aiji of Tabini's house had asked that humans hadn't done, or given, or tried to comply with, since the War of the Landing itself, right down to his current paper regarding processed meat, which tried . . . *tried* to explain to Mospheira that commercialization of meat production was deeply offensive to Ragi, no matter that Nisebi saw nothing wrong with it and were willing to sell. That cultural adaptation went both ways, and Mospheira ought to rely on the sea, and fish, which had no season, and thereby *show* their hosts on the planet that they had made an effort to change themselves to conform to atevi sensibilities, the way atevi had changed their behaviors toward humans. . . .

Sometimes his job seemed like rolling the proverbial boulder uphill. Just not losing ground seemed hard.

But atevi were on the very threshold of manned spaceflight. They had satellite communications. They had a reliable light launch system. They were on the verge of developing the materials that, with human advice, could leapfrog them past the steps humans had taken getting down here, right to powered descent, interlinked maneuvering—terms *he* was having to learn, concepts that he was studying up on during his so-called fall vacations, cramming into his head the details behind the next policy paper he might give—that he *ached* to give—some time in the next five years, granted the intermediate heavy-lift rocket was going to work.

Not even that they absolutely needed to take that step; but the office on Mospheira said stall, let atevi develop the intermediate lift capacity. The quality in the synthetic materials wasn't there yet, and the chemical rocket lifter and the early manned experience would give atevi the experience and the political and emotional investment in space—atevi were much on heroes.

It was a cultural decision, a scientific decision . . . it disappointed hell out of him, because he wanted to be the paidhi that put them a hundred percent into the business of space, and he wanted it while he was young enough to go up himself. That was his secret, personal dream, that if atevi were going to trust any human to go, they might trust the paidhi, and he wanted to be that person, and steer the attitudes if not the spacecraft—

That was the dream he had. The nightmare was less specific, only the apprehension which, long before the assassin tried his bedroom, he had been trying to communicate to Hanks and the rest of the office, that you couldn't go on giving atevi bits and pieces of tech without accelerating the randomness in the process, meaning that atevi minds didn't work the same as human minds, and that atevi cultural bias was going to view certain technological advances differently than humans did, and atevi inventiveness was going to put more and more items together into their own inventions, about which they didn't consult the Mospheira Technology Commission.

Thank God so far the independent inventions hadn't been ICBMs or atomic bombs. But he knew, as every paidhi before him had known, that, if someday the Treaty broke down, he'd be the first to know.

He watched the land pass under the wings, the farmland, the free ranges and forests . . . eventually a tide of cloud rolled under them, with the black, snow-capped peaks of the Bergid thrusting up like steep-sided islands—fascinating, to see the edge of his visible world go past, and exciting, in a disturbing way, to be seeing country humans never saw. Everything was new, hitherto forbidden.

But after a time, cloud closed in around the peaks, and while the sky remained blue, there was a sheet of wrinkled white under them, hiding the land.

Disappointing. This sort of thing set in over the strait and didn't let up. Even the planet kept atevi secrets.

Which didn't mean there wasn't useful work he could

do while he was being kidnapped. He'd rescued his computer from baggage. He set it up on the table and brought up his notes for the end of the quarter development conference, his arguments for creating a computer science center in Costain Bay, modem-linked to atevi students in Wingin.

If there is, he wrote now, *one area of technological difficulty, it is ironically in mathematics, in which the different uses of mathematics by our separate cultures and languages have led to different expressions of mathematics at an operational level. While these different perceptions of math are a rich field for speculation by mathematicians and computer designers for the future, for the present, these foundational differences in concept remain an obstacle particularly to the beginning atevi computer student attempting to comprehend a logical machine which ignores certain of his expectations, which ignores the operational conveniences and shortcuts of his language, and which proceeds by a logical architecture adapted over centuries to the human mind.*

The development of a computer architecture in agreement with atevi perceptions is both inevitable and desirable for the economic progress of the atevi associations, particularly in materials development, but the paidhi respectfully urges that many useful and lifesaving technologies are being delayed in development because of this difficulty.

While the paidhi recognizes the valid and true reasons for maintaining the doctrine of Separation in the Treaty of Mospheira, it seems that computer technology itself can become the means to link instructors on Mospheira with students on the mainland, so that atevi students may have the direct benefit of study with human masters of design and theory, to bring computers with all their advantages into common usage—while encouraging atevi students to devise interfacing software which may take advantage of atevi mathematical skills.

Such a study center may serve as a model program,

moreover, for finding other areas in which atevi may, without harm to either culture, interface directly in the territory of empirical science and form working agreements which seem appropriate to both cultures.

I call to mind the specific language of the Treaty of Mospheira which calls for experimental contacts in science leading to agreements of definition and unequivocal terminology, with a view to future intercultural cooperations under the appointment of appropriate atevi officials.

This seems to me one of those areas in which cooperation could work to the benefit of atevi, widening intercultural understanding, fulfilling all provisions of the Treaty wherein . . .

Banichi dropped into the seat opposite.

"You're so busy," Banichi said.

"I was writing my text for the quarterly conference. I trust I'll get back for it."

"Your safety is of more concern. But if it should be that you can't attend, certainly I'll see that it reaches the conference."

"There surely can't be a question. The conference is four weeks away."

"Truthfully, I don't know."

Don't know, he thought in alarm. Don't know— But Jago set a drink in front of Banichi, and sat down, herself, in the other seat facing his. "It's a pleasant place," Jago said. "You've never been there."

"No. To Taiben. Not to Malguri." Politeness, he could do on autopilot, while he was frantically trying to frame a euphemism for kidnapping. He saved his work down hard and folded up the computer. "But four weeks, nadi! I can't do my work from halfway across the country."

"It's an opportunity," Banichi said. "No human before you, nand' paidhi, has made this trip. Don't be so glum."

"What of the aiji-dowager? Sharing accommodations with a member of the aiji's family, with a woman I don't know—has anyone told her I'm coming?"

Banichi drew back his lip from his teeth, a fierce amusement.

"You're resourceful, paidhi-ji. Surely you can deal with her. She'd have *been* the aiji, for your predecessor, at least. . . ."

"Except for the hasdrawad," Jago said.

The hasdrawad had chosen her son, whom she'd wished aloud she'd aborted when she'd had the chance, as the story ran; then, adding insult to injury, the hasdrawad had passed over her a second time when her son was assassinated—ignoring her claims to the succession, in favor of her grandson, Tabini.

"She *favors* Tabini," Banichi said. "Contrary to reports. She always has favored him."

She'd fallen, riding in the hunt, at seventy-two. Broke her shoulder, broke her arm and four ribs, got up and rode through the rest of the course, until they'd caught the quarry.

Then she'd attacked the course manager with her riding crop, for the lost hide on her precious, high-bred Matiawa jumper—as the story went.

"Her reputation," Bren said judiciously, "is not for patience."

"Oh, very much it is," Jago said "When she wants something that needs it."

"Is it true, what people say about the succession?"

"That Tabini-aiji's father died by assassination?" Banichi said. "Yes."

"They never found the agency," said Jago. "And very competent people searched."

"Not a clue to be had—except in the dowager's satisfaction," said Banichi. "Which isn't admissible evidence.—She wasn't, of course, the only one so motivated. But her personal guard is no slight matter."

"Licensed?" Bren asked.

"Oh, yes," said Banichi.

"Most of her guard are old," Jago said. "A bit behind the times."

"Now," said Banichi. "But I wouldn't say they were, then."

"And this is where Tabini-aiji sends me for safety?"

"The aiji-dowager does favor him," Jago said.

"Well, in most regards," Banichi said.

The plane thumped onto the runway in a blinding downpour—other planes had been diverted out to the lowland airport. Banichi said so. But the aiji's crew went right on through. Engines reversed thrust, brakes screeched on wet pavement, the plane veered into a controlled right turn and blazed a fast track to the small terminal.

Bren stared glumly at the weather, at guards and trucks hurrying out to the aiji's plane—a more elaborate reception than he got at Mospheira. But, then, the people meeting him on Mospheira didn't carry guns.

He unbelted, got up with his computer, and followed Banichi to the door as the pilot opened it, with Jago close in attendance.

Rain whipped into their faces, a mist thick enough to breathe. Rain spattered the pavement of the runway. It veiled the scenery in gray, so the lake visible from the airport melded seamlessly with the sky, and the hills around it were banks of shadow against that sky.

Malguri, he thought, must be somewhere on those high shores, overlooking the lake.

"They're sending a car," Jago yelled into their ears—had pocket-com in hand, as a crew began pulling up a movable stairs for their descent. The device had no rain canopy such as Shejidan airport afforded. One supposed they were expected to make a dash for it, down the steps.

One wondered whether, if Tabini had been on the plane, they would have found such a canopy. Or parked the car closer.

Thunder rumbled, and lightnings glared off the wet concrete.

"Auspicious," Bren muttered, far from anxious to venture metal steps in the frequent lightning. But the stairs thumped against the side of the plane, rocking it; rain gusted in, cold as autumn.

The raincoated attendants yelled and beckoned them to come ahead. Banichi went. Hell, he thought, and ducked through the door and hurried after, clinging to the cold, slick metal hand-grip, flinching as lightning lit the ladder and the pavement and thunder cracked overhead. Light up like a candle, they would. He reached the bottom and left the metal ladder with relief, spied Banichi at the open door of the transport van, and, trying not to slip on the pavement, ran for it, with Jago rattling her way down the steps behind him.

He reached shelter. Jago arrived, close behind him, flung herself into the seat, rain glistening on her black skin, as the van driver got out to close the van door and stopped to stare, wide-eyed, while the cold mist gusted in. Evidently no one had told the driver a human was in the party.

"Shut the door!" Banichi said, and the drenched driver slammed it and made haste to climb in his seat in front.

"Algini and Tano," Bren protested, leaning to glance back at the plane, through a rain-spotted window, as the driver's door shut.

"They'll bring the baggage," Jago said. "In another car."

In case of bombs, Bren supposed glumly, as the driver took off the brake, threw the van into gear and launched into what must be the standard verbal courtesies, gamely wishing them Welcome to Maidingi, Jewel of the Mountains, a practiced patter that went on into the felicitous positioning of the mountains, cosmically harmonious and fortunate, and the 'grateful influences' of the mountain springs above the Lake, the Mirror of Heaven.

The Mirror of Heaven reflected nothing, at the moment. Rain shattered the images of drowned buildings and gray void beyond the glass as the car sped along—Bren had expected them to pull up at the terminal and catch a train to Malguri, but the van had whisked them right past the terminal entrances, one and the next and the next, as they headed for the wire fence and the lake.

"Where are we going?" Bren asked, casting anxious glances at Banichi—surely, he thought, Banichi would protest this strange detour; possibly they were all in danger and he should keep his mouth shut.

"This is scheduled, nadi," Jago said, laying a hand on his knee. "Everything as arranged."

"*What's* arranged?" He was short of temper. He divided his attention nervously between the oncoming fence and Jago's placid face, then paid it all to the fence, as collision seemed imminent.

But the driver swung toward a gate, which opened automatically in front of them. And Jago hadn't answered him. "Where are we going?"

"Be calm," Banichi said quietly. "Please take my assurances, nand' paidhi, everything is quite in order."

"Aren't we taking the rail?"

"There's no rail to Malguri," Banichi said. "One goes by car."

One wasn't supposed to go by car. There wasn't supposed to be a car link between an airport and any end destination, no matter how rich one was: the nearest rail link was supposed to be the rule . . . and was there no rail at all between Malguri and the airport?

The designation on the van, written in large letters right above the driver, was, Maidingi Air . . . and did an airline vehicle regularly serve private destinations? They weren't licensed to be a ground transport.

Maybe it was a special authorization security had. But was it that dire an emergency?

"Are we afraid to hire a bus?" he asked, and indicated, right in front of them, and clear to be read, Maidingi Air.

"There's no bus to Malguri."

"It's the law. There's supposed to be a hired bus. . . ."

The van caught an abrupt turn and threw him against Jago's arm.

Jago patted his leg, and he folded his arms and sank back to reassemble the pieces of his dignity and his self-possession, while the thunder rumbled.

There were places where the local tech hadn't caught up to the regulations. There were places with economic exceptions.

But the aiji's own holding damned sure wasn't one. Tabini couldn't hire a bus? Or the bus to Maidingi Township didn't serve Malguri, when it was right next door? The aiji was supposed to set an example of environmental compliance. *Kabiu.* Good precedent. Correct behavior. Appearances.

Where in hell was the estate, that the town bus couldn't get them there?

Gravel scattered under the tires, and the van jolted onto a road in which gray void was on one side and a mountain on the other. The road ceased to be Improved in any sort, and one recalled the vetoes of one's predecessor, overriding the access highway bill from the high villages—and one's own assertion to the aiji, mildly tipsy, that such would 'undermine the rail priority,' that the appeal from the mountain villages was a smoke screen—the aiji had taken to that expression with delight, once he understood it—covering provincial ambitions and leading provincial aijiin to sedition.

It was the identical argument his predecessors had used—he had been queasy about the paranoid logic it encouraged in Tabini, from an ethical standpoint—but Tabini had seemed to accept it as perfectly reasonable atevi logic, and the paidhi didn't vary from his predecessors' arguments for mere human reasons: the paidhi adhered to what had worked with past administrations, argued by atevi logic, unless he had very carefully worked out a change and passed it by council.

And this road was evidently the by-product of that logic, founded on his predecessor's vetoes over the highway system, and sustained on his own.

No bus. No pavement.

He skiied, on his vacations. He was a passionate skiier. He had been on interesting roads, up Mt. Allan Thomas, on Mospheira.

Paved roads. Thank you. Going down a mountain on skis was one thing.

This . . .

. . . vehicle was not designed to climb. It slipped on the turns.

He clutched his computer to keep it from sliding to the rear of the van. He thought he might change his recommendation on the non-township roads proposal.

The van ground its way for what felt like well over an hour up rainwashed gravel, whined and slipped and struggled around an uphill serpentine curve with a spit of gravel from beneath the wheels at the last. Gray space and driving rain filled the windows on every side but one. The van lurched upward into void, tilted, and Bren held to the seat white-knuckled with his free hand, Jago swaying into him, with what might be Lake Maidingi or empty air beside and below and in front of him—he didn't want to look. He didn't want to imagine.

How long would it take searchers to find them if a tire slipped off the rain-washed edge, and they plunged off into the lake?

Another jolt—a slip. "God!"

The driver gave him a startled look in the rearview mirror that took his attention from the wheel. Bren clamped his mouth shut after that. But Banichi and the driver started a conversation—during which the driver kept looking to the back seat to make his points.

"Please, nadi!" Bren said.

Gravel went over the edge. Their right tires bridged a washout and narrowly missed the rim. He was certain of it.

Then, around that curve, curtained in rain, a mass of shadow towered on the gray brink. Stone towers and spires rose there, in a rain-crystaled spatter on the glass—he couldn't tell where the road was, now, except the rattle of gravel under the tires assured him they were still on it.

"Malguri," Banichi said in his deep tones.

"A fortress of the forty-third century," the driver said, "the architectural jewel of this province ... maintained under the provincial trust, an autumn residence of the aiji-major, currently of the aiji-dowager ..."

He sat and hugged his computer case and watched as the towers grew larger in the windshield, as they gathered detail out of the universal gray of the mist, the lake below, and the clouds ... then acquired colors, the dark gray of stone and the rain-soaked drip of heraldic banners from the uppermost tiers.

He was used to atevi architecture, was accustomed to antiquity in the City, and found it in the customs of the aiji's hall, but this place, bristling with turrets and castellations, was not the style of the Landing, like so much of Shejidan. The date the driver had given them was from long, long before humans had ever come into the system, from long before there had ever been a strayed ship or a space station—before—he made a fast re-reckoning—there'd been a human in space at all.

The wipers cleared the scene in alternate blinks, a world creating and recreating itself out of primeval deluge as wooden gates yawned for them and let them inside, onto a stone-paved road that curved beneath a broad, sheltering portico, where the rain only scarcely reached.

The van stopped. Banichi got up and opened the door from inside, on a darkly shadowed porch and open wooden doors. A handful of atevi hastened out of that warm, gold-lit darkness to meet the van—in casual dress, all of them, which fit what Bren knew of country life. Except the boots, it was attire appropriate to a hunting lodge like Taiben, which Bren supposed that Malguri was, in fact, considering the wild land around it ... probably very good hunting, when some more energetic member of the aiji's family was in residence.

He followed Banichi out of the van, computer in hand, reckoning, now that he saw the style of the place, that there might even be formal hunts while they were here, if the staff lent itself to entertaining the guests. Banichi and Jago would certainly be keen for it. He wouldn't: tramping through dusty weeds, getting sunburn, and staring at his supper down a gun barrel was not his favorite sport. He was concerned for his computer in the cold mist that was whirling about them, sucked under the portico by the drafts; and he was more than anxious to conclude the welcome and get in out of the wet.

"The paidhi," Banichi was saying, and Banichi laid a heavy hand on his shoulder. "Bren Cameron, the close associate of Tabini-aiji, the very person, give him good welcome . . ." It was the standard formality. Bren bowed, murmured, "Honor and thanks," in reply to the staff's courtesies, while Jago banged the van door shut and dismissed the driver. The van whined off into the storm and somehow the whole welcoming party advanced, by degrees and inquiries into the aiji's health and well-being, across the cobbles toward the main doors—thank God, Bren thought. A backward glance in response to a question spotted an antique cannon in the paved courtyard, through veils of rain; a forward glance met gold, muted light coming through the doors on a wave of warmer air.

It was a stone-paved hall, with timbered and plastered walls. The banners that hung from the time-blackened rafters looked centuries old themselves, with their muted colors and complex serpentine patterns of ancient writing that, no, indeed, the paidhi didn't know. He recognized Tabini's colors, and the centermost banner had Tabini's personal emblem, the *baji* on a red circle, on a blue field. There were weapons on every wall—swords and weapons the names of which he didn't know, but he'd seen them in the lodge at Taiben, with similar hides, spotted and shaded, pinned on walls, thrown over chairs that owed nothing to human designs.

Banichi seized him by the shoulder again and made

further introductions, this time to two servants, both male, introductions which required another round of bows.

"They'll take you to your rooms," Banichi said. "They'll be assigned to you."

He'd already let the names slip his attention. But, was on his tongue to say, —but what about Algini and Tano, on their way from the airport? Why someone else?

"Excuse me," he said, and bowed in embarrassment. "I lost the names." The paidhi was a diplomat, the paidhi didn't let names get away like that, even names of servants—he wasn't focussing, even yet, asking himself whether these servants were ones Banichi knew, or Jago did, or how they could trust these people.

But they bowed and patiently and courteously said their names again: Maigi and Djinana, honored to be at his service.

Dreadful beginning, with atevi trying to be polite to him. He was being pushed and shoved into places he didn't know in a culture already full of strangenesses, and he was overwhelmed with the place.

"Go with them," Banichi said gently, and added something in one of the regional languages, to which the servants nodded and bowed, regarding him with faces as impassive as Banichi's and Jago's.

"Nand' paidhi," one said. Maigi. He had to get them straight.

Maigi and Djinana, he said over and over to himself, as he followed them across the hall, through the archway, and to the foot of bronze-banistered stone stairs. He realized of a sudden they had just passed out of the sight of Jago and Banichi, but Banichi had said go, Banichi evidently believed they were trustworthy. He had no wish to insult the servants twice by doubting them.

So it was up the stairs, into the upper floor of a strange house ruled by a stranger old woman. The servants he followed talked together in a language the paidhi didn't know, and the place smelled of stone and antiquity. Plastering didn't exist in these wooden-floored upper halls, which, he supposed, were for lesser guests. Pipes and wires ran across ceilings clearly ancient, and bare tungsten-based bulbs hung in brackets festooned by aged copper-centered insulated wire, covered with dust.

This is Tabini's hospitality? he asked himself. This is how his grandmother lives?

He didn't believe it. He was offended, outright offended, *and* somewhat hurt, that Tabini sent him to this dingy, depressing house, with out-of-date plumbing and God knew what kind of beds.

They were running out of hallway. Two huge doors closed off the end. More hiking, he supposed glumly, into some gloomy cubbyhole remote from the activity of the dowager and her staff.

It probably wasn't Tabini's fault. It might be the dowager had countermanded Tabini's arrangements. Grandmother might not *want* a human in her house, and might lodge him under a stairs or in a storeroom somewhere. Banichi and Jago would object when they found out. Grandmother would take offense, Tabini would take offense . . .

The servants opened the doors, on carpet, a spacious sitting room and furniture . . . God, gilt, carved over every surface, carpets that weren't, Bren suddenly realized, mill-produced. The soft, pale light came from a large, pointed-arched window with small rectangular panes, bordered in amber and blue panes—a beautiful frame on a gray, rain-spattered nothing.

"This is the paidhi's reception room," Maigi said, as Djinana opened another, side door and showed him into an equally ornate room with a blazing fireplace—illicit heating source, he said to himself in a remote, note-taking, area of his brain; but the forebrain was busy with other details, the heads and hides and weapons on the walls, the carved wooden furniture, the antique carpet with the *baji-naji* medallions endlessly repeated, identical windows in the next room, which, though smaller, was no less ornate.

"The private sitting room," Maigi said, then flung open the doors on a windowless side room of the same style, with a long, polished wood table from end to end. "The dining room," Maigi said, and went on to point out the hanging bell-pull that would summon them, "Like that in the sitting room," Maigi said, and drew him back to be assured he saw it.

Bren drew a deep breath. Everywhere it was stone walls and polished wooden floors, and dim lights, and gilt . . . a museum tour, it began to be, with Maigi and Djinana pointing out particular record heads of species three of which they confessed to be extinct, and explaining certain furnishings of historical significance.

"Given by the aiji of Deinali province on the marriage of the fourth dynasty aiji's heir to the heir of Deinali, which, however, was never consummated, due to the death of the aiji's heir in a fall from the garden walk. . . ."

What garden walk? he asked himself, determined, under the circustances, to avoid the fatal area himself.

It was the paranoia of the flight here working on his nerves. It must be.

Or it might be the glass eyes of dead animals staring at him, mute and helpless.

Maigi opened yet another door, on a bedroom far, far larger than any reasonable bedroom needed to be, with— Bren supposed at least it was a bed and not a couch—an affair on a dais, with spears upholding the curtains which mostly enfolded it, a bed smothered in skins of animals and set on a stonework dais. Maigi showed him another bellpull, and briskly led him on to yet—God!—a farther hall.

He followed, beginning to feel the entire matter of the paidhi's accommodations ridiculously out of control. Maigi opened a side door to a stone-floored room with a hole in the floor, a silver basin, and a stack of linen towels. "The accommodation," Maigi pronounced it, euphemismistically. "Please use the towels provided. Paper jams the plumbing."

He supposed his consternation showed. Maigi took up a dipper from the polished silver cauldron, an ornate dipper, and poured it down the hole in the floor.

"Actually," Djinana said, "there's continual water action. The aiji Padigi had it installed in 4879. The dipper remains, for the towels, of course."

It was genteel, it was elegant, it was . . . appalling, was the feeling he had about it. Atevi weren't animals. He wasn't. He couldn't use this. There had to be something else, downstairs, perhaps; he'd find out, and walk that far.

Djinana opened a double door beyond the accommodation, which let into a bath, an immense stone tub, with pipes running across the floor. "Mind your step, nadi," Djinana said. Clearly plumbing here was an afterthought, too, and the volume of water one used for a single bath had to be immense.

"Your own servants will light the fires for you each evening," Djinana said, and demonstrated that there was running water, while he absorbed that small advisement that Algini and Tano were not lost, his luggage might yet make it, and he might not be alone with Djinana and Maigi after all.

Meanwhile Maigi had opened up the boiler, which was mounted on the stone wall, and which had two pipes running into it from overhead, down the wall: the larger one had to be cold water entering the boiler and a hot water conduit carried it out and across to the tub; but he was puzzled by the second, thinner pipe—until he realized that small blue flame in the boiler compartment must be supplied by that smaller gauge pipe. Methane gas. An explosion waiting to happen. An asphyxiation, if the little flame went out and let gas accumulate in the bath.

My God, he thought, racking up violation after violation, several of them potentially lethal as the two servants led the way back through the accommodation and into the hall.

Had Tabini sent him here for safety? Now that he understood what some of these pipes and electric lines must be, he traced other after-thought installations in the ancient stonework, some of which he realized now were certainly carrying methane, throughout the apartments and elsewhere, others of which were an antique electric supply, a source of sparks.

The building was still standing. The wiring was very old. So were the pipes. Evidently the staff had been careful . . . thus far.

"We, of course, are at your service," Maigi said as they walked. "Your own staff should be arriving soon. They'll lodge in the servants' quarters, too. One ring for them, for personal needs; two for us, for food, for adjustment in the accommodations. We serve Malguri itself, and of course, provide its hospitality in any special requirements the paidhi might have."

Djinana led the way back to the sitting room—an expedition in itself—and taking a small leather-bound codex from a table, presented it to him along with a pen. "Please add your name to the distinguished guests," Djinana requested of him, and, as he prepared to do so: "It would be a further distinction, nadi, if you'd sign in your own language. That's never been, before."

"Thank you," he said, quite touched, actually, at the implication of genuine welcome in this shrine, and duly signed in atevi script and, with, ironically, less practice, in Mosphei'.

He heard thumping in the hall. He looked up.

"Doubtless your servants," Maigi said, and a moment later saw Tano with two big boxes, headed in through the outer door, and, imperiling an antique table, through the reception room.

"Nand' paidhi," Tano said, out of breath, and rain-soaked, like the boxes. Djinana hastened to show Tano through into the bedroom, to save the furniture, Bren supposed—and hoped those boxes were his clothes, particularly his sweaters and middle-weight coat.

"Would the paidhi like tea?" Maigi asked, as a thump of the outer door announced some other arrival, probably

Algini. A draft fluttered the fire in the fireplace, and immediately, true to his guess, Algini came through the sitting room, equally soaked, and managed to bow in transit, difficult with two huge boxes in his arms.

Everything he owned, he thought, remembering the pile of boxes they had loaded on the train—God, how long did they propose he stay here?

"Tea," he recalled distractedly. "Yes—" He felt chilled in spite of the fire, having come, a few hours ago, from a much more southerly and coastal climate, and having suffered a long drive over a trying road. Hot tea appealed to him, and it came to him that, in the confusion, he hadn't had breakfast, or lunch, except a few wafers on the plane. "Is there a cheese pie, do you think?" That was usually safe, whatever the season.

"Of course, nadi. Although I should remind the paidhi that dinner is only an hour away...."

The time zones, he realized. He'd never been far enough from Mospheira to meet one. But not only was the climate colder, the time zones had to be at least two hours advanced. He wasn't sure how his stomach agreed with that sudden piece of information, or whether he could last an hour until supper, now that he was thinking about food.

Thunder rumbled, and lightning flashed, whiting out the windows. "No pie, then," he said, and decided life was not necessarily fast-paced here: he might find diversion in a leisurely, lodge-style supper. "Just the tea, please."

But he was thinking, hearing another furious spate of rain hit the windows, God, I understand why there's a lake here.

Supper arrived, after the tea, elegantly served in the dining room. Definitely lodge-style cuisine, and he certainly had no complaint against the menu—the seasonal game, thank God, was different here in the highlands.

But it was a solitary supper—himself alone at the very

long and silent table—at the endmost seat, so he could see the window in the sitting room, which he thought would be pleasant, but they were so high up, on the second floor, he had no view but the gray sky, which was darkening sullenly to dusk. Tano and Algini ate in their quarters, Maigi and Djinana served, and he hardly knew either set of servants well enough to make conversation. Attempts died in, Yes, nand' paidhi, thank you, nand' paidhi, the cook will be glad, nand' paidhi.

Finally, though, during the second, post game-dish soup course, Jago came, leaned her arms on the back of the nearest of the ten chairs on either side of the table, and made idle chatter with him, how did he find the accommodations, how did he find the staff?

"Wonderful," he said. "Though I haven't seen a phone connection. Or the wires. Is there a portable I could borrow?"

"There's one, I believe, in the security station. But it's raining."

Still.

"You mean the security station is outside."

"I fear it is. And I really don't think it prudent to call out, nadi Bren."

"Why?" It came out angry, and he hadn't meant that. Jago had instantly withdrawn her elbows from the chair back and stood up straight. "Forgive me, nadi," he said more moderately. "But I do need to reach my office on some regular basis. I urgently need to have my mail. I do hope my mail is going to get up that difficult road."

Jago heaved a sigh and set her hands on the chair back. "Nadi Bren," she said patiently, "while I don't think our moving you from the capital necessarily deceived anyone, it would hardly be wise to have you phoning out. They'll expect decoys. Let them think our flight to Malguri was exactly that."

"Then you know something about them."

"No. Not actually."

He was tired, he had had the self-restraint scared out of

him, on the drive up, and no matter how much the atevi liked their courtesies and facades, he had felt the situation slipping farther and farther from his control for two days, now. He wanted something to be clear to him. He was ready to lose all patience.

Instead he said, mildly, "I know you've done your best. Probably you'd rather be elsewhere than here."

Jago's brow furrowed. "Have I given such an impression?"

God help him, he thought. "No, of course not. But I suppose you have other duties than me."

"No."

Jago had a habit of doing that to conversations, he decided, once you inquired about anything useful, anything you really wanted to know. He took a spoonful of soup, hoping Jago would find something to say.

She didn't. She leaned on the chair back, evidently at her ease.

He took another spoonful, and a third, and still Jago leaned on the chair, evidently content to watch him, or guarding him, or something. Thunder was still rumbling outside.

"Are you going to stay at Malguri?" he asked.

"Most likely."

"Do you expect whoever invaded my room can reach here, too?"

"Less likely."

It went like that, by one syllable and two, and never much more, once he'd started asking questions.

"When do you think the rain will stop?" he asked her finally, only to make Jago carry the conversation for more than three beats.

"Tomorrow," she said. And stopped.

"Jago, do you *favor* me? Or am I in your disfavor?"

"Of course not, nadi Bren."

"Have I done something for Tabini to be put out with me?"

"Not that I know."

"Are they sending my mail?"

"Banichi's asking about that. It takes authorizations."

"Whose?"

"We're working on it."

Thunder rolled above the fortress. He finished his supper, intermittent with question and answer with Jago, had a drink or two in which Jago did not share, and even wished, if, as Banichi had said, Jago found him in the least attractive, she would stay in his sitting room and at least make some polite pass at him, if it meant she initiated four consecutive sentences. He just wanted someone to talk to.

But Jago left, all business, seeming preoccupied. The servants cleared supper away in silence.

He cast about for what to do with himself, and thought about a resumption of his regular habits, watching the evening news ... which, now that he thought about it, he had no television to receive.

He didn't ask the servants about the matter. He opened cabinets and armoires, and finally made the entire circuit of the apartments, looking for nothing more basic now than a power tap.

Not one. Not a hint of accommodation for television or telephones.

Or computer recharges.

He thought about ringing the bell, rousing the servants and demanding an extension cord, at least, so he could use his almost depleted computer tonight, if they had to run the cord up from the kitchens or via an adapter, which had to exist in some electronics store in this benighted district, down from an electric light socket.

But Banichi hadn't put in an appearance since they parted company downstairs, Jago had refused the request for a phone already, and after pacing the carpeted wooden floors awhile and investigating the small library for something to do, he went to bed in disgust—flung himself into the curtained bed among the skins of dead animals and discovered that one, there was no reading light, two, the lights were all controlled from a switch at the doorway; and, three, a dead and angry beast was staring straight at him, from the opposite wall.

It wasn't me, he thought at it. It wasn't my fault. I probably wasn't born when you died.

My species probably hadn't left the homeworld yet.

It's not my fault, beast. We're both stuck here.

IV

Morning dawned through a rain-spattered glass, and breakfast didn't arrive automatically. He pulled the chain to call for it, delivered his request to Maigi, who was at least prompt to appear, and had Djinana light the fire for an after-breakfast bath.

Then there was the "accommodation" question; and, faced with trekking downstairs before breakfast in search of a modern bathroom, he opted for privacy and for coping with what evidently worked, in its fashion, which required no embarrassed questions and no (diplomatically speaking) appearance of despising what was—with effort—an elegant, historic hospitality. He managed. He decided that, left alone, he could get used to it.

The paidhi's job, he thought, was to adapt. Somehow.

Breakfast, God, was four courses. He saw his waistline doubling before his eyes and ordered a simple poached fish and piece of fruit for lunch, then shooed the servants out and took his leisurely bath, thoroughly self-indulgent. Life in Malguri was of necessity a matter of planning ahead, not just turning a tap. But the water was hot.

He didn't ask Tano and Algini in for their non-conversation while he bathed ("Yes, nadi, no, nadi.") or their help in dressing. He found no actual purpose for dressing: no agenda, nowhere to go until lunch, so far as Banichi and Jago had advised him.

So he wrapped himself in his dressing gown and stared out the study window at a grayness in which the blue and amber glass edging was the only color. The lake was silver gray, set in dark gray bluffs and fog. The sky was milky gray, portending more rain. A last few drops jeweled the glass.

It was exotic. It damned sure wasn't Shejidan. It wasn't Mospheira, it wasn't human, and it wasn't so far as he could see any safer than Tabini's own household, just less convenient. Without a plug-in for his computer.

Maybe the assassin wouldn't spend a plane ticket on him.

Maybe boredom would send the rascal back to livelier climes.

Maybe after a week of this splendid luxury he would hike to the train station and join the assassin in an escape himself.

Fancies, all.

He took the guest book from its shelf—anything to occupy his mind—took it back to the window where there was better light and leafed through it, looking at the names, realizing—as the leaves were added forward, rather than the reverse, after the habit of atevi books—that he was holding an antiquity that went back seven hundred years, at least; and that most of the occupants of these rooms had been aijiin, or the in-laws of aijiin, some of them well-known in history, like Pagioni, like Dagina, who'd signed the Controlled Resources Development Treaty with Mospheira—a canny, hard-headed fellow, who, thank God, had knocked heads together and eliminated a few highly dangerous, warlike obstacles in ways humans couldn't.

He was truly impressed. He opened it from the back, as atevi read—the right-left direction, and down—and discovered the foundation date of the first fortress on the site, as the van driver had said, was indeed an incredible two thousand years ago. Built of native stone, to hold the valuable water resource of Maidingi for the lowlands, and to prevent the constant raiding of hill tribes on the villages of the plain. The second, expanded, fortress—one supposed, including these very walls—dated from the sixty-first century.

He leafed through changes and additions, found a tour schedule, of all things, once monthly, confined to the lower hall—*(We ask our guests to ignore this monthly visit, which the aiji feels necessary and proper, as Malguri represents a treasure belonging to the people of the provinces. Should a guest wish to receive tour groups in formal or informal audience, please inform the staff and they will be most happy to make all arrangements. Certain guests have indeed done so, to the delight and honor of the visitors. . . .)*

Shock hell out of them, I would, Bren thought glumly. Send children screaming for their parents. None of the people here have seen a human face-to-face.

Too much television, Banichi would say. Children in Shejidan had to be reassured about Mospheira, that humans weren't going to leave there and turn up in their houses at night—so the report went. Atevi children knew about assassins. From television they knew about the War of the Landing. And the space station the world hadn't asked to have. Which was going to swoop down and destroy the earth.

His predecessor twice removed had tried to arrange to let humans tour the outlying towns. Several mayors had backed the idea. One had died for it.

Paranoia still might run that deep—in the outlying districts—and he had no wish to push it, not now, not at this critical juncture, with one attempt already on his life. Lie low and lie quiet, was the role Tabini had assigned him, in sending him here. And he still, dammit, didn't know what else he could have done wiser than he had, once the opportunity had passed to have made a phone call to Mospheira.

If there'd ever been such an opportunity.

Human pilots, in alternation with atevi crews, flew cargo from Mospheira to Shejidan, and to several coastal towns and back again ... that was the freedom humans had now, when their forebears had flown between stars none of them remembered.

Now the paidhi would be arrested, most likely, if he took a walk to town after an extension cord. His appearance could start riots, economic panics, rumors of descending space stations and death rays.

He was depressed, to tell the truth. He had thought he had a good rapport with Tabini, he had *thought,* in his human way of needing such things, that Tabini was as close to a friend as an ateva was capable of being.

Something was damned well wrong. At least wrong enough that Tabini couldn't confide it to him. That was what everything added up to—either officially or personally. And he put the codex back on the shelf and took to pacing the floor, not that he intended to, but he found himself doing it, back and forth, back and forth, to the bedroom and back, and out to the sitting room, where the view of the lake at least afforded a ray of sunlight through the clouds. It struck brilliant silver on the water.

It was a beautiful lake. It was a glorious view, when it wasn't gray.

He could be inspired, if his breakfast wasn't lying like lead on his stomach.

Hell if he wanted to go on being patient. The paidhi's job might demand it. The paidhi's job might be to sit still and figure out how to keep the peace, and maybe he hadn't done that very well by discharging firearms in the aiji's household. But ...

He hadn't looked for the gun. He hadn't even thought about it. Tano and Algini and Jago had done the actual packing and unpacking of his belongings.

He blazed a straight course back to the bedroom, got down on his knees and felt under the mattress.

His fingers met hard metal. Two pieces of hard metal, one a gun and one a clip of shells.

He pulled them out, sitting on the floor as he was, in his dressing robe, with the gun in his hands and a sudden dread of someone walking in on him. He shoved the gun and the clip back where they belonged, and sat there asking himself—what in hell is this about?

Nothing but that the paidhi's in cold storage. And armed. And guarded. And his guards won't tell him a cursed thing.

Well, *damn,* he thought.

And gathered himself up off the floor in a sudden fit of resolution, intending to push it as far as he had latitude and find out where the boundaries (however nebulous) might be. He went to the armoire and pulled out a good pair of pants; a sweater, obstinately human and impossible for atevi to judge for status statements; and his good brown hunting boots, that being the style of this country house.

His favorite casual coat, the leather one.

Then he walked out the impressive front doors of his suite and down the hall, an easy, idle stroll, down the stairs to the stone-floored main floor, making no attempt whatsoever at stealth, and along the hall to the grand central room, where a fire burned wastefully in the hearth, where the lights were all candles, and the massive front doors were shut.

He walked about, idly examined the bric-a-brac, and objects on tables that might be functional and might be purely decorative—he didn't know. He didn't know what to call a good many of the objects on the walls, particularly the lethal ones. He didn't recognize the odder heads and hides—he determined to find out the species and the status of those species, and add them to the data files for Mospheira, with illustrations, if he could get a book . . . or a copy machine . . .

. . . or plug in the computer.

His frustration hit new levels, at the latter thoughts. He

thought about trying the front doors to see if they were locked, taking a walk out in the front courtyard, if they weren't—maybe having a close up look at the cannon, and maybe at the gates and the road.

Then he decided that that was probably pushing Banichi's good humor much too far; possibly, too, and more to the point, risking Banichi's carefully laid security arrangements . . . which might catch him instead of an assassin.

So he opted to take a stroll back into the rest of the building instead, down an ornate corridor, and into plain ones, past doors he didn't venture to open. If assassins might venture in here looking for him, especially in the dark, he wanted a mental map of the halls and the rooms and the stairways that might become escape routes.

He located the kitchens. And the storerooms.

And a hall at a right angle, which offered slit windows and a view out toward the mountains. He took that turn, having discovered, he supposed, the outside wall, and he walked the long corridor to the end, where he found a choice: one hallway tending off to the left and another to the right.

The left must be another wing of the building, he decided, and, seeing double doors down that direction, and those doors shut, he had a sudden chilling thought of personal residence areas, wires, and security systems.

He reasoned then that the more prudent direction for him to take, if he had come to private apartments of some sort, where security arrangements might be far more modern than the lighting, was back toward the front of the building, boxing the square toward the front hall and the foyer.

The hall he walked was going that direction, at about the right distance of separation, he was increasingly confident, to end up as the corridor that exited near the stairs leading up to his floor. He walked past one more side hall and a left-right-straight-ahead choice, and, indeed, ended up in the archway entry to the grand hall in front of the main doors, where the fireplace was.

Fairly good navigation, he thought, and walked back to the warmth of the fireplace, where he had started his exploration of the back halls.

"Well," someone said, close behind him.

He had thought the fireside unoccupied. He turned in alarm to see a wizened little ateva, with white in her black hair, sitting in one of the high-backed leather chairs . . . diminutive woman—for her kind.

"Well?" she said again, and snapped her book closed. "You're Bren. Yes?"

"You're . . ." He struggled with titles and politics—different honorifics, when one was face to face with an atevi lord. "The esteemed aiji-dowager."

"Esteemed, hell. Tell that to the hasdrawad." She beckoned with a thin, wrinkled hand. "Come here."

He moved without even thinking to move. That was the command in Ilisidi. Her finger indicated the spot in front of her chair, and he moved there and stood while she looked him up and down, with pale yellow eyes that had to be a family trait. They made the recipient of that stare think of everything he'd done in the last thirty hours.

"Puny sort," she said.

People didn't cross the dowager. That was well reputed.

"Not for my species, nand' dowager."

"Machines to open doors. Machines to climb stairs. Small wonder."

"Machines to fly. Machines to fly between stars." Maybe she reminded him of Tabini. He was suddenly over the edge of courtesy between strangers. He had forgotten the honorifics and argued with her. He found no way back from his position. Tabini would never respect a retreat. Neither would Ilisidi, he was convinced of that in the instant he saw the tightening of the jaw, the spark of fire in the eyes that were Tabini's own.

"And you let us have what suits our backward selves."

Gave him back the direct retort, indeed. He bowed.

"I recall you won the War, nand' dowager."

"*Did* we?"

Those yellow, pale eyes were quick, the wrinkles around her mouth all said decisiveness. She shot at him. He shot back,

"Tabini-aiji also says it's questionable. We argue."

"Sit down!"

It was progress, of a kind. He bowed, and drew up the convenient footstool rather than fuss with a chair, which he didn't think would further his case with the old lady.

"I'm dying," Ilisidi snapped. "Do you know that?"

"Everyone is dying, nand' dowager. I know that."

Yellow eyes still held his, cruel and cold, and the aiji-dowager's mouth drew down at the corners. "Impudent whelp."

"Respectful, nand' dowager, of one who *has* survived."

The flesh at the corner of the eyes crinkled. The chin lifted, stern and square. "Cheap philosophy."

"Not for your enemies, nand' dowager."

"How *is* my grandson's health?"

Almost she shook him. Almost. "As well as it deserves to be, nand' dowager."

"How well does it deserve to be?" She seized the cane beside her chair in a knobby hand and banged the ferule against the floor, once, twice, three times. "Damn you!" she shouted at no one in particular. "*Where's the tea?*"

The conversation was over, evidently. He was glad to find it was her servants who had trespassed her good will. "I'm sorry to have bothered you," he began to say, and began to get up.

The cane hammered the stones. She swung her scowl on him. "Sit down!"

"I beg the dowager's pardon, I—" Have a pressing engagement, he wanted to say, but he didn't. In this place the lie was impossible.

Bang! went the cane. Bang! "Damnable layabouts! Cenedi! The tea!"

Was she sane? he asked himself. He sat. He didn't know what else he could do, but sit. He wasn't even sure there were servants, or that tea had been in the equation until it crossed her mind, but he supposed the aiji-dowager's personal staff knew what to do with her.

Old staffers, Jago had said. Dangerous, Banichi had hinted.

Bang! Bang! "Cenedi! Do you hear me?"

Cenedi might be twenty years dead for all he knew. He sat frozen like a child on a footstool, arms about his knees, ready to defend his head and shoulders if Ilisidi's whim turned the cane on him.

But to his relief, someone did show up, an atevi servant he took at first glance for Banichi, but it clearly wasn't, on the second look. The same black uniform. But the face was lined with time and the hair was streaked liberally with gray.

"Two cups," Ilisidi snapped.

"Easily, nand' dowager," the servant said.

Cenedi, Bren supposed, and he didn't want tea, he had had his breakfast, all four courses of it. He was anxious to escape Ilisidi's company and her hostile questions before he said or did something to cause trouble for Banichi, wherever Banichi was.

Or for Tabini.

If Tabini's grandmother was, as she claimed, dying . . . she was possibly out of reasons to be patient with the world, which in Ilisidi's declared opinion, had not done wisely to pass over her. This could be a dangerous and angry woman.

But a tea service regularly had six cups, and Cenedi set one filled cup in the dowager's hand, and offered another to him, a cup which clearly he was to drink, and for a moment he could hear what wise atevi adults told every toddling child, don't take, don't touch, don't talk with strangers—

Ilisidi took a delicate sip, and her implacable stare was on him. She was amused, he was sure. Perhaps she thought him a fool that he didn't set down the cup at once and run for Banichi's advice, or that he'd gotten himself this far in over his head, arguing with a woman no few atevi feared, and not for her insanity.

He took the sip. He found no other choice but abject flight, and that wasn't the course the paidhi ever had open to him. He stared Ilisidi in the eyes when he did drink, and when he didn't feel any strangeness from the cup or the tea, he took a second sip.

A web of wrinkles tightened about Ilisidi's eyelids as she drank. He couldn't see her mouth behind her hand and the cup, and when she lowered that cup, the web had all relaxed, leaving only the unrealized map of her years and her intentions, a maze of lines in the firelit black gloss of her skin.

"So what vices does the paidhi have in his spare time? Gambling? Sex with the servants?"

"It's the paidhi's business to be circumspect."

"And celibate?"

It wasn't a polite question. Nor politely meant, he feared. "Mospheira is an easy flight away, nand' dowager. When I have the time to go home, I do. The last time . . ." He didn't feel invited to chatter. But he preferred it to Ilisidi's interrogation. " . . . was the 28th Madara."

"So." Another sip of tea. A flick of long, thin fingers. "Doubtless a tale of perversions."

"I paid respects to my mother and brother."

"And your father?"

A more difficult question. "Estranged."

"On an island?"

"The aiji-dowager may know, we don't pursue blood-feud. Only law."

"A cold-blooded lot."

"Historically, we practiced feud."

"Ah. And is this *another* thing your great wisdom found unwise?"

He sensed, perhaps, the core of her resentments. He wasn't sure. But he had trod that minefield before—it was known territory, and he looked her straight in the face. "The paidhi's job is to advise. If the aiji rejects our advice . . ."

"You wait," she finished for him, "for another aiji, another paidhi. But you expect to get your way."

No one had ever put it so bluntly to him. He had wondered if the atevi did understand, though he had thought they had.

"Situations change, nand' dowager."

"Your tea's getting cold." He sipped it.. It was indeed cold, quickly chilled, in the small cups. He wondered if she knew what had brought him to Malguri. He had had the image of an old woman out of touch with the world, and now he thought not. He emptied the cup.

Ilisidi emptied hers, and flung it at the fire. Porcelain shattered. He jumped—shaken by the violence, asking himself again if Ilisidi was mad.

"I never favored that tea service," Ilisidi said.

He had the momentary impulse to send his cup after it. If Tabini had said the like, Tabini would have been testing him, and he would have thrown it. But he didn't know Ilisidi. He had to take that into account for good and all. He rose and handed his cup to Cenedi, who waited with the tray.

Cenedi hurled the whole set at the fireplace. Tea hissed in the coals. Porcelain lay shattered.

Bren bowed, as if he had received a compliment, and saw an old woman who, dying, sitting in the midst of this prized antiquity, destroyed what offended her preferences, broke what was ancient and priceless, because *she* didn't like it. He looked for escape, murmured, "I thank the aiji-dowager for her attention," and got two steps away before *bang!* went the cane on the stones, and he stopped and faced back again, constrained by atevi custom—and the suspicion what service Cenedi was to her.

He had amused the aiji-dowager. She was grinning, laughing with a humor that shook her thin body, as she leaned both hands on the cane. "Run," she said. "Run, nand' paidhi. But where's safe? Do you know?"

"This place," he shot back. One *didn't* retreat from direct challenges—not if one wasn't a child, and wasn't anyone's servant. "Your residence. The aiji thought so."

She didn't say a thing, just grinned and laughed and rocked back and forth on the pivot of the cane. After an anxious moment he decided he was dismissed, and bowed, and headed away, hoping she was through with jokes, and asking himself was Ilisidi sane, or had Tabini known, or *why* had she destroyed the tea service?

Because a human had profaned it?

Or because there was something in the tea, that now was vapor on the winds above the chimney? His stomach was upset. He told himself it was suggestion. He reminded himself there were some teas humans shouldn't drink.

His pulse was hammering as he walked the hall and climbed the stairs, and he wondered if he should try to throw up, or where, or if he could get to his own bathroom to do it . . . not to upset the staff . . . or lose his dignity . . .

Which was stupid, if he was poisoned. Possibly it was fear that was making his heart race. Possibly it was one of those stimulants like midarga, which in overdoses could put a human in the emergency room, and he should find Banichi or Jago and tell them what he'd done, and what he'd drunk, that was already making its way into his bloodstream.

A clammy sweat was on his skin as he reached the upper hall. It might be nothing more than fear, and suggestion, but he couldn't get air enough, and there was a darkening around the edges of his vision. The hall became a nightmare, echoing with his steps on the wooden floor. He put out a hand to the wall to steady himself and his hand vanished into a strange dark nowhere at the side of his vision.

I'm in serious trouble, he thought. I have to get to the

door. I mustn't fall in the hallway. I mustn't make it obvious I'm reacting to the stuff . . . never show fear, never show discomfort. . . .

The door wobbled closer and larger in the midst of the dark tunnel. He had a blurred view of the latch, pushed down on it. The door opened and let him into the blinding glare of the windows, white as molten metal.

Close the door, he thought. Lock it. I'm going to bed. I might fall asleep awhile. Can't sleep with the door unlocked.

The latch caught. He was sure of that. He faced the glare of the windows, staggered a few steps and then found he was going the wrong way, into the light.

"Nadi Bren!"

He swung around, frightened by the echoing sound, frightened by the darkness that loomed up on every side of him, around the edges and now in the center of his vision, darkness that reached out arms and caught him and swept him off his feet in a whirling of all his concept of up and down.

Then it was white, white, until the vision went gray again and violent, and he was bent over a stone edge, with someone shouting orders that echoed in his ears, and peeling his sweater off over his head.

Water blasted the back of his head, then, cold water, a battering flood that rattled his brain in his skull. He sucked in an involuntary, watery gasp of air, and tried to fight against drowning, but an iron grip held his arms and another—whoever it was had too many hands—gripped the back of his neck and kept him where he was. If he tried to turn his head, he choked. If he stayed where he was, head down to the torrent, he could breathe, between spasms of a gut that couldn't get rid of any more than it had.

A pain stung his arm. Someone had stuck him and he was bleeding, or his arm was swelling, and whoever was holding him was still bent on drowning him. Waves of nausea rolled through his gut, he could feel the burning of tides in his blood that didn't have anything to do with this world's moons. They weren't human, the things that surrounded him and constrained him, and they didn't like him—even at best, atevi wished humanity had never been, never come here . . . there'd been so much blood, holding on to Mospheira, and they were guilty, but what else could they have done?

He began to chill. The cold of the water went deeper and deeper into his skull, until the dark began to go away, and he could see the gray stone, and the water in the tub, and feel the grip on his neck and his arms as painful. His knees hurt, on the stones. His arms were numb.

And his head began to feel light and strange. Is this dying? he wondered. Am I dying? Banichi's going to be mad if that's the case.

"Cut the water," Banichi said, and of a sudden Bren found himself hauled over onto his back, dumped into what he vaguely decided was a lap, and felt a blanket, a very welcome but inadequate blanket, thrown over his chilled skin. Sight came and went. He thought it was a yellow blanket, he didn't know why it mattered. He was scared as someone picked him up like a child and carried him, that that person was going to try to carry him down the stairs, which were somewhere about, the last he remembered. He didn't feel at all secure, being carried.

The arms gave way and dumped him.

He yelled. His back and shoulders hit a mattress, and the rest of him followed.

Then someone rolled him roughly onto his face on silken, skidding furs, and pulled off his blanket, his boots and his trousers, while he just lay there, paralyzed, aware of all of it, but aware too of a pain in his temples that forecast a very bad headache. He heard Banichi's voice out of the general murmur in the room, so it was all right now. It would be all right, since Banichi was here. He said, to help Banichi,

"I drank the tea."

A blow exploded across his ear. "Fool!" Banichi said,

from above him, and flung him over onto his back and covered him with furs.

It didn't help the headache, which was rising at a rate that scared him and made his heart race. He thought of stroke, or aneurism, or an impending heart attack. Only where Banichi had hit his ear was hot and halfway numb. Banichi grabbed his arm and stuck him with a needle—it hurt, but not near the pain his head was beginning to have.

After that, he just wanted to lie there submerged in dead animal skins, and breathe. He listened to his own heartbeat, he timed his breaths, he found troughs between the waves of pain, and lived in those, while his eyes ran tears from the daylight and he wished he was sane enough to tell Banichi to draw the drapes.

"This isn't Shejidan!" Banichi railed at him. "Things don't come in plastic packages!"

He knew that. He wasn't stupid. He remembered where he was, though he wasn't sure what plastic packages had to do with anything. The headache reached a point he thought he was going to die and he wanted to have it over with—

But you didn't say that to atevi, who didn't think the same as humans, and Banichi was already mad at him.

Justifiably. This was the second time in a week Banichi had had to rescue him. He kept asking himself had the aiji-dowager tried to kill him, and tried to warn Banichi that Cenedi was an assassin—he was sure he was. He looked like Banichi—he wasn't sure that was a compelling logic, but he tried to structure his arguments so Banichi wouldn't think he was a total fool.

"Cenedi did this?"

He thought he'd said so. He wasn't sure. His head hurt too much. He just wanted to lie there in the warm furs and go to sleep and not have it hurt when and if he woke up, but he was scared to let go, because he might never wake up and he hadn't called Hanks.

Banichi crossed the room and talked to someone. He

wasn't sure, but he thought it was Jago. He hoped there wasn't going to be trouble, and that they weren't under attack of some kind. He wished he could follow what they were saying.

He shut his eyes. The light hurt them too much. Someone asked if he was all right, and he decided if he weren't all right, Banichi would call doctors or something, so he nodded that he was, and slid off into the dark, thinking maybe he had called Hanks, or maybe just thought about calling Hanks. He wasn't sure.

V

Light hurt. Moving hurt. There wasn't any part of him that didn't hurt once he tried to move, particularly his head, and the smell of food wasn't at all attractive. But a second shake came at his shoulder, and Tano leaned over him, he was sure it was Tano, though his eyes wouldn't focus, quite, and light hurt.

"You'd better eat, nand' paidhi."

"God."

"Come on." Pitilessly, Tano began plumping up the cushions about his head and shoulders—which made his head ache and made him uncertain about his stomach.

He rested there, figuring that for enough cooperation to satisfy his tormentors, and saw Algini in the doorway to the bath and the servants' quarters, talking to Jago, the two of them speaking very quietly, in voices that echoed and distorted. Tano came back with a bowl of soup and some meal wafers. "Eat," Tano told him, and he didn't want it. He wanted to tell Tano go away, but his servants didn't go away, Tabini hired them, and he had to do what they said.

Besides, white wafers was what you ate when your

stomach was upset and you wanted not to be sick—he flashed on Mospheira, on his own bedroom, and his mother—but it was Tano holding his head, Tano insisting he have at least half of it, and he nibbled a crumb at a time, while the room and everything tilted on him, and kept trying to slide off into the echoing edges of the world.

He rested his eyes after that, and waked to the smell of soup. He didn't want it, but he took a sip of it, when Tano put the cup to his lips, and burned his mouth. It tasted like the tea. He wanted to stop right there, but Tano kept trying to feed it to him, insisting he had to, that it was the only way to flush the tea out of his system. So he put an arm into the cold air, located the cup handle with his own hand, let Tano prop his head with pillows, and drank at the cup without dropping it, until his stomach decided it absolutely couldn't tolerate any more.

He rested the cup in both hands, then, exhausted, unable to decide whether he wanted to put his arm back under the covers to get warm or whether the heat from the porcelain was better. Stay where he was, he thought. He didn't want to move, didn't want to do anything but breathe.

Then Banichi walked in, dismissed Tano and stood over his bed with arms folded.

"How are you feeling, nand' paidhi?"

"Very foolish," he muttered. He remembered, if he was not hallucinating, the aiji-dowager, a pot of tea, smashed in the fireplace. And a man, Banichi's very image.

Who was standing in the doorway.

His heart jumped.

Cenedi walked in when he saw him looking his way, and stood on the other side of his bed.

"I wish to apologize," Cenedi said. "Professionally, nand' paidhi. I should have known about the tea."

"I should have known. I will know, after this." The taste of the tea was still in his mouth. His head ached if he blinked. He was upset that Banichi allowed this stranger into the room, and he asked himself whether Banichi was playing some angle he didn't understand, pretending to believe Cenedi. It only made sense to keep his answers moderate, and to be polite, and not to offend anyone unnecessarily.

"They compound the aiji-dowager's tea," Banichi said, "from a very old local recipe. There's a strong stimulant involved, which the dowager considers healthful, or at least bracing. With humans' small body weight and adverse reaction to alkaloids—"

"God."

"The compound is a tea called dajdi, which I counsel you to avoid in future."

"The cook requests assurances of your good will," Cenedi said from the other side of his bed. "He had no idea a human would be in the company."

"Assure him, please." His head was going in circles. He lay back against the pillow, and almost spilled the half cup of soup. "No ill will. My damn fault."

"These are human manners," Banichi said. "He wishes to emphasize his confidence it was an accident, nadi."

There was silence. He knew he hadn't said what he hoped to have said, and he shouldn't swear doing it, but his head hurt too much. "No wish to offend," he murmured, which was the universal way out of confusing offenses. "Only good will." His head was beginning to hurt again. Banichi rescued the soup and set it aside with a clank on the table that sounded like thunder.

"The aiji-dowager wants her doctor to examine the paidhi," Cenedi said, "if you would stand by as a witness for both sides in this affair, Banichi-ji."

"Thank the aiji-dowager," Banichi said. "Yes."

"I don't need a doctor," Bren said. He didn't want to have the dowager's doctor near him. He only wanted a little while to rest, lie in the pillows, and let the soup settle.

But no one paid any attention to his wishes. Cenedi went out with Jago, came back with an elderly ateva with a bag full of equipment, who threw back the warm furs, exposed his skin to chill, listened to his heart, looked into his eyes, took his pulse, and discussed with Banichi what he'd been given, how many cups of tea he'd had ... "One," he insisted, but no one listened to the victim.

Finally the doctor came and stared down at him like a specimen in a collection, asked if he had a residual taste in his mouth, or smelled something like tea, and residual taste did describe it.

"Milk," the doctor said, "a glass every three hours. Warm or cold."

"Cold," he said, shuddering.

When it came, it was heated, it tasted of the tea, and he complained of it; but Banichi tasted it, swore it was only the taste in his mouth and said that when it went away it would tell him he was free of the substance.

Meanwhile Algini, the one without a sense of humor, kept bringing him fruit juice and insisting he drink, until he had to make repeated trips to what Maigi termed, delicately, the accommodation.

And meanwhile Banichi disappeared, again, and Algini didn't know a thing about his mail, couldn't authorize a power outlet ...

"This is an historical monument, nand' paidhi. It's my understanding that any change to these walls has to be submitted to the Preservation Commission. We can't even remove a hanging picture to put up our schedule board, on the very same pins."

It didn't sound encouraging.

"What are my chances," he asked, "of going back to the City any time soon?"

"I can certainly present your request, nand' paidhi. I have to say, I don't think so. I'm sure the same considerations that brought you here, still apply."

"What considerations?"

"The protection of your life, nand' paidhi."

"It doesn't seem safe here, does it?"

"We've warned the kitchen to ask if you're in any party

it serves. The cook is extremely concerned. He assures you of his caution in the future."

He sulked, childlike, and, feeling Algini's frustration, struggled to mend his expression—but he felt like a child, hemmed about, decided for, and talked past by towering people with motives too dark and hushed to share with him. It inspired him to do childish things, like sending Algini for something complicated so he could sneak downstairs and out the front door and down the road to town.

But he sat still in bed like a good adult, and tried not to be surly with the staff, and drink the damned milk— "Cold!" he insisted to Algini, deciding he couldn't manage the rest of it.

Whereupon the kitchen, evidently never having heard of such a procedure, sent it over ice.

The milk at last stopped tasting of the tea, the fruit juice had run through him until he had fruit juice running in his veins, he said as much to Djinana, who thought that was exceptionally, originally funny.

He didn't. He asked for books on Maidingi, read about Malguri castle, out of books liberal in color pictures of his apartments, with notes on what century which piece dated from.

The bed, for instance, was seven hundred years old. There were tours into this section of the castle, if there happened to be no guest in residence. He imagined tourists walking through, children gazing fearfully at the bed, and the guide talking about the paidhi, who'd died in Malguri castle, said to walk the halls at night, haunting the kitchens, looking for a cup of tea . . .

But it was all history that humans hadn't had access to—he knew: he'd read every writing of his predecessors. He wanted to make a note, to request *Annals of Maidingi* by Tagisi of Maidingi township, of Polgini clan, Carditi-Aigorana house, for the paidhiin's permanent research library in Mospheira . . . and then remembered the power outlet that it wasn't possible to have. And nobody, of course, could remove an historic damned lightbulb to put in a tap. It might pull down the historic damned wiring right off its track across the historic wooden rafters.

Solar recharger, he thought. He wondered if the nearby town had any such thing compatible with his computer, and if he could charge his account via the local bank— certainly Banichi could.

Meanwhile . . . paper and pen. He got up and searched the desks in the study, and found paper. No pen. He searched for the one he'd used to sign the guest register. Gone.

Maddening. He rang for the servants, told Djinana he wanted one immediately, and got the requisite pen from the servants' quarters. It skipped and it spat, but it wrote; and he wrapped himself in a warm robe, put stockings on his cold feet, and sat and wrote morbid notes to his successor.

. . . *If,* he added glumly, *this ever gets to human eyes. I've a gun under my mattress. Whom shall I shoot? Algini, who can't get his schedule board hung? Cenedi, who probably didn't have a clue about the tea being lethal to humans?*

Tabini-aiji sent me here for my protection. So far, I've come far nearer dying at the hands of Malguri's kitchen than Shejidan's assassins . . .

Some things he didn't write, fearing his room wasn't immune to search, if only by the servants and his own security, who were probably one and the same—but he asked himself about the aiji-dowager, and asked himself twice what Tabini had had on his mind with that throw-away comment, "Grandmother's in residence."

Not in the least likely, of course, that Tabini had foreseen his invitation to a fatal tea: even for the aiji-dowager, it was too serendipitous and too strange, over all—even if one grew extremely suspicious when accidents happened in the presence of persons of twice-denied ambition.

The obvious thought, of course, was that Ilisidi didn't like humans.

But what if—a poisoned, delirious brain could form very strange ideas—what if Tabini's sending him here hadn't been to send *him* here, but to get Banichi and Jago inside Malguri, past Ilisidi's guard?

A try on Ilisidi?

Thinking about it made his head hurt.

His appetite was still off, at supper. He didn't feel up to formal dinner, and ordered simply a bowl of soup and wafers—which tasted better than they had yesterday, and he decided he felt up to a second bowl of it, in his televisionless, fellowless, phoneless exile.

Mealtimes had become a marker in the day, which thus far, lacking even a clock, he measured in paces of his quarters, in pages turned, in the slow progress of clouds across the sky, or boats across the wind-wrinkled lake.

He forced himself to drink an ordinary tea, and lingered over a sweet milk pudding, in which there was only one questionable and lumpy substance, exceedingly bitter to the taste—but one could, with dexterity, pick the bits out.

Food became an amusement, a hobby, an adventure despite cook's assurances. The book he had open beside his plate was an absorbing enough account of lingering and resentful spirits of Malguri's murdered and accident-prone dead. The lake also was given to be haunted by various restless fishermen and by one ill-fated lord of Malguri who leapt in full armor from the cliffs, thus evading what the book called 'a shameful marriage.'

Curious idea. He resolved to ask someone about that, and to find out the doubtless prurient details.

He discarded the last bitter bit in the pudding, and had his final spoonful as Djinana came in, to take the dishes, as he supposed.

"I'll have another cup of tea," he said. He was feeling

much better. Djinana laid a tiny silver scroll-case, with great ceremony, beside his plate.

"What's this?" he asked.

"I don't know, nand' paidhi. Nadi Cenedi conveyed it."

"Would you open it?"

"It's the dowager's own ..." Djinana protested.

"Nadi. Would you open it?"

Djinana frowned and took it up—broke the seal and spread out the paper.

He took it, once Djinana had proven it only the scroll it seemed to be. But he was thinking of the Bu-javid post office, and Jago's comment about needles in the mail.

It was almost as welcome. An invitation. From the aiji-dowager. For an early breakfast.

The hospitality of an aiji of any degree was not easy to refuse. He had to share a roof with this woman. She'd nearly killed him. Refusal could convey a belief it wasn't an accident. And *that* could mean hostilities. "Tell Banichi I need to talk to him."

"I'll try, nadi."

"What, 'try?' Where *is* he, nadi?"

"I believe he and nadi Jago drove somewhere."

"Somewhere." He'd become reluctantly well acquainted with the vicinity, at least the historical sites within driving distance of Malguri. There wasn't anywhere to drive to, except the airport and the town just outside. "Then I need to talk to Tano."

"I don't know where he is, either, nand' paidhi. I rather thought he'd gone with your security staff."

"Algini, then."

"I'll look for him, nand' paidhi."

"They wouldn't have left me here."

"I would think not, nand' paidhi. But I assure you Maighi and I are perfectly well at your service."

"Then what would *you* advise?" He handed Djinana the scroll, case and all. Djinana scanned it, and frowned.

"It's unusual," Djinana said. "The aiji-dowager doesn't receive many people."

Fine, he thought. So she's making an extraordinary gesture. The stakes go up.

"So what do I answer, nadi? Is it safe?"

Djinana's face assumed a very official serenity. "I couldn't possibly advise the paidhi."

"Then çan we find Algini? I take it there's some urgency to respond to this."

"A certain amount. I believe nand' Cenedi elected to wait—"

"He knows Banichi's not here."

"I'm not sure, nadi." The facade cracked. Worry did come through. "Perhaps I can find Algini."

Djinana left on that errand. He poured himself another cup of tea. He had to answer the summons, one way or the other. The thought unworthily crossed his mind that the aiji-dowager might indeed have waited until Banichi and Jago were otherwise occupied, although what might legitimately have drawn the whole damned staff to the airport when Tabini had *said* he was in their charge, he didn't know. He carefully rolled up the little scroll, shoved it into the case, and capped it. And waited until Djinana came back, and bowed, with a worried look. "Nadi, I don't know—"

"—where Algini is," he said.

"I'm sorry, nand' paidhi. I truly don't know what to say. I can't imagine. I've made inquiries in the kitchen and with nand' Cenedi—"

"Is he still waiting?"

"Yes, nand' paidhi. I've told him—you wished to consult protocols."

Tell Cenedi he was indisposed? That might save him—if the dowager wasn't getting her own reports from the staff.

Which he couldn't at all guarantee.

"Nadi Djinana. If your mother had a gun, and your mother threatened me—whose side would you take?"

"I—assure you, nadi, my mother would never . . ."

"You're not security. I don't come under your *man'chi*."

"No, nadi. I work for the Preservation Commission. I'm a caretaker. Of the estate, you understand."

If there was one ateva in the world telling him the truth, he believed it by that one moment of absolute shock in Djinana's eyes, that minute, dismayed hesitation.

He hadn't phrased it quite right, of course, not, at least, inescapably. Banichi would have said, You're within my duty, nand' paidhi. And that could have meant anything.

But, caretaker of Malguri? One knew where Djinana stood. Firmly *against* the hanging of schedule boards and the importation of extension cords and the sticking of nails in Malguri's walls. He knew that—but he didn't know even that much about Banichi at the present moment. Certainly Banichi hadn't been wholly forthcoming with him, either that, or Banichi had been damned lax—which wasn't Banichi's style as he knew it.

Unless something truly catastrophic had happened. Something like an attempt on Tabini himself.

That surmise upset his stomach.

Which, dammit, he didn't need to happen to him when he had just gotten his stomach used to food again. No, Tabini wasn't in danger. Tabini had far better security than he did; Tabini had the whole damned City to look out for him, while *his* staff was down at the airport, leaving *him* to Cenedi, who could walk in here and blow him and Djinana to small bits, if Cenedi were so inclined to disregard *biichi-ji* and stain the historic carpets.

"Appropriate paper and pen."

"With your own scroll-case, nadi?"

"The paidhi doesn't know where his staff put it. They don't let him in on such matters. Try some appropriate drawer. If you don't find it, it can go bare. —And if Banichi isn't back by tomorrow morning, *you'll* go with me."

"I—" Djinana began a protest. And made a bow, instead. "I have some small skill at protocols. I'll look for the scroll-case. Or provide one from the estate. Would the paidhi wish advice in phrasing?"

"Djinana, tell me. *Am* I frightening? *Am* I so foreign? *Would* I give children bad dreams?"

"I—" Djinana looked twice distressed.

"Do I disturb *you,* nadi? I wouldn't want to. I think you're an honest man. And I've met so few."

"I wish the paidhi every good thing."

"You *are* skilled in protocol. Do you think you can get me there and back tomorrow unpoisoned?"

"Please, nand' paidhi. I'm not qualified—"

"But you're honest. You're a good man. You'd defend your mother before you'd defend me. As a human, I find that very honest. You owe your mother more than you do me. As I owe mine, thank you. And in that particular, you could be human, nadi, which I don't personally consider an outrageous thing to be."

Djinana regarded him with a troubled frown. "I truly don't understand your figure of speech, nadi."

"Between Malguri, and your mother, nadi—if it were the ruin of one or the other—*which* would you choose?"

"That of my mother, nadi. My *man'chi* is with this place."

"For Malguri's reputation—would you die, nadi-ji?"

"I'm not nadi-ji. Only nadi, nand' paidhi."

"Would you die, nadi-ji?"

"I would die for the stones of this place. So I would, nadi-ji. I couldn't abandon it."

"We also," he said, in a strange and angry mood, "we human folk, understand antiquities. We understand preserving. We understand the importance of old stories. Everything we own and know—is in old stories. I wish we could give you everything we know, nadi, and I wish you could give us the same, and I wish we could travel to the moon together before we're both too old."

"To the moon!" Djinana said, with an anxious, uncertain laughter. "What would we do there?"

"Or to the old station. It's your *inheritance*, nadi-ji. It should be." The paidhi was vastly upset, he discovered, and saying things he ordinarily reserved for one man, for Tabini, things he dared not bring out in open council, because there were interests vested in suspicion of humans and of everything the paidhi did and said, as surely misguidance and deception of atevi interests.

So he told the truth to a caretaker-servant, instead.

And was angry at Banichi, who probably, justifiably, was angry with the paidhi. But the paidhi saw things slipping away from him, and atevi he'd trusted turning strange and distant and withholding answers from him at moments of crisis they might have foreseen.

He'd puzzled Djinana, that was certain. Djinana simply gathered up the dessert dish and, when he couldn't find the scroll-case, brought him an antique one from the estate, and pen and paper and sealing-wax.

He wrote, in his best hand, *Accepting the aiji-dowager's most gracious invitation for breakfast at the first of the clock, the paidhi-aiji, Bren Cameron, with profound respect . . .*

It was the form—laying it on, perhaps, but not by much. And he trusted that the dowager wouldn't have *her* mail censored. He passed the text by Djinana's doubtless impeccable protocol-sense, then sealed it with his seal-ring and dismissed him to give it to Cenedi, who was probably growing very annoyed with waiting.

After that, with Djinana handling those courtesies, he composed another letter, to Tabini.

I am uneasy, aiji-ma. I feel that there must be duties in the City which go wanting, as there were several matters pending. I hope that your staff will provide me necessary briefings, as I would be distressed to fall out of current with events. As you may know, Malguri is not computerized, and phone calls appear out·of the question.

Please accept my warm regards for auspicious days and fortunate outcome. Baji-naji *be both in your favor. The paidhi-aiji Bren Cameron with profound respect and*

devotion to the Association and to Tabini-aiji in the con-
tinuance of his office, the ...

He had to stop and count up the date on his fingers, figuring he had lost a day. Or two. He became confused—decided it was only one, then wrote it down and sealed the letter with only a ribbon seal, but with the wax directly on the paper.

That one was for Banichi to take on his *next* trip to the airport, and, one presumed, to the post.

Then, in the case that one never made it, he wrote a copy.

Djinana came back through the room, reporting he'd delivered the scroll, and asking would the paidhi need the wax-jack further.

"I've a little correspondence to take care of," he said to Djinana. "I'll blow out the wick and read awhile after, thank you, nadi. I don't think I'll need anything. Is the dowager's gentleman out?"

"The door is locked for the night, nand' paidhi, yes."

"Banichi has a key."

"He does, yes. So does nadi Jago. But they'll most probably use the kitchen entry."

The kitchen entry. Of course there was one. The food arrived, not from the stairs, but from the back halls, through the servants' quarters, his bedroom, and the sitting room, before it reached his dining table.

"I'll be fine, then. Good night, nadi Djinana. Thank you. You've been extremely helpful."

"Good night, nand' paidhi."

Djinana went on back to his quarters, then. He finished his paraphrase of the note, and added:

If this is found, and no note of similar wording has reached you before this, Tabini-ji, suspect the hand that should have delivered the first message. After one poisoned cup, from the dowager, I am not reassured of anyone in Malguri, even my own staff.

He put it in the guest book, figuring that the next occupant would find it, if he didn't remove it himself. It wasn't a book Banichi would necessarily read.

And, as he had just written, he was far from certain of anything or anyone in Malguri, tonight.

Thunder rumbled outside, and lightning lit rain-drops on the night-dark window glass, flared brief color from the stained glass borders.

Bren read, late, in no mood to sleep, or to share a bed with his morbid thoughts. He looked at pictures, when the words began to challenge his focus or his acceptance of atevi attitudes. He read about old wars. Betrayals. Poisonings.

Banichi arrived on a peal of thunder, walked in and stood by the fire. A fine mist glistened on his black, silver-trimmed uniform, and he seemed not pleased. "Nadi Bren, I wish you'd consult before decisions."

The silence hung there. He looked at Banichi without speaking, without an expression on his face, and thought of saying, Nadi, I wish *you'd* consult before leaving.

But Banichi, for what he cared, could guess what he was thinking, the way he was left to guess what Banichi was thinking, or where Jago was, or why the so-called servants they'd brought for him from the City were absent or unavailable.

And maybe it wasn't justified that he be angry, and maybe Banichi's business at the airport or wherever he'd just been was entirely justified and too secret to tell him, but, *damn,* he was angry, a peculiar, stinging kind of anger that, while Banichi was standing there, added up to a hurt he hadn't realized he felt so keenly, a thoroughly unprofessional and foolish and human hurt, which began with Tabini and extended to the two atevi besides Tabini that he'd thought he understood.

Heaving up his insides on a regular basis probably had something to do with it. Mineral balance. Vitamins. Unaccustomed foods that could leach nutrients out of you instead of putting them in, or chemically bind what you needed . . . he could think of a dozen absolutely plausible excuses for calculatedly self-destructive behavior, half of them dietary and the other half because, dammit, his own hard-wiring or his own culture wanted to *like* some single one of the people he'd devoted his life to helping.

"I don't *have* to be the paidhi," he said, finally, since Banichi persisted in saying nothing. "I don't have to leave my family and my people and live where I'm not welcome with nine tenths of the population."

"How *do* they choose you?" Banichi asked.

"It's a study. It's something you specialize in. If you're the best, and the paidhi quits, you take the job. That's how. It's something you do so there'll be peace."

"You're the best at what you do."

"I try to be," he retorted. "I do try, Banichi. Evidently I've done something amiss. Possibly I've offended the aiji-dowager. Possibly I've gotten myself into a dangerous situation. I don't know. That's an admission of failure, Banichi. *I don't know.* But you weren't here to ask. Jago wasn't here. I couldn't raise Algini. Tano wasn't on duty. So I asked Djinana, who didn't know what maybe you could have told me. If you'd been here."

Banichi frowned, darkly.

"Where *were* you, Banichi? Or should I ask? If you intended to answer my questions, you'd have told me you were leaving, and if you didn't intend me to worry you wouldn't trail the evidence past me and refuse my reasonable questions, when I rely on you for protection the Treaty doesn't let me provide for myself."

Banichi said nothing, nor moved for the moment. Then he removed his elbow from the fireplace stonework and stalked off toward the bedroom.

Bren snapped the book shut. Banichi looked back in startlement, he had that satisfaction. Banichi's nerves were that tightly strung.

"Where's Jago?" Bren asked.

"Outside. Refusing your reasonable questions, too."

"Banichi, dammit!" He stood up, little good it did—he

still had to look up to Banichi's face, even at a distance. "If I'm under arrest and confined here, —tell me. And where's my mail? Don't regular planes come to Maidingi? It looked like an airport to me."

"From Shejidan, once a week. Most of the country, nadi, runs at a different speed. Be calm. Enjoy the lake. Enjoy the slower pace."

"Slower pace? I want a solar recharge, Banichi. I want to make a phone call. Don't tell me this place doesn't have a telephone."

"In point of fact, no, there isn't a telephone. This is an historical monument. The wires would disfigure the—"

"Underground lines, Banichi. Pipes overhead. The place has plenty of wires."

"They have to get here."

"There's gas. There's light. Why aren't there plug-ins? Why can't someone go down to the town, go to a hardware and get me a damned power extension and a screw-in plug? I could sacrifice a ceiling light. The historic walls wouldn't suffer defacement."

"There isn't a hardware. The town of Maidingi is a very small place, nadi Bren."

"God." His head was starting to hurt, acutely. His blood pressure was coming up again and he was dizzy, the light and warmth and noise of the fire all pouring into his senses as he groped after the fireplace stonework. "Banichi, why is Tabini doing this?"

"Doing what, nadi? I don't think the aiji-ji has a thing to do with hardwares in Maidingi."

He wasn't amused. He leaned his back against the stones, folded his arms and fixed Banichi with an angry stare, determined to have it out, one way or the other. "You know, 'doing what.' I could feel better if I thought it was policy. I don't feel better thinking it might be something I've done, or trouble I've made for Tabini—I *like* him, Banichi. I don't want to be the cause of harm to him, or to you, or to Jago. It's *my man'chi*. Humans are like that. We *have* unreasonable loyalties to people we like, and you're going far past the surface of my politeness, Banichi."

"Clearly."

"And I still *like* you, damn you. You don't shake one of us, you don't fling our *liking* away because your *man'chi* says otherwise, you can't get rid of us when we *like* you, Banichi, you're stuck with me, so make the best of it."

There wasn't a clear word for *like*. It meant a preference for salad greens or iced drinks. But *love* was worse. Banichi would never forgive him that.

Banichi's nostrils flared, once, twice. He said, in accented Mosphei', "What meaning? What meaning you say, nand' paidhi?"

"It means the feeling I have for my mother and my brother and my job, I have for Tabini and for you and for Jago." Breath failed him. Self-control did. He flung it all out. "Banichi, I'd walk a thousand miles to have a kind word from you. I'd give you the shirt from my back if you needed it; if you were in trouble, I'd carry you that thousand miles. What do you call that? Foolish?"

Another flaring of Banichi's nostrils. "That would be very difficult for you."

"So is liking atevi." That got out before he censored it. "Baji-naji. It's the luck I have."

"Don't joke."

"I'm not joking. *God,* I'm not joking. We have to *like* somebody, we're bound to like somebody, or we die, Banichi, we outright die. We make appointments with grandmothers, we drink the cups strangers offer us, and we don't ask for help anymore, Banichi, what's the damned point, when you don't see what we need?"

"If I don't guess what you like, you threaten to ruin my reputation. Is this accurate?"

The headache was suddenly excruciating. Things blurred. "Like, like, like—get off the damned word, Banichi. I cross that trench every day. Can't you cross it once? Can't you cross to where I am, Banichi, just once, to know what I think? You're clever. I know you're hard to mislead. *Follow*, Banichi, the solitary trail of my thoughts."

"I'm not a cursed dinner-course!"

"Banichi-ji." The pain reached a level and stayed there, tolerable, once he'd discovered the limits of it. He had his hand on the stonework. He felt the texture of it, the silken dust of age, the fire-heated rock, broken from the earth to make this building before humans ever left the home-world. Before they were ever lost, and desperate. He composed himself—he remembered he was the paidhi, the man in the middle. He remembered he'd chosen this, knowing there wouldn't be a reward, believing, at the time, that of course atevi had feelings, and of course, once he could find the right words, hit the right button, *find* the clue to atevi thought—he'd win of atevi everything he was giving up among humankind.

He'd been twenty-two, and what he'd not known had so vastly outweighed what he'd known.

"Your behavior worries me," Banichi said.

"Forgive me." There was a large knot interfering with his speech. But he was vastly calmer. He chose not to look at Banichi. He only imagined the suspicion and the anger on Banichi's face. "I reacted unprofessionally and intrusively."

"Reacted to what, nand' paidhi?"

A betraying word choice. He *was* slipping, badly. The headache had upset his stomach, which was still uncertain. "I misinterpreted your behavior. The mistake was mine, not yours. Will you attend my appointment with me in the morning, and guard me from my own stupidity?"

"What behavior did you misinterpret?"

Straight back to the attack. Banichi refused the bait he cast. And he had no ability to argue, now, or to deal at all in cold rationality.

"I explained that. It didn't make sense to you. It won't." He stared into the hazy corners beyond the firelight, and remembered the interpretation Banichi had put on his explanation. "It wasn't a threat, Banichi. I would never do that. I value your presence and your good qualities. Will you go with me tomorrow?"

Back to the simplest, the earliest and most agreed-upon words. Cold. Unfreighted.

"No, nadi. No one invites himself to the dowager's table. You accepted."

"You're assigned—"

"My *man'chi* is to Tabini. My actions are his actions. The paidhi can't have forgotten this simple thing."

He was angry. He looked at Banichi, and went on looking, long enough, he hoped, for Banichi to think in what other regard his actions were Tabini's actions. "I haven't forgotten. How could I forget?"

Banichi returned a sullen stare. "Ask regarding the food you're offered. Be sure the cook understands you're in the party."

The door in the outermost room opened. Banichi's attention was instant and wary. But it was Jago coming through, rain-spattered as Banichi, in evident good humor until the moment she saw the two of them. Her face went immediately impassive. She walked through to his bedroom without comment.

"Excuse me," Banichi said darkly, and went after her.

Bren glared at his black-uniformed back, at a briskly swinging braid—the two of Tabini's guards on their way through his bedroom, to the servant quarters; he hit his fist against the stonework and didn't feel the pain until he walked away from the fireside.

Stupid, he said to himself. Stupid and dangerous to have tried to explain anything to Banichi: Yes, nadi, no, nadi, clear and simple words, nadi.

Banichi and Jago had gone on to the servants' quarters, where they lodged, separately. He went through to his own bedroom and undressed, with an eye to the dead and angry creature on the wall, the expression of its last, cornered fight.

It stared back at him, when he was in the bed. He picked up his book and read, because he was too angry to sleep, about ancient atevi battles, about treacheries and murders.

About ghost ships on the lake, and a manifestation that haunted the audience hall on this level, a ghostly beast that sometimes went snuffling up and down the corridors, looking for something or someone.

He was a modern man. They were atevi superstitions. But he took one look and then evaded the glass, glaring eyes of the beast on the wall.

Thunder banged. The lights all went out, except the fire in the next room, casting its uncertain glow, that didn't reach all the corners of this one, and didn't at all touch the servants' hall.

He told himself lightning must have hit a transformer.

But the place was eerily quiet after that, except for a strange, distant thumping that sounded like a heartbeat coming through the walls.

Then far back in the servants' hall, beyond the bath, steps moved down the corridor toward his bedroom.

He slid off the bed, onto his knees.

"Nand' paidhi," Jago's voice called out. "It's Jago."

He withdrew his hand from beneath the mattress, and slithered up onto the bed, sitting and watching as an entire brigade of staff moved like shadows through his room and outward. He couldn't see faces. He saw the spark of metal on what he thought was Banichi's uniform.

One lingered.

"Who is it?" he asked, anxiously.

"Jago, nadi. I'm staying with you. Go to sleep."

"You're joking!"

"It's most likely only a lightning strike, nand' paidi. That's the auxiliary generator you hear. It keeps the refrigeration running in the kitchen, at least until morning."

He got up, went looking for his robe and banged his knee on a chair, making an embarrassing scrape.

"What do you want, nadi?"

"My robe."

"Is this it?" Jago located it instantly, at the foot of his

bed, and handed it to him. Atevi night vision was that much better, he reminded himself, and took not quite that much comfort from knowing it. He put the robe on, tied it about him and went into the sitting room, as less provocative, out where the fireplace provided one kind of light and a whiter, intermittent flicker of lightning came from the windows.

A padding, metal-sparked shadow followed him. Atevi eyes reflected a pale gold. Atevi found it spooky that human eyes didn't, that humans could slip quietly through the dark. Their differences touched each others' nightmares.

But there was no safer company in the world, he told himself, and told himself also that the disturbance was in fact nothing but a lightning strike, and that Banichi was going to be wet, chilled, and in no good mood when he got back in.

But Jago wasn't in her night-robe. Jago had been in uniform and armed, and so had Banichi been, when the lights had gone.

"Don't you sleep?" he asked her, standing before the fire.

The twin reflections of her eyes eclipsed, a blink, then vanished as she came close enough to rest an elbow against the stonework mantel. Her shadow loomed over him, and fire glistened on the blackness of her skin. "We were awake," she said.

Business went on all around him, with no explanations. He felt chilled, despite the robe, and thought how desperately he needed his sleep—in order to deal with the dowager in the morning.

"Are there protections around this place?" he asked.

"Assuredly, nadi-ji. This is still a fortress, when it needs to be."

"With the tourists and all."

"Tourists. Yes. —There is a group due tomorrow, nadi. Please be prudent. They needn't see you."

He felt himself more and more fragile, standing shiver-

ing in front of the fire in his night-robe. "Do people ever
... slip away from the tour, slip out of the guards' sight?"

"There's a severe fine for that," Jago said.

"Probably one for killing the paidhi, too," he muttered.
His robe had no pockets. You could never convince an
atevi tailor about pockets. He shoved his hands up the
sleeves. "A month's pay, at least."

Jago thought that was funny. He heard her laugh, a rare
sound. That was her reassurance.

"I'm supposed to be at breakfast with Tabini's grandmother," he said. "Banichi's mad at me."

"Why did you accept?"

"I didn't know I could refuse. I didn't know what trouble it would make—"

Jago made a soft, derisive sound. "Banichi said it was
because you thought he was a dessert."

He couldn't laugh for a moment. It was too grim, and
on the edge of pain; and then it *was* funny, Banichi's
glum perplexity, his human desperation to find a focus for
his orphaned affections. Jago's sudden, unprecedented
willingness to converse.

"I take it this was confused in translation," Jago said.

"I expressed my extreme respect for him," he said.
Which was cold, and distant, and proper. The whole futile
argument loomed up, insurmountable barriers again. "Respect. Favor. It's all one thing."

"How?" Jago asked—a completely honest question.
The atevi words didn't mean what he tried to make them
mean. They couldn't, wouldn't, ever. The whole atevi
hardwiring was different, the experts said so. The dynamics of atevi relationships were different ... in ways no
paidhi had ever figured out, either, possibly because
paidhiin invariably tried to find words to fit into human
terms—and then deceived themselves about the meanings, in self-defense, when the atevi world grew too much
for them.

God, why did she decide to talk tonight? Was it policy?
An interrogation?

"Nadi," he said wearily, "if I could say that, you'd understand us ever so much better."

"Banichi speaks Mosphei'. You should say it to him in Mosphei'."

"Banichi doesn't *feel* Mosphei'." It was late. He was extremely foolish. He made a desperate, far-reaching attempt to locate abstracts. "I tried to express that I would do favorable things on his behalf because he seems to me a favorable person."

It at least threw it into the abstract realm, that perception of luck in charge of the universe, which somewhat passed for a god in Ragi thinking.

"Midei," Jago declared in seeming surprise. It was a word he'd not heard before, and there weren't many, in ordinary usage, that he hadn't. "Dahemidei. You're midedeni."

That was three in a row. He was too tired to take notes and the damned computer was down. "What does that mean?"

"Midedeni believe luck and favor reside in people. It was a heresy, of course."

Of course it was. "So it was a long time ago."

"Oh, half of Adjaiwaio still believes something like that, in the country, anyway—that you're supposed to Associate with *everybody* you meet."

An entire remote Association where people *liked* other people? He both wanted to go there and feared there were other essential, perhaps Treaty-threatening, differences.

"You really believe in that?" Jago pursued the matter. And it was indeed dangerous, how scattered and longing his thoughts instantly grew down that track, how difficult it was to structure logical arguments against the notion, the very seductive notion that atevi *could* understand affection. "The lords of technology truly think this is the case?"

Jago clearly thought intelligent people weren't expected to think so.

Which made him question himself, in the paidhi's internal habit, whether humans *were* somehow blind to the primitive character of such attachments.

Then the dislocation jerked him the other direction, back into belief humans were right. "Something like that," he said. The experts said atevi *couldn't* think outside hierarchical structure. And Jago said they could? His heart was pounding. His common sense said hold back, don't believe it, there's a contradiction here. "So you *can* feel attachment to one you don't have *man'chi* for."

"Nadi Bren, —are you making a sexual proposition to me?"

The bottom dropped out of his stomach. "I— *No*, Jago-ji."

"I wondered."

"Forgive my impropriety."

"Forgive my mistaken notion. What *were* you asking?"

"I—" Recovering objectivity was impossible. Or it had never existed. "I'd only like to read about midedeni, if you could find a book for me."

"Certainly. But I doubt there'd be one here. Malguri's library is mostly local history. The midedeni were all eastern."

"I'd like a book to keep, if I could."

"I'm sure. I have one, if nothing else, but it's in Shejidan."

He'd made a thorough mess. And left a person who was probably reporting directly to Tabini with the impression humans belonged to some dead heresy they probably didn't even remotely match.

"It probably isn't applicable," he said, trying to patch matters. "Exact correspondence is just too unlikely." Jago had a brain. A very quick one; and he risked something he ordinarily would have said only to Tabini. "It's the apparent correspondences that can *be* the most deceptive. We want to believe them."

"At very least, we're polite in Shejidan. We don't shoot people over philosophical differences. *I* wouldn't take such a contract."

God help him. He thought that was a joke out of Jago. The second for the evening. "I wouldn't think so."

"I hope I don't offend you, nadi."

"I like you, too."

In atev', it was very funny. It won Jago's rare grin, a duck of the head, a flash of that eerie mirror-luminance of her eyes, quite, quite sober.

"I haven't understood," she said. "It eludes me, nadi."

The best will in the world couldn't bridge the gap. He looked at her in a sense of isolation he hadn't felt since his first week on the mainland, his first unintended mistake with atevi.

"But you try, Jago-ji. Banichi tries, too. It makes me less—" There *was* no word for lonely. "Less single."

"We share a *man'chi*," Jago said, as if she *had* understood something he was saying. "To Tabini's house. Don't doubt us, paidhi-ji. We won't desert you."

Off the meaning again. There was nothing there, nothing to make the leap of logic. He stared at her, asking himself how someone so fundamentally honest, and *kind,* granted the license she had—could be so absolutely void of what it might take to make that leap of emotional need. It just didn't click into place. And it was a mistake to pin anything on the Adjaiwaio and any dead philosophy.

Philosophy was the keyword: intellectual, not emotional structure. And a human being, having embraced it, went away empty and in pain.

He said, "Thank you, nadi-ji," and walked away from the fire to the window, which showed nothing but rain-spots against the dark.

Something banged, or popped. It echoed off the walls, once, twice.

That was no loose shutter. It was off somewhere outside the walls, to the southwest, he thought, beyond the driveway.

The house seemed very still, except the rain and the sound of the fire on the hearth.

"Get away from the window," Jago said, and he stepped

back immediately, his shoulder to solid stone, his heart beating like a hammer as he expected Jago to leave him and rush off to Banichi's aid. His imagination leapt to four and five assassins breaching the antique defenses of the castle, enemies already inside the walls.

But Jago only stood listening, as it seemed. There was no second report. Her pocket-com beeped—he had not seen it on her person, but of course she had it; she lifted it and thumbed on to Banichi's voice, speaking in verbal code.

"Tano shot at shadows," she translated, glancing at him. She was a black shape against the fire. "It's all right. He's not licensed."

Understandable that Tano would make a mistake in judgement, she meant. So Tano, at least, and probably Algini, was out of Tabini's house guard—licensed for firearms, for defense, but not for their use in public places.

"So was it lightning?" he asked. "Is it lightning they're shooting at out there?"

"Nervous fingers," Jago said easily, and shut the com off. "Nothing at all to worry about, nadi-ji."

"How long until we have power?"

"As soon as the crews can get up here from Maidingi. Morning, I'd say, before we have lights. This happens, nadi. The cannon on the wall draw strikes very frequently. So, unfortunately, does the transformer. It's not at all uncommon."

Breakfast might be cancelled, due to the power failure. He might have a reprieve from his folly.

"I suggest you go to bed," Jago said. "I'll sit here and read until the rest of us come in. You've an appointment in the morning."

"We were discussing *man'chi*," he said, unnerved, be it the storm or the shot or his own failures. He'd gotten far too personal with Jago, right down to her assumption he was trying to approach her for sex, God help him. He was tangling every line of communication he had, he was on an emotional jag, he felt entirely uneasy about the impression he'd left with her, an impression she was doubtless going to convey to Banichi, and both of them to Tabini: the paidhi's behaving very oddly, they'd say. He propositioned Jago, invited Djinana to the moon, and thinks Banichi's a dessert.

"Were we?" Jago left the fire and walked over to him, taking his arm. "Let's walk back to your bedroom, nand' paidhi, you'll take a chill—" She outright snatched him past the window, bruising his arm, he so little expected it.

He walked with her, then, telling himself if she were really concerned she'd have made him crawl beneath it—she only wanted him away from a window that would glow with conspicuous light from the fire, and cast their shadows. There were the outer walls, between that window and the lake.

But was it lightning hitting the cannon that she feared?

"Go to bed," Jago said, delivering him to the door of his bedroom. "Bren-ji. Don't worry. They'll be assessing damage. We'll need to call down to the power station with the information. And of course we take special precautions when we do lose power. It's only routine. You may hear me go out. You may not. Don't worry for your safety."

So one *could* call the airport on the security radio. One would have thought so. But it was the first he'd heard anyone admit it. And having security trekking through his room all night didn't promise a good night's sleep.

But he sat down on the bed and Jago walked back to the other room, leaving him in the almost dark. He took off his robe, put himself beneath the skins, and lay listening, watching the faint light from the fireplace in the other room make moving shadows on the walls and glisten on the glass eyes of the beast opposite his bed.

They say it's perfectly safe, he thought at it. Don't worry.

It made a sort of sense to talk to it, the two of them in such intimate relationship. It was a creature of this planet.

It had died mad, fighting atevi who'd enjoyed killing it. Nobody needed to feel sorry for anybody. It wasn't the last of its species. There were probably hundreds of thousands of its kind out there in the underbrush as mad and pitiless as it was.

Adapted for this earth. It didn't make attachments to its young or its associates. It didn't need them. Nature fitted it with a hierarchical sense of dominance, survival positive, proof against heartbreak.

It survived until something meaner killed it and stuck its head on a wall, for company to a foolish human, who'd let himself in for this—who'd chased after the knowledge and then the honor of being the best.

Which had to be enough to go to bed with on nights like this. Because there damned sure wasn't anything else, and if he let himself—

But he couldn't. The paidhi couldn't start, at twenty-six atevi years of age, to humanize the people he dealt with. It was the worst trap. All his predecessors had battled it. He knew it in theory.

He'd been doing all right while he was an hour's flight away from Mospheira. While his mail arrived on schedule, twice a week. While . . .

While he'd believed beyond a doubt he was going to see human faces again, and while things were going outstandingly well, and while Tabini and he were such, such good friends.

Key that word, Friend.

The paidhi had been in a damned lot of trouble, right there. The paidhi had been stone blind, right there.

The paidhi didn't know why he was here, the paidhi didn't know how he was going to get back again, the paidhi couldn't *get* the emotional satisfaction out of Banichi and Jago that Tabini had been feeding him, laughing with him, joking with him, down to the last time they'd met.

Blowing melons to bits. Tabini patting him on the back—gently, because human backs fractured so easily—

and telling him he had real talent for firearms. How good was *Tabini*, more to the point? How good at reading the paidhi was the atevi fourth in line of *his* side of the bargain?

Tipped off, perhaps, by *his* predecessor, that the paidhiin had a soft spot for personal attachments?

That the longer you knew them, the greater fools they became, and the more trusting, and the easier to get things from?

There was a painful lump in his throat, a painful, human knot interfering with his rational assessment of the situation. He'd questioned, occasionally, how long he was good for, whether he *could* adjust. Not every paidhi made it the lifelong commitment they'd signed on for, the pool of available advice had dried up—Wilson hadn't been a damned bit of help, just gotten strange and so short-fused the board had talked about replacing him against Tabini's father's expressed refusal to have him replaced. Wilson had had his third heart attack the first month he was back on Mospheira, maintained a grim, passionless demeanor in every meeting the two of them had had, never told him a damned thing of any use.

The board called it burn-out. He'd taken their word for it and tried not to think of Wilson as a son of a bitch. He'd *met* Tabini on his few fill-ins for Wilson's absences, a few days at a time, the two last years of Valasi's administration—he'd thought Tabini's predecessor Valasi a real match for Wilson's glum mood, but he'd *liked* Tabini—that dangerous word again—but, point of fact, he'd never personally believed in Wilson's burn-out. A man didn't get that strange, that unpleasant, without his own character contributing to it. He'd not *liked* Wilson, and when he'd asked Wilson what his impression was of Tabini, Wilson had said, in a surly tone, "The same as the rest of them."

He'd not *liked* Wilson. He *had* liked Tabini. He'd thought it a mistake on the board's part to have ever let

Wilson take office, a man with that kind of prejudice, that kind of attitude.

He was scared tonight. He looked down the years he might stay in office and the years he might waste in the foolishness he called friendship with Tabini, and saw himself in Wilson's place, never having had a wife, never having had a child, never having had a friend past the day Barb would find some man on Mospheira a better investment: life was too short to stay at the beck and call of some guy dropping into her life with no explanations, no conversation about his job—a face that began to go dead as if the nerves of expression were cut.

He could resign. He could go home. He could ask Barb to marry him.

But he had no guarantee Barb *wanted* to marry him. No questions, no commitment, no unloading of problems, a fairy-tale weekend of fancy restaurants and luxury hotels ... he didn't know what Barb really thought, he didn't know what Barb really wanted, he didn't *know* her in any way but the terms they'd met on, the terms they still had. It wasn't love. It wasn't even close friendship. When he tried to think of the people he'd called friends before he went into university ... he didn't know where they were now, if they'd left the town, or if they'd stayed.

He hadn't been able to turn the situation over to Deana Hanks for a week. Where did he think he was going to find it in him to turn the whole job over to her and walk out—irrevocably, walk out on what he'd prepared his whole life to do?

Like Wilson—a man seventy years old, who'd just seen Valasi assassinated, who'd just come home, because his career ended with Valasi—with nothing to show for forty-three years of work but the dictionary entries he'd made, a handful of scholarly articles, and a record number of vetoes on the Transmontane Highway Project. No wife, no family. Nothing but the university teaching post waiting for him, and he couldn't communicate with the students.

Wilson couldn't communicate with the human students.

He was going to write a paper when he got out of this, however damning it was, a paper about Wilson, and the atevi interface, and the talk he'd had with Jago, and *why* Wilson, with that face, with that demeanor, with that attitude, couldn't communicate with his classes.

Thunder crashed, outside his wall. He jumped, and lay there with his heart doing double beats and his ears still ringing.

The cannon, Jago said. Common occurrence.

He lay there and shook, whether because of the noise, or the craziness of the night. Or because he couldn't understand any longer why he was here, or why a Bu-javid guard like Tano drew a gun and fired, when they were out there looking at transformers.

Looking at lightning-struck transformers, while the lightning played over their heads and the rain fell on them.

Like hell, he thought, like hell, Jago. Shooting at shadows. What *shadows*, Jago, is Tano expecting out there in the rain?

Shadows that fly in on scheduled airliners . . . and the tightest security on the planet, except ours, doesn't know who it is and where they are?

Like hell *again*, Jago.

VI

"**A** lively night," the aiji-dowager said, over tea she swore was safe. "Did you sleep, nand' paidhi?"

"Intermittently."

Ilisidi chuckled softly, and pointed out the flight of a dragonette above the misty, chill lake. The balcony railing dripped with recent rain. The sun came up gold above the mountains across the lake, and the mist began to glow with it. The dragonette dived down the face of the cliff, membranous wings spread against the sun, and swept upward again, with something in its claws.

Predator and prey.

"They're pests," Ilisidi said. "The mecheiti hate them, but I won't have the nest destroyed. They were here first. What does the paidhi say?"

"The paidhi agrees with you."

"What, that those that were here first—have natural ownership?"

Two sips of tea, one bite of roll, and Ilisidi was on the attack. Banichi had said be careful. Tabini had said he could handle it.

He thought a moment, first to agree, then to quibble. Then: "The paidhi agrees that the chain of life shouldn't be broken. That the loss of that nest would impoverish Malguri."

Ilisidi's pale eyes rested on him, impassive as Banichi's could ever be—she was annoyed, perhaps, at his changing the subject back again.

But he hadn't changed her proposition, not entirely.

"They're bandits," Ilisidi said.

"Irreplaceable," he said.

"Vermin."

"The past needs the future. The future needs the past."

"Vermin, I say, that I choose to preserve."

"The paidhi agrees. What do you call them?"

"Wi'itkitiin. They make that sound."

"Wi'itkitiin." He watched another scaled and feathered diver, and asked himself if Earth had ever known the like. "Nothing else makes that sound."

"No."

"Reason enough to save it."

Ilisidi's mouth tightened. The grimace became a hint of a laugh, and she spooned up several bites of cereal, put away several thin slices of breakfast steak.

Bren kept pace, figuring one didn't speak to the aiji-dowager when she was thinking, and an excellent breakfast was going to get cold. Cooked over wood fire, Cenedi had said, when he wondered how there was anything hot, or cooked. He supposed they managed that in the kitchen fireplace, if there was a fireplace in the kitchen. The thumping Jago had called the generator had stopped sometime during the night. The machine was out of fuel, perhaps, or malfunctioning itself. Maidingi Power swore on their lives and reputations that Malguri would have power, as soon, they said, as they had restored power to the quarter of Maidingi township that was dark and chill this morning.

Meanwhile the castle got along, with fireplaces to warm the rooms and cook the food, with candles to light the halls where light from windows didn't reach—systems which had once been The System in Malguri. The aiji-dowager had ordered breakfast set outside, on the balcony, in a chill mountain summer morning—fortunate, Bren thought, that he'd worn his heavier coat this morning, because of the chill already in the rooms. The cold had steam going up from his tea-cup. It was nippishly pleasant—hard to remember the steamy nights that were the rule in the City in this month, the rainstorms rolling in from the sea.

And with the candles and the wood fires and the ancient stones, it was a blink of the eye to imagine, this misty morning, that he had come unfixed in time, that oared vessels with heraldic sails might appear out of the mist on the end of the lake.

Another dragonette had flown, with its eye on some prey. Its cry wailed away down the heights.

"What are you thinking, paidhi? Some wise and revelatory thought?"

"Thinking about ships. And wood fires. And how Malguri doesn't need anything from anywhere to survive."

The aiji-dowager pursed her lips, rested her chin on her fist. "Aei, a hundred or so staff to do the laundry and carry the wood and make the candles, and it survives. Another five hundred to plow and tend and hunt, to feed the launderers and the wood-cutters and the candlemakers and themselves, and, oh, yes, we're self-sufficient. Except the iron-workers and the copy-makers to supply us and the riders and the cannoneers to defend it all from the Un-associated who won't do their share and had rather prey on those who do. Malguri had electric lights before you came, nadi, I do assure you." She took a sip of tea, set the cup down and waved her napkin at Cenedi, who hovered in the doorway and mediated the service.

He thought the breakfast ended, then. He prepared to rise, but Ilisidi waved a hand toward the terrace stairs.

"Come."

He was caught, snared. "I beg the dowager's pardon. My security absolutely forbids me—"

"*Forbids* you! Outrageous. —Or did my grandson set them against me?"

"No such thing, I assure you, with utmost courtesy. He spoke very positively—"

"Then let your guards use their famous ingenuity." She shoved her chair back. Cenedi hastened to assist, and to put her cane under her hand. "Come, come, let me show you the rest of Malguri. Let me show you the Malguri of your imagination."

He didn't know what to do. She wasn't an enemy—at least he hoped she wasn't, and he didn't want to make one. Tabini, damn him, had put him here, when he'd known his grandmother was here. Banichi was all re-proach for the invitation he'd accepted without having Banichi's doubtless wise advice—and there was nothing the paidhi saw now to do, being committed to the dowa-ger's hospitality, except to fall to the floor moaning and plead indisposition—hardly flattering to an already upset cook; or to get up from the table and follow the old woman and see what she wanted him to see.

The latter seemed less damaging to the peace. He doubted Banichi would counsel him differently. So he fol-lowed Ilisidi to the outer edge of the terrace and down, and down the stone steps, to yet another terrace, from which another stairs, and then a third terrace, and so below to a paved courtyard, all leisurely, Cenedi going before the dowager, four of the dowager's security bringing up the rear.

It was farther down than he expected. It involved walking quite far back in the fortress, first through a walled courtyard, then across an earthy-smelling second walled court, at which he truly began to doubt the direction they were going, and the wisdom of following this party of strangers.

Banichi is going to kill me, Bren thought. Jago is going to file Intent on me. If the dowager's guard doesn't have it in mind from the start. Banichi can't have any idea where I've gone, if he isn't watching already—

Which, thinking of it, he well might—

Something banged, hammerlike, at the gate in front of them, and as Cenedi opened it there came fierce squeals the like of which he'd never heard at close range, only in machimi plays. . . .

Mecheiti, he thought with trepidation, seeing first Cenedi and then the dowager walk through that gate. *Horse* was what the Remote Equivalencies said.

But *horse* didn't cover this utter darkness beyond the gates, defying the servants to hold it, shaking its head, threatening with its formidable rooting-tusks—it was *horse* only because atevi rode it, it was *horse* on the atevi scale of things, the creature that had helped them cross the continents and pull their wagons and patrol their borders. It threw its head in defiance of its handlers, it gnashed its formidable teeth, its tusks capped with gold. Its head-harness glittered with beads, in the mop of flying mane—it was violent, frightening in its nearness and in the heedless strength with which it pulled the handlers about.

He stopped at the gate, counting it only prudence—but Ilisidi kept walking, after Cenedi. The other guards— there were three more of them than they had started with—passed him where he stood, telling him his fear was inappropriate, whatever the evidence of his senses, and he gathered his resolve and walked out behind the last, suffering, in that tall company, a sudden revision of perspectives: the world had suddenly become all atevi size, and the fragile old ateva leaning on her cane next to this terrible creature, and reaching out her hand to it, was of the same giant scale, the same fearsome darkness. It might have been centuries ago in Malguri. It might have been some aiji of the warlike age—

He watched in trepidation as the mecheita dipped his huge head and took something from Ilisidi's hand. It gulped that down and began to make little snatches at her fingers with its overshot upper lip as if it expected more—playing games, he realized, delicate in its movements, reacting to her fingers with a duck of its head and a gentleness in its touch he would not have believed from its behavior with the handlers.

Bluff and bluster, he said to himself. The creature was a pet. It was all a show to impress the paidhi, the stupid human.

"Come, come," Ilisidi said, looking back at him. She leaned the hand with the cane against the mecheita's neck, using the animal for a prop instead, and wanted *him* to come up to it.

Well, atevi had tried to bluff him before—including Tabini. Atevi in the court had set up traps to destroy his dignity, and with it his credibility. So he knew the game. He summoned up the mild anger and the amusement it deserved, walked up with his heart in his throat and tentatively offered his hand, expecting the dowager would dissuade him if there was a real threat

But not putting all his faith in it. He was ready to snatch his hand back as it stretched its neck toward him— and jerked away.

He did the same, heart thumping.

"Again," said Ilisidi. "Again, paidhi. Don't worry. He hasn't taken fingers in a year or two."

He gathered a breath and held out his hand a second time—this time he and the creature were more cautious of each other, the mecheita's nostrils opening and shutting rapidly, smelling him, he supposed, recalling from his studies that such animals did rely heavily on smell. Its head was as long as his arm from shoulder to fingertip. Its body shadowed him from the sun. It grew bolder, feeling over his hand with its prehensile upper lip, not seeming to threaten, but dragging his fingers down against the gold-capped rooting tusks.

It had a little lump of bony plate on its nose, that was bare and gray and smooth. The inquisitive lip was barred with wrinkles, and came to a narrow point between the two gold-capped tusks. It explored his fingers, snuffling and blowing its great breaths on him in evident enthusiasm, flicking its ears as it had with the dowager, seeming not offended that he had no treat for it. It tickled the soft skin between his fingers, and tasted his fingertips with a file-like tongue.

It didn't flinch away from him, that curious rough contact, it took to his whole fingers with skin-abrading enthusiasm, and he was delighted and afraid and enchanted, that something in the world met him with such complete, uncomplicated curiosity—accepting what it met. It wasn't offended at his strange taste, *that* for the dowager's hopes of his discomfiture.

Then it took the ultimate, unanticipated liberty of nosing him in the face. His hands flew up to fend it off, and his next view of it was from the pavings looking up at its looming shadow.

"Hei," Ilisidi said, holding the creature's harness, and standing over him, "don't push on the nose, nand' paidhi. Babs is sorry, aren't you, Babs? Didn't expect a hand on your nose, did you, poor Babs?"

He gathered himself up—he had saved his skull from the pavings, but not his backside. He brushed himself off and doggedly offered his hand again to the mecheita— one *didn't* admit an embarrassment, among atevi, even while the dowager chuckled at his discomfort and said he should take Nokhada, as a relatively placid mount.

"Take . . . where, aiji-mai?"

"To see Malguri, of course," Ilisidi declared, as if his agreement had encompassed everything. She gave her cane to Cenedi, hiked up the skirt of her coat and hit Babs on the shoulder, the signal—he knew it from television— for Babs to put out a foreleg. Another man helped Ilisidi with his joined hands, and Ilisidi swung up to a practiced landing on the riding-pad as Babs surged up again, smooth and quick as a courtly bow. They towered above him, Ilisidi and the mecheita, black against the sky, the beast that was wholly shadow, and Ilisidi, whose pale eyes were the only brightness, like a figure out of Malguri's violent past, that swept past him, and turned about and fidgeted to be moving.

There was a great deal of activity out of the further building, a stable from which other mecheiti came with their handlers, a crowd of black shapes, as tall, as ominous from where he stood, one for every man in Ilisidi's party.

And himself. "Forgive me," he began, when Cenedi signaled the handlers to bring one of the creatures to him. "This isn't cleared. I don't know how to ride. I beg to recall that I was sent here for my safety, at considerable difficulty of my absence from critical matters in court—I've not consulted with my own security, whose reputations—"

Nokhada's passage cut off his view, a living mountain between him and the stone wall of Malguri. "Let her have your scent," Cenedi said, having the lead rope, and holding the creature still. "Just don't press on the nose. The reaction is quite involuntary. The tusks are capped, but all the same—one could deal damage."

The mecheita stretched out its neck for a lazy sniff of his hand, and a more curious examination of his clothing, and a lick at his face and a try for his neck. He stepped back, not quite in time, from the swing of its head—a blunt tusk bruised his jaw and brought stars to his eyes, while Cenedi restrained it and the servants, nothing heeding his protests, prepared to help him up the way they had helped Ilisidi.

"Just put your foot here, nand' paidhi, it's quite all right."

"I can't ride, dammit, I don't know how!"

"It's quite all right," Cenedi said. "Just hold to the pad-rings. Leave the reins alone. She'll follow Babs."

"Where?" he asked bluntly. "Where are we going?"

"Just out and back. Come. I'll assure your safety, nand' paidhi. It's quite all right."

Call Cenedi a liar, in Cenedi's domain? He was sur-rounded by the people he'd left safety to follow, because he wouldn't be bluffed into retreat. Cenedi vowed he was safe. It was Cenedi's responsibility, and Banichi would hold him to it—with his life.

The paidhi could only be a certain degree dead. He was replaceable, in an hour, once Mospheira knew he'd bro-ken his neck.

"It's your responsibility," he said to Cenedi, taking up the reins. "Tabini-aiji *has* filed Intent, on my behalf. I trust you're aware what went on last night."

With which he prepared to put his foot in the stirrup, and let Cenedi worry. He resolutely struck Nokhada on the shoulder, to make him or her or it extend the foreleg: he knew from television *how* one got up.

But as Nokhada inclined in the brief bow, and he couldn't get the stirrup situated, or his foot situated in it, the handlers gave him a shove up toward the rings. His light weight went up from their hands in a greater hurry than he expected, and he had only just landed on the riding-pad when Nokhada came up on her feet.

He went off the other side with a wild snatch at the riding-pad, into the hands of security, as Nokhada went in a circle.

Atevi seldom laughed aloud. Ilisidi did, as Babs threw

his head and circled and snorted and handlers tried to collect Nokhada.

There was no choice, now. Absolutely none. He dusted himself off, asked Cenedi for the rein, and, shaking in the knees, remade his acquaintance with Nokhada, who had been made a fool along with him.

"Make both of us look good," he muttered to a mountainous shoulder, and tried a second time to make Nokhada extend the leg. "Hit harder," Cenedi said, so he hit harder, and Nokhada sighed wearily and put the leg out.

A second time he put his foot in the stirrup, and a second time Nokhada came up with him.

This time he expected it. This time he grabbed the pad-rings and leaned into Nokhada's motion—landed astride, then tilted as Nokhada continued to turn in circles.

"Loosen the rein, *loosen the rein, nand' paidhi!*"

He heard the dowager laughing uproariously and clung to the rings as he let the rein slip through his thumb and forefinger. Nokhada shook herself and turned around and around again.

"Ha!" Ilisidi said, as his circular, humiliating course showed him other riders getting mounted, with far less spectacle. He tried to straighten the reins out. He tried with pats of his hand to make friends with Nokhada, who in her now slower circles, seemed more interested in investigating his right foot, which he moved anxiously out of range.

Then Ilisidi shouted out, Babs passed him in a sudden rush of shadow, Nokhada took it for permission and made the last revolution a surge forward that jerked the rein through his hand so hard it burned. The stone face of the building passed in a lurching blur, the gate did, and while he was clinging to the pad-rings and trying to find his balance, they were across the courtyard, headed through an arch and down a stone chute beside the stairs that ended in an open gate, and sunlight.

A cliff was in front of them. He saw Ilisidi and Babs

turn to the road, and he jerked on Nokhada's head to make her turn, too, which Nokhada took for an insult, dancing deliberately out on the brink of disaster, with the misty lake beyond and empty air below.

"Don't jerk her head, nand' paidhi!" someone shouted from close behind him, and Cenedi came riding past, bumping his leg, sending Nokhada on a perverse course along the very edge, the creature shaking her head and kicking at nothing in particular.

On the upward course ahead, Ilisidi stopped, and turned about and waited until they caught up, among the rest of her guard. Nokhada was sweating and snorting as he jogged them to a stop beside Cenedi, and he was perfectly content, trembling in every joint, that Nokhada should stop and stand as the other riders gathered about them.

He'd survived. He was on a solid part of the mountain. Nokhada couldn't fling them both into the lake. That was a hard-won triumph.

"Caught your breath?" Ilisidi asked him. "How are you doing, nand' paidhi?"

"All right," he lied, out of breath.

"The lake trail's a little steep for a novice," Ilisidi said, and he thought she had to be joking. There *was* no trail over that edge back there. Surely there wasn't. "Are we ready? —Thumb and finger, nand' paidhi. Gently, gently. She'll follow. Just hold on."

Babs moved, Nokhada moved, as if she was on an invisible string. Babs made a running rush at the slope, and Nokhada waited and did the same, right behind, with Cenedi behind him. But two of the men were ahead of Ilisidi, and over the ridge and out of sight—security, he supposed, though he supposed that any sniper would just wait for a more profitable target.

"Someone did try to kill me," he said breathlessly to Cenedi, in case no one had ever quite made all the details clear, in case Cenedi had thought he was other than serious. "In Shejidan. Under the aiji's own roof. Without filing. I supposed Banichi must have mentioned that. It's not just a supposed threat."

"We're well aware," Cenedi said. "The tea was our best chance."

Cenedi was joking, he hoped. Deadpan retaliation for his remark when they mounted up.

But Cenedi claimed he'd known all along that there was a hazard, and Cenedi, or Ilisidi, had insisted all the same on bringing him outside the walls, and risking his neck with Nokhada. On one level, it was Tabini's kind of gesture, absolute defiance of his restrictions and the better thoughts of his security—but he remained uneasy in spite of Cenedi's assurances. The thought flitted through his head that if there were enemies or kidnappers in Malguri . . . he could be riding with them.

But Banichi hadn't warned him anything of the sort. Banichi had brought Cenedi into his bedroom. Cenedi said he knew why they were at Malguri, and thought he could guarantee his safety.

Nokhada dipped her head of a sudden to investigate the ground—not the most opportune moment for Nokhada to do that, and he made a grab at the rings and jerked Nokhada's head to bring it up—which brought Nokhada to an inglorious, sulking halt for two heartbeats before Nokhada moved on her own, still ducking her head, nose to the ground while she was climbing.

"She has a scent," Cenedi said. Cenedi's own mecheita was doing much the same, and so was Babs, up the hill. "I'd hang on, nand' paidhi. Babs is lead."

"Lead what?" he asked.

"Mecheit'-aiji," Cenedi said, and he had a sudden recollection of televised hunts, of the legendary ability of mecheiti to track atevi fugitives or four-footed game. He remembered Babs going over his hand, and Nokhada smelling him over. He had the sudden apprehension that it wasn't just television, wasn't anything made-up, or exaggerated.

And he couldn't control the damned mecheita he was

on to prevent it taking him wherever Ilisidi took a whim
to go.

Babs gave a sudden whip of his tail and with a scatter
of gravel took out diagonally across the slope. Nokhada
and Cenedi's mount and the rest pivoted and launched
themselves as if they'd been shot at—Nokhada recklessly,
roughly surging uphill in Babs' tracks, outpacing Cenedi
and the rest. He didn't *want* the lead—and all he could do
was hang on to the rings and not drop the rein.

A gully loomed ahead, a wash of soft earth down the
hill, and Ilisidi showed no disposition to slow Babs down.

Babs took it.

Oh, God, he thought, envisioning himself bleeding on
the ground, run over by the mecheiti behind. He tucked
down, he gripped the rings with all his might—he didn't
mass much, he didn't mass much, he kept telling himself
as Nokhada thundered across the slope—Nokhada was
going to go and Nokhada didn't intend to fall—Nokhada
took a four-beat turn into the jump, hind legs shoved,
shoulders rose—

Then came a floating feeling, a headlong plunge
against which his body instinctively reacted backward—
and a teeth-cracking jolt as somehow he went forward
again and his mouth hit the back of Nokhada's neck.

Nokhada's legs were under them again, all four of
them, in a pounding rhythm—Babs' dark rump showed in
front of them as Babs suddenly darted left and right on
the close track of something brown and white running
ahead of them. Nokhada ran a straighter course, other
mecheiti running like earthquake behind her.

A shot rang out ahead, from Ilisidi. Whatever it was—
went down in a cloud of dust and flattening grass as it
skidded downslope.

The guards all cheered the shot, as Babs stopped and
the mecheiti came to a blowing, stamping halt around
Babs, laying back ears and snorting and sidling about.

Bren's mouth was cut. He blotted it, watching one of
the guards ride down the slope to where the game had

fallen. Everyone thought it a wonderful shot on Ilisidi's part. He supposed it was. He was shaking. His lip was swelling already, and he must have bruised Nokhada's ribs with the clenching of his legs—his inner thigh muscles were sore and shuddery, and he was sweating, after doing nothing whatsoever in the chase but hold on.

While the aiji-dowager had just shot supper for herself and her staff, and the mecheiti were all wild-eyed and excited, at, one supposed, the smell of blood and gunpowder in the air.

"How do we fare, nand' paidhi?"

"I'm still here, nai-ji." That sounded too much like a challenge. "Credit to the mecheita, not myself."

"Are you hurt, nand' paidhi?"

Dependable. *Exactly* like Tabini. *Now* the concern.

"Her neck and my face," he said ruefully.

"Too far forward," Ilisidi said, and started off again at a brisk clip, uphill, while—a glance over his shoulder—the one guard was hauling the carcass up onto the riding-pad.

The beasts' abilities weren't just television. Machimi plays that showed a fugitive ripped apart by those tusks *wasn't* exaggeration, he was convinced of it. He didn't want to be on the ground in front of those feet, or in the way of those teeth, which, in war, they'd not blunt-capped.

Cenedi's assurances of safety with them began to seem more and less substantial. But—he began to recall with a shudder Babs smelling him over, a smell Babs could never have met before. The mecheiti-aiji, Cenedi had called him, Babs having fixed that smell in his beast-brain and the associative group hierarchy the experts swore extended right into the animal kingdom—

Politics. Four-footed politics. Colony behavior, they called it on Mospheira, where they studied small indigenous animals, but nothing—nothing like the mecheita, nothing like these hunters, that *ate*—he remembered his history—anything they could root up or catch. Omnivores. Pack hunters.

His legs were limp. His hand was shaking, holding the rein, from the excess of adrenalin, he said to himself.

Like the gunshot. He wasn't used to such things. They engaged his senses wholly, insanely, on a level a professional risk-taker like Cenedi surely didn't deal with anymore: he didn't know what was important, so he took in everything that hit his senses, like a madman, and tried to do something when, to a well-ordered mind like Cenedi's, there wasn't anything to do.

The single guardsman they had left overtook them at a diagonal on the hill, with a small, graceful creature tied to the back of his riding-pad. Its head lolled. Its eyes were like the beast's on the bedroom wall, not angry, though: soft, and astonished. A small trickle of blood ran from black, fine nostrils, a pretty nose, a pretty face. Bren *didn't* want dinner with the dowager tonight.

Sausages didn't have such mortality about them. He preferred distance from his meals. Tabini called it a moral flaw. He called it civilization and Tabini called it delusion: You eat meat out of season, Tabini would say. Out of time with the earth, you sell flesh for profit. You eat what never runs free: you call that *civilized?*

He hadn't an argument against that reasoning. He rode at Babs' swishing tail, as the company remarked to each other again how fine a shot the dowager had made, and Ilisidi said that now that they had stocked the larder, they could enjoy the rest of the ride.

At a slower pace, Bren hoped: the insides of his legs, even relaxing, now, were finding the riding-pad an unnatural stretch, and when he tried to find a comfortable posture, he kicked Nokhada by accident and went humiliatingly off the trail, right down the mountainside, before he could get the mecheita stopped and redirected.

"Nand' paidhi?" Cenedi asked from above.

"We're coming," he said. He supposed Nokhada made a 'we.' Nokhada certainly expressed an opinion, in flattened ears and plodding gait, once they reached the trail again, overtaking the rear of the column, where Cenedi waited.

"What happened?" Cenedi asked.

"We're figuring it out," he muttered. But Cenedi gave him a fast rundown of the signals: touch of the feet for direction, light tugs of the rein for attention signals, or to restrain outright rebellion. Don't touch the nose, don't pull down on the head. Left foot, go right, right foot, go left; tug lightly, go faster, tug hard, go slow, don't kick a man in the groin or a mecheita behind the ribs.

Which seemed a civilized arrangement.

"If he intends to jump," Cenedi told him, "do as you did. Your weight won't bother him. —Are the stirrups short enough?"

"I fear, nadi, I wouldn't possibly know."

"If your legs cramp, say so."

"They don't." He didn't complain of the rubbery condition. He put that down to sheer fright and a workout of muscles he wasn't used to using.

"Good," Cenedi said, and rode off at a steep diagonal up the ridge, Cenedi's mechieta ducking its head and sniffing the ground intermittently, while its long legs never broke stride.

Curious ability. It was smelling for something along the ground, and lifted its head to smell the wind as they reached the crest of the ridge.

And Cenedi kept the creature under control so damned effortlessly. Cenedi stopped, signalled them with a wave of his hand, and Ilisidi put Babs up the ridge at a fair clip.

Nokhada took the diagonal course uphill, then, hellbent on regaining second place to Babs. Dammit! Bren thought, cutting the guards off in their climb; but he was afraid to pull on the rein, among the rocks and sliding gravel.

"Excuse me!" he called back over his shoulder. "Nadiin, it's her idea!" That drew laughter from the guards, as Nokhada fell in at Babs' tail.

Better than resentment, at least. There *was* a hierarchy among mecheiti, and Ilisidi and everyone in the party had known Nokhada was going to follow Babs, come hell or high water. They'd had their joke. He'd gained a cut lip and sore muscles, but he hadn't fallen off and he'd been a fair sport about the joke—it was the way he'd learned to deal with Tabini's court, at least, and the way he'd learned to deal with Tabini, early on.

One just didn't back away from a challenge—and atevi *would* try a newcomer, if for nothing more than to determine his place in the order of things: they did it to anyone and they did it as a matter of course, on an instant's judgment to find out a fool or a leader . . . neither of which he planned to be with them, not to threaten Ilisidi or Cenedi or any of them.

And after he had realized Ilisidi's joke at his expense and let them know he saw it, then things were easier, then he could ride at Babs' lazily switching tail and be easy about the position in which Ilisidi had set him, giving him a mecheita proper to a high-ranking visitor from Tabini's own staff; he could quite well appreciate the humor in that, too—a mecheita that was going to give the unskilled visitor hell, especially if he thought he was going to adjust his position in line, or argue with Ilisidi.

Humiliate him? Ilisidi could do that with a flick of her riding crop. Follow a competition jumper in terrain like this? The paidhi-aiji would be extremely lucky if only his dignity fractured.

But he must have passed Ilisidi's trial of him, since Cenedi had given him at least a fair sketch of left, right, go, and stop—enough knowledge to put a fool in trouble or keep a wiser man from outright folly—like that business on the exit from the gate, and the cliff, which now he was convinced must not have been so sheer as his immediate impression of it, or Nokhada more in command of her footing than she seemed. Dump the paidhi down-slope? Yes. Lose a high-bred mecheita? The woman who'd attacked a course official with her riding crop, over scratches?

He wasn't wholly certain. The tea service had certainly been calculated to send some message; and he wasn't wholly certain Ilisidi was innocent in the matter of the tea—although he would bet the severity of his reaction had left the dowager and Cenedi some little chagrined: a general atevi recklessness toward questions of life and death and *bihawa,* that aggressive impulse to test strangers, had betrayed them and left them somewhat at disadvantage: to that degree he suspected it was in fact an accident—a blemish on mutual dignity they had to repair.

Had to. And he couldn't have accepted the breakfast invitation and then declined to come with Ilisidi on this ride. He'd read it right, let Banichi say what he would, he'd read it correctly.

And, having achieved something of a Place in the dowager's party, he hoped hereafter simply to enjoy the sun and the mountain—the very height of the mountain, the world spread out below in a spectacular view.

They rode in tall, windswept grass, and yellow, ragged flowers that abounded along the ridge, with an unobstructed view across the lake to the mountains on the other side. The breaths he drew were freighted with rich smells of the earth and the grass and crushed flowers, the oiled leather of the harness, and the dusty, musky smell of the mecheiti themselves. The grass and the pebbly rubble at the roots brought back vividly the last time he and Tabini had hunted at Taiben, slogging afoot through the dusty hills—

Tabini trying to show him the finer points of hunting and stalking—

Everything came back to him so very clearly: that day, that exact time, as if the realities of the countryside and the reality of the city compartmentalized themselves so thoroughly they maintained separate time-streams, so that, entering one ... he took up where he had left off, with no events between. Time slipped wildly on him,

turned treacherous. Today's foolish hazard had slid un-
awares to chancy, intoxicating success, the paidhi riding
a thousand, two thousand miles from the safety of Mospheira and enjoying the sights and smells and sounds no
human had ever experienced. The mecheiti of the
machimi plays had turned real as the dust and the flowers
and the sun.

And strangest of all to his ears came the silence that
wasn't silence, but the total absence, for the first time in
his life that he was ever aware, of machine sounds. The
sounds that reached his ears were rich enough, the wind
and the creak of leather and jingle of harness and bridle
rings, the scuff of gravel, the sighing of the grass along
the hill—but he'd never been anywhere, even Taiben,
where he couldn't see power lines, or hear, however
faintly, the sound of aircraft, or a passing train, or just the
generalized hum of machinery working—and he'd never
known it existed, until he heard its absence.

Below them, the miniaturized walls of Malguri, as few
atevi surely ever were privileged to view them. There
wasn't a road, wasn't a rail, wasn't a trace of habitation
aparent in all the hills and the lake shore, except those
walls.

Time slipped again. He imagined the wind-stirred banners of the machimi plays, the meetings of treachery and
connivance in the hills, the fortress destined for attack—
how to get the lord into the open, or assassins within the
walls, engaging single individuals, instead of armies . . .
saving lives, saving resources, saving the land from future
feuds.

And always, in such plays, the retainer with an ancestral grudge, the trusted assassin with the unevident
man'chi, the thing the aiji on the windy ridge or the aiji
within the fortress should have known and didn't. One
could all but hear the banners cracking in the wind, hear
the rattle of armor . . . atevi civilization, atevi history that
flourished now only in the machimi, on television—
where human history flourished not at all.

There was something unexpectedly seductive about the textures . . . from the brightness of blood on the kill to the white and brown fur of the animal, from the casual drop of dung to the smell of flowers and the scent of crushed grass and the lazy switch of mecheita ears. It wasn't the same reality as in the halls of the Bu-javid. It certainly wasn't Mospheira. It was the atevi world as humans might never see it, neighboring, as they did, only the smoke-stacks and steam-engines of Shejidan.

It was a world that, given a hundred years, atevi themselves might never see again, or never understand, because the future that might have naturally grown from Malguri's past—never would grow at all in a solely atevi way, now that Mospheira had given atevi the railroads and communications satellites, now that jets sped atevi travellers across the country too high and too fast to see a place like Malguri.

He argued with Tabini about meat, and seasons, and thought atevi ways . . . inconvenient.

But that argument was the same thing as the jets and the satellites. Another little piece of Malguri under attack.

Thinking of that word . . .

"Have you talked specifically to Banichi, nadi?" he asked Cenedi, who rode behind him. "I would hate to ride into security installations."

Cenedi gave him an expressionless stare. "So would we, nadi."

He knew *that* response. Helpful as a stone wall. Which said the paidhi wasn't supposed to know about the installations—or that Cenedi didn't know, and wasn't in Banichi's confidence, and now thought that *he* was, which couldn't help matters if they rode into something he couldn't foresee.

But the two men that had ridden out from their number at the beginning still hadn't rejoined them—or even shown up again. They must be the other side of the ridge. And now and again Babs in particular would drop his head to sniff at the trail, Nokhada likewise—unexpected little jolts and a pitch of Nokhada's shoulder, but he learned to read the intent in the set of Nokhada's ears and the general rhythm of her stride.

Not easy beasts to trap, he began to think. Not beasts that would go blindly into something wrong on the trail.

But he began to be easier on that account. Malguri's grounds weren't, then, the sort of weed-grown, desolate place where enterprising assassins could just come and go at will. The very presence of the mecheiti would dissuade intruders.

And one could legitimately believe, after all, that the power outage that still held in Malguri this morning was the legitimate result of a lightning strike, considering that power seemed to have gone out over a quarter of the township in the valley.

Ilisidi had asked if he had slept through the disturbance—no, Ilisidi had called it a lively night, and asked whether he'd slept through it.

Through what? Power failures? Or gunshots in the night, Tano's nervous finger on the trigger, and Banichi on the radio?

Neither Banichi nor Jago had clued him what to do, if they'd had any idea of the proposed morning hunt. Neither of them had forewarned him he might be asked ... had trusted him as the paidhi, maybe. Or just not known.

But Tabini, who doubtless knew the aiji-dowager as well as anyone in Shejidan, had said, regarding his dealings with Ilisidi—use your diplomacy.

Ilisidi slowed and stopped ahead of him, where the trail began a downward pitch again.

"From this place," Ilisidi said, waving her hand to the view ahead, "you can see three provinces, Maidingi, Didaini, Taimani. How do you regard my land?"

"Beautiful," he said honestly.

"*My land,* nand' paidhi."

Nothing Ilisidi said was idle, or without calculation.

"Your land, nai-ji. I confess I resisted being sent to Malguri. I thought it remote from my duties. I was mistaken. I wouldn't have known about the dragonettes otherwise. I wouldn't have ridden, in all my life." In the moment, he agreed inside with what he was saying, enjoying his brief respite from Banichi, Jago, and sane responsibility, enjoying—the atevi attitude was contagious—his chance to push the restrictions under which the paidhi necessarily lived and conducted business. "But Banichi will kill me when I get back."

Ilisidi looked askance at him, and the corners of her mouth tightened.

Literal atevi minds. "Figuratively speaking, nai-ji."

"You're sure of my grandson."

Disquieting question. "Should I have doubt, nai-ji?" Ilisidi was certainly the one to ask, but one couldn't trust the answer. No one knew Ilisidi's *man'chi*, where it lay. She had never made it clear, at least that he knew, and, presumably, if Banichi or Jago knew, they would have told him.

But no more did he know where Tabini's was. That was always the way with aijiin—that they had none, or had none in reach of their subordinates.

"Tabini's a steady lad," Ilisidi said. "Young. Very young. Tech solves everything."

A hint of her thoughts and her motives? He wasn't sure. "Even the paidhi doesn't maintain that to be the case, nai-ji."

"Doesn't the Treaty forbid—I believe this was your insistence—interference in our affairs?"

"That it does, nai-ji." Dangerous ground. Very dangerous ground. Hell if this woman was as fragile as she looked. "Have I seemed to do contrary things? Please do me the kindness of telling me so."

"Does my grandson tell you so?"

"If he told me I was interfering, I do swear to you, nai-ji, I would certainly reconsider my actions."

She said nothing for a space. It left him, riding beside her in the windy silence, to think anxiously whether anything he had said or done or supported in the various councils could be controversial, or as the dowager hinted, interfere in atevi affairs, or push technology too fast.

"Please, aiji-ji. Be blunt. Am I opposing or advancing a position with which you disagree?"

"What a strange question," Ilisidi said. "Why should I tell you that?"

"Because I would try to find out your reasons, nai-ji, not to oppose your interests, not to preempt your resources—but to avoid areas of your extreme interest. Let me recall to you, we don't use assassins, nai-ji. That's not even a resource for us."

"But they are, for atevi who may support you in your positions."

He'd heard that argument before. He could get around it with Tabini. He longed after Tabini's company, he longed only to ask him, forthrightly to learn things ... that no one else was telling him lately.

And as now and again in the hours since he'd come to Malguri, he suffered another of those moments of dislocation—at one instant convinced that things were all right, and then, with no particular reason, doubting that, and recalling how completely he was isolated, more isolated than the paidhi had ever been from his resources.

"Forgive my question," he said to Ilisidi. "But the paidhi isn't always wise enough to understand his position in your affairs. I hope for your good opinion, nai-ji."

"What do you hope to accomplish in your tenure?"

He hadn't expected that question. But he'd answered it, repeatedly, in councils. "An advancement for atevi and humans, nai-ji. An advancement, a step toward technological equality, at a pace which won't do harm."

"That's a given, isn't it? By the Treaty, a dull and tedious given. Be less modest. Name the specific, wondrous thing you'd have done before you die ... the gift you wish most, in your great wisdom, to bestow on us."

He didn't think it a harmless question. He could name certain things. He honestly didn't have a clear answer.

"I don't know," he said.

"What, the paidhi without a notion what he wishes to do?"

"A step at a time, nai-ji. I don't know what may be possible. And telling you ... would in itself violate the principles ..."

"The most ambitious thing you've ever advanced."

"The rail system."

"Pish. We invented the rail. You improved it."

That was true, though atevi trains and steamships had been only the most rudimentary design, and boilers had burst with frightening regularity.

"So what more, paidhi? Rockets to the moons? Travel amongst the stars?"

A far more dangerous topic. "I'd like, yes, to see atevi at least reach that threshold in my lifetime. Nai-ji, so much is possible from there. So much you could do then. But we aren't sure of the changes that would make, and I want to understand what would result. I want to give good advice. That's my job, nai-ji." He had never himself seen it so clearly, until now. "We're at the edge of space. And so much changes once you can look down on the world."

"What changes?"

One more dangerous question, this one cultural and philosophical. He looked outward, at the lake, the whole world seeming to lie below the path they rode.

"Height changes your perspective, nai-ji. We see three provinces from here. But my eye can't see the treaty-boundaries."

"Mine can. That mountain ridge. The river. They're quite evident."

"But were this mountain as high as the great moon, nai-ji, and if were you born on this very high mountain, would you see the lines? Or, if you saw them, would they mean to you what they mean to people born on the plain, these distant, invisible lines?"

"*Man'chi* is *man'chi*. *Man'chi* is important. And to a

dweller on the border—what meaning, these lines aijiin agree on? *Man'chi* is never visible."

It was gratifying to expect the answer one got, the same that Tabini inevitably gave. It was gratifying to think one did accurately forecast atevi sentiments. It was useful to know about Ilisidi.

"So that wouldn't change," he said. "Even if you stood on the highest mountain."

"*Man'chi* would never change," Ilisidi said.

"Even if you left the sight of the world for years and years."

"In hell and on earth, *man'chi* would not change. But you don't understand this, you humans." Babs struck a slight rise, and for a moment walked solitary, until Nokhada caught up. Ilisidi-dowager said, "Or you never tell your enemies, if you do change."

That, too, was in the machimi plays. The catastrophic event, the overturning of a life's understandings. But always toward the truth, as he saw it. Always toward what *man'chi* should have been.

Ilisidi offered no explanation of her remark. Perhaps he was supposed to have asked something wise. But imagination failed him.

"We truthfully didn't understand your view of things, nai-ji, when we first arrived. We didn't understand atevi. You didn't understand us. That's one of the great and unfortunate reasons of the War."

"The unfortunate reason of the War was humans taking Mospheira, to which they had no right. It was hundreds of thousands of atevi dislodged from their homes. It was *man'chi* broken, because we couldn't deal with your weapons, nand' paidhi." The dowager's voice wasn't angry, only severe, and emphatic. "And slowly you raise us up to have technology, and more technology. Does this not seem a foolish thing to do?"

Not the first time he'd met that question, either. Atevi asked it among themselves, when they thought the paidhi would hear no report of their discussion. Thwarted councillors shouted it at the paidhi in council. Not even to Tabini could he give the untranslatable, the true answer: We thought we could make you our friends.

So he gave the official, the carefully worked out, translatable reply: "We saw association possible. We saw advantage to us in your good will in this region where fortune had cast us."

"You tell us whether we shall have roads, or rail. You deny us what pleases you to deny. You promise us wonders. But the great wonders, as I hear, are on Mospheira, for the enjoyment of humans, who have paved roads."

"A very few. Fewer than you have."

"On a continent a thousand times the size of Mospheira. Be honest, nand' paidhi."

"With vehicles that don't use internal combustion. Which will come, nai-ji, which will come to atevi."

"In your lifetime . . . or in mine?"

"Perhaps in thirty years. Perhaps less. Depending on whether we have the necessary industry. Depending on finding resources. Depending on the associations and the provinces finding it politic to cooperate in producing scarce items, in depending on computers. Depending on *man'chi,* and who's willing and not willing to work together, and how successful the first programs are . . . but I needn't tell that to the aiji-dowager, who knows the obstinacy of vested interests."

He had made the dowager laugh, if briefly and darkly. The sun cast Ilisidi's black profile in shadow against the hazy distances of the sky and the lake. They rode a while in silence, there on the crest of the mountain, with the wind picking up the mecheiti's manes and himself rocking, child-sized, on the back of a creature bred to carry atevi into their infrequent and terrible wars.

"There's the airport," Ilisidi said, pointing ahead of them.

Straining his eyes, he could make out what he thought was Maidingi Airport, beside a hazy sprawl he decided must be Maidingi township. Nearer at hand, he could just make out the road, or what he took for it, wending down the mountain.

"Is that the town?" he asked, knowing it was a stupid question, but only to break the silence; and Ilisidi said it was Maidingi.

After that, looking out over the broad plain, Ilisidi pointed out the direction of villages outlying Maidingi township, and told him the names of plants and regions and the mountains across the lake.

But in his mind was the history he had seen in the books in his room, the castle standing against attack from the Association across the lake, even before cannon had come into the question. Malguri had stood for centuries against intrusion from the east. Banners flying, smoke of cannon on the walls. . . .

Don't romanticize, his predecessor had told him. Don't imagine. See and observe and report.

Accuracy. Not wishful thinking.

Lives relied on the paidhi's accuracy. Billions of lives relied on the truth of his perception.

And relied equally on his representing both sides accurately to each other.

But, he thought, how much have we forgotten about them? How much have we encouraged them to lose? How much have we overridden, imposing our priorities and our technological sequence over theirs?

Or are those possibilities really forgotten here? Have they ever wholly been forgotten?

They rode to the very end of the ridge. Clouds were rolling in over the southern end of the lake, dark gray beneath, flashing with lightnings, brooding over slate-gray waters. But sunlight slanted over the blue peaks to the east, turning the water along the Malguri shore as bright as polished silver. A dragonette leapt from its nest among the rocks, crying protest to the winds, and thunder rumbled. Another dragonette was creeping back up the mountain the long, slow way they must, once they'd flown, wings folded, wing-claws finding purchase on the steep rocks.

Dragonettes existed in Shejidan. Buildings near the park had slanted walls, he'd heard, specifically to afford them purchase. Atevi still valued them, for their stubbornness, for their insistence on flying, when they knew the way back was uncertain and fraught with dangers.

Predator on the wing and potential prey on the return.

Ilisidi turned Babs about on the end of the trail, and took a downward, slanting course among the rocks. He followed.

In a time more of riding, they passed an old and ruined building Cenedi said was an artillery installation from a provincial dispute. But its foundations, Cenedi said, had been older than that, as a fortress called Tadiiri, the Sister, once bristling with cannon.

"How did it go to ruins?" he asked.

"A falling out with Malguri," Cenedi said. "And a barrel of wine that didn't agree with the aiji of Tadiiri or his court."

Poison. "But the whole fortress?" he blurted out.

"It lacked finesse," Cenedi said.

So he knew of a certainty then what Cenedi was, the same as Banichi and Jago. And he believed now absolutely that his near demise had embarrassed Cenedi, as Cenedi had said, professionally.

"After that," Cenedi said, "Tadiiri was demolished, its cannon taken down. You saw them at the front entrance, as you drove in."

He had not even been sure they were authentic. A memorial, he had thought. He didn't know such things. But the age of wars and cannon had been so brief—and war on the earth of the atevi so seldom a matter of engagement, almost always of maneuver, and betrayal, with leaders guarded by their armies. It was assassination one most had to guard against, on whatever scale.

And here he rode with Ilisidi, and her guard, leaving the one Tabini had lent him.

Or was it, in atevi terms, a maneuver, a posturing, a declaration of position and power, their forcing him to join them? He might have found something else unhealthful to drink, or eat. There were so many hazards a human could meet, if they meant him harm.

And Banichi and Cenedi did speak, and did intrude into each other's territory—Banichi had been angry at him for accepting the invitation, Banichi had said there was no way to retrieve him from his promise—but all of it was for atevi reasons, atevi dealing with a situation between Tabini and his grandmother, at the least, and maybe a trial of Banichi's authority in the house: he simply couldn't read it.

Maybe Ilisidi and Tabini had made their point and maybe, hereafter, he could hope for peace between the two wings of the house—Tabini's house, Tabini's politics with generations before him, and paidhiin before himself.

Diplomacy, indeed, he thought, falling back to Babs' tail again, in his place and deftly advised of it.

He understood who ruled in Malguri. He had certainly gotten that clear and strong. He supposed, through Banichi, that Tabini had.

But in the same way he supposed himself a little safer now, inside Ilisidi's guardianship as well as Tabini's.

VII

In a courtyard echoing with shouts and the squeals of mecheiti, Nokhada extended a leg at his third request, mostly, Bren thought, because the last but her had already done the same.

He slithered down Nokhada's sun-warmed side, and viewed with mistrust the mecheita's bending her neck around and nibbling his sleeve, butting capped but still formidable tusks into his side as he tried to straighten the twisted rein. But he wasn't so foolish as to press on Nokhada's nose again, and Nokhada lifted her head, sniffing the air, a black mountain between him and the mid-morning sun, complaining at something unseen——or only liking the echoes of her own voice.

The handlers moved in to take the rein. He gave Nokhada a dismissing pat on the shoulder, figuring that was due. Nokhada made a rumbling sound, and ripped the rein from his hand, following the rest of the group the handlers were leading away into the maze of courtyards.

"Use her while you're here," Ilisidi said, near him. "At any time, at any hour. The stables have their instructions to accommodate the paidhi-aiji."

"The dowager is very kind," he said, wondering if there was skin left on his palm.

"Your seat is still doubtful," she said, took her cane from an attendant and walked off toward the steps.

He took that for a dismissal.

But she stopped at the first step and looked back, leaning with both hands on her cane. "Tomorrow morning. Breakfast." The cane stabbed the air between them. "No argument, nand' paidhi. This is your host's privilege."

He bowed and followed Ilisidi up the steps in the general upward flow of her servants and her security, who probably overlapped such functions, like his own.

His lip was swollen, he had lost the outer layer of skin on his right hand, intimate regions of his person were sore and promising to get sorer, and by the dowager's declaration, he was to come back for a second try tomorrow, a situation into which he seemed to have opened a door that couldn't be shut again.

He followed all the way up the steps to the balcony of Ilisidi's apartment, that being the only way up into the castle he knew, while the dowager, on her way into her inner apartments, paid not the least further attention to his being there——which was not the rudeness it would have been among humans: it only meant the aiji-dowager was disinterested to pursue business further with an inferior. At their disparity of rank she owed him nothing; and in that silence, he was free to go, unless some servant should deliver him some instruction to the contrary.

None did. He trailed through the dowager's doorway, and on through the public reception areas of her apartment, tagged all the way by her lesser servants, who opened the outermost doors for him and bowed and wished him good fortune in his day as he left.

Good fortune, he wished them, in his turn, with appropriate nods and bows on their part, after which he trekked off down the halls, bruised and damaged, but with a knowledge now of the land, the provinces, the view and the command of the castle, and even what was the history and origin of the cannon he could see through the open front doors.

Where—God help him—several vehicles were parked. Perhaps some official had come up from the township. Perhaps the promised repair crew had arrived and they were putting the electricity back in service. In any event, the paidhi wasn't a presence most provincial atevi would take without flinching. He decided to hurry, and traversed the front room at a fast, sore-legged walk.

Straight into an inbound group of the castle staff and a flock of tourists.

A child screamed, and ducked behind its parents. Parents stood stock still, a black wall with wide yellow eyes. He made an apologetic and sweeping bow, and—it was the paidhi's minimal job—knew he had to patch the damage, wild as he must look, with a cut lip, and dust on his coat.

"Welcome to Malguri," he said. "I'd no idea there were visitors. Please reassure the young lady." A pause for breath. A second bow. "The paidhi, Bren Cameron, at your kind disposal. May I do you any grace?"

"May we have a ribbon?" an older boy was forward to ask.

"I don't know that I have ribbons," he said. He did,

sometimes, have them in his office for formalities. He didn't know whether Jago had brought such things. But one of the staff said they could procure them, and wax, if he had his seal-ring.

He was trapped. Banichi *was* going to kill him.

"Excuse me," he said. "I've just come in from the stable court. I need to wash my hands. I'll be right back down. Excuse me, give you grace, thank you ..." He bowed two and three times more and made the stairs, was halfway up them when he looked up.

Tano was standing at the top of the stairs with no pleased expression on his face, a gun plainly on his hip. Tano beckoned him to come upstairs, and he ran the rest of the steps, the whole transaction between them at such an angle, he hoped, that the tourists couldn't see the reason for his sudden burst of energy.

"Nand' paidhi," Tano said severely. "You were to use the back hall."

"No one told me, nadi!" He was furious. And held his temper. The culprit was Banichi, who was in charge—and the second party responsible was clearly himself. "I need to clean up. I've promised these people—"

"Ribbons, nand' paidhi. I'll see to it. Hurry."

He flew up the stairs past Tano, aches and all, down the hall to his apartment, with no time to bathe. He only washed, flung on fresh shirt and trousers, a clean coat, and passed cologne-damp hands over his windblown hair, which was coming out of its braid.

Then he stalked out and down the hall, and made a more civilized descent of the stairs to what had been set up as a receiving line, a place ready at the table in the hall in front of the fireplace, with wax-jack, with ribbons, with small cards, and an anxious line of atevi—for each of them, a card to sign, ribbon and seal with wax, and, with the first such signature and seal, a pleased and nervous tourist who'd received a bonus for his trip, while a line of thirty more waited, stealing glances past one another at the only living human face they'd likely seen, unless they'd been as far as Shejidan.

The paidhi was used to adult stares. The children were far harder to deal with. They'd grown up on machimi about the War. Some of them were sullen. Others wanted to touch the paidhi's hand to see if his skin was real. One asked him if his mother was that color, too. Several were afraid of his eyes, or asked if he had a gun.

"No, nadi," he lied to them, with mostly a clear conscience, "no such thing. We're at peace now. I live in the aiji's house."

A parent asked, "Are you on vacation, nand' paidhi?"

"I'm enjoying the lake," he said, and wondered if his attempted assassination was on the television news yet, in whatever province the man came from. "I'm learning to ride." He poured wax and sealed the ribbon to the card. "It's a beautiful view."

Thunder rumbled. The tourists looked anxiously to the door.

"I'll hurry," he said, and began to move the line faster, recalling the black cloud that they had seen from the ridge, down over the end of the lake—the daily deluge, he said to himself, and wondered whether it was the season and whether perhaps there was a reason why Tabini came here in the autumn, and not mid-summer. Perhaps Tabini knew better, and sent the paidhi here to be drowned.

The electricity was still off. "It looks so authentic," one visitor said to another, regarding the candlelight.

Tour the bathrooms, he thought glumly, and longed for the hot bath that would take half an hour at least to heat. He felt the least small discomfort sitting on the hard chair, that had everything to do with the riding-pad and Nokhada's gait, and the stretching of muscles in places he'd been unaware separate muscles existed.

A humid, cold gust of wind swept in the open front doors, fluttering the candles and making a sputter of wax from the wax-jack that sprinkled the polished wood of the table. He thought of calling out to the staff to shut the door before the rain hit, but they were all out of convenient range, and he was almost finished. The tourists would be outbound in only another moment or two, and the door was providing more light to the room than the candles did.

Thunder boomed, echoing off the walls, and he was down to the last two tourists, an elderly couple who wanted "Four cards, if the paidhi would, for the grandchildren."

He signed and sealed, while the tourists with their ribboned cards were congregating by the open doors. The vans were pulling around, and the air smelled like rain, sharp contrast to the smell of sealing-wax.

He made an extra card, his last ribbon, for the old man, who told him his grandchildren were Nadimi and Fari and Tabona and little Tigani, who had just cut her first teeth, and his son Fedi was a farmer in Didaini province, and would the paidhi mind a picture?

He stood, feeling the stretch of stiffening muscles, he smiled at the camera, and at the general click of shutters as others took it for permission. He felt much better about the meeting, encouraged that the tourists proved approachable, even the children behaving far more easily toward him. It was the closest he supposed he'd ever come to meeting ordinary folk, except the very few he met in audience in Shejidan, and in the success of the gesture and in the habits of his job he felt constrained to a reciprocal courtesy, seeing them to the doors and onto their buses—always good policy, the extra gesture of good will, despite the chill; and he *liked* the old couple, who were following at his elbow and asking him about his family. "No, I don't have a wife," he said, "no, I've thought about it—"

Barb would die of boredom and frustration, in the cloister the paidhi lived in. Barb would stifle in the surrounding security, and as for being circumspect—her life wouldn't tolerate the board's questions, she wouldn't pass

... and Barb ... he didn't *love* her, but she was what he needed.

A boy crowded near him, right up against his arm, and said, not too discreetly, "I'm that tall, look." Which was the truth. But his parents hastily snatched him away, declaring that that was a very *insheibi* thing to say, very indiscreet, rude and dangerous, and begging the paidhi's pardon could they possibly take a picture with him if a member of the paidhi's staff could possibly snap the shutter?

He smiled, atevi-style, waited while they arranged the shot, and looked civilized and as comfortable as possible, standing with the couple as the camera clicked.

More cameras went off, the moment he stepped away, a veritable barrage of shutters.

And a random three pops outside the open doors. He turned in a heart-frozen shock, recognizing the sound of gunfire, as someone grabbed him by the arm and slammed him against the open door—as the tourists all rushed out under the portico in the rain.

Another shot rang out. The tourists cheered.

It was Tano half-smothering him, when he hadn't even known Tano was close. "Stay here," Tano said, and went outside, his hand on his gun.

He couldn't stand there not knowing what was happening, or what the danger was. He risked a glance after Tano's departing back, keeping the rest of him behind the substantial door. He saw, in the gaps of a screen of tourists, a man lying on the pavings out in the rain, and at the same remove, atevi figures coming from the lawn to the circular drive, near the cannon, mere shadows through the veils of rain. A bus driver, ignoring the whole affair, was shouting for his tourists to get aboard, that they had a long drive today, and a schedule for lunch on the lake, if the weather passed.

The tourists boarded, while the atevi shadows stood around the man lying on the cobbles. He supposed the shooting was over. He came out and stood in front of the door as the damp gusts hit him. Tano came back in haste.

"Get inside, nand' paidhi," Tano said. The first van was moving out, tourists pressing their faces to the windows, a few waving. He waved back, helpless habit, frozen by the grotesqueness of the sight. The van made the circular drive past the cannon and the second bus passed him.

"It's handled, nand' paidhi, get inside. They think it was machimi for the tourists, it's all right."

"All right?" He held his indignation in check and steadied his voice. "Who's been killed? Who is it?"

"I don't know, nand' paidhi, I'll try to find out, but I can't leave you down here. Please go upstairs."

"Where's Banichi?"

"Out there," Tano said. "Everything's all right, nadi, come, I'll take you to your rooms." Tano's pocket-com sputtered, and Tano turned it on, one-handed. "I have him," Tano said. It was Banichi's voice, Bren thought, thank God it was Banichi, but where was Jago? He heard Banichi saying something in verbal code, about a problem solved, and then another voice—telling gender with atevi voices wasn't always easy—saying something about a second team and that being all right.

"The dowager," Bren said in a low voice, suddenly asking himself—one had to ask, with the evidence of death on the grounds—was Ilisidi somehow involved, was she all right, was she somehow the author of what was happening out there, with Banichi?

"Perfectly safe," Tano said, and gave him another gentle shove. "Please, nadi, Banichi's fine, everyone is fine—"

"Who's dead? An outsider? Someone on staff?"

"I'm not quite sure," Tano said, "but please, nadi, don't make our jobs more difficult."

He let himself be maneuvered away from the doors, then, away from the blowing mist that made his clothing damp and cold, and across the dim hall and up the stairs. All the while he was thinking about the shadows in the rain, about Banichi out there, and someone lying dead on the cobbled drive, right by the flower beds and the memorial cannon—

Thinking uneasily, too, about the alarm last night, and about riding up on the ridge not an hour ago, with Ilisidi and Cenedi, where any rifle might have picked them off. The vivid memory came back, of that night in Shejidan, and the shock of the gun in his hands, and Jago saying, like a bad dream, that there was blood on the terrace. Like outside, on the lawn, in the rain.

His knees started shaking as he climbed the stairs to the upper hall. His gut was upset before he reached the doors to his apartment, as if it *were* that night, as if everything was slipping again out of his control.

Tano strode two steps ahead of him at the last and opened the door to his receiving room, to what should feel like refuge, where warm air met him like a wall and light flooded in from a window blind with rain. Lightning flashed, making the window white for an instant. The tourists were having a rain-drenched ride down the mountain. Their lunch on the lake seemed uncertain.

Someone had invaded the grounds last night and that someone was dead on the drive, all his plans cancelled. It hardly seemed reasonable that no one knew what they were.

Tano rang for the other servants, and assured him in a low voice that hot tea was forthcoming. "A bath," Bren said, "if they can." He didn't want to deal with Djinana and Maigi right now, he wanted Tano, he wanted people he knew were Tabini's—but he was scared to protest that to Tano, as if a question to their plans could turn into a challenge to their conspiracy of silence, a sign that the prisoner had gained the spirit to rebel, a warning that his guards should be more careful—

Another stupid thought. Banichi and Jago were the ones he wanted near him, and Tano had said it, his personal needs could only hinder whatever investigation Banichi was pursuing out there. He didn't *need* to know on the same level that Banichi needed to be following that trail in the rain, needed to be asking questions among the staff, like how that person had gotten in or whether he had come with the bus or whether Banichi had somehow made a terrible mistake and it was just some poor, mistaken tourist out on the lawn for a special camera angle.

The people on the bus would miss one of their own number, wouldn't they? Wouldn't one or the other busloads be asking why a seat was vacant, or who that had been, or had it all been machimi, just an actor, all along, an entertainment for their edification? Wasn't it historic, and educational, here at Malguri, where fatal accidents happened on the walks?

Djinana and Maigi were quick to answer his summons, and hastened him out of Tano's care and into the drawing room in front of the fire—peeling him out of his damp coat as they went and asking him how breakfast had gone with the dowager . . . as if no tourists had come in, as if nothing was going on out there, with any possible relevancy to anyone's life—

Where was Algini? he suddenly wondered. He hadn't seen Tano's partner since yesterday, and someone was dead out there. He hadn't *seen* Algini last night, just shadows passing through his room. He hadn't seen Algini maybe since the day before . . . what with the incident with the tea, he'd lost his sense of time since he'd left Shejidan.

Tano hadn't looked worried. But atevi didn't always express things with their faces. Didn't always express what they felt, if they felt, and you didn't know . . .

"Start the heater," Maigi said to Djinana, and flung a lap-robe about him. "Nadi, please sit down and stay warm. I'll help you with the boots."

He eased down into the chair in front of the fire, while Maigi tugged the boots off. His hands were like ice. His feet were chilled, for no good reason at all. "Someone was shot outside," he said in a sudden reckless mood, challenging Maigi's silence on the matter. "Do you know that?"

"I'm sure everything's taken care of." Maigi knelt on the carpet, warming his right foot with vigorous rubbing. "They're very good."

Banichi and Jago, Maigi seemed to mean. Very good. A man was dead. Maybe it was over, and he could go back tomorrow, where his computer would work and his mail would come.

With the electricity still out, and tourists coming and going, and the dowager exposing all of them to danger on a morning ride?

Why *hadn't* Banichi interposed some warning, if Banichi had any warning there was someone loose on the grounds, and why *hadn't* Banichi's warning gotten to him about the tourists?

Or hadn't Jago said something to him, yesterday—something about a tour, —but he hadn't remembered, dammit, he'd been thinking about the other mess he'd gotten himself into, and it hadn't stuck in his mind.

So it wasn't their fault. Somebody had been chasing him, and he had walked in among the tourists, where someone else could have gotten shot—if his guards hadn't, in the considerations of finesse, somehow protected him by being there.

He felt cold. Maigi tucked him into the chair with the robe and brought in hot tea. He sat with his robe-wrapped feet propped in front of the fire, while the thunder boomed outside the window and the rain whipped at the glass, a level above the walls. The window faced the straight open sweep off the lake. It sounded like gravel pelting the glass. Or hail. Which made him wonder how the windows withstood it: whether they were somehow reinforced—and whether they were, considering the wall out there, and the chance of someone climbing it, also bulletproof.

Jago had wanted him clear of it, last night. Algini had

disappeared, since before last night. The power had failed.

He sat there and kept replaying the morning in his head, the breakfast, the ride, Ilisidi and Cenedi, and the tourists and Tano, most of all the happy faces and the hands waving at him from the windows of the buses, as if everything was television, everything was machimi. He'd made a slight inroad into the country, met people he'd convinced not to be afraid of him, like the kids, like the old couple, and someone got shot right in front of them.

He'd fired a gun, he'd learned he *would* shoot to kill, for fear, for—he was discovering—for a terrible, terrible anger he had, an anger that was still shaking him—an anger he hadn't known he had, didn't know where it had started, or what it wanted to do, or whether it was directed at himself, or atevi, or any specific situation.

It hadn't been a false alarm last night—or it was, Barb would say, one hell of a coincidence. Maybe Banichi had thought last night he was safe, and whoever it was had simply gotten that far within Banichi's guard. Maybe they'd been tracking the assassin all along, and let him go off with Ilisidi this morning in the hope he'd draw the assassin out of cover.

Too much television, Banichi had said, that night with the smell of gunpowder in his room, and rain on the terrace. Too many machimi plays.

Too much fear in children's faces. Too many pointing fingers.

He wanted his mail, dammit, he wanted just the catalogs, the pictures to look at. But they weren't going to bring it.

Hanks might have missed him by now, tried to call his office and not gotten through.

On vacation with Tabini, they'd say. Hanks might know better. They monitored atevi transmissions. But they wouldn't challenge the Bu-javid on the point. They'd go on monitoring, once they were alert to trouble, trying to find him—and blame him for not doing his job. Hanks would start packing to assume his post. Hanks always had resented his winning it over her.

And Tabini would detest Hanks. He could tell the Commission that, if they didn't think it self-serving, and part of the feud between him and Hanks.

But if he was so damned good at predicting Tabini—or reading situations—he couldn't prove it from where he sat now. He hadn't made the vital call, he hadn't put Mospheira alert to the situation—

God, that was stupid. He had the willies over some misguided lunatic and now he saw the Treaty collapsing, as if atevi had been waiting all these centuries only to resume the War, hiding a missile program they'd built on their own, launching warheads at Mospheira.

It was as stupid as atevi with their planet-skimming satellites shooting death rays. Relations between Mospheira and Shejidan *had* bad periods. Tabini's administration was the least secretive, the easiest to deal with of all the administrations they'd ever dealt with.

"Death rays," Tabini would say, and laugh, invite him to supper and a private drink of the vice humans and atevi held in common. Laugh, Tabini would say. Bren, there are fools on Mospheira and fools in the Bu-javid. Don't take them seriously.

Steady hand, Bren-ji, like pointing the finger, there's no difference.

Good shot, *good* shot, Bren. . . .

Rain . . . pelted the window. Washed evidence away. Buses rolled away down the road, the tourists laughed, amazed and amused by their encounter.

They hadn't hated him. They'd wanted photographs to prove his existence to their neighbors . . .

"Nadi," Djinana said, from the doorway. "Your bathwater's ready."

He gathered the fortitude to move, tucked his robe about him and went with Djinana through the bedroom, through the hall and the clammy accommodation, into the overheated air of the bath, where he could shed the blanket and the rest of his clothes, to sink neck-deep into warm, steamy water.

Clouds rose around him. The water invaded the aches he wouldn't admit to. He could lie and soak and stare stupidly at the ancient stonework around him—ask himself important questions such as why the tub didn't fall through the floor, when the whole rest of the second floor was wood.

Or things like . . . why hadn't the two staffs advised each other about the alarm last night, and why had Cenedi let them go out there?

They'd talked about cannon, and ancient wars.

Everything blurred. The stones, the precariousness, the age, the heat, the threat to his life. The storm noise didn't get here. There was just the occasional shock of thunder through the stones, like ancient cannon shots.

And everyone saying, It's all right, nand' paidhi, it's nothing for you to worry about, nand' paidhi.

He heard footsteps somewhere outside. He heard voices that quickly died away.

Banichi coming back, maybe. Or Jago or Tano. Even Algini, if he was alive and well. Nothing in the house seemed to be an emergency. In the failure of higher technology, the methane burner worked.

The paidhi was used to having his welfare completely in others' hands. There was nothing he could do. There was nowhere he could go.

He lay still in the water, wiggling his toes, which were cramped and sore from the boots, and ankles which were stiffening from the stress of staying on the mecheita's back. He must have clenched his legs all the way. He sat there soaking away the aches until the water began to cool and finally climbed out and toweled himself dry—Djinana would gladly help him, but he had never had that habit with his own servants, let alone with strangers. Let alone here.

So he put on the dressing-robe Djinana had laid out, and went back to the study to sit in front of his own safe fire, read his book and wait for information, or release, or hell to freeze over, whichever came first.

Maybe they'd caught the assassin alive. Maybe they were asking questions and getting answers. Maybe Banichi would even tell him if that was the case—

Or maybe not.

"When will we have power?" he asked Djinana, when Djinana came to ask if the paidhi wanted anything else. "Do they give any estimate?"

"Jago said something about ordering a new transformer," Djinana said, "by train from Raigan. Something blew out in the power station between here and Maidingi. I don't know what. The paidhi probably understands the systems far better than I do."

He did. He hadn't realized there was a secondary station. Nobody had said there was—only the news that a quarter of Maidingi was waiting on the same repair. It was logical a power station should attract lightning, but it wasn't reasonable that no one within a hundred miles could bring power back to a major section of a township without parts freighted in.

"This isn't a poor province. This has to happen from time to time. Does it happen every summer?"

"Oh, sometimes," Djinana said. "Twice last."

"Does it happen assassins get in? Does *that* happen?"

"Please be assured not, nand' paidhi. And it's all right now."

"Is he dead? Do they know who he was?"

"I don't know, nand' paidhi. They haven't told us. I'm sure they're trying to find out. Don't worry about such things."

"I think it's natural I worry about such things," he muttered, looking at his book. And it wasn't fair to take his frustration out on Djinana and Maigi, who only worked here, and who would take Malguri's reputation very personally. "I would like tea, Djinana, thank you."

"With sandwiches?"

"I think not, Djinana, thank you, no. I'll sit here and read."

There were ghost ships on the lake. One was a passenger ship that still made port on midwinter nights, once at Maidingi port itself, right under the lights, and tried to take aboard the unwary and the deservedly damned, but only a judge-magistrate had gone aboard, a hundred years ago, and it had never made port again.

There was a fishing boat which sometimes appeared in storms—once, not twenty years ago, it had appeared to the crew of a stranded net-fisher that was taking on water and sinking. All but two had gone aboard, the captain and his son electing to stay with their crippled trawler. The fishing boat, which everyone had remarked to be old and dilapidated, had sailed away with the crew, never to be seen again.

Everything in the legends seemed to depend on misplaced trust, though atevi didn't quite have the word for it: ghosts lost all power if the victims didn't believe what they saw, or if they knew things were too good to be true, and refused to deceive themselves.

Banichi still hadn't come back. Maigi and Djinana came asking what he wanted for dinner, and recommended a game course, a sort of elusive, cold-blooded creature he didn't find appetizing, though he knew his servants thought it a delicacy. He asked for shellfish, instead, and Maigi thought that easy, though, Djinana said, the molluscs might not be the best this time of year: they would send down to town and they might have them, but it might be two or three hours or so before they could present them.

"Waiting won't matter," he said, and added, "they might lay in some more for lunch tomorrow."

"There's no ice," Djinana said apologetically.

"Perhaps in town."

"One could find out, nadi. But a great deal of the town

is without power, and most houses will buy it up for their own stock. We'll inquire. . ."

"No, no, nadi, please." He survived on shellfish, in seasons of desperation. "Others doubtless need the ice. And if they can't preserve it—please, take no chances. If the household could possibly arrange to find me fruited toast and tea, that would do quite well. I've no real appetite this evening."

"Nadi, you must have more than toast and tea. You missed lunch."

"Djinana-nadi, I must confess, I find the season's dish very strong . . . a difference in perceptions. We're quite sensitive to alkaloids. There may be some somewhere in the preparations, and it's absolutely essential I avoid them. If there were any *kabiu* choice of fruit or vegetables . . . The dowager-aiji had very fine breakfast rolls, which I very much favor."

"I'll most certainly tell the cook. And—" Djinana had a most conspiratorial look. "I do think there's last month's smoked joint left. It's certainly not un-*kabiu,* if it's left over. And we always put by several."

Preserved meat. Out of season. God save them.

"We never know how many guests," Djinana said, quite straight-faced. "We'd hate to run short."

"Djinana-nadi, you've saved my life."

Djinana was highly amused, very pleased with their solution, and bowed twice before leaving.

Whereupon, for the rest of the afternoon, he went back to his ghost ships, and his headless captains of trawlers that plied Malguri shores during storms. A bell was said to ring in the advent of disasters.

Instead there was an opening of the door, a squishing of wet boots across the drawing room, and a very wet and very tired-looking Banichi, who walked into the study, and said, "I'll join you for dinner, nadi."

He snapped his book shut, and thought of saying that most people waited to be asked, that he hadn't had any courtesy and that he was getting damned tired of being walked past, ignored, talked down to and treated in general like a wayward child.

"Delighted to have company," he said, and persuaded himself he really was glad to have someone to talk to. "Tell Djinana to set another place. —Is Jago coming?"

"Jago's on her way to Shejidan." Banichi's voice floated back to him from the bedroom, as he headed for the servants' quarters and the bath. "She'll be back tomorrow."

He didn't even ask why. He didn't ask why a plane bothered to take off in the middle of a thunderstorm, the second since noon, when it was presumably the aiji's plane, and could observe any schedule it liked. Banichi disappeared into the back hall, and after a while he heard water running in the bath. The boiler must still be up. Banichi didn't have to wait for *his* bath.

As for himself, he went back to his ghost bells and his headless victims, and the shiploads of sailors lost to the notorious luck of Maidingi, which always fed on the misfortune of others when an aiji was resident in Malguri.

That was what the book said; and atevi, who believed in no omnipotent gods, who saw the universe and its quasi god-forces as ruled by *baji* and *naji*, believed at least that *naji* could flow through one person to the next—or they had believed so, before they became modern and cynical and enlightened, and realized that superior firepower could redistribute luck to entirely undeserving people.

He had sat about in the dressing-robe all afternoon, developing sore spots in very private areas. He declined to move, much less to dress for dinner, deciding that if Banichi had invited himself, Banichi could certainly tolerate his informality.

Banichi himself showed up in the study merely in black shirt, boots, and trousers, somewhat more formal, but only just, without a coat, and with his braid dripping wet down his back. "Paidhi-ji," Banichi said, bowing, and, "Have a drink," Bren said, since he was indulging, cautiously, in a before-dinner drink from his own stock, which he knew was safe. He did have a flask of Dimagi, which he couldn't drink without a headache, and eventual more serious effects, very excellent Dimagi, he supposed, since Tabini had given it to him, and he poured a generous glass of that for Banichi.

"Nadi," Banichi said, taking the glass with a sigh, and invited himself to sit by the fire in the chair angled opposite to his.

"So?" The liquor stung his cut lip. "A man's dead. Was he the same one who invaded my bedroom?"

"We can't be sure," Banichi said.

"No strayed tourist."

"No tourist at all. Professional. We know who he is."

"And still no filing?"

"A very disturbing aspect of this business. This man was licensed. He had everything to lose by doing what he did. He'll be stricken from the rolls, he'll be denied benefits of the profession, his instructors will be disgraced. These are no small matters."

"Then I feel sorry for his instructors," Bren said.

"So do I, nadi. They were mine."

Dead stop, on that point. Banichi—and this unknown man—had a link of some kind? Fellow students?

"You know him?"

"We met frequently, socially."

"In Shejidan?"

"A son of distinguished family." Banichi took a sip and stared into the fire. "Jago is escorting the remains and the report to the Guild."

Not a good day, Bren decided, having lost all appetite for supper. Banichi regarded him with a flat, dark stare that he couldn't read—not Banichi's opinion, nor what obligation Banichi had relative to Tabini versus his Guild or this man, nor where the *man'chi* lay, now.

"I'm very sorry," was all he could think to say.

"You have a right to retaliate."

"I don't want to retaliate. I never wanted this quarrel, Banichi."

"They have one now."

"With you?" He grew desperate. His stomach was upset. His teeth ached. Sitting was painful. "Banichi, I don't want you or Jago hurt. I don't want anybody killed."

"But they do, nadi. That's abundantly clear. A professional agreed with them enough to disregard Guild law—for *man'chi,* nadi. That's what we have to trace—to whom was his *man'chi?* That's all that could motivate him."

"And if yours is to Tabini?"

Banichi hesitated in his answer. Then, somberly: "That makes them highly unwise."

"Can't we arrest them? They've broken the *law,* Banichi. Don't we have some recourse to stop this through the courts?"

"That," Banichi said, "would be very dangerous."

Because it wouldn't restrain them. He understood that. It couldn't legally stop them until there *was* a judgment in his favor.

"All they need claim is affront," Banichi said, "or business interests. And how can you defend anything? No one understands your associations. The court hardly has a means to find them out."

"And my word is worth nothing? My *man'chi* is to Tabini, the same as yours. They have to know that."

"But they don't know that," Banichi said. "Even *I* don't know that absolutely, nadi. I know only what you tell me."

He felt quite cold, quite isolated. And angry. "I'm not a liar. I am *not* a liar, Banichi. I didn't contest with the best my people have for fifteen years to come here to lie to you."

"For fifteen years."

"To be sent to Shejidan. To have the place I have. To interpret to atevi. I don't lie, Banichi!"

Banichi looked at him a long, silent moment. "Never? I thought that *was* the paidhi's job."

"Not in this."

"How selective dare we be? When do you lie?"

"Just find out who hired him."

"No contract could compel his action."

"What could?"

Banichi didn't answer that question. Banichi only stared into the fire.

"What *could*, Banichi?"

"We don't know a dead man's thoughts. I could only wish Cenedi weren't so accurate."

"Cenedi shot him." So Cenedi and Ilisidi's loyalties at least were accounted for. He was relieved.

But Banichi didn't seem wholly pleased with Cenedi. Or, at least, with the outcome. Banichi took a sip of the drink warming in his hands and never looked away from the fire.

"But you're worried," Bren said.

"I emphatically disapprove these delivery vehicles. This is an unwarrantable risk. The tourists at least have a person counting heads."

"You think that's how he got in?"

"Very possible."

"They're not going to continue the tours. Are they?"

"People have had their reservations for months. They'd be quite unhappy."

Sometimes he ran straight up against atevi mindset in ways he didn't understand. Or expect.

"Those people were in danger, Banichi!"

"Not from him or us."

Finesse. *Biichi-ji.*

"There were children in that crowd. They saw a man shot."

Banichi looked at him as if waiting for the concluding statement that would make sense. As if they had totally left the subject.

"It's not right, Banichi. They thought it was a machimi! They thought it was television!"

"Then they were hardly offended. Were they?"

Before he could follow *that* line of reasoning, Djinana and Maigi arrived down the inner hall with the dinner cart.

With a selection of dishes, the seasonal and slices from the leftover joint. Banichi's eyes brightened at the offering, as they seated themselves in the dining room and the covers came off the dishes. State of mourning or murderous intent, Banichi had no hesitation in loading his plate, and no diminution of appetite.

The cook had provided a selection of prepared fruits, very artistically arranged. That appealed. One could have exempted the prepared head of the unseasonal game as a cap for the stewpot, but Banichi lifted it by the ears and set it delicately aside, gratefully out of view behind the stewpot. Other dead animals stared down from the walls.

"This is excellent," Banichi said.

Bren poked at the sliced meat. His nerves were jangled. The dining chair hurt. He took up his knife and cut a bite, trying to put ghost stories and assassins out of his mind. He found the first taste excellent, and helped himself to the sliced meat and a good deal of the spicy sauce he enjoyed over the vegetables.

"Is there," he asked, in the lull eating made, "possibly any word on my mail? I know you've had your hands full, but—"

"I have, as you quaintly express it, had my hands full. Perhaps Jago will remember to check the post."

"You could call her." Temper flared up. Or a sense of muddled desperation. "Has *anyone* explained to my office where I am, or why?"

"I frankly don't know that, paidhi-ji."

"I want you to convey a message to them. I want you to patch me through on your communications. I know you can do that, from the security station."

"Not without clearance. It's a public move, if the

paidhi takes to our security channels. You understand the policy statement that would make, absolute encouragement to your detractors and Tabini's."

"What happened to security?"

"Courier is still far better. Far better, nadi. Prepare your statement. I'll send it the next time one of us carries a report."

Banichi didn't refuse him. Banichi didn't say no. But it kept coming out to procrastination, I forgot, and, There's a reason.

He ate the rest of the meat course in silence, favoring his sore mouth.

And questions still nagged him.

"*Was* it an accident, the power outage?"

"Most probably. To put a quarter of the homes in Maidingi township in the dark? Hardly the Guild's style."

"But you knew it last night. You *knew* someone was loose on the grounds."

"I didn't know. I suspected it. We had a perimeter alarm."

Did we? he thought bitterly. And asked, instead: "*Where* is Algini?"

"He'll return with Jago."

"Did he leave with Jago?"

"He took the commercial flight. Yesterday."

"Carrying a report?"

"Yes."

"For *what?* Forgive my frankness, Banichi-ji, but I don't believe there's any possible investigation to be done—to find the precise agency at work here, yes, but I don't for a moment believe Tabini doesn't know exactly what's wrong and who's behind it. I don't believe you don't know. I don't believe you didn't know where I was this morning."

"Behind the ridge, mostly, for quite a while. I noticed your limping."

Soreness didn't help his mood. "You might have warned me."

"Regarding what? That Ilisidi would go riding? She often does."

"Dammit, if you'd told me there was the chance of a sniper, if you'd told me we'd be leaving the house, I might have come up with a reasonable objection."

"You had a reasonable objection. You might have pleaded your recent indisposition. I doubt they would have carried you to the stables."

"You didn't tell me there was a danger!"

"There's a constant danger, nadi."

"Don't shove me off, dammit. You let me go out there. It's harder to find an excuse for tomorrow, when I'm also committed to go. And am I safe *then?* I don't always understand your sense of priorities, Banichi, and in this, I truly confess I don't."

"The tea was Ilisidi's personal opportunity. And Cenedi was with us last night, during the search. Cenedi would have taken me if he'd intended to. I made that test."

It took a moment for that to sink in. "You mean you gave Cenedi a chance to kill you?"

"When you *will* make promises to strangers without consulting me, paidhi-ji, you do make my job more difficult. Jago was advised of the situation. Possibly Cenedi knew it, and knew that he had Jago yet to deal with, but Cenedi is *not* contracted against you, I made amply certain of that. And I was between you and the estate at all times this morning."

"Banichi, I apologize. Profoundly."

Banichi shrugged. "Ilisidi is an old and clever woman. What did you talk about? The weather? Tabini?"

"Breakfast. Not breaking my neck. A mecheita called Babs—"

"Babsidi." It meant 'lethal.' "And nothing else?"

He desperately tried to remember. "How it was her land. What plants grow here. Dragonettes."

"And?"

"Nothing. Nothing of consequence. Cenedi talked about the ruin up there, and the cannon on the front lawn.

—She ran me up a hill, I cut my lip . . . after that they were polite to me. And the *tourists* were polite to me. I gave them ribbons and signed their cards and we talked about families and where they came from. —Was either one a disaster, Banichi-ji—before some fool tried to cross the lawn? Advise me. I *am* asking for advice."

Another of Banichi's long, sober stares. Banichi's eyes were the clearest, incredible yellow. Like glass. Just as expressive. "We're both professionals, paidhi-ji. You *are* quite good."

"You think I'm lying?"

"I mean that you're no more off duty than I am." Banichi lifted the flask and poured moderately for them both. "I have confidence in your professional instincts. Have confidence in mine."

It came down to the fruit, and a creme and liqueur sauce. A man could be seduced by that, if his stomach weren't uncertain from dinner conversation.

"If you're running courier," Bren said, when the atmosphere felt easier, "you can handle a written dispatch from me to my office on Mospheira."

"We might," Banichi said. "If Tabini approves."

"Any word about that solar unit I wanted?"

"I'm afraid they're prioritied, if they can find one. We've donated the generator we have. We have homes in the valley without power, elderly and ill persons—"

"Of course." He couldn't fault that answer. It was entirely reasonable. Everything was.

Confidence, Bren said to the creatures on the wall. Patience. Glass eyes stared back at him, some angry, some placidly stupid, having awaited their hunters with equanimity, one supposed.

Banichi said he had business to attend—reports to write. In longhand, one supposed.

Or not. Djinana came and took the dishes away, and lit the oil lamps, having blown out the candelabra in the dining room.

"Will you need anything more?" Djinana asked; and, "No," Bren said, thinking to himself that of individuals who didn't get regular hours or a fair explanation around this place, Djinana was chief. One wondered where Tano was—Tano, who was supposed to be his personal staff. While Algini was off in Shejidan. "I'm sure I won't. I'll read until bedtime."

"I'll lay out your night things," Djinana said.

"Thank you," he murmured, and picked up his book and took the chair by the fire, where, if he sat at an angle, with the lamps on the table beside him, the two light sources made reading at least moderately possible. Live flame flickered. He had discovered that primary good reason for light bulbs.

Djinana whisked the cart away with the dishes—the man never so much as rattled a glass when he worked. The candles were out in the dining room, leaving it a dark cavern. Elsewhere the fire cast horned and large-eared shadows about the room, and danced in the glass eyes of the beasts.

He heard Djinana open the armoire in the bedroom, and heard him go away again.

After that was a curious quiet about the place. No rain, no thunder, nothing but the crackle of the fire. He read, he turned pages—which sounded amazingly loud, on a rare romance in the histories, no one bent on feud, no inter-clan struggles, no dramatic leaps from Malguri tower, and not a drowning to be had, just a romantic couple who met and courted at Malguri, who happened to be the aijiin of two neighboring provinces, and who had a plethora of talented children.

Pleasant thought, that someone who slept in these rooms hadn't come to a bad end; interesting, to have a notion of romantic goings-on, the gifts of flowers, the long and tender relationship of two people who, being heads of state, never quite had a domicile except Malguri, in the fall. It was a side of themselves atevi didn't show to the paidhi—unless one counted flirtations he never

knew whether he should take seriously. But that was how
it went, a number of small gifts, tied to each other's gates,
or sent by third parties. Atevi marriages didn't always
mean cohabitation. Often enough they didn't, except
when there were minor children in question—and sometimes then cohabitation lasted and sometimes it didn't.
What atevi *thought* or what atevi *felt* still eluded him
through the atevi language.

But he *liked* the aijiin of Malguri the way he'd *liked* the
old couple with the grandchildren, touring together, he
supposed, looking for adventures ... maybe not cohab-
iting: nothing guaranteed that.

And long as paidhiin had been on the continent, they
had discovered no graceful way to ask, through atevi ret-
icence to discuss their living arrangements, their ad-
dresses, their routines or their habits—it all fell under
'private business,' and no one else's.

He thought he might ask Jago. Jago at least found
amusement in his rude questions. And Jago was amazingly well read. She might even know the historic couple.

He *missed* Jago. He wouldn't have had a near-fight
with Banichi if Jago had been here. He didn't know why
Banichi had insisted on inviting himself to supper, if he
had to spend it in a surly mood.

Something hadn't gone well, perhaps.

In a day which had included Cenedi shooting a man
and that man turning out to be one Banichi knew—
damned right something hadn't gone right today, and
Banichi had every reason to be in a rotten state of mind.
That atevi *didn't* show it and habitually understated the
case didn't mean Banichi wasn't upset—and didn't mean
Banichi might not himself wish Jago were here. He supposed Banichi hadn't had a good time himself, having a
surly human displaying an emotional load an atevi
twelve-year-old wouldn't own to.

He supposed he even owed Banichi an apology.

Not that he wanted to give one. Because he understood
didn't mean he was reconciled, and he wished twice over

that Jago hadn't gone to Shejidan today, Jago being just slightly the younger, a little more reticent, as he read her now, even shy, but just slightly more forthcoming than Banichi once she decided to talk, whether Jago was more so by nature or because Tabini's *man'chi* didn't lie lightly on anyone's shoulders, least of all Banichi's.

His eyes stung with reading in the flickering light; keeping the fire lively enough to cast light to the chair made the fireside uncomfortably warm, and the oil lamps made the air thick. He found himself with a mild headache, and got up and walked, quietly, so as not to disturb the staff, into the cooler part of the room—too restless to sleep, yet.

He missed his late-night news. He missed being able to call Barb, or even, God help him, Hanks, and say the things he dared say over lines he knew were bugged. He was all but down to talking to himself, just to hear the sound of human language in the silence, to get away, however briefly, from immersion in atevi thoughts and atevi reasoning.

A motor started, somewhere. He stopped still and listened, decided someone was leaving the courtyard and going down to the town, or somewhere in between, and who *that* was, he had a fair notion.

Damn, he thought, and went to the window, but one couldn't see the courtyard from there because of the sideways jut of the front hall. A pin held the latch of the side window panels, and he pulled that to see if he could tell whether the car was going down the main road or off into the hills, or whether he was about to trigger a nonhistorical security alarm by opening the latch.

Only the airline transport van, hell. Malguri had a van of its own. Food and passengers came up the road. They could have gotten him from the airport.

But Banichi had thought otherwise, perhaps. Perhaps he wanted to sound things out before relying on Cenedi.

Perhaps he still had his doubts.

The sound of the motor went up and around the walls.

He couldn't tell. But the night air coming in was crisp and cold after the stuffiness of the room. He drew in a great breath and a second one.

First night he had been here that it hadn't been raining, the first hour of full dark, and the sky above the lake and the mountains to the east were so clear and black and cold one could see Maudette aloft, faintly red, and Gabriel's almost invisible companion, a real test of eyesight, on Mospheira.

The night air smelled wonderful, loaded with wildflowers, he supposed; and he hadn't realized how he'd missed the garden outside his room, or how pent up he'd felt.

He'd been able, on clear nights on Mt. Allan Thomas, to see the station just around sunset or sunrise. He didn't keep up with its schedule the way he had in his youth, when Toby and he had used to go hiking in the hills, when they'd used to tell stories about the Landing, and imagine—it was embarrassing, nowadays—that there were atevi guerrillas hiding in the high hills. They had used to have imaginary wars up there, shooting atevi by the hundreds, being shot at by fictitious atevi villains, about as good as the atevi machimi about secret human guerrillas supported by egomaniacs secretly concealing their base aboard the station . . . the Foreign Star, as atevi had called it in those long past and warlike days.

At least they'd achieved a common mythology, a common past, a common set of heroes and villains—and which was which only depending on point of view.

He never had mentioned to Tabini that his father was Polanski's descendant several illegitimate generations down the line, the Polanski who'd generaled the standoff on Half Moon Beach, the one that had kept atevi reinforcements off Mospheira.

Nothing Polanski's remote descendant had anything to do with—nothing, in his present job, that he wanted to admit to.

One made progress as one could. He wished atevi children didn't see humans as shadow-players and madmen;

he wished human children didn't play at shooting atevi in the woods. The idea came to him of making that a major theme in his winter speech to the assembly ... but he didn't know how one got at all the film and all the television on both sides which kept reinforcing it all.

But not totally smart, with realities as they were, to be standing with the fire at his back. Jago had pulled him away from this very window last night ... a danger from the windows or the roof of the other wing seemed stupid.

But anybody could have a boat on the lake, he supposed, though not close enough to give an assassin a good target. Anybody could land on Malguri's shore, give or take the walls and the cliffs below the walls, which were formidable.

He stepped back and began to close the window.

Lights flashed on all about him. An alarm began to ring as he blinked in the glare of electric light, and slammed the window shut and latched it, heart beating in utter startlement, with the sound of bare feet crossing the wooden floor of the next room.

Tano showed up, stark naked, gun in hand, Djinana close behind him, and Maigi after that, Maigi dripping wet and wrapped in a towel, with the thump of people running out in the halls, everywhere in Malguri, the alarm still sounding.

"Did you open a window?" Tano asked.

"Nadiin, I did, I'm sorry."

His rescuers drew a collective breath as the latch rattled in the next room, and Tano dismissed Djinana in that direction with a wave of his hand.

"Nadi, they've brought us on-line again," Tano said. "Your security had rather you not open the windows, for your own protection. Particularly at night."

Djinana had let someone in from the outside hall. Cenedi showed up with Djinana and a couple of the dowager's guard, to hear Tano say, "The paidhi opened the window, nadi."

"Nand' paidhi," Cenedi said. "Please, hereafter, don't."

"I beg your pardons," he said. The alarm was still going, jangling his nerves. "Can someone please turn off the alarm?"

Cenedi gave the orders. It still took time to sort out, and the oil lamps all had to be put out before he could get his rooms clear of staff.

He sank down on the side of his bed after the clatter and the commotion had died, after the doors and windows were shut, asking himself where Banichi had been and what black thoughts the dowager must be having about him at the moment.

Damned sloppy, having an alarm system down with the power. It wasn't Banichi's style. He didn't think it was Cenedi's. He didn't think he'd seen everything that guarded Malguri. Solar-batteried security, he'd bet on it. They had the technology.

It didn't keep the paidhi from waking the house and looking like a fool.

It didn't make Ilisidi happier with him. He could bet on that, too.

VIII

"A noisy night," Ilisidi said, pouring her own tea—the smell of it drifted with the steam, across the table, and Bren's stomach went queasy.

"I'm extremely sorry," he said, "and embarrassed, aiji-mai."

Ilisidi grinned, positively grinned, and added sugar.

It was little barbs all during breakfast. Ilisidi was in an excellent humor. She wolfed down four fish, a bowl of cereal and two cakes with sweet oil, while he stayed to the cereal and the breakfast rolls, thinking that, considering the pain he was in sitting on a hard chair this morning, he would almost rather drink Ilisidi's tea than get onto Nokhada's back again.

But it was downstairs, Ilisidi reveling in the stiff breeze blowing in off the lake, a breeze that tore at coat-skirts and knifed right through sweaters when one passed out of the sunlight and into the stable court.

Nokhada at least was willing to get down for him this morning, and this time, at least, he was ready for the snap of Nokhada's rising before he was quite astride.

It hurt. God, it hurt. Not exactly the kind of pain a man could admit to, or beg off from. He only hoped for early numbness, and told himself his human ancestors had been riders, and somehow continued the species.

He brought a quick stop to Nokhada's milling about, determined to have the final word on their course this morning—which lasted until Ilisidi moved Babs out and Nokhada jostled Cenedi's mecheita for position at Babs' tail in a sudden dash out onto the road.

Straight out. Ilisidi and Babs vanished over the cliff, a stride or two before Nokhada won out over Cenedi's mount and took the same downward plunge.

Onto what thank God was trail and not empty air.

He didn't yell, and didn't object, though his legs did, and for a moment the pain was acute, in a dozen jolting strides down a dusty slot of a trail that began above the point where Nokhada had thrown the fit yesterday about the rein.

If they had gone off then, they would *not* have fallen, damn the creature. Gone an embarrassing long distance down to a second terrace above the lake, indeed they would, but there was such a terrace, whether or not, yesterday, at the start of the ride, he might have had the ability to stay on Nokhada's back.

And he found it equally interesting that, with the plunge over the cliff available for the novice fool, Ilisidi had taken them straight up the mountain yesterday, however rough the course. A second chance missed, then. So maybe the tea was, after all, an accident.

Although, given there had been an intruder on the grounds yesterday, maybe getting them over the ridge or above line-of-sight from the fortress had been a priority.

And given Banichi's comment about having had them under direct surveillance ...

"Why didn't you tell me yesterday that there was a possibility of someone out there?" he asked Cenedi, with the rest of the dowager's guard trailing behind. "You knew we were in danger yesterday. Banichi informed you."

"The outriders," Cenedi said, "were well alert. And Banichi was never far."

"Nadi, a risk to the dowager? In all respect, is that reasonable?"

"With Tabini's man?" Cenedi's face had things in common with Banichi's. Just as expressive. "No. It wasn't a risk."

Not a risk? A compliment to Banichi, perhaps, but damned well a risk, under any human interpretation of the word, unless, the thought that had jogged his attention last night, there were more security systems about than either Banichi or Cenedi was going to own to. He rode by Cenedi in thinking silence, with the waves lapping the rocks below. The sky was blue. The waters danced. A dragonette soared past Nokhada's face and made her jump, a single heart-stopping moment, close to the edge.

"Damn!" he said, and he and Nokhada had a silent war for a moment, at which Cenedi maintained complete lack of expression, and complete control of his mecheita.

Ilisidi rode ahead of them, oblivious, seemingly, to all of it. When he tilted his head back and looked up he couldn't see the fortress walls at all, just the bowed face of the rocks and, behind them, the very edge of the modern wall that divided off the paved court from the trail. Ahead, the trail wound higher on the mountain, until they came to a promontory with a dizzying view, where Ilisidi stopped and let Babs stand, and where, when he arrived, he sat doing the same with Nokhada, telling himself that if Babs didn't fling himself over the cliff, Nokhada wouldn't, and he needn't worry.

"Glorious day," Ilisidi said.

"An unforgettable view," he said, and thought that he never *would* forget it, the chanciness of their height, the power of the creature under him, the startling panorama of the lake spread out around them as far as the eye could see. Skiing with Toby, he had had such sights, but never one fraught with atevi significances, never one once foreign and now freighted with names, and identity, and history. The Bu-javid—with its pressures, its schedules, its crowds of political favor-seekers—had no such views, no such absolute, breath-taking moments as Malguri offered ... between hours, as yesterday, of cloistered, stifling silence, headaches from oil-burning lamps, cold, dark spots in the corners of cavernous halls and knees blistered from proximity to a warming fire.

Not to mention the plumbing.

But it had its charm. It *had* its moments, it had the incredible texture of life that didn't measure by straight lines and standardized measures, that didn't go by streets and straight edges, with people living stacked up on top of each other, and lights blotting out the stars at night. Here, one could hear the wind and the waves, one could find endless variety in weathered stones and pebbles and there was no schedule but the inescapable fact that riding out and riding back were the same distance. . . .

Ilisidi talked about the trading ships and the fishermen, while the high, thin trail of a jet passed above Malguri on its way east, across the continental divide, across the barrier that had held two atevi civilizations from meeting for thousands of years—a matter of four, five hours, now, that easy. But Ilisidi talked about crossings of Maidingi that took days, and involved separate aijiin's territory.

"In those days," Ilisidi said, "one proceeded very carefully into the territory of foreign aijiin."

Not without a point. Again.

"But we've learned so much more, nand' dowager."

"More than what?"

"That walling others out equally walls us in, nand' dowager."

"Hah," Ilisidi declared, and with a move he never saw, spun Babs about and lit out along the hill, scattering stones.

Nokhada followed. All of them had to. And it hurt, God, it hurt when they struck the downhill to the lake. Ahead of them, Ilisidi, with her white-shot braid flying—no ribbon of rank, no adornment, just a red and black coat, and Babsidi's sleek black rump, tail switching for nothing more than excess energy—nothing more in Ilisidi's mind, perhaps, than the free space in front of her.

Catching up was Nokhada's idea; but with the rest of the guard behind, and Cenedi beside, there was nothing to do but follow.

At another time they stopped, on the narrow half-moon of a sandy beach, where the lake curved in, and a man thinking of assassins could only say to himself that there were places on the shore where a boat could land and reach Malguri.

But standing while the mecheiti caught their breaths, Ilisidi talked about the lake, its depth, its denizens—its ghosts. "When I was a child," she said, "a wreck washed up on the south shore, just the bow of it, but they thought it might be from a treasure ship that sank four hundred years ago. And divers went out for it, all up and down this shore. They say they never found it. But a number of antiquities turned up in Malguri, and the servants were cleaning them in barrels in the stable court, about that time. My father sent the best pieces to the museum in Shejidan. And it probably cost him an estate. But most people in Maidingi province would have melted them for the gold."

"It's good he saved them."

"Why?"

"For the past," he said, wondering if he had misunderstood something else in atevi mindset. "To save it. Isn't that important?"

"Is it?" Ilisidi answered him with a question and left him none the wiser. She was off again up the hill, and he forgot all his philosophy, in favor of protecting what he feared might have progressed to blisters. Damn the woman, he thought, and thought that if he pulled up and lagged behind as long as he could hold Nokhada's instincts in check, the dowager might take that for a surrender and slow down, but *damned* if he would, *damned* if he would cry help or halt. Ilisidi would dismiss him from her company then, probably lose all interest in him, and he could lie about in a warm bath, reading ghost stories until his would-be assassins flung themselves against the barriers Banichi had doubtless set up, and killed themselves, and he could go home to air-conditioning, the morning news, and tea he could trust. From moment to moment it seemed like the only escape.

But he kept Ilisidi's pace. Atevi called it *na'itada*. Barb called it being a damned fool. He had never spent so long an hour as it took to get home again, an hour in which he told himself repeatedly he had rather fall off the mountain and be done.

Finally the gates of the stable court were in front of them, then behind them, with the mecheiti anxious for stables and grain. He managed to get Nokhada to drop a shoulder, and climbed down off Nokhada's towering height onto legs he wasn't sure would bear his weight.

"A hot bath," Ilisidi called out to him. "I'll send you some herbs, nand' paidhi. I'll see you in the morning!"

He managed to bow, and, among Ilisidi's entourage, to walk up the stairs without conspicuously limping.

"The soreness goes," Cenedi said to him quietly, "in four or five days."

A hot bath was all he was thinking of, all the long way up to the front hall. A hot bath, for about an hour. A soft and motionless chair. Soaking and reading seemed an excellent way to spend the remainder of the day, sitting in the sun, minding his own business, evading aijiin and their athletic endeavors. He limped down the long hall and started the stairs up to his floor, at his own pace.

Quick footsteps crossed the stone floor below the stairs. He looked back in some concern for his safety in the halls and saw Jago coming toward the stairs, all energy and anxiousness. "Bren-ji," she called out to him. "Are you all right?"

The limp showed. His hair was flying loose from its braid and there was dust and fur and spit on his coat. "Fine, nadi-ji. Was it a good flight?"

"Long," she said, overtaking him in a handful of double steps a human would struggle to make. "Did you fall, Bren-ji? You *didn't* fall off . . ."

"No, just sore. Perfectly ordinary." He made a determined effort not to limp the rest of the way up the stairs, and went beside her down the hall . . . which was supposing she wanted the company of sweat and mecheita fur. Jago smelled of flowers, quite nicely so. He'd never noticed it before; and he was marginally embarrassed—not polite to sweat, the word had passed discreetly from paidhi to paidhi. Overheated humans smelled different, and different was not good with atevi, in matters of personal hygiene; the administration had pounded that concept into junior administrative heads. So he tried to keep as discreetly as possible apart from Jago, glad she was back, wishing he might have a chance for a bath before debriefing, and wishing most of all that she'd been here last night. "Where's Banichi? Do you know? I haven't seen him since yesterday."

"He was down at the airport half an hour ago," Jago said. "He was talking to some television people. I think they're coming up here."

"Why?"

"I don't know, nadi. They came in on the flight. It could have to do with the assassination attempt. They didn't say."

Not his business, he concluded. Banichi would handle it with his usual discretion, probably put them on the next flight out.

"Not any other trouble here?"

"Only with Banichi."

"How?"

"Just not happy with me. I seem to have done something or said something, nadi-ji, —I'm not even sure."

"It isn't a comfortable business," Jago said, "to report an associate to his disgrace. Give him room, nand' paidhi. Some things aren't within your office."

"I understand that," he said, telling himself he hadn't understood: he'd been unreasonably focussed on his own discomforts last night, to the exclusion of Banichi's own reasonable distress. It began to dawn on him that Banichi might have wanted things of him he just hadn't given, before they'd parted in discomfort with each other. "I think I was very rude last night, nadi. I shouldn't have been. I wasn't doing my job. I think he's right to be upset with me. I hope you can explain to him."

"You *have* no 'job' toward him, Bren-ji. Ours is toward you. And I much doubt he took offense. If he allowed you to see his distress, count it for a compliment to you."

Unusual notion. One part of his brain went ransacking memory, turning over old references. Another part went on vacation, wondering if it meant Banichi did after all *like* him.

And the sensible, workaday part of his brain told the other two parts to pay attention to business and quit expecting human responses out of atevi minds. Jago meant what Jago said, point, endit; Banichi let down his guard with him, Banichi was pissed about a dirty business, and neither Banichi nor Jago was suddenly, by being cooped up with a bored human, about to break out in human sentiment. It wasn't contagious, it wasn't transferable, and probably he frustrated hell out of Banichi, too, who'd just as busily sent him clues he hadn't picked up on. As a dinner date, he'd been a dismal substitute for Jago, who'd been off explaining to the Guild why somebody wanted to kill the paidhi; and probably by the end of the evening, Banichi had ideas of his own why that could be.

They reached the door. He had his key from his pocket, but Jago was first with hers, and let them into the receiving room.

"So glum," she said, looking back at him. "Why, nand' paidhi?"

"Last night. We were saying things—I wished I hadn't. I wish I'd said I was sorry. If you could convey to him that I am . . ."

"Said and did aren't even brothers," Jago said. She pulled the door to, pocketed her key and took the portfolio from under her arm. "This should cheer you. I brought your mail."

He'd given up. He'd accepted that it wasn't going to get through security; and Jago threw over all his suppositions about his situation in Malguri.

He took the bundle she handed him and sorted through it, not even troubling to sit down in his search for personal mail.

It was mostly catalogs, not nearly so many as he ordinarily got; three letters, but none from Mospheira—two from committee heads in Agriculture and Finance, and one with Tabini's official seal.

It *wasn't* all his mail, not, at least, his ordinary mail—nothing from Barb or his mother. No communication from his office, messages like, Where are you? Are you alive?

Jago surely knew what was missing. She had to know, she wasn't that inefficient. And what did he say about it? She stood there, waiting, probably in curiosity about Tabini's letter.

Or maybe knowing very well what was in it.

He began to be scared of the answers—scared of his own ignorance and his own failure to figure out what the silence around him was saying, or what of Tabini's signals he was supposed to have picked up.

He ran his thumbnail under the seal on Tabini's letter, hoping for rescue, *hoping* it held some sort of explanation that didn't add up to disaster.

Tabini's handwriting—was not the clearest hand he had ever dealt with. The usual declaration of titles. *I hope for your health,* it began, with Tabini's calligraphic flourish. *I hope for your enjoyment of Malguri's resources of sun and water.*

Thanks, Tabini, he thought sourly, thanks a lot. The rainy season, no less. He rested a sore backside against the table to read it, while Jago waited.

Something about television. *Television,* for God's sake. *... my intention by this interview to give people around the world an exposure to human thought and appearance far different than the machimi have presented. I feel this is a useful opportunity which should not be wasted, and have great confidence in your diplomacy, Bren. Please be as frank with these professionals as you would be with me, privately.*

"Nadi Jago. Do you know what's in this?"

"No, Bren-ji. Is there a problem?"

"Tabini's sent the television crew!"

"That would explain the people on the flight. I am surprised we weren't advised. Though I'm sure they have credentials."

Under the circumstances which have made advisable your isolation from the City and its contacts, I can think of no more effective counter to your enemy than the cultivation of increased public favor. I have spoken personally to the head of news and public awareness at the national network, and authorized a reputable and highly regarded news crew to meet with you at Malguri, for an interview which may, in my hopes and those of the esteemed lord Minister of Education, lead to monthly news conferences ...

"He wants me to do a monthly news program! Do you *know* about this?"

"I plead not, nadi-ji. I'm sure, however, if Tabini-aiji

has cleared these individuals to speak to you, they're very reputable people."

"Reputable people." He scanned the letter for more devastating news, found only *I know the weather in this season is not the best, but I hope that you have found pleasure in the library and accommodation with the esteemed aiji-dowager, to whom I hope you will convey my personal good wishes.*

"This is impossible. I have to talk to Tabini. —Jago, I need a phone. Now."

"I've no authorization, Bren-ji. There *isn't* a phone here, and I've no authorization to remove you from our—"

"The hell, Jago!"

"I've no authorization, Bren-ji."

"Does Banichi?"

"I doubt so, nadi-ji."

"Well, neither do I. I can't talk to these people."

Jago's frown grew anxious. "The paidhi tells me that Tabini-aiji has authorized these people. If Tabini-aiji has authorized this interview, the paidhi is surely aware that it would be a very great embarrassment to these people and their superior, extending even to the aiji's court. If the paidhi has any authorization in this letter to refuse this, I must ask to see this letter."

"It's not Tabini. I've no authorization from Mospheira to do any interview. I absolutely can't do this without contacting my office. I certainly can't do it on any half-hour notice. I need to contact my office. Immediately."

"Is not your *man'chi* to Tabini? Is this not what you said?"

God, *right* down the predictable and unarguable slot.

"My *man'chi* to Tabini doesn't exclude my arguing with him or my protecting my position of authority among my own people. It's my obligation to do that, nadi-ji. I have no force to use. It's all on your side. But my *man'chi* gives me the moral authority to call on you to do my job."

The twists and turns of a trial lawyer were a necessary part of the paidhi's job. But persuading Jago to reinterpret *man'chi* was like pleading a brief against gravity.

"Banichi would have to authorize it," Jago said with perfect composure, "if he has the authority, which I don't think he does, Bren-ji. If you wish me to go down to the airport, I will tell him your objection, though I fear the television crew will come when their clearance says to come, which may be before any other thing can be arranged, and I cannot conceive how Tabini could withdraw a permission he seems to have granted without—"

"I feel faint. It must be the tea."

"*Please,* nadi, don't joke."

"I can't deal with them!"

"This would reflect very badly on many people, nadi. Surely you understand—"

"I cannot decide such policy changes on my own, Jago! It's not in the authority I was given—"

"Refusal of these people must necessarily have far-reaching effect. I could not possibly predict, Bren-ji, but can you not comply at least in form? This surely won't air immediately, and if there should be policy considerations, surely there could be ameliorations. Tabini has recommended these people. Reputations are assuredly at stake in this."

Jago was no mean lawyer herself—versed in *man'chi* and its obligations, at least, and the niceties on which her profession accepted or didn't accept grievances. Life and death. Justified and not. And she had a point. She had serious points.

"May I see the letter, Bren-ji? I don't, of course, insist on it, but it would make matters clearer."

He handed it over. Jago walked over to the window to read it, not, he thought, because she needed the light.

"I believe," she said, "you're urged to be very frank with these people, nadi. I think I understand Tabini-aiji's thinking, if I may be so forward. If anything should happen to you—it would be very useful to have popular sympathy."

"If anything should happen to me."

"Not fatally. But we have taken an atevi life."

He stood stock still, hearing from Jago what he thought he heard. It was her impeccable honesty. She could not perceive that there was prejudice in what she said. She was thinking atevi politics. That was her job, for Tabini and for him.

"An atevi life."

"We've taken it in defense of *yours,* nand' paidhi. It's our *man'chi* to have done so. But not everyone would agree with that choice."

He had to ask. "Do you, nadi?"

Jago delayed her answer a moment. She folded the letter. "For Tabini's sake I certainly would agree. May I keep this in file, nadi?"

"Yes," he said, and shoved the affront out of his mind. What did you expect? he asked himself, and asked himself what was he to do without consultation, what might they ask and what dared he say?

Jago simply took the letter and left, through his bedroom, without answering his question.

An honest woman, Jago was, and she'd given him no grounds at all to question her protection. It wasn't precisely what he'd questioned—but she doubtless didn't see it that way.

He'd alienated Banichi and now he'd offended Jago. He wasn't doing well at all today.

"Jago," he called after her. "Are you going down to the airport?"

Atevi manners didn't approve yelling at people, either. Jago walked all the way back to answer him.

"If you wish. But what I read in the letter gives me little grounds on which to delay these people, nand' paidhi. I can only advise Banichi of your feelings. I don't see how I could do otherwise."

He was at the end of his resources. He made a small,

weary bow. "About what I said. I'm tired, nadi, I didn't express myself well."

"I take no offense, Bren-ji. The opinion of these people is uninformed. Shall I attempt to reach Banichi?"

"No," he said in despair. "No. I'll deal with them. Only suggest to Tabini on my behalf that he's put me in a position which may cost me my job."

"I'll certainly convey that," Jago said. And if Jago said it that way, he did believe it.

"Thank you, nadi," he said, and Jago bowed and went on through the bedroom.

He followed, with a vacation advertisement and a crafts catalog, which he figured for bathtub reading.

Goodbye to the hour-long bath. He rang for Djinana to advise him of the change in plans, he shed the coat in the bedroom, limped down the hall into the bathroom and shed dusty, spit-stained clothes in the hamper on the way to the waiting tub.

The water was hot, frothed with herbs, and he would have cheerfully spent half the day in it, if Djinana would only keep pouring in warm water. He drowned the crafts catalog, falling asleep in mid-scan—just dropped his hand and soaked it: he found himself that tired and that little in possession of his faculties.

But of course Tano came in to say a van had pulled up in the portico, and it was television people, with Banichi, and they were going to set up downstairs. Would the paidhi care to dress?

The paidhi would care to drown, rather than put on court formality and that damned tailored coat, but Tabini had other plans.

He'd not brought his notes on the transportation problems. He thought he should have. It went to question after question, until at least numbness had set in where he met the chair and where an empty stomach protested the lack of lunch.

"What," the interviewer asked then, "determines the

rate of turnover of information? Isn't it true that all these systems exist on Mospheira?"

"Many do."

"What wouldn't?"

"We don't use as much rail. Local air is easier. The interior elevations make air more practical for us."

"But you didn't present that as an option to the aiji two hundred years ago."

"We frankly worried that we'd be attacked."

"So there *are* other considerations than the environment."

Sharp interviewer. And empowered by someone to ask questions that might not make the broadcast, but—might, still. Tabini had confidence in this man, and sent him.

"There's also the risk," he said, "of creating problems among atevi. You had rail—you almost had rail at the time of the Landing. If we'd thrown air travel into Shejidan immediately, it might have provoked disturbances among the outlying Associations. Not everyone believed Barjida-aiji would share the technology. And better steam trains were a lot less threatening. We could have turned over rockets. We could have said, in the very first negotiations—here's the formula for dynamite. And maybe irresponsible people would have decided to drop explosives on each other's cities. We'd just been through a war. It was hard enough to get it stopped. We didn't want to provide new weapons for another one. *We* could have dropped explosives from planes, when we built them. But we didn't want to do that."

"That's a good point," the interviewer said.

He hoped it was. He hoped people thought about it.

"We don't ever want a war," he said. "We didn't have much choice about being on this planet. We caused harm we didn't intend or want. It seems a fair repayment, what the Treaty asked."

"Is there a limit to what you'll turn over?"

He shook his head. "No."

"What about highways?"

Damn, *that* question again. He drew a breath to think about it. "Certainly I've seen the realities of transportation in the mountains. I intend to take my observations to *our* council. And I'm sure the nai-aijiin will have recommendations to me, too."

A little laughter at that. And a sober next question: "Yet you alone, rather than the legislature, determine whether a town gets the transport it needs."

"Not myself alone. In consultation with the aiji, with the councils, with the legislatures."

"Why not road development?"

"Because—"

Because mecheiti followed the leader. Because Babs was the leader, and Nokhada hadn't a choice, without fighting that Nokhada didn't want, damned stupid idea, and he had to say something to that question, something that didn't insult atevi.

"Because," he said, trapped. "We couldn't predict what might happen. Because we saw the difficulties of regulation." He panicked. He was losing the threads of it, not making sense, and not making sense sounded like a lie. "We feared at the outset the allocation of road funds might cause division within the Association. A breakdown of an authority we didn't understand."

The interviewer hesitated, politely expressionless. "Are you saying, nand' paidhi, that this policy was based on misapprehension?"

Oh, God. "Initially, perhaps." The mind snapped back into focus. The *village* problem was the atevi concern. "But we don't think it would have led to a solution for the villages. *If* there'd been highways a hundred, two hundred years ago, there'd have been a growth in unregulated commerce. If *that* had happened—the commercial interests would build where the biggest highways were, and the straighter the highways, the more big population centers in a row, the more attraction they'd be—while no one but the aiji would have defended the remote villages, who *still* would have trouble getting transportation, very much what we have now, but we'd also have the pollution from the motors and the concentration of even more political power into the major population strings, along those roads. I see a place for a road system—in the villages, not the population centers, as spur lines to the centralized transport system."

He didn't engage the interviewer's interest. He'd gotten too detailed, too technical, or at least promised to lead to technical matters the interviewer didn't want or felt his audience didn't want. He sensed the shift in intention, as the interviewer shifted position and frowned. He was glad of it. The interviewer posed a few more questions, about where he lived, about family associations, about what he did on vacation, thank God, none of them critical. He was sweating under the lights when the interview wound to its close and the interviewer went through the obligatory courtesies.

"Thank you, nand' paidhi," the man said, and Bren withheld the sigh of relief as the lights went out.

"I'm sorry," he said at once, "I'm not used to cameras. I'm afraid I wasn't very coherent at all."

"You speak very well, nand' paidhi, *much* better than some of our assignments, I assure you. We're very pleased you found the time for us." The interviewer stood up, he stood up, Banichi stood up, from the shadowed fringes, where the lights had obscured his presence. Everyone bowed. The interviewer offered a hand to shake. Someone must have told him that.

"You've been informed on our customs," he ventured to say, and the interviewer was pleased and bowed, shaking hands with a crushing grip.

There was the commercial plane returning at sunset. The news crew had another assignment in Maidingi, on the electrical outage. Thank God. The crew was packing up lights, disconnecting cable run like an infestation of red and black vines across the ancient carpets, from the remote hallways. Maigi went to retrieve the far end somewhere near the kitchens, where, Bren was sure, the staff was not eager to admit strangers. Everything folded away into boxes. The glass-eyed animals stared back from the walls, as amazed and dazed as the paidhi.

What have I done? he asked himself, asked himself if he could justify everything he'd said, when he wrote his report to Mospheira, but they'd kept off sensitive topics—he'd accomplished that much, give or take his mental lapse on the highway question.

"We'd like to do more such interviews," the man said—he could *not* recall the name: Daigani or something like it. "We'd be delighted to tape one, nand' paidhi, actually in Mospheira. Perhaps reciprocal arrangements with your television, but one of our crews actually on site—interviews with ordinary people, that sort of thing."

"Certainly if something of the sort could be worked out," he answered. It was the answer to any unlikely proposal. He couldn't have it go to Mospheira as something he'd agreed to. "I could contact the appropriate people—" It was a deliberate, *Give me a phone,* challenge to Banichi and Jago *and* Tabini. A dozen uneasy thoughts slithered through the back of his mind. The news services had to know that someone had tried to kill him, and no one had mentioned that fact. *He* hadn't. The Bu-javid's conspiratorial attitude about security seeped into the blood and bone of those who lived there—one *didn't* talk to the press without authorization, one didn't carry gossip, one left it to the departments with authority to state official policy.

But he couldn't tell the news that a man had died here yesterday? Or they knew and didn't ask?

He didn't know what had gone out on the news in the last week. He didn't know what *was* common knowledge and what wasn't, and the policy of his office said keep quiet when you didn't know.

So he made polite expressions and bowed and sweated, still, in spite of the cooling of the air. A front was moving in. The crew hoped their flight would beat it out. They'd ridden through the front this morning, a choppy, bumpy flight, what Jago called 'long,' and the news crew called 'uncomfortable.'

But the front doors were open now, with the wind blowing through, and the light coming in, brighter than the electric bulbs in this hall, which only managed a wan, golden glow. The crew carried out their lights, the interviewer lingered for small talk, and Tano and Algini had their heads together over by the door, watching the crew carry the equipment—Algini had come up with them. So had Banichi. Jago was ... somewhere, probably resting; and meanwhile the thoughts about what he'd said and what he'd thought kept jostling one another at the back of his mind, clamoring for attention and further analysis.

Banichi carefully disengaged the interviewer, then, and walked him as far as the door, where one last round of bows was obligatory.

Bren made his own courtesies, and, with the last of the crew outside, leaned his shoulders against the shadowed back of the door and sighed in relief.

"Tano and Aligini will see them down to the airport," Banichi said, turning up as a shadow out of the sunlight. "They may stay down, for supper. I discovered a good restaurant."

"That's fine," he said, and didn't ask Why don't we all go? because most patrons didn't like assassinations during the salad course. He realized he'd been nervous as hell about the interview, not alone because of the questions that might turn up, but because he didn't trust the crew with all those boxes of equipment, and because he didn't know these people.

He'd become, he decided, thoroughly paranoid. Afraid. And he *didn't* think a crew from the national news network was going to produce explosive devices.

It was stupid.

"You did very well, nand' paidhi."

"I couldn't get my thoughts together. I could have done better."

"Tabini thinks there should be more of these interviews," Banichi said. "He thinks it's time the paidhi became more public. More in touch with the people."

"Is that going to stop the people that don't want me alive?" He didn't mean to be negative. Doubtless the move was a good idea. Doubtless Tabini thought so. But his uneasy feeling persisted.

"Why don't you go upstairs, nadi, and get out of the coat? You can relax now."

He didn't know if he could manage to relax, for the rest of the day, but the coat collar chafed, and he'd gotten stiff, sitting still. It was more than a good idea, to go up and change clothes. It was the only thing they'd let him do or decide for the rest of the day. His grand single decision.

Until tomorrow.

He said, because it was politic at the moment and because he'd meant it, earlier, and sullenly told himself he would, again: "I was rude last night, Banichi, forgive me."

"I didn't notice," Banichi said. Banichi's attention was out the door, toward the van, the doors of which were slamming shut.

"I'm sorry about your associate. And for your instructors."

"It was none of your doing. Or mine. One only wishes he had been wiser—but no more successful." Banichi laid a hand on his shoulder, only half welcome. "Go upstairs, nadi."

Go away, don't bother me. The paidhi could translate. Banichi's thoughts were elsewhere, and he—after the heat of the lights—decided he was going to go back upstairs and finish the bath he'd had to leave. People didn't bother him in the bath. He didn't have to talk philosophy in the bath. And it helped a soreness he didn't want to discuss with the servants.

It took no little time to fire up the boiler again, and run water. He took the time for a light lunch, in which he read the first committee letters, then thought—how quickly the mind dropped into familiar ruts—that he should take computer notes.

But they didn't run extension cords from the kitchen for the paidhi, no, just for news cameramen, and no one mentioned going back to Shejidan.

So he had his bath, leaned his head back on the rim of the tub, steam rising around him. He had a glass of the human-compatible liquor sitting by him, and a stack of catalogs ... the vacation catalog, among them, plus one for sports equipment—not that he had any reasonable use for a second pair of skis, or another ski suit, but, then, almost all his catalog-perusing was wishful.

Thunder rumbled through the stones. He wondered idly if the news crew's commercial flight had made it out on schedule. He truly hoped so. He wanted them out and away. He wondered, too, what Algini and Tano were up to in the rustic pleasures of Maidingi township. Sightseeing around the lake shore, maybe. One hoped they wouldn't be soaked.

He had a sip from the sweating glass—*ice* in good liquor? Tabini had asked him incredulously, early in their acquaintance.

Djinana, presented with such a request, had raised his brows and blinked, much more diplomatic. And with the power on again, and the lights working, ice did exist in the kitchens.

He turned the page and considered ski boots, scanned the art and culture inset, a service of the company, which described the recovery of old art from the data banks. Read the article on the building of the Mt. Allan Thomas resort, the first luxury establishment on Mospheira, where a hardy few had resurrected the idea of skiing.

Atevi were lately showing an interest in the sport, on their own mountains. Tabini called it suicide—then seemed to show a grudging flicker of interest himself, when he'd seen the homemade skiing tapes the paidhi had cleared through the Commission.

A potential common passion, human and atevi. Good for relations.

He'd almost talked Tabini into trying it, if the damned security crisis hadn't blown up. He might yet. There were, supposedly, good slopes in the Bergid, only an hour away from Shejidan—where fools risked their necks, as Tabini put it.

The interview still bothered him. He still worried over what he'd said, or what expression he'd had, when atevi didn't show expression . . . and *he* wasn't used to television cameras and talking to glaring lights. . . .

Thunder crashed. The lights flickered. And went out.

Incredible. He cast a baleful look at the dimmed ceiling, in which the bulb was out.

But he refused, this time, to be inconvenienced. Hot water didn't become unhot instantly. The candles were still in the sconce. He got out in the warm air, took a candle from the candelabrum on the table, lit it from the boiler flame, and with the one candle, lit the candles in the sconce. He heard the servants shouting at each other down the hall, not panicked, except perhaps the cook, who probably had reason, at this hour. But come lightning, come storm, Malguri managed.

He settled back into the hot water, complacent and competent in his atevi past—the paidhi having learned the world didn't stop when the power failed. He sipped his iced drink, and went back to the contemplation of safety ski bindings, buyer's choice, black, white, or glowing green.

Hurried footsteps arrived from the accommodation. He looked up as a flashlight beam flared into his eyes, with a black, metal-sparked figure behind it.

"Bren-ji?" Jago asked. "Our apologies. It's general, I'm afraid. Are you all right?"

"Perfectly fine," he said. "—Do you mean to tell me that that piece of equipment they just freighted in and installed—just went out?"

"We truly don't know, at this point. We suspect the first

incident was arranged. We're investigating this one. Please stay put."

Away went the sense of security. The thought of intruders in the halls, while he was sitting in the bath—was not comfortable. "I'm getting out."

"I'm going to be here," Jago said. "You don't have to, nadi-ji."

"I'd rather. It's fine. I was just going to read."

"I'll be in the reception room. I'll tell Djinana."

Jago left. He climbed out and dressed by candlelight, took a candle with him, but someone had already lit the lamps in the bedroom and in the sitting room.

Rain spattered the sitting room windows, a gray sameness that began to seem natural. He felt sorry for Banichi—who was probably out in that. Sorry, and worried for his safety. He didn't understand how someone faked a lightning strike, or what they could have found out that changed things.

He walked into the reception room, found Jago standing in front of the window, the clouded light making a mask of her profile and glittering on her uniform. She was staring out at the lake, or at the featureless sky.

"They wouldn't try the same thing again," he said. "They can't be that crazy."

Jago looked at him—gave a small, strange laugh. "Perhaps that makes them clever. They expect us not to take it for granted."

"They?"

"Or he or she. One doesn't know, nadi. We're trying to find out."

Don't bother me, he decided that meant. He stood and looked out the window, which gave him nothing at all.

"Go read if you like," Jago said.

As if the mind could leap, that quickly, back to ski catalogs. His damned well couldn't. It didn't like informational voids; it didn't like silent guards lurking in his reception room, or the chance there was a reason to need them, possibly slipping up the stairs outside.

Read, hell. He wanted a window that overlooked something but gray.

He hadn't the disposition, he decided. He was far too nervous.

"Nadi Bren. Come away from the window."

He didn't think about such things. He was chagrined, to be caught twice, shook his head and walked back—

Jago was staring at him with disturbing worry—set to shepherd a fool, he supposed, who walked in front of windows. "Sorry," he said.

"Think as one thinks trying to reach you," she said. "Do them no favors. Go, sit, relax."

Guild assassin, Banichi had said. Someone Banichi knew. Socialized with.

And didn't yet know why a man had broken the rules?

"Jago,—how does a person get a license?"

"To do what, Bren-ji?"

"You know. The Guild." He wanted not to tread on sensibilities with Jago. He was sorry he'd wandered into the territory.

"To be licensed to the Guild? One elects. One chooses."

It told him no more than before, what pushed a sane person in that direction. Jago didn't seem the type—if there was a type to the profession.

"Bren-ji. Why do you ask?"

"Wondering—what sort of person is after me."

Jago seemed to ignore his question then, looking off to the window. Into rain-spatter and nothing.

"We're not one kind, Bren-ji. We're not one face."

None of your business, he supposed. "Nadi," he said, departing, willing to leave her to her own thoughts, if he could only shake his own.

"What sort becomes paidhi?" she asked him, before he could take a second step.

Good question, he thought. Solid hit. He had to think about it, and didn't find the answer he'd used to have . . . couldn't even locate the boy who'd started down that track, couldn't believe in him, even marginally.

"A fool, probably."

"One doubts, nadi-ji. Is that a requirement?"

"I think so."

"So . . . how do you vie for this honor? In what foolishness?"

"Curiosity. Wanting to know more than Mospheira. Doing good to the planet we're on, the people we live next to."

"Is this also Wilson?"

Dead hit. What could he say?

"You," Jago said, "do not act like Wilson-paidhi."

"Valasi-aiji," he countered, "wasn't Tabini, either."

"True," Jago said. "Very true."

"Jago, I—" He was up against that word, which only governed salad courses. He shook his head and started to walk away.

"Bren-ji. Please finish."

He didn't want to talk. He wasn't sure of his rationality, let alone his self-control. But Jago waited.

"Jago-ji, I've worked all my life, best I can do. I don't know what else I can do. Now we've lost the lights again. I don't think I've deserved this. But I ask myself, nadi, is it my fault, have I gone too far and too fast, have I done Tabini harm by trying to help him, and is someone that damned persistent in trying to kill me? *Why,* Jago? Do you have the remotest notion?"

"You bring change," Jago said. "To some, this is frightening."

"The damned *railroad?*" The emphasis of the interview bewildered him. Jago was all but a shadow to him, expressionless, unreachable. He made a frustrated dismissal with his hand and walked away toward the sitting room, only to gain a space to think, to sit down and read and take his mind off the day's bizarre turn, maybe before supper, which she might share, if no one poisoned the cook.

But he stopped again, fearing he might insult her. "If someday," he said, "this television business ever works out to bring news crews onto Mospheira, I'll ask for you and Banichi to come visit my family. I'd like you to see what we are. I'd like you to know us, nadi-ji."

"I'd be most honored," Jago said solemnly.

So perhaps he'd patched things. He walked away into the sitting room and threw another piece of wood onto the fire, while thunder echoed off the walls. Jago had followed him in, evidently conceiving that as what he wanted, but she said nothing, only took up looking through the sitting room library shelves instead.

There was no interfering with Jago's notions of duty, or what she might conceive as being sociable. He took up his book, began to sit down.

The lights came on again.

He looked up, frustrated, at the ceiling fixtures.

"It must have been a fuse," Jago said, from across the room. "That's good."

He recalled dusty old wires running beside bare natural gas pipes, along the hall ceiling, and envisioned the whole apartment going up in an electrical disaster. "Malguri needs a new electrical system," he muttered. "Where do they have that gas tank?"

"What gas?"

"Methane."

"In the cellar," Jago said.

"Under the building. It's a damned bomb, nadi. The place *needs* electric furnaces. If they've installed electric lights, surely electric furnaces can't hurt."

"Funding," Jago said.

"While they're looking for assassins—do they watch that tank?"

"Every access to this building," Jago said, "is under surveillance."

"Except when the power's out."

Jago made a small shrug.

"Those windows," he said, "aren't watched. I found that out last night, when the power came back on."

Jago frowned, went close to the window, and ran a finger around the edge of the casement, looked up and around—at what, he couldn't see.

"How did you find out, Bren-ji?"

"I opened a window to look out. The power came back on. The alarm went off. I take it that's an old system."

"It certainly is," Jago said. "Did you report this?"

"It woke the whole staff."

Jago didn't look happier, but what she saw, examining the window, he couldn't tell.

"Except Banichi," he said.

"Except Banichi."

"I don't know where he was. I told you. We had an argument. He went off somewhere." He had an entirely unwelcome thought but kept his mouth shut on it, watched while Jago walked to the door, pulled it half-shut, and looked at the wall behind it, still frowning. Security *didn't* talk about security. He doubted an explanation was forthcoming.

"Nadi Jago," he said. "Banichi wasn't here. Do you have any notion where he was last night?"

He might have remarked it was raining outside. Jago's expression never varied. She opened the door again to its ordinary position, walked out and into the reception room.

The lights went out again. He looked up in frustration, then followed her into the other room to protest the silence and the confusion of his security. She was at the window. She unlatched the side panel, opened it and shut it again, without an alarm.

"What in hell's going *on*, Jago?"

Jago took out her pocket-com and thumbed it on, rattled off a string of code he didn't understand.

Banichi answered. He was relatively certain it was Banichi's voice. And Jago's stance showed some small reassurance. She answered, and cut the com off, and put it away.

"It did register," she said. "*Our* system registered."

"Yours and Banichi's?" he asked—but the com beeped and Jago thumbed it on again and answered it, frowning.

Banichi's voice replied. Jago's frown deepened. She answered Banichi shortly, a sign-off, clipped the com to her belt and headed for the door.

"What was that?" he asked. "What's happening? Jago?"

She crossed back in two strides, seized his shoulders and looked down at him. "Bren-ji. I've never betrayed you. I will *not*, Bren-ji."

After which she was out the hall door at the same pace. She shut it. Hard.

Jago? he thought. His shoulders still felt the force of her fingers. And her footsteps were fading at a rapid pace down the hall outside, while he stood there asking himself where Banichi had been last night when he'd set the alarm off.

If there *was* another system—Banichi had known about him opening that window, if Banichi had been monitoring it. And for whatever reason—Banichi hadn't come back when the general alarm went.

Maybe because Banichi had already discounted it as a threat. But that *wasn't* the Banichi he knew, to take something like that for granted.

It was craziness, from breakfast with the dowager to the television crew arriving in the middle of a security so tight he couldn't get a telephone. He didn't like the feeling he was having. He didn't like the reasons that might make Jago go running out of here, saying, in a language that didn't have a definite word for trust—*trust* me to take care of you.

He double-checked the window latch. What kind of person could get in on the upper floor overlooking a sheer drop, he didn't know, but he didn't want to find out. He checked the outer door lock, although he'd heard it click.

But what good that was when everyone on staff had keys to the back hall of this place—

He had a sudden and anxious thought, went straight to

his bedroom and, on his knees by the bed, reached under the mattress.

The gun Banichi had given him ... wasn't there.

He searched, thinking that the Malguri staff, making the bed, might have shifted it without knowing it was there. He lifted the mattress to be sure—found nothing; no gun, no ammunition.

He let the mattress back down and arranged the bedclothes and the furs—sat down then, on the edge of the bed, trying to keep panic at arm's length, reasoning with himself that he had as much time to discover the gun missing as they thought it might take him, before they grew anxious; and if they hadn't devised visual surveillance in the rooms he didn't know about, whoever had taken it didn't know yet that he'd discovered the fact.

Fact: someone had it. Someone was armed with it, more to the point, who might or might not ordinarily have access to that issue pistol, or its caliber of ammunition. It was Banichi's—and if Banichi hadn't taken it himself, then *somebody* had a gun with an identification and a distinctive marking on its bullets that could report it right back to Banichi's commander in the Bu-javid.

No matter what it was used for.

If Banichi didn't know what had happened—Banichi needed to know it was gone—and he didn't have a phone, a pocket-com, or any way he knew to get one, except to walk out the door, go violate some security perimeter and hope it was Banichi who answered the alarm.

Which was the plan he had. Not the most discreet way to attract attention.

But, again, so long as he called no one's bluff—things *might* stay quiet until Banichi or Jago got back. The missing gun wasn't a thing to bring to the staff's attention. He could probably trust Tano and Algini, who'd come with them from Shejidan—but he didn't know that.

He was rattled. He was tired, after an uneasy night and a nerve-wracking afternoon. He wasn't, perhaps, making his best decisions—wasn't up to cleverness, without knowing more than he did.

His nerves twitched to distant thunder—that also was how tired he was. He could go try to trip alarms—but Banichi and Jago were out in the rain, chasing someone, or worse, chasing someone *inside* the house. His imagination pictured a tank of methane sitting in the basement, someone with explosives—

But they mustn't deface Malguri. Atevi wouldn't take that route. *Mishidi.* Awkward. Messy. No *biichi-ji.*

So they wouldn't explode the place. If anything happened, and a bullet turned up where it shouldn't, with marks that could trace it to Banichi, he could swear to what had really happened.

Unless he was the corpse in question.

Not a good time to go walking the halls, he decided, or startling his own security, who thought they knew where he was. He'd planned to spend the afternoon reading. He found he had no better or wiser plans. He got his dressing gown for a little extra warmth, went back to the sitting-room fire and picked up his book, back in the histories of Malguri.

About atevi. And loyalty. And expectations that didn't work out.

Expectations on his side, too—about feelings that just weren't there. Flat weren't there, and no use—no *possibility*—of changing anything to do with biology. What could one do? Pour human hormones into atevi bloodstreams, crosswire atevi brains to send impulses atevi brains didn't have?

And ask how humans had to fail atevi expectations, at what emotional level. There had to be an emotional level.

No. There didn't have to be. Terracentric thinking again. There was nothing in the laws of the universe that said what let atevi achieve a very respectable society on their own *had* to have human attributes, or respond when humans tried to attach to them in human ways. In a reasonable universe, it didn't have to happen; more, in a reasonable universe, it was more reasonable for atevi locomotives to resemble human-built locomotives than for atevi to resemble humans psychologically. Locomotives, designed by whatever species, had tracks for easy rolling, shafts to drive the wheels, steam or diesel, and gears to power the shafts, and a pipe to vent the smoke—that was physics. Airplanes flying through an equal density of air wouldn't tend to look like locomotives. Rockets wouldn't resemble refrigerators. Physics had its constraints for machines and structures with one job to do, and physics on old Earth and physics on the earth of the atevi wasn't a smidge different.

But biology, for intelligent beings with a whole damned lot of jobs to do, with microenvironments, evolutionary pressures, and genetic baroque sifted into the mix—had one hell of a lot of variables in potential makeup.

Not anybody's fault. Not anybody's fault they'd come to this star—wormhole, discontinuity of some kind—the physics people had their theories, but no human could prove the cause from where they sat, which was on the far side of God-knew-what galactic disk, for all they knew: no spectrum matched Sol or its neighbors, the pulsars, which the physicists said could peg their location . . . hadn't.

They hadn't known where they were then, and they didn't know now—as if where they were had any absolute referent when they didn't know how long it had taken them to get there: hundreds of years in subspace, for all anyone knew—stuck here, able to cobble the station together—

But it was a long, slow haul to the star's frozen debris belt and back to the life-zone, where they'd built the station: that, the way he'd understood it, had been the real politics, whether to build in the life-zone or at the edge of it; and the life-zone had won out, even knowing it was around a living world, even knowing someday it was going to mean admitting they were making a dangerous choice on very little data. . . .

Political compromise. Accepting a someday problem to solve a near-term worry.

Add in the refinery wreck and the solar storms, which no one at the time knew the limit of, and the attractive planet just lying there under their feet, hell—they'd do no damage, they'd get along, the natives already had steam, they were bound to encounter anyway, and why should they risk their precious lives trying to hold together against the odds.

At least, that was how a descendant nine or so generations down reconstructed the decision-making process . . . the atevi couldn't be too different. They had locomotives. They had steam mills. They had industry.

They had one hell of a different hard-wiring, but you couldn't tell that from the physics they used.

Couldn't tell that meeting an atevi. Hello, how are you, how's the weather? *Nice* people. Arrange a little trade, a little tech for an out-of-season game animal or two . . .

Right bang into the cultural rift.

Try to settle it—make it right with the local leaders: right into the cultural whirlpool.

Count the ways the first settlement had screwed it up. Count the ways they'd gotten good and deep into the interface before they'd begun to figure out betrayal wasn't betrayal and murder wasn't murder and that you couldn't promote one local aiji and fight another one without involving a continent-spanning Association with *everything* that conflict dragged into it. You didn't *expect* a steam-powered civilization to have world government . . .

But, then, if you were an early human colonist, maybe you didn't expect anyone to behave in any way you wouldn't.

Fifty years and two paidhiin ago, Mospheira had taken a collective deep breath and thrown satellite communications and rocket science onto the table, with the fervent hope that by hooking it to advanced communications, *biichi-ji* and *kabiu* together would keep some enterprising atevi entity from combining the explosive with the propellant technology and blowing their rivals to hell.

Because they thought now they'd gotten to know the atevi.

God help fools and tourists.

He flipped an unread page of the history, realized he hadn't read it, and flipped it back again, trying to concentrate on the doings of aijiin and councillors long since drifting on the Malguri winds, washed into its soil with the rains, down to the sea from Lake Maidingi rather more rapidly in this season than in fall.

He was bitterly angry and his mind was wandering, back and forth inside known limits, like a caged creature, when the real answers had to lie outside the bars of his understanding.

Maybe it was a point all paidhiin got to. Maybe he was the most naive, maybe because he'd gone into a relationship with the most friendly of aijiin, and it was so damned easy to ignore the warnings in every text he'd ever studied and fall right into the same trap as the first humans on the planet ... expecting atevi to be human. Expecting atevi to do what one naturally expected nice, sane human people to do and, God help him twice, what he *wanted* atevi to do, what he emotionally *needed* atevi to do, instead of himself waking up, paying attention to danger signals, and doing the job he'd been sent here for.

He *should* have made that phone call, back in Shejidan, if he'd had to make it with Bu-javid guards battering down the door. He shouldn't be thinking, even at this hour, that Tabini was under some sort of pressure and desperately *needed* him back in Shejidan, because if that was the case, then the television network Tabini tightly managed wouldn't be looking for interviews to prove the paidhi was a nice, easy-going friendly fellow, not some shadow-villain plotting world domination or contriving death-rays to level cities.

I will *not* betray you, Bren-ji?

What in hell did that mean, before Jago lit out the door and down the hall at the next thing to a dead run?

And where's the gun, Jago? Where is Banichi's gun?

The logs burned down and fell, showering sparks up the flue. He put on another, and settled back to his book.

Not a word back from Banichi or Jago about what was wrong out there—whether someone had breached the security perimeter, or whether someone odd had simply arrived at the airport or whether they'd had some dire word from Tabini.

He flipped the page, figured out he'd stopped reading the second time somewhere in the middle of it, and turned it back, with a dogged effort to concentrate on the text, in atevi directions, and to make sense out of the antique, ornate type style.

The lights went on again, out again.

Damn, he thought, and looked at the window. The rain was down to spatters now, gray cloud and a scattering of bright drops on the glass. The candles cast a golden glow. White light came from the window, as if the clouds were finally thinning up there.

He laid the book down, got up with the intention of having a look at the weather—heard someone in his bedroom and saw Djinana coming through from the back hall.

"The transformer or a bad wire?" he asked Djinana conversationally.

"One hopes, a wire," Djinana said, and bowed, at the door. "Nadi, a message for you."

Message? In this place of no telephones?

Djinana offered him a tiny scroll—Ilisidi's seal and ribbon, he judged before he even looked, because the red and black was Tabini's house. He opened it with his thumbnail, wondering was it something to do with the after-breakfast engagement. A cancellation, perhaps, or postponement due to the weather.

I need to speak with you immediately, it said. *I'll meet you in the downstairs hall.*

It had *Cenedi's* signature.

IX

Downstairs all the oil lamps were lit and a fire burned in the hearth. The outer hall, with its ancient weapons and its trophy heads and its faded, antique banners, was all golds and browns and faded reds. The upward stairs and the retreating hall below them were cast in shadow, interrupted by circles of lamplight from upstairs and down. Power was still out. Power looked to stay out, this time, and Bren regretted not wearing his coat downstairs. Someone must have had the front door open recently. The whole lower hall was cold.

But he expected no long meeting, no formality, and the fire moderated the chill. He stood warming his hands, waiting—heard someone coming from Ilisidi's part of the house, and cast a glance toward that recessed, main-floor hallway.

It was indeed Cenedi, dark-uniformed, with sparks of metal about his person, epitome of the Guild-licensed personal bodyguard. He thought that Cenedi would come as far as the fire, and that Cenedi would deliver him some private word and then let him go back to his supper—but Cenedi walked only far enough to catch his eye and beckoned for him to follow.

Follow him—where? Bren asked himself, not as easy about this little shadow-play as about the simple summons downstairs—as difficult to refuse as the rest of Ilisidi's invitations.

But in this turn of events he had a moment's impulse to excuse himself upstairs on the pretext of getting his coat, and to send Djinana to find Banichi or Jago—which he knew now he should already have done. Dammit, he said to himself, if he had been half thinking upstairs ...

But he no longer knew which side of many sides was dealing in truth tonight—no longer knew for certain how many sides there were. The gun was missing. Someone had it ... possibly Cenedi, possibly Banichi. Possibly Banichi had taken it to keep Cenedi from finding it: the chances were too convoluted to figure. If Djinana and Maighi had discovered it and taken it to Cenedi, he believed in his heart of hearts that Djinana could not have faced him without some visible sign of guilt. Not every atevi was as self-controlled as Banichi or Jago.

But while his guards were out and about on whatever business they were pursuing, he had been making his own decisions this far and come to no grief, and if Cenedi did want to talk to him about the gun, best not try to bluff about it and make Cenedi doubt his truthfulness, bottom line. He could take responsibility on himself for it being there. Cenedi had no way of knowing he hadn't packed the luggage himself. If the paidhi had to leave office in scandal ... God knew, it was better than seeing Tabini implicated, and the Association weakened. It was his own mess. He might have to face the consequences of it.

But if Cenedi had the gun and the serial number, surely the aiji-dowager's personal guard had the means to contact the police and have that gun traced through records—*by* the very computers the paidhi had hoped to make a universal convenience. And a lie trying to cover Banichi could make matters worse.

There were just too damn many things out of place: Banichi's behavior, Jago's rushing off like that, this man, dead in the driveway, being some old schoolmate of Banichi's ... or whatever licensed assassins called their fellows.

Cenedi at least had missed opportunity after opportunity to fling the paidhi off the mountainside with no one the wiser. The near-fatal tea could have been stronger. If

there was something sinister going on within the household, if Tabini had sent him here simply to get Banichi
and Jago inside Ilisidi's defenses—that was his own
nightmare scenario—the paidhi was square in the middle
of it; he *liked* Ilisidi, dammit, Cenedi had never done him
any harm, and what in the name of God had he gotten
himself into, coming down here to talk to Cenedi in private? He could lie with an absolutely innocent face when
he had an official, canned line to hand out. But he
couldn't lie effectively about things like guns, and
whether Banichi was up to anything . . . he didn't know
any answers, either, but he couldn't deal with the questions without showing an anxiety that an ateva would read
as extreme.

He walked through the circles of lamplight, back and
back into the mid-hall where Cenedi stood waiting for
him, a tall shadow against the lamplight from an open
door, a shadow that disappeared inside before he reached
the door.

He expected only Cenedi. Another of Ilisidi's guards
was in the office, a man he'd ridden with that morning.
He couldn't remember the name, and he didn't know at
first, panicked thought what that man should have to do
with him.

Cenedi sat down and offered the chair at the side of his
desk. "Nand' paidhi, please." And with a wry irony:
"Would you—I swear to its safety—care for tea?"

One could hardly refuse that courtesy. More, it explained the second man, there to handle the amenities, he
supposed, in a discussion Cenedi might not want bruited
about outside the office. "Thank you," he said gratefully,
and took the chair, while the guard poured a cup for him
and one for Cenedi.

Cenedi dismissed the man then, and the man shut the
door as he left. The two oil lamps on the wall behind the
desk cast Cenedi's broad-shouldered shape in exaggerated, overlapping shadows, emitted fumes that made the
air heavy, as, one elbow on the desk, one hand occasion-

ally for the teacup, Cenedi sorted through papers on his desk as if those had the reason of the summons and he had lost precisely the one he wanted.

Then Cenedi looked straight at him, a flash of lambent yellow, the quirk of a smile on his face.

"How are you sitting this evening, nand' paidhi? Any better?"

"Better." It set him off his guard, made him laugh, a little frayed nerves, there, and he sat on it. Fast.

"Only one way to get over it," Cenedi said. "The dowager's guard sympathizes, nand' paidhi. They laugh. But we've suffered. Don't think their humor aimed at you."

"I didn't take it so, I assure you."

"You've a fair seat for a beginner. I take it you don't spend all your time at the desk."

He was flattered. But not set off his guard a second time. "I spend it on the mountain, when I get the chance. About twice a year."

"Climbing?"

"Skiing."

"I've not tried that," Cenedi said, shuffling more paper, trimming up a stack. "I've seen it on television. Some young folk trying it, up in the Bergid. No offense, but I'd rather a live instructor than a picture in a contraband catalog and some promoter's notion how not to break your neck."

"Is *that* where my mail's been going?"

"Oh, there's a market for it. The post tries to be careful. But things do slip."

Is that what this is about? Bren asked himself. Someone stealing mail? Selling illicit catalogs?

"If you get me to the Bergid this winter," he said, "I'd be glad to show you the basics. Fair trade for the riding lessons."

Cenedi achieved a final, two-handed stack in his desk-straightening. "I'd like that, nand' paidhi. On more than one account. I'd like to persuade the dowager back to Shejidan. Malguri is *hell* in the winter."

They still hadn't gotten to the subject. But it wasn't uncommon in atevi business to meander, to set a tone. Atevi manners.

"Maybe we can do that," he said. "I'd like to."

Cenedi sipped his tea and set the cup down. "They don't ride on Mospheira."

"No. No mecheiti."

"You hunt."

"Sometimes."

"On Mospheira?"

Were they talking about guns, now? Was that where this was going? "I have. A few times. Small game. Very small."

"One remembers," Cenedi said—as if any living atevi *could* remember. "Is it very different, Mospheira?"

"From Malguri?" One didn't quite go off one's guard. "Very. From Shejidan—much less so."

"It was reputed—quite beautiful before the War."

"It still is. We have very strict rules—protection of the rivers, the scenic areas. Preservation of the species we found there."

Cenedi leaned back in his chair. "Do you think, nadi, there'll be a time Mospheira will open up—to either side of the strait?"

"I hope it will happen."

"But do you think it *will* happen, nand' paidhi?"

Cenedi might have gotten to his subject, or might have led away from the matter of the gun simply to make him relax. He couldn't figure—and he felt more than a mild unease. The question touched policy matters on which he couldn't comment without consultation. He didn't want to say no to Cenedi, when Cenedi was being pleasant. It could target whole new areas for Cenedi's curiosity. "It's my hope. That's all I can say." He took a sip of hot tea. "It's what I work very hard for, someday to have that happen, but no paidhi can say when—it's for aijiin and presidenti to work out."

"Do you think this television interview is—what is your expression?—a step in the right direction?"

Is *that* it? Publicity? Tabini's campaign for association with Mospheira? "Honestly, nadi Cenedi, I was disappointed. I don't think we got to any depth. There are things I wanted to say. And they never asked me those. I wasn't sure what they wanted to do with it. It worried me—what they might put in, that I hadn't meant."

"I understand there's some thought about monthly broadcasts. The paidhi to the masses."

"I don't know. I certainly don't decide things like that on my own. I'm obliged to consult."

"By human laws, you mean."

"Yes."

"You're not autonomous."

"No. I'm not." Early on, atevi had expected paidhiin to make and keep agreements—but the court in Shejidan didn't have this misconception now, and he didn't believe Cenedi was any less informed. "Though in practicality, nadi, paidhiin aren't often overruled. We just don't promise what we don't think our council will accept. Though we do argue with our council, and sometimes we win."

"Do you favor more interviews? Will you argue for the idea?"

Ilisidi was on the conservative side of her years. Probably she didn't like television cameras in Malguri, let alone the idea of the paidhi on regular network broadcasts. He could imagine what she might say to Tabini.

"I don't know what position I'll argue. Maybe I'll wait and see how atevi like the first one. Whether people *want* to see a human face—or not. I may frighten the children."

Cenedi laughed. "Your face has already been on television, nand' paidhi, at least the official clips. 'The paidhi discussed the highway program with the minister of Works, the paidhi has indicated a major new release forthcoming in microelectronics . . .'"

"But that's not an interview. And a still picture. I can't understand why anyone would want to hear me discuss the relative merits of microcircuits for an hour-long program."

"Ah, but your microcircuits work by numbers. Such intricate geometries. The hobbyists would deluge the phone system. 'Give us the paidhi,' they'd say. 'Let us hear the numbers.' "

He wasn't sure Cenedi was joking at first. A few days removed from the Bu-javid and one could forget the intensity, the passion of the devout number-counters. He decided it *was* a joke—Tabini's sort of joke, irreverent of the believers, impatient of the complications their factions created.

"Or people can think my proposals contain wicked numbers," Bren said, himself taking a more serious turn. "As evidently some do think." And a second diversion, Cenedi delaying to reveal his reasons. "—*Is* it a blown fuse, this time, nadi?"

"I think it's a short somewhere. The breaker keeps going off. They're trying to find the source."

"Jago received some message from Banichi a while ago that distressed her, and she left. It worried me, nadi. So did your summons. Do you have any idea what's going on?"

"Banichi's working with the house maintenance staff. I don't know what he might have found, but he's extremely exacting. His subordinates do hurry when they're asked." Cenedi took another drink of tea, a large one, and set the cup down. "I wouldn't worry about it. He'd have advised me, I think, if he'd found anything irregular. Certainly house maintenance would, independent of him. —Another cup, nadi?"

He'd diverted Cenedi from his conversation. He was obligated to another cup. "Thank you," he said, and started to get up to get his own tea, in the absence of a servant, and not suggesting Cenedi do the office, but Cenedi signaled otherwise, reached a long arm across the corner of the desk, picked up the pot and poured for him and for himself.

"Nadi, a personal curiosity—and I've never had the paidhi at hand to ask: all these years you've been dealing out secrets. When will you be out of them? And what will you do then?"

Odd that no one had ever asked the paidhiin that quite that plainly ... on *this* side of the water, although God knew they agonized over it on Mospheira.

And perhaps that *was* Cenedi's own and personal question, though not *the* question, he was sure, which Cenedi had called him downstairs specifically to answer. It was the sort of thing an astute news service might ask. The sort of thing a child might ... not a political sophisticate like Cenedi, not officially.

But it was very much the sort of question he'd already begun to hint at in technical meetings, testing the waters, beginning, one hoped, to shift attitudes among atevi, and knowing atevi couldn't go much farther down certain paths without developments resisted for years by vested interests in other departments.

"Things don't only flow one way across the strait, nadi. We learn from *your* scientists, quite often. Not to say we've stood still ourselves since the Landing. But the essential principles have been on the table for a hundred years. I'm not a scientist—but as I understand it, it's the intervening steps, the things that atevi science has to do before the principles in other areas become clear—those are the things still missing. There's materials science. There's the kind of industry it takes to support the science. And the education necessary for new generations to understand it. The councils are still debating the shape of baffles in fuel tanks—when no one's teaching the students in the schools *why* you need a slosh baffle in the first place."

"You find us slow students?"

That trap was obvious as a pit in the floor. And damned right they'd expected atevi to pick things up faster—give or take aijiin who wouldn't budge and committees that wouldn't release a process until they'd debated it to death. An incredibly short path to flight and advanced metallurgy. An incredibly difficult one to get a damn bridge built as it needed to be to stand the stresses of heavy-hauling trains.

"Extremely quick students," he said, "interminable debaters."

Cenedi laughed. "And humans debate nothing."

"But we don't have to debate the technology, nadi Cenedi. We *have* it. We *use* it."

"Did it bring you success?"

Watch it, he thought. *Watch* it. He gave a self-deprecating shrug, atevi-style. "We're comfortable in the association we've made. The last secrets *are* potentially on the table, nadi. We just can't get atevi conservatives to accept the essential parts of them. Our secrets are full of numbers. Our numbers describe the universe. And how can the universe be unfortunate? We are confused when certain people claim the numbers add in anything but felicitous combination. We can only believe nature." He was talking to *Ilisidi's* seniormost guard, Ilisidi, who chose to reside in Malguri. Ilisidi, who hunted for her table—but believed in the necessity of dragonettes. "Surely, in my own opinion, not an expert opinion, nadi, someone must have added in what nature didn't put in the equations."

It was a very reckless thing to say, on one level. On the other, he hadn't said *which* philosophy of numbers he faulted and which he favored, out of half a dozen he personally knew in practice, and, human-wise, *couldn't* do in his head. He personally wanted to know where Cenedi, personally, stood—and Cenedi's mouth tightened in a rare amusement.

"While the computers you design secretly assign unlucky attributes," Cenedi said wryly. "And swing the stars in their courses."

"Not that I've seen happen. The stars go where nature has them going, nadi Cenedi. The same with the reasons for slosh baffles."

"Are we superstitious fools?"

"Assuredly not. There's nothing *wrong* with this world. There's nothing wrong with Malguri. There's nothing *wrong* with the way things worked before we arrived. It's just—if atevi want what we know—"

"Counting numbers is folly?"

Cenedi wanted him to admit to heresy. He had a sudden, panicked fear of a hidden tape recorder—and an equal fear of a lie to this man, a lie that would break the pretense of courtesy with Cenedi before he completely understood what the game was.

"We've given atevi true numbers, nadi, I'll swear to that. Numbers that work, although some doubt them, even in the face of the evidence of nature right in front of them."

"Some doubt human good will, more than they doubt the numbers."

So it *wasn't* casual conversation Cenedi was making. They sat here by the light of oil lamps—*he* sat here, in Cenedi's territory, with his own security elsewhere and, for all he knew, uninformed of his position, his conversation, his danger.

"Nadi, my predecessors in the office never made any secret how we came here. We arrived at this star completely by accident, and completely desperate. We'd no idea atevi existed. We didn't want to starve to death. We saw our equipment damaged. We knew it was a risk to us and, I admit it, to you, for us to go down from the station and land—but we saw atevi already well advanced down a technological path very similar to ours. We *thought* we could avoid harming anyone. We *thought* the place where we landed was remote from any association—since it had no buildings. That was the first mistake."

"Which party do you consider made the second?"

They were charting a course through ice floes. Nothing Cenedi asked was forbidden. Nothing he answered was controversial—right down the line of the accepted truth as paidhiin had told it for over a hundred years.

But he thought for a fleeting second about the mecheiti, and about atevi government, while Cenedi waited—too long, he thought, to let him refuse the man some gain.

"I blame the War," he said, "on both sides giving wrong signals. We thought we'd received encouragement to things that turned out quite wrong, fatally wrong, as it turned out."

"What sort of encouragement?"

"We thought we'd received encouragement to come close, encouragement to treat each other as . . ." There wasn't a word. "Known. After we'd developed expectations. We went to all-out war *after* we'd had a promising beginning of a settlement. People who think they were betrayed don't believe twice in assurances."

"You're saying you weren't at fault."

"I'm saying atevi weren't, either. I believe that."

Cenedi tapped the fingers of one hand, together, against the desk, thinking, it seemed. Then: "An accident brought you to us. Was it a mistake of numbers?"

He found breath scarce in the room, perhaps the oil lamps, perhaps having gone in over his head with a very well-prepared man.

"We don't know," he said. "Or I don't. I'm not a scientist."

"But don't your numbers describe nature? Was it a supernatural accident?"

"I don't think so, nadi. Machinery may have broken. Such things do happen. Space is a vacuum, but it has dust, it has rocks—like trying to figure which of millions of dust motes you might disturb by breathing."

"Then your numbers aren't perfect."

Another pitfall of heresy. "Nadi, engineers approximate, and nature corrects them. We *approach* nature. Our numbers work, and nature doesn't correct us constantly. Only sometimes. We're good. We're not perfect."

"And the War was one of these imperfections?"

"A very great one. —But we can *learn,* nadi. I've insulted Jago at least twice, but she was patient until I figured it out. Banichi's made me extremely unhappy—and I know for certain he didn't know what he did, but I don't cease to value associating with him. I've probably done harm to others I don't know about,—but at least, at least, nadi, at very least we're not angry with each other, and we each *know* that the other side means to be fair. We make a lot of mistakes . . . but people can make up their minds to be patient."

Cenedi sat staring at him, giving him the feeling . . . he didn't know why . . . that he had entered on very shaky ground with Cenedi. But he hadn't lost yet. He hadn't made a fatal mistake. He wished he knew whether Banichi knew where he was at the moment.

"Yet," Cenedi said, "someone wasn't patient. Someone attempted your life."

"Evidently."

"Do you have any idea why?"

"I have *no* idea, nadi. I truly don't, in specific, but I'm aware some people just don't like humans."

Cenedi opened the drawer of his desk and took out a roll of paper heavy with the red and black ribbons of the aiji's house.

Ilisidi's, he thought apprehensively, as Cenedi passed it across the desk to him. He unrolled it and saw instead a familiar hand.

Tabini's.

I send you a man, 'Sidi-ji, for your disposition. I have filed Intent on his behalf, for his protection from faceless agencies, not, I think, agencies faceless to you, but I make no complaint against you regarding a course of action which under extraordinary circumstances you personally may have considered necessary.

What is this? he thought and, in the sudden, frantic sense of limited time, read again, trying to understand was it Tabini's threat *against* Ilisidi or was he saying Ilisidi was *behind* the attack on him?

And Tabini sent him *here?*

Therefore I relieve you of that unpleasant and danger-

ous necessity, 'Sidi-ji, my favorite enemy, knowing that others may have acted against me invidiously, or for personal gain, but that you, alone, have consistently taken a stand of principle and policy against the Treaty.

Neither I nor my agents will oppose your inquiries or your disposition of the paidhi-aiji at this most dangerous juncture. I require only that you inform me of your considered conclusions, and we will discuss solutions and choices.

Disposition of the paidhi? Tabini, Tabini, for God's sake, what are you *doing* to me?

My agents have instructions to remain but not to interfere.

Tabini-aiji with profound respect

To Ilisidi of Malguri, in Malguri, in Maidingi Province . . .

His hands shook. He tried not to let them. He read the letter two and three times, and found no other possible interpretation. It *was* Tabini's handwriting. It *was* Tabini's seal. There was no possible forgery. He tried to memorize the wording in the little time he reasonably had to hold the document, but the elaborate letters blurred in his eyes. Reason tried to intervene, interposing the professional, intellectual understanding that Tabini *was* atevi, that friendship didn't guide him, that Tabini couldn't even comprehend the word.

That Tabini, in the long run, had to act in atevi interests, and as an ateva, not in any human-influenced way that needed to make sense to him.

Intellect argued that he couldn't waste time feeling anything, or interpreting anything by human rules. Intellect argued that he was in dire and deep trouble in this place, that he had a slim hope in the indication that Banichi and Jago were to stay here—an even wilder hope in the possibility Tabini might have been compelled to betray him, and that Tabini had kept Banichi and Jago on hand for a reason . . . a wild and improbable rescue . . .

But it was all a very thin, very remote possibility, considering that Tabini had felt constrained to write such a letter at all.

And if Tabini was willing to risk the paidhi's life and along with it the advantage of Mospheira's technology, one could only conclude that Tabini's power was threatened in some substantial way that Tabini couldn't resist.

Or one could argue that the paidhi had completely failed to understand the situation he was in.

.Which offered no hope, either.

He handed Cenedi back the letter with, he hoped, not quite so obvious a tremor in his hands as might have been. He wasn't afraid. He found that curious. He was aware only of a knot in his throat, and a chill lack of sensation in his fingers.

"Nadi," he said quietly. "I don't understand. Are you the ones trying to kill me in Shejidan?"

"Not directly. But denial wouldn't serve the truth, either."

Tabini had armed him contrary to the treaty.

Cenedi had *killed* an assassin on the grounds. Hadn't he?

The confusion piled up around him.

"Where's Banichi? And Jago? Do they know about this? Do they know where I am?"

"They know. I say that denial of responsibility would be a lie. But I will also own that we are embarrassed by the actions of an associate who called on a licensed professional for a disgraceful action. The Guild has been embarrassed by the actions of a single individual acting for personal conviction. I personally—embarrassed myself, in the incident of the tea. More, you accepted my apology, which makes my duty at this moment no easier, nand' paidhi. I assure you there is *nothing* personal in this confrontation. But I will do whatever I feel sufficient to find the truth in this situation."

"What situation?"

"Nand' paidhi. Do you ever mislead us? Do you ever tell us less—or more—than the truth?"

His hazard didn't warrant rushing to judgment head-long—or dealing in on-the-spot absolutes, with a man the extent of whose information or misinformation he didn't know. He tried to think. He tried to be absolutely careful.

"Nadi, there are times I may know . . . some small technical detail, a circuit, a mode of operation—sometimes a whole technological field—that I haven't brought to the appropriate committee; or that I haven't put forward to the aiji. But it's not that I don't intend to bring it forward, no more than other paidhiin have ever withheld what they know. There is no technology we have that I *intend* to withhold—ever."

"Have you ever, in collaboration with Tabini, rendered additional numbers into the transmissions from Mospheira to the station?"

God.

"Ask the aiji."

"Have those numbers been supplied to you by the aiji?"

"Ask him."

Cenedi looked through papers, and looked up again, his dark face absolutely impassive. "I'm asking you, nand' paidhi. Have those numbers been supplied to you by the aiji?"

"That's Tabini's business. Not mine." His hands were cold. He worked his fingers and tried to pretend to himself that the debate was no more serious than a council meeting, at which, very rarely, the questions grew hot and quick. "If Tabini-aiji sends to Mospheira, I render what he says accurately. That's my job. I wouldn't misrepresent him, or Mospheira. *That* is my integrity, nadi Cenedi. I don't lie to either party."

Another silence, long and tense, in which the thunder of an outside storm rumbled through the stones.

"Have you always told the truth, nadi?"

"In such transactions? Yes. To both sides."

"*I* have questions for you, in the name of the aiji-dowager. Will you answer them?"

The walls of the trap closed. It was the nightmare every paidhi had feared and no one had yet met, until, God help him, he had walked right into it, trusting atevi even though he couldn't translate the concept of trust to them, persisting in trusting them when his own advisors said no, standing so doggedly by his belief in Tabini's personal attachment to him that he *hadn't* called his office when he'd received every possible warning things were going wrong.

If Cenedi wanted to use force now . . . he had no help. If Cenedi wanted him to swear that there *was* a human plot against atevi . . . he had no idea whether he could hold out against saying whatever Cenedi wanted.

He gave a slight, atevi shrug, a move of one hand. "As best I can," he said, "I'll answer, as best I personally know the answers."

"Mospheira has . . . how many people?"

"About four million."

"No atevi."

"No atevi."

"Have atevi ever come there, since the Treaty?"

"No, nadi. There haven't. Except the airline crews."

"What do you think of the concept of a paidhi-atevi?"

"Early on, we wanted it. We tried to get it into the Treaty as a condition of the cease fire, because we wanted to understand atevi better than we did. We knew we'd misunderstood. We knew we were partially responsible for the War. But atevi refused. If atevi were willing, now, absolutely I'd support the idea."

"You've nothing to hide, you as a people? It wouldn't provoke resentment, to have an ateva resident on Mospheira, admitted to your councils?"

"I think it would be very useful for atevi to learn our customs. I'd sponsor it. I'd argue passionately in favor of it."

"You don't fear atevi spies any longer."

"I've told you—there are no more secrets. There's nothing to spy on. We live very similar lives. We have very similar conveniences. You wouldn't know the difference between Adams Town and Shejidan."

"I would not?"

"We're very similar. And not—" he added deliberately, "not that all the influence has come from us to you, nadi. I tell you, we've found a good many atevi ideas very wise. You'd feel quite at home in some particulars. We have learned from you."

He doubted Cenedi quite believed that. He saw the frown.

"Could there," Cenedi asked him, "regarding the secrets you say you've provided—be any important area held back?"

"Biological research. Understanding of genetics. That's the last, the most difficult."

"Why is that the last?"

"Numbers. Like space. The size of the numbers. One hopes that computers will find more general acceptance among atevi. One *needs* computers, nadi, adept as you are in mathematics—you still need them. I confess I can't follow everything you do in your heads, but you have to have the computers for space science, for record-keeping, and for genetics as we practice it."

"The number-counters don't believe that. Some say computers are inauspicious and misleading."

"Some also do admit a fascination with them. I've heard some numerologists are writing software ... and criticizing our hardware. They're quite right. Our scientists are very interested in their opinions."

"In atevi invention."

"Very much so."

"What can we possibly invent? Humans have done it all."

"Oh, no, no, nadi, far from all. It's a wide universe. And our ship did once break down."

"Wide enough, this universe?"

He almost said—beyond calculation. But that was heresy. "At least beyond what I know, nadi. Beyond any limit we've found with our ships."

"Is it? But what use is it?"

Occasionally he met a new atevi attitude—inevitably astonishing. "What use is the earth, nadi? What use is the whole world except that we're in it? It's where we *are*, nadi. Its use is that we exist. There may be more important positions in the universe, but from where we stand, it's all that *is* important."

"You believe that some things are uncountable?"

The heresy pit again. He reached for an irrefutable answer, knowing that, if the wrong thing went down on tape—the extremists had him. "If one had the vision to see them, I'm sure one could count them."

"Does anyone have universal vision?"

Another atevi sect, for all he knew. "I wouldn't know, nadi. I'm certainly not that person."

Damned if Cenedi believed the numerologists. But what Cenedi might want for political reasons, he had no way to guess. He wanted out of this line of questioning.

"More tea?" Cenedi asked him.

"Nadi, thank you, I have some left."

"Do you suspect me personally as an enemy?"

"I don't know. I certainly hope not. I've found your company pleasant and I hope it to continue."

"There is nothing personal in my position, nand' paidhi."

"I trust so. I don't know how I could have offended you. Certainly not by intent."

"Heresy is not the charge here, understand. I find all the number-counting complete, primitive foolishness."

"But tapes can be edited."

"So can television," Cenedi said. "You provided Tabini-aiji with abundant material today."

The television? He'd put it from his mind, in the shock of reading Tabini's letter. But now that Cenedi said it, he factored it in with that letter—all the personal, easy questions, about himself, his life, his associations.

Double-cross, by the only ateva he absolutely trusted with his life, double-cross by the aiji who held all the agreements with human civilization.

Tabini had armed him against assassins—and in the light of that letter he couldn't prove the assassins weren't Tabini's. Tabini gave him a gun that could be found and traced by the markings on its bullets.

But when he'd used it, and drawn blood, Banichi had given him another. He didn't understand that.

Although perhaps Banichi hadn't understood then, either, and done the loyal thing, not being in on the plot. All his reckonings ran in circles—and now Banichi's gun was gone from under his mattress, when they could photograph anything, plant any piece of evidence, and fill in the serial numbers later ... he knew at least some of the tricks they could use. He'd studied them. The administration had *made* him study them until his head rattled with them, and he hadn't wanted to believe he'd ever need to know.

Not with Tabini, no.

Not with a man who confided in him, who told him official secrets he didn't, out of respect for this man, convey to Mospheira.... "How many people live on Mospheira?" Cenedi asked.

"You asked that, nadi. About four million. Four million three hundred thousand."

"We'll repeat questions from time to time, just to be sure.—Does that count children?"

Question after question, then, about support for the rail system, about the vetoes his predecessor had cast, about power plants, about dams and highways and the ecological studies, on Mospheira and on the mainland.

About the air link between the island and the mainland, and the road system in Mospheira's highland north and center. Nothing at any point that was classified. Nothing they couldn't find out from the catalogs and from his private mail, wherever that was going.

Probably they *had* found it out from his mail, long be-

fore the satellites. They might have, out of the vacation
catalogs, assembled a mosaic of Mospheira's roads, cities,
streets, might have photographed the coastal cities, where
regular cargo flights came in from Shejidan and flew out
with human-manufactured electronics, textiles, seafood
and pharmaceuticals.

"Do you have many associates on Mospheira, nadi?
What are their names?"

"What do you do regularly when you go back to
Mospheira, nadi? Surely you spend some official time. . . ?"

"You had a weapon in your quarters, nadi. What did
you plan to do with it?"

Admit nothing, he thought. There *was* no friendly question.

"I'm unaware of any gun."

"An object that size, under your mattress."

"I don't know. Maybe it arrived and departed the same
day."

"Please don't joke, nadi. This is an extremely serious
business."

"I'm aware it is. But I assure you, I didn't bring it here
and I didn't put it under my mattress."

"It appeared spontaneously."

"It must have. I've no other answer. Nadi, what would
I do with it? I'm no marksman. I'm no danger with a gun,
except to myself and the furniture."

"Nadi. We know this gun didn't originate in Malguri.
We have its registration."

He looked elsewhere, at the double-edged shadows on
the wall. Maybe Tabini had lost politically, somehow, in
some way that mandated turning him over to a rival entity. He didn't know who he was defending, now, in the
matter of the disappearing gun, whether Tabini from his
rivals or Banichi from prosecution, or whether Banichi's
substitution of that gun had muddied things up so badly
that everyone looked guilty.

But he had no question now where the gun had gone.

And, as for lying, he adopted his own official line.

"Nadi," Cenedi said. "Answer the question."

"I thought it was a statement, nadi. Forgive me. I don't own a gun. I didn't put it there. That's all I can say."

"You *fired* at the assassin in Shejidan, nand' paidhi."

"No. I raised an alarm. Banichi fired when the man ran."

"Banichi's aim is not, then, what I'd expect of him."

"It was dark, it was raining, and the man was running."

"And there was no one but yourself in the room."

"I heard a noise. I roused the guard."

"Banichi regularly stands guard by your door at night?"

"I don't know, I suppose he had some business in the halls—some lady. I didn't ask him."

"Nadi, you're lying. This doesn't help anyone."

"Only three people in the world know what happened that night: myself, Banichi, and the man on that balcony—who was surely not you, Cenedi-ji. *Was* it?"

"No. It's not my method of choice."

That was probably a joke. He didn't know whether to take it as one. He was scared, and sure that Cenedi had information from sources he didn't know about. Cenedi was building a case of some kind. And while there were laws against kidnapping, and against holding a person by force, there were none against what Tabini had done in sending him here.

"You have no idea how the gun got there," Cenedi said. "You state emphatically that you didn't know it was there."

"Yes."

Cenedi leaned back in his chair and stared at him, a long, long moment.

"Banichi gave you the gun."

"No, nadi. He did not."

"Nand' paidhi, there are people of the dowager's acquaintance, closely associated people, whose associations with Tabini-aiji are *through* the aiji-dowager. They don't accept this piece of paper, this *Treaty* with Mospheira. Pieces of paper don't impress them at all, and, quite frankly, they don't consider the cession of Mospheira legitimate or effective."

That crowd, he thought with a chill. The conservative fringe. The attack-the-beaches element. He didn't want to believe it.

"We've received inquiry from them," Cenedi said. "In fact, their agents have come to Malguri requesting you be turned over to them, urging the aiji-dowager to abandon association with Tabini altogether. They argue the Treaty is valueless. That Tabini-aiji is leading in a wrong direction. We've arranged a compromise. They need certain information, I've indicated we can obtain it for them, and they'll not request you be turned over to them."

It was a nightmare. He didn't know what aspect of it to try to deal with. Finding out where Cenedi stood seemed foremost.

"Are you working for the aiji-dowager, nadi?"

"Always. Without exception."

"And what side is *she* taking? For or against Tabini?"

"She has no *man'chi*. She acts for herself."

"To replace him?"

"That would be a possibility, nadi. She would do nothing that reduces her independence."

Nothing that reduces her independence. Ilisidi had lost the election in the hasdrawad. Twice. Once five years ago, to Tabini.

And Tabini had to write that letter and send *him* to Ilisidi?

"Will you give me the statements I need, nand' paidhi?"

It wasn't an easy answer. Possibly—possibly Tabini hadn't really betrayed him. Possibly Tabini's administration was on its way down in defeat, and he'd never felt the earthquake. He couldn't believe that. But atevi politics had confounded paidhiin before him.

"Nand' paidhi," Cenedi said. "These people have sent to Malguri to bring you back to their authorities. If I give you over to them, I don't say we can't get you back—but in what condition I can hardly promise. They might carry their questioning much further, into technology, weapons, and space-based systems, things in which we have no interest, and in which we have no reason to believe you haven't told the truth. Please don't delude yourself: this is not machimi, and no one keeps secrets from professionals. If you give me the statement I want, that will bring Tabini down, we can be cordial. If I can't show them that—"

His mind was racing. He was losing bits of what Cenedi was saying, and that could be disastrous.

"—I've no choice but to let them obtain it their way. And I had much rather keep you from that, nand' paidhi. Again: who fired the gun?"

"Banichi fired the gun."

"Who *gave* you the gun?"

"No one gave me a gun, nadi."

Cenedi sighed and pressed a button. Not a historical relic, a distracted corner of his mind objected. But probably a great deal else around Cenedi's office wasn't historical, or outmoded.

They waited. He could, he thought, change his mind. He could give Cenedi what he wanted, change sides—but he had Cenedi's word . . . and that letter . . . to tell him what was really going on, and he didn't believe it, not wholly. Tabini had been too canny, too much the politician, to go down without a maneuver tried, and he might, for all he knew, be a piece Tabini still counted his. Still relied on.

Which was stupid to think. If Tabini wanted him to take any active role in this, if that letter wasn't to take seriously, Tabini could have told him, Banichi or Jago could have told him—*someone* could have told him what in hell they wanted him to do.

And he could have called his office, the way he was supposed to, and filed a report.

X

The door behind him opened. He had no illusions about making an escape from Malguri—half the continent away from human territory, with no phone and no one to rely on except Jago and Banichi—and that was, perhaps, a chance; but out-muscling two strong atevi who stood head and shoulders taller than he did, who loomed over him and laid hands on his arms as he got up from the chair . . . that hardly felt like a sane chance, either.

Cenedi looked at him, and said nothing as they took him out into the dim hall. They were taking him further back into Malguri's farther wing, outside the territory he knew, farther and farther from the outside door, and he had at least a notion Banichi might be on the grounds, if Cenedi had told the truth, working wherever the power lines came into the building. He might reach Banichi, at least raise an alarm—if he could overpower two atevi, three, counting Cenedi, and one had *better* count Cenedi.

And get out of Cenedi's hearing.

"I need the restroom," he said, planting his feet, his heart beating like a hammer. It was stupid, but after two cups of tea, it was also the truth. "Just wait a damned minute, I need the restroom. . . ."

"Restroom," one said, and they brought him further down the hall to a backstairs room he judged must be under his own accommodation, and no more modern.

The one shut the outside door. The other stayed close to him, and stood by while he did what he'd complained he needed to, and washed his hands and desperately measured his chances against them. It had been a long time since he'd studied martial arts, a long time since he'd last worked out, and not so long for them, he was certain of that. He walked back toward the door in the hope the one would make the mistake of opening it in advance of him—the man didn't, and that moment of transition was the only and last chance. He jabbed an elbow into the man at his left, tried to come about for a kick to clear the man from the door, and knew he was in trouble the split second before he found his wrist and his shoulder twisted around in a move that could break his arm.

"All right, all right," he gasped, then had the unforgiving stone wall against the side of his face and found the breath he desperately needed to draw brought that trapped arm closer to breaking.

A lot of breathing then, theirs, his. The venue didn't lend itself to complex reasoning, or argument about anything but the pain. He felt a cord come around his wrist, worse and worse, and he made another try at freeing himself as the one man opened the bathroom door. But the cord and the twist and lock on his arm gave the other guard a compelling argument.

He went where they wanted: it was all he could do—a short walk down the hall and to a doorway with lamplit stone steps leading downward to a basement he hadn't known existed in Malguri. "I want to talk to Banichi," he said at the top step, and balked.

Which convinced him they had no idea of the fragility of human joints and the guard was imminently, truly going to break the arm. He tried to take the step and missed it, lost his balance completely, and the guard shoved him along regardless, using the arm for leverage until he got his feet marginally under him and made the next several steps down on his own. Vision blurred, a teary haze of lamplight from a single hanging source. Stone walls, no furniture but that solitary, hanging oil lamp and a table and chair. Thunder shook the stones, even this deep into the rock, seeming like a last message from the outside world. There was another doorway, open on a dark corridor. They shoved him at it.

There wasn't any help. Unless Banichi was on some side of this he couldn't figure, there wasn't going to be any. He'd lost his best bid, thrown it away in a try at fighting two atevi hand to hand—but if he could get leverage to get free . . . before they could get a door shut on him—and he could get the door behind them shut—

It wasn't a good chance. It wasn't any chance. But he was desperate as they took him aside, through a door into a dark cell with no light except from the room down the hall. He figured they meant to turn him loose here, and he prepared to come back at them, duck low and see if he could get past them.

But when the guard let go, he kept the wrist cord, swung him about by that and backed him against the wall while his fellow grabbed the other arm. He kicked and got a casual knee in the gut for his trouble, the atevi having their hands full.

"Don't," that one said, while he was trying to get his wind back. "No more, do you hear me?"

After which they hooked his feet out from under him, stretched his one arm out along a metal bar, while the second guard pulled the other arm in the other direction, and tied it tight with cord from wrist to elbow.

For most of it, he was still trying to breathe—damned mess, was all he could think, over and over, classic atevi way of handling a troublesome case, only the bar wasn't average human height and he couldn't get his knees on the ground or his feet under him. Just not damned comfortable, he thought—couldn't get out of it by any means he could think of—couldn't even find a place to put his knees to protect vital parts of his body from the working-over he expected.

But they went away and left him instead, without a word, only brushing off their hands and dusting their clothes, as if he had ruffled their dignity. He dreaded their shutting the door and leaving him in the dark . . . but they left it as it was, so there was an open door within sight, and their shadows retreating on the hall floor outside. He heard their voices echoing, the two of them talking about having a drink, in the way of workmen with a job finished.

He heard them go away up the steps, and heard the door shut.

After that was—just—silence.

They had told him at the very outset of his training, that if the situation ever really blew up like this, suicide was a job requirement. They didn't want a human in atevi hands spilling technological information ad lib and indefinitely—a very serious worry early on, when atevi hadn't reached the political stability they had had for a century, and when rivalry between associations had been a constant threat to the Treaty ... oh, no, it couldn't happen, not in remotest imagination.

But they still taught the course—he knew a dozen painless methods—and they still said, if there was no other option, take it—because there was no rescue coming and no way anyone would risk the peace to bring him out.

Not that there was much he could tell anybody, except political information against Tabini. Technology nowadays was so esoteric the paidhi didn't know it until he had his briefing on Mospheira, and he worked at it until he could translate it and make sense of it to atevi experts. There was no way they could beat atomic secrets out of him, no more than he could explain trans-light technology.

But he couldn't let them use him politically, either—couldn't make statements for them to edit and twist out of context, not without marks on him to show the world he was under duress.

And he'd made the television interview—sitting there quite at ease in front of the cameras.

He'd let Cenedi get his answers on tape, including his damning refusal to attribute the gun. They had all the visuals and sound bites they could want.

Damn, he thought. He'd screwed it. He'd screwed it beyond any repair. Hanks was in charge, as of now, and damn, he wished there was better, and more imaginative, and *somebody* to realize Tabini was still the best bet they had.

Overthrow Tabini, replace him with the humanophobes, and him with Deana Hanks, and watch everything generations had built go to absolute hell. He believed it. And the hard-liners among humans who thought he'd gotten entirely too friendly with Tabini . . . they weren't right, he refused to believe they were right; but they'd have their field day saying so.

The irony was, the hard-liners, the nuke-the-opposition factions, were alike on both sides of the strait. And he couldn't turn the situation over to them.

Mistake to have taken himself out of Cenedi's hands. He believed that now. He had to tough it out somehow, find out if Banichi was involved, or a prisoner, or what— get them to bring Cenedi back in, get the ear of somebody who'd listen to reason.

Plenty of time for the mind to race over plans and plans and plans.

But when the cold got into his bones and the muscles started to stiffen and then to hurt—the mind found other things to occupy it besides plans for how to fix what he'd screwed up, the mind found the body was damned uncomfortable, and it hurt, and he might never get out of this cellar if he didn't give these people everything they wanted.

But he couldn't do that. He couldn't, wouldn't, hadn't done his job half right or he wouldn't be here, but he wasn't going to finish it by bringing Tabini down.

Only hope he had, he kept telling himself. Tabini was a canny son of a bitch when he had to be. Damn him, he'd given up a card he'd known he had to cede—*knew* humans wouldn't fight over him; and having not a human bone in his body, didn't *feel* what a human would. He'd gotten his television interview. He'd show the world and the humans that Bren Cameron was well-disposed to him—he'd slipped that television crew in neatly as could be and gotten his essential interview just before the other side moved in their agents with their demands on Ilisidi, who was probably fence-sitting and playing neutral.

Check, and mate.

Put him in one hell of a position, Tabini had. Thanks a lot, he thought. Thanks a lot, Tabini.

But we need you. Peace—depends on you staying in power. You know they'll replace me. Give you a brand new paidhi, a new quantity for the number-counters to figure out and argue over. Switch the dice on them—leave them with a new puzzle and humans not reacting the way atevi would.

You son of a *bitch*, Tabini-ji.

The time seemed to stretch into hours, from terror to pain, to boredom and an acute misery of stiffened muscles, numb spots, cold metal and cold stone. He didn't hear the thunder anymore. He couldn't find an angle to put his legs that didn't hurt his back or his knees or his shoulders, and every try hurt.

Imagination in the quiet and the dark was no asset at all—too much television, Banichi would tell him.

But Banichi had either turned coat—which meant Banichi's *man'chi* had always been something other than even Tabini thought—or Banichi had landed in the same trouble as he was.

In his fondest hope, Banichi or Jago would come through that door and cut him free before the opposition put him on their urgent list. Maybe the delay in dealing with him *was* because they were looking for Banichi and Jago. Maybe Jago's quick exit when he'd last talked with her, and that com message from Banichi—had been because Banichi knew something, and Banichi had called her, knowing *they* had to be free in order to do anything to free him. . . .

It was a good machimi plot, but it didn't happen. It wasn't *going* to happen. He just hung there and hurt in various sprained places, and finally heard the outer hall door open.

Footsteps descended the stone steps into the outer room—two sets of footsteps, or three, he wasn't entirely

sure, then decided on three: he heard voices, saying something he couldn't make out. He reached a certain pitch of
panic fear, deciding whatever was going to happen was
about to happen. But no one came, so he thought the hell
with it and let his head fall forward, which could relieve
the ache in his neck for maybe five minutes at a time.

Then voices he'd decided were going to stay in the
next room became noises in the hall; and when he looked
up, a shadow walked in—someone in guard uniform, he
couldn't see against the light, but he could see the sparks
of metal off the shadows that filled his field of vision.

"Good evening," he said to his visitor. "Or is it the
middle of the night?"

The shadow left him, and nerves ratcheted to the point
of pain began a series of tremors that he decided must be
the stage before paralysis set into his legs, like that in his
fingers. He didn't want that. He hoped maybe that was
just a guard checking on him, and they'd go away.

The steps came back. He was supposed to be scared by
this silent coming and going, he decided—and that, with
the pain, made him mad. He'd hoped to get to mad . . . he
always found a state of temper more comforting than a
state of terror.

But this time more arrived, bringing a wooden chair
from somewhere, and a tape recorder—all of them shadows casting other shadows in the light from the doorway.
The recorder cast a shadow, too, and a red light glowed
on it when one of them bent and pressed the button.

"Live, on tape," he said. He saw no reason to forbear
anything, and he stayed angry, now, though on the edge of
terror. He'd not deserved this, he told himself—not deserved it of Tabini, or Cenedi, or Ilisidi. "So who are
you? What do you want, nadi? Anything reasonable? I'm
sure not."

"No fear at all?" the shadow asked him. "No remorse,
no regret?"

"What should I regret, nadi? Relying on the dowager's

hospitality? If I've passed my welcome here, I apologize, and I'd like to—leave—"

One shadow separated itself from the others, picked up the chair, turned it quietly face about and sat down, arms folded on the low back.

"Where did you get the gun?" this shadow asked, a stranger's voice.

"I didn't have a gun. Banichi fired. I didn't."

"Why would Banichi involve himself? And why did it turn up in your bed?"

"I've no idea."

"Has Banichi ever gone with you to Mospheira?"

"No."

"Gone to Mospheira at all?"

"No. No ateva has, in my lifetime."

"You're lying about the gun, aren't you?"

"No," he said.

The tic in his left leg started again. He tried to stay calm and to think, while the questions came one after the other and periodically circled back to the business of the gun.

The tape ran out, and he watched them replace it. The tic never let up. Another one threatened, in his right arm, and he tried to change position to relieve it.

"What do you project," the next question was, on a new tape, "on future raw metals shipments to Mospheira? Why the increase?"

"Because Mospheira's infrastructure is wearing out." It was the pat answer, the simplistic answer. "We need the raw metals. We have our own processing requirements."

"And your own launch site?"

Wasn't the same question. His heart skipped a beat. He knew he took too long. "What launch site?"

"We know. *You* gave us satellites. Shouldn't we know?"

"Don't launch from Mospheira latitude. Can't. Not practical."

"Possible. Practical, if that's the site you have. Or do

any boats leave Mospheira that don't have to do with fishing?"

What damned boats? he asked himself. If there was anything, *he* didn't know it, and he didn't rule that out. "We're not building any launch site, nadi, I swear to you. If we are, the paidhi isn't aware of it."

"You slip numbers into the dataflow. You encourage sectarian debates to delay us. Most clearly you're stockpiling metals. You increase your demands for steel, for gold—you give us industries, and you trade us microcircuits for graphite, for titanium, aluminum, palladium, elements we didn't know existed a hundred years ago and, thanks to you, now we have a use for. Now you import them, minerals that don't exist on Mospheira. For what? For what do you use these things, if not the same things you've taught us to use them for, for light-lift aircraft you don't fly, for—"

"I'm not an engineer. I'm not expert in our manufacturing. I know we use these things in electronics, in high-strength steel for industry—"

"And light-lift aircraft? High-velocity fan blades for jets you don't manufacture?"

He shook his head, childhood habit. It meant nothing to atevi. He was in dire trouble, and he couldn't tell anybody who urgently needed to know the kind of suspicions atevi were entertaining. He feared he wouldn't have the chance to tell anybody outside this room if he didn't come up with plausible, cooperative answers for this man.

"I've no doubt—no doubt there are experimental aircraft. We haven't anything but diagrams of what used to exist. We build test vehicles. Models. We *test* what we think we understand before we give advice that will let some ateva blow himself to bits, nadi, we know the dangers of these propellants and these flight systems—"

"Concern for us."

"Nadi, I assure you, we don't want some ateva blowing up a laboratory or falling out of the sky and everybody saying it was our fault. People find fault with the programs. There are enough people blaming us for planes that don't file flight plans and city streets piled full of grain because the agriculture minister thought the computer was making up the numbers—damned right we have test programs. We try to prevent disasters before we ask you to risk your necks—it's not a conspiracy, it's public relations!"

"It's more than tests," the interrogator said. "The aiji is well aware. Is he not?"

"He's not aware. I'm not aware. There *is* no launch site. There's nothing we're holding back, there's nothing we're hiding. If they're building planes, it's a test program."

"Who gave you the gun, nadi?"

"Nobody gave me a gun. I didn't even know it was under my mattress. Ask Cenedi how it got there."

"Who gave it to you, nadi-ji? Just give us an answer. Say, The aiji gave it to me, and you can go back to bed and not be concerned in this."

"I don't know. I said I don't know."

The man nearest drew a gun. He saw the sheen on the barrel in the almost dark. The man moved closer and he felt the cold metal against his face. Well, he thought, That's what we want, isn't it? No more questions.

"Nand' paidhi," the interrogator said. "You say Banichi fired the shots at the intruder in your quarters. Is that true?"

Past a certain point, to hell with the game. He shut his eyes and thought about the snow and the sky around winter slopes. About the wind, and nobody else in sight.

Told him something, that did, that it wasn't Barb his mind went to. If it mattered. It was, however, a curious, painful discovery.

"Isn't that true, nand' paidhi?"

He declined to answer. The gun barrel went away. A powerful hand pulled his head up and banged it against the wall.

"Nand' paidhi. Tabini-aiji has renounced you. He's

given your disposition into our hands. You've read the letter. Have you not?"

"Yes."

"What is our politics to you? —Let him go, nadi. Let go. All of you, wait outside."

The man let him go. They changed the rules of a sudden. The rest of them filed out the door, letting light past, so that he could see at least the outlined edges of the interrogator's face, but he didn't think he knew the man. He only wondered what the last-ditch proposition was going to be, or what the man had to offer him he wasn't going to say with the others there. He wasn't expecting to like it.

The interrogator reached down and cut off the recorder. It was very quiet in the cell, then, for a long, long wait.

"Do you think," the man said finally, "that we dare release you now, nand' paidhi, to go back to Mospheira? On the other hand, if you provided the aiji-dowager the necessary evidence to remove the aiji, if you became a resource useful on our side—we'd be fools to turn you over to more radical factions of our association."

"Cenedi said the same thing. And sent me here."

"We support the aiji-dowager. We'd keep you alive and quite comfortable, nand' paidhi. You could go back to Shejidan. Nothing essential would change in the relations of the association with Mospheira—except the party in power. If you're telling the truth, and you don't know the other information we'd like to have, we're reasonable. We can accept that, so long as you're willing to provide us statements that serve our point of view. It costs you nothing. It maintains you in office, nand' paidhi. All for a simple answer. What do you say?" The interrogator bent, complete shadow again, and turned the tape recorder back on. "Who provided you the gun, nand' paidhi?"

"I never had a gun," he said. "I don't know what you're talking about."

The interrogator cut off the tape recorder, picked it up, got up, and left him.

He hung against the bar, shaking, telling himself he'd just been a complete fool, telling himself Tabini didn't deserve a favor that size, if there was a real chance that he could get himself out of this alive, stay in office, and go back to dealing with Mospheira, business as usual—

The hell they'd let him. Trust was a word you couldn't translate. But atevi had fourteen words for betrayal.

He expected the guards would come back, maybe shoot him, maybe take him somewhere else, to the less reasonable people the man had talked about. If you had a potential informer, you didn't turn him over to rival factions. No. It was all Cenedi. It was all the dowager. All the same game, no matter the strategy. It just got rougher. Cenedi had warned him that people didn't hold out.

He heard someone go out of the room down the hall, heard the doors shut, and in the long, long silence asked himself how bad it could get—and had ugly, ugly answers out of the machimi. He didn't like to think about that. Breathing hurt, now, but he couldn't feel his legs.

A long while later the outer room door opened. Again the footsteps, descending the stone steps—he listened to them, drawing quick, shallow breaths that didn't give him enough oxygen, watched the shadows come down the darker corridor, and tried to keep his wits about him— find a point of negotiation, he said to himself. Engage the bastards, just to get them talking—stall for time in which Hanks or Tabini or somebody could *do* something.

The guards walked in. —Cenedi's, he was damned sure, now.

"Tell Cenedi I've decided," he said, as matter of factly as if it was his office and they'd shown up to collect the message. "Maybe we can find an agreement. I need to talk to him. I'd rather talk to him."

"That's not our business," one said—and he recognized the attitude, the official hand-washing, the atevi official who'd taken a position, broken off negotiations, and told his subordinates to stonewall attempts, officially. Cenedi might have given orders not to hear about the methods.

He didn't take Cenedi for that sort. He thought Cenedi would insist to know what his subordinates did.

"There's an intermediate position," he said. "Tell him there's a way to solve this." Anything to get Cenedi to send for him.

But the guards had other orders. They started untying his arms. Going to take him somewhere else, then. Inside Malguri, please God.

Four of them to handle him. Ludicrous. But his legs weren't working well. One foot was asleep. His hands wouldn't work. He tried to get up before they found a way of their own, and two of them dragged him up and locked arms behind him to hold him on his feet, although one of them could have carried him. "Sorry," he said, with the foot collapsing at every other step as they took him out the door, and he felt the fool for opening his mouth—he was so damned used to courtesies, and they seemed so damned useless now. "Just *tell* Cenedi," he said as they were going down the corridor. "Where are we going?"

"Nand' paidhi, just walk. We're ordered not to answer you."

Which meant they wouldn't. They owed him nothing. That they gave him back courtesy was comforting, at least indicating that they didn't personally hold a grudge, but it didn't mean a thing beyond that. *Man'chi* was everything—wherever theirs was, you couldn't argue that.

At least they took him up the steps, into the hall. He held out a hope they might pass Cenedi's office, and they did—but that door was shut, and no light showed under it. Damn, he thought, one more hope gone to nothing—it shook him, ever so small a shaking of his remaining understanding, but the thoughts kept wanting to scatter to what was happening, what might happen, whose these men were—and that wasn't important, because he couldn't *do* anything about it. He could sort through the questions they'd asked, and try to figure what they *would* ask—that . . . that was the only thing that would do any

good; and he couldn't trust that the persistent question
about the gun was even the important one—it might be
what they wanted him to focus on while they chipped
away at what he did know ... while they figured out
where the limits of his knowledge were and how useful
he was likely to be to them.

There wasn't any damned launch facility—that was the
scariest question, and they were wrong about that, they
had to be wrong about that: he couldn't make it true by
any stretch of the imagination. But the stockpiling—they
had the trade figures. He couldn't lie about that. Atevi
had finally gotten the lesson humans had taught, knew
they were accumulating materials useful in certain kinds
of development, and he could tell them far too much, if
they asked the right questions and used the right drugs.
Cenedi had said the same thing his own administrators
had said: he wasn't going to be any hero, unless he could
think of a better lie than he'd thought of, impromptu, already ... and build on what he'd said.

God, only *hope* tying the gun to Tabini was their immediate objective, and not the rest of it—they hadn't beaten
Tabini, couldn't have, and still be asking what they were
asking—

But he couldn't give them any more on that score.

Couldn't. Daren't. Couldn't play the game down that
dangerous path. He needed to use his head, and his head
wasn't all that clear at the moment—he hurt, and the
thoughts went tumbling and skittering at every distraction, into what might happen and what he could do and
daren't do and how much choice he might have.

They brought him around by the kitchens, and down
the corridor to the stairs he'd once suspected might be
wired—Ilisidi's back stairs, her apartment, and her wing
of the fortress, completely away from the rest of Malguri.

"Banichi!" he yelled as they began that climb—and his
guards took a numbing, tighter grip on him. "Banichi!
Tano! Help!" He shoved to pitch them all down the
stairs—grabbed the railing with one hand and couldn't

hold on to it. One guard got an arm around him, tore him loose and squeezed the breath out of him as his partner recovered his balance.

"Banichi!" he yelled till his throat cracked; but he wasn't strong enough to throw them once they were on their guard. They carried him upstairs between them, and down the upstairs hall, and through the massive doors to Ilisidi's apartments.

Thick doors. Soundproof doors, once they shut. Ilisidi's premises smelled of floral scent, of wood fire, of lamp oil. There was no more point in fighting them. He caught his breath and went on his own feet as best he could— he'd done his best and his worst: he let them steer him without violence, now that they were out of hearing of help—across polished wooden floors and antique carpets, past delicate furniture and priceless art and, as everywhere in Malguri, the heads of dead animals—some extinct, hunted out of existence.

A gasping breath caught the clean, cold scent of rain-washed air. Windows or balcony doors were open somewhere, wafting a breeze through the rooms, the next of which were in shadow, lamps unlit, air colder and colder as they went, finally through a dark drawing room he remembered, and toward the open-air chill of the balcony.

A table was set there, in the dark—a dark figure, hair streaked with white, sat having tea and toast, wrapped in robes against the cold. Ilisidi looked up at their intrusion on her before-dawn breakfast and, quite, quite madly, to his eyes, waved a gesture toward the empty chair, while icy gusts whipped at the lace table-covering.

"Good morning," she said, "nand' paidhi. Sit. What lovely hair you have. Does it curl on its own?"

He fell into the chair as the guards deposited him there. His braid had come completely undone. His hair flew in the wind that whipped the steam off Ilisidi's cup. Guards stood behind his chair while the dowager's servant poured him a cup. The wind took that steam, too, chilling him to the bone as it skirled in off the shadowed lake, out of the mountains. The faintest redness of dawn showed in the lowest notches.

"It's the hour for ghosts," Ilisidi said. "Do you believe in them?"

He caught a quick, cold breath—caught up the pieces of his sanity . . . and engaged.

"I believe in unrewarded duty, nand' dowager. I believe in treachery, and invitations one shouldn't take at face value. —Come aboard my ship, said the lady to the fisherman." He picked up the teacup in a shaking hand. Tea spilled, scalding his fingers, but he carried it to his lips and sipped it. He tasted only sweet. "Not Cenedi's brew. What effect does this one have?"

"Such a prideful lad. I heard you enjoyed sweets. —Hear the bell?"

He did. The buoy bell, he supposed, far out in the lake.

"When the wind blows, it carries it," Ilisidi said, wrapped in her robes, and wrapping them closer. "Warning of rocks. We had the idea long before you came bringing gifts."

"I've no doubt. Atevi had found so much before us."

"Shipwrecked, were you? Is that still the story? No buoy bells?"

"Too far from our ordinary routes," he said, and took another, warming sip, while the wind cut through his shirt and trousers. Shivers made him spill scalding liquid on his fingers as he set the cup down. "Off our charts. Too far to see the stars we knew."

"But close enough for this one."

"Eventually. When we were desperate." The ringing came and went by turns, on the tricks of the wind. "We never meant to harm anyone, nand' dowager. That's still the truth."

"Is it?"

"When Tabini sent me to you—he said I'd need all my diplomacy. I didn't understand, then. I understood his grandmother was simply difficult."

Ilisidi gave him no expression, none that human eyes

could see in the dim morning. But she might have been amused. Ilisidi was frequently amused at such odd points. The cold had penetrated all the way to his brain, maybe, or it was the tea: he found no particular terror left, with her.

"Do you mind telling me," he asked her above the wind, "what you're after? Launch sites on Mospheira is a piece of nonsense. Wrong latitude. Ships leaving for other places is the same. So, is arresting me just politics, or what?"

"My eyes aren't what they were. When I was your age I could see your orbiting station. Can you, from here?"

He turned his head toward the sun, toward the mountains, searching above the peaks for a star that didn't twinkle, a star shining with reflected sunlight.

His vision blurred on him. He saw it distorted, and he looked instead for dimmer, neighboring stars. He had no trouble seeing them, the sky was still so dark, without electric lights to haze the dawn with city-glow.

And when he looked fixedly at the station he could still see its deformation, as if—he feared at first thought—it had yawed out of its habitual plane, making a minute exaggeration of its round into an ellipse.

Was it possibly the central mast coming into view? The station tilted radically out of plane?

Logical explanations chased through his head—the station further along to deterioration than they had reckoned, a solar storm, maybe—and Mospheira might be transmitting like mad, trying to salvage it. It would engage atevi notice: they had perfectly adequate optics.

Maybe it was some solar panel come loose from the station and catching the sun. The station rotated once every so many minutes. If it was something loose, it ought to go away and come back.

"Well, nand' paidhi?"

He got up from his chair and stared at it, trying not to blink, trying until his eyes hurt in the gusts that blasted cold through his clothing.

But it didn't do those things—didn't dim, or change. It remained a steady, minute irregularity that stayed on the same side of a station that was supposed to be spinning on its axis ... slower and slower over the centuries, as entropy had its way, but—

But, he thought, my God, not in my lifetime, the station wasn't supposed to break apart, barring total, astronomical calamity. . . .

And it wouldn't just hang there like that—unless I *am* looking at the mast. . . .

He took a step toward the balcony. Atevi hands moved to stop him, and held his arms, but it wasn't flinging himself off the side of Malguri that he had in mind, it was insulation from the very faint light still reaching them from the farther rooms. He still couldn't resolve it. His brain kept trying to make sense out of the configuration.

"Eight days ago," Ilisidi said, "this—appeared and joined the station."

Appeared.

Joined the station.

Oh, my God, my God—

XI

"Transmissions between Mospheira and the station have been frequent," Ilisidi said. "An explanation, nand' paidhi. What do you see?"

"It's the ship. Our ship—at least, *some* ship—"

He was speaking his own language. His legs were numb. He couldn't trust himself to walk—it was a good thing the guards caught his arms and steered him back to safety at the table.

But they didn't let him sit. They faced him toward Ilisidi, and held him there.

"Some call it treachery, nand' paidhi. What do *you* call it?"

Eight days ago. The emergency return, bringing him and Tabini back from Taiben. The cut-off of his mail. Banichi and Jago with him constantly.

"Nand' paidhi? *Tell* me what you see."

"A ship," he managed to say in their language—he was bone-cold, incapable of standing, except for the atevi hands holding him. He was almost incapable of speaking, the breath was so short in his chest. "It's the ship that left us here, aiji-mai, that's all I can think."

"Many of us think many more things," Ilisidi said, "nand' paidhi. What do you suppose they're saying ... this supposed ship ... and your people across the strait? Do you suppose we figure in these conversations at all?"

He shivered and looked at the sky again, thinking, It's impossible—

And looked at Ilisidi, a darkness in the dawn, except only the silver in her hair and the liquid anger in her eyes.

"Aiji-mai, I *don't* understand. I didn't know this was happening. No one expected it. No one told me."

"Oh, this is a little incredible, paidhi-ji, that no one knew, that this appearance in our skies is so totally, utterly a surprise to you."

"Please." His legs were going. The blood was cut off to his hands. For what he knew, the dowager would have the guards pitch him off the edge from here, a gesture of atevi defiance, in a war the world couldn't win, a war the paidhiin were supposed to prevent. "Nand' dowager, I'm telling you the truth. I didn't expect this. But I know why they're here. I know the things you want to know."

"Do you, now. And the paidhiin are only interpreters."

"And human, aiji-mai. I know what's going on up there, the way I know what humans did in the past and what they want for the future—nothing in their plans is to your detriment."

"As the station wasn't. As your coming here wasn't. As your interference in our affairs wasn't, and your domina-

tion of our trade, our invention, our governance of ourselves wasn't. You led us to the technology *you* wanted,
you lent us the industry *you* needed, you perverted our
needs to your programs, you pushed us into a future of
television and computers and satellites, all of which we
grow to love, oh, to rely on—and forget every aspect of
our own past, our own laws, our own course that *we*
would have followed to use our own resources. We are
not so stupid, nand' paidhi, *not* so stupid as to have destroyed ourselves as you kept counseling us we would do
without your lordly help, we are *not* so stupid as to believe we weren't supplying you with materials for which
you had your own uses, in an agenda we hadn't set.
Tabini placed great confidence in you—too damned *much*
confidence in you. When he knew what had happened he
sent you to me, as someone with her wits still about her,
someone who hasn't spent her life in Shejidan watching
television and growing complacent. So tell *me* your truth,
nand' paidhi! Give *me* your assurances! Tell me why all
the other lies are justified and why the truth in our skies
this morning is good for us!"

The blasts of wind came no colder than Ilisidi's anger.
It was the truth, all of it, all justified, he knew that the
way he'd known the unspoken truth of his dealings with
atevi—that the paidhiin were doing the best they could do
in a bad bargain, keeping a peace that wasn't viable between ordinary people of their two species, saving what
they'd almost entirely destroyed, things like this reality
around him, the ancient stones, the lake, the order of life
in an atevi fortress, remote from the sky and the stars he
couldn't reach from here. He looked up at that truth and
the lights blurred in his eyes. The wind gave him no direction, whether up or down, whether he was falling into
the sky or standing on stones he couldn't feel. He was
afraid—terrified as atevi must be of that human presence
up there—and didn't comprehend why.

"Aiji-mai, I can't say it's good that it's there, it's just
there, it's just what's happened, and if you kill me, it

won't make anything any better than it is. Mospheira didn't plan this. Yes, we've guided your technology—we wanted to get back into space, aiji-mai, we didn't have the resources ourselves, our equipment was half-destroyed, and we didn't *think* the ship still existed. We took a chance coming down here—it was a disaster for us and for you. Two hundred years we've worked to get back up there, and we never wanted to destroy the atevi—only to give you the same freedom we want for ourselves."

"Damned nice of you. Did you ask?"

"We were naive. But we hadn't a choice as we saw it, and we hadn't a way to leave once we were down. It's easier to fall onto a planet than to fly free of one. It was our calculated decision, aiji-mai, and we thought we could build our way back to space and bring atevi with us. We never intended to go to war—we didn't want to *take* anything from you . . ."

"Baji-naji, nand' paidhi. Fortune has a human face and bastard Chance whores drunken down your streets. —Let him go, nadiin. Let him go where he likes. If you want to go down to the township, nand' paidhi,—there's a car that can take you."

He blinked into the wind, staggering in a freedom that all but dumped him down to his knees. The guards' grip lingered, keeping him steady. It was all that did. It was like the other crazed things Ilisidi had done—sending him out of here, setting him free.

But he didn't know he'd reach the airport. She didn't promise more than freedom to leave Malguri. She didn't say his leaving was what she wanted—*If you want to go* still rang in his ears; and she'd given him crazy signals before this, challenging him to stay behind her—atevi-fashion: *follow* me if you dare.

He shook off the guards and stumbled forward to grab the vacant chair at the table, as guns came out and safeties went off. He slid it back and fell into it, too cold to feel the lace-covered glass under his arms, his sense of balance tilting this way and that on this narrow strip of a balcony.

"Tabini sent me *here*," he said. "Aiji-mai, your grandson couldn't believe his own judgement, so he sent me *here*, relying on yours. So I do rely on it. What do you want me to do?"

A long, long moment Ilisidi stared at him, a shadow wrapped in robes, immune to the cold. He was too cold to shiver. He only flinched in the blasts and hunched his arms together. But he didn't doubt what he was doing. He didn't doubt the challenge Ilisidi had laid in front of him, offering him an escape—by everything he'd learned of her and of atevi, Ilisidi would write off him and every human alive if he took her up on that invitation to escape.

"In reasonable fear of harm," Ilisidi said finally, "you would not give us a simple statement against my grandson. In pain, you refused to give it. What good is *man'chi* to a human?"

"Every good." Of a sudden it was dazzlingly, personally clear to him. "A place to stand. An understanding of who I am, and where I am. If Tabini-aiji sent me here, he relied on your judgement—of me, of the situation, of the use I am to him."

Another long silence. "I'm old-fashioned. Impractical. Without appreciation of the modern world. What can my grandson possibly want from me?"

"Evidently," he said, and found, after all, the capacity to shiver, "evidently he's come to value your opinion."

Ilisidi's mouth made a hard line. That curved. "In Maidingi there are people waiting for you—who expect me to turn you over to them, who demand it, in fact— people who rely on me as my grandson hasn't. Your choice to stay here—is wise. But what excuse for holding you should I tell them, nadi?"

The shivers had become violent. He gave a shake of his head, tried to answer, wasn't sure Ilisidi wanted an answer. The rim of the sun cast a sudden, fierce gleam over the mountains across the lake, flaming gold.

"This young man is freezing," Ilisidi said. "Get him inside. Hot tea. Breakfast. I don't know when he may get another."

When he may get another? He wanted explanation, but Ilisidi's bodyguard hauled him out of his chair—the ones he knew, who knew him, not the ones who had brought him from below. He couldn't coordinate his getting up. He couldn't walk without staggering, the cold had set so deeply into his joints. "My apartment," he protested. "I want to talk to Banichi. Or Jago."

Ilisidi said nothing to that request, and the guards took him from the balcony into the dead air of the inside, guided him by the arms through the antiques and the delicate tables—opened a door to a firelit room, Ilisidi's study, he supposed, by the books and the papers about. They brought him to the chair before the fire, wrapped a robe about him and let him sit down and huddle in the warmthless wool. They piled more logs on the fire, sent embers flying up the chimney, and he was still numb, scarcely feeling the heat on the soles of his boots.

A movement in the doorway caught his eye. Cenedi was watching him silently. How long Cenedi had been there he had no idea. He stared back, dimly realizing that Cenedi along with Ilisidi had just gained his agreement—and Cenedi had arranged the whole damned shadow-show.

Cenedi only nodded as if he'd seen what he came to see, and left, without a word.

Anger sent a shiver through him, and he hugged the robe closer to hide the reaction. One of Ilisidi's guards—he remembered the name as Giri—had lingered, working with the fire. Giri looked askance at him. "There's another blanket, nadi," Giri said, and in his sullen silence got up and brought it and put it over him. "Thin folk chill through faster," Giri said. "Do you want the tea, nand' paidhi? Breakfast?"

"No. Enough tea. Thank you." Cenedi's presence had upset his stomach. He told himself—intellectually—that

Cenedi could have done him far greater hurt: Cenedi could have put enough pressure on to make him confess anything Cenedi wanted. He supposed Cenedi had done him a favor, getting what he needed and no more than that.

But he couldn't be that charitable, with the livid marks of atevi fingers on his arms. He'd little dignity left. He made a desultory, one-handed twist of his hair at the nape of his neck—he wanted to make a plait or two to hold it, but the arm they'd twisted wouldn't lift while he was shivering. He was angry, in pain, and in the dim, dazed way his brain was working, he didn't know who to blame for it: not Cenedi, ultimately; not Ilisidi—not even Tabini, who had every good reason to suspect human motives, with the evidence of human space operations over his head and his own government tottering around him.

While he'd been doing television interviews with newscasters and talking to tourists who hadn't said a damned thing about it.

His office had probably rung the phone off the desk trying to get hold of him, but atevi news was controlled. Nothing of that major import got out until Tabini wanted it released, not in this Association and not in others: atevi notions of priority and public rights and the duties of aijiin to manage the public welfare took precedence over democracy.

The tourists might *not* have known, if they hadn't been near a television for some number of days. Even the television crew might not have known. The dissidents who must have gravitated to Ilisidi as a rival to Tabini . . . they would have had their sources, in the hasdrawad, in the way atevi associations had no borders. They would have wanted to get to the paidhi and the information he had, urgently. At any cost.

Maybe the rival factions had wanted to silence his advice, the character of which they might believe they knew without hearing him.

Or maybe they had wanted something else. Maybe

there had never been an assassination attempt against him—maybe they'd wanted to snatch him away to question, to find out what a human would say and what it meant to their position, before Tabini took some action they didn't know how to judge.

Tabini had ordered their rushed and early return from Taiben—after arming him against the logical actions of the people Tabini already intended to send him to?

Had the attempt on his bedroom been real in any sense—or something Tabini himself had done for an excuse?

And why did someone of Banichi's rank just happen to be in his wing that night? The cooks and the clerks didn't merit Banichi's level of security. It *was* his room they'd been guarding—Tabini had already been advised of the goings-on in the heavens.

But somebody of Banichi's experience let a man he was guarding sleep with the garden doors and the lattice open?

Things blurred. He felt a clamminess in his hands, was overwhelmed, of a sudden, with anger at the games-playing. He'd believed Cenedi. He'd believed the game in the cellar, when they'd put the gun to his head—they'd made him think he was going to die, and in such a moment, dammit, he'd have thought he'd think of Barb, he'd have thought he'd think of his mother or Toby or someone human, but he hadn't. They'd made him stand face-to-face with that disturbing, personal moment of truth, and he hadn't discovered any noble sentiments or even human reactions. The high snows and the sky was all he'd been able to see, being alone was all he could imagine—just the snow, just the sky and the cold, up where he went to have his solitude from work and his own family's clamoring demands for his time, that was the truth they'd pushed him to, not a warm human thought in him, no love, no humanity—

His hand flew up to his face scarcely in time to bury the sudden rush of helpless, watery reaction that he told himself at once was nerves, the psychological crash after the crisis—that, at least, was human, if anything he did was human, or natural, if anything he did was anything but one damned calculated move after technologically, politically calculated move—

"Nadi." Giri was hovering over him. He didn't know Giri. Giri didn't know him. Giri just saw the paidhi acting oddly, and the dowager didn't want him to die because she had use for him.

It was good that someone did.

He wiped his eyes, leaned his head back against the chair and composed his face, mentally severing the nerves to it, drawing smaller and smaller breaths until he could be as statue-calm as Banichi or Tabini.

"Are you hurting, nand' paidhi? Do you need a doctor?"

Giri's confusion was funny, so wildly, hysterically funny, it all but shattered him. He laughed once, a strangled sound, and got control of it, and wiped his eyes a second time.

"No," he said, before Giri could escape in alarm. "*No,* dammit, I don't need a doctor. I'm all right. I'm just tired." He shut his eyes against further ministrations, felt the leak of tears and didn't open his eyelids, just kept his breathing calm, down a long, long, head-splitting spiral of fire-warmth and lack of oxygen, that bottomed out somewhere in a dizzy dark. He heard a confused set of voices talking in the background, probably discussing him. Hell, why not? he asked himself.

Usually it was the servants that betrayed you, the likes of Djinana and Maigi, Tano and Algini. But in the flutter of banners, the clashing of weapons, the smoke of shattered buildings, the rules of all existence changed. Hell broke loose. Or maybe it was television. Machimi and shadows.

Blood on the terrace, Jago had said, coming back out of the rain, and Banichi's face had turned up in the mirror.

The beast walked Malguri's halls after midnight, when

everyone was asleep . . . looking for its head, and damned upset about it.

It's my gun, Banichi had said, and it was. He'd been used, Banichi had been used, Jago had been used—everyone had been used, in every way. It was all machimi, and ordinary atevi didn't know the game either—ordinary atevi had never understood the feud between the humans who'd had to stay on the station and those who'd taken the ship and gone, for two hundred cursed, earthbound years. . . .

They'd fallen through a hole in space and found not a single star they knew, in the spectra of a thousand suns that fluttered on atevi banners, banners declaring war, declaring ownership of the world that seemed, for stranded strangers, the surest chance to live in freedom.

He lay still in the chair, listening to the snap of the fire, letting the tides of headache come and go—exhausted emotionally and physically—aching in a dozen places, now that he was warm, but hurting less than he did when he moved.

Build the station for a base and go and search for resources at the next likely star, that was what the Pilots' Guild had decided they would do. The hell with the noncrew technicians and construction workers. Every kid on Mospheira knew the story. Every kid knew how *Phoenix* had betrayed them, and why *Phoenix* wasn't a factor in their lives any longer. Time ran long between the stars and age didn't pass the way it ought to—like in the stories, the man that slept a hundred years and never knew.

An atevi story or human, he wasn't personally sure.

Goseniin and eggs. They daren't kill the paidhi. Otherwise, how could they find out anything they needed to know?

"Bren-ji."

He flashed on the cellar, and the shadows around him, and the cold metal against his head. No. A less definite touch than that, brushing his cheek.

"Bren-ji."

A second touch. He blinked at a black, yellow-eyed face, a warm and worried face.

"Jago!"

"Bren-ji, Bren-ji, you have to leave this province. Some people have come into Maidingi, following rumors—the same who've acted against you. We need to get you out of here, now—for your protection, and theirs. Far too many innocents, Bren-ji. We've received advisement from the aiji-dowager, from her people inside the rebel movement . . . certain of them will take her orders. Certain of that group she knows will not. The aijiin of two provinces are in rebellion—they've sent forces to come up the road and take you from Malguri." The back of her fingers brushed his cheek a third time, her yellow eyes held him paralyzed. "We'll hold them by what tactics we can use. Rely on Ilisidi. We'll join you if we can."

"Jago?"

"I've got to go. *Got* to go, Bren-ji."

He tried to delay her to ask where Banichi was or what they meant by *hold them*—but her fingers slipped through his, and Jago was away and out the door, her black braid swinging.

Alarm brought him to his feet—sore joints, headache, and lapful of blankets and all—with half that Jago had said ringing and rattling around a dazed and exhausted brain.

Hold them? Hold a mob off from Malguri? How in hell, Jago?

And for what? One damned more *illusion,* Jago? Is *this* one real?

Innocents, Jago said.

People who wanted to kill him? Innocents?

People who were just scared, because the word had begun to spread of what had arrived in their skies. Malguri was still candle-lit and fire-lit. The countryside around about had had no lights. People in cities didn't spend their time on rooftops looking at a station you couldn't see in city haze without a telescope, no, but a quarter of Maidingi township had been in blackout, and ordinary atevi could have had pointed out to them what astronomers and amateurs would have seen in their telescopes days ago.

Now the panic began, the fear of landings, the rumor of attack on their planet from an enemy above their reach.

What were they to think of this apparition, absent a communication from the paidhi's office, but a resumption of the War, another invasion, another, harsher imposition of human ways on the world? They'd had their experience of humans seeking a foothold in their territory.

He stood lost in the middle of a nightmare—realized Ilisidi's guards were watching him anxiously, and didn't know what to do, except that the paidhi was the only voice, the *only* voice that could represent atevi interests to Mospheira's authorities—and to that ship up there.

No contact, the Guild had argued; but that principle had fallen in the first stiff challenge. To get the deal they wanted out of the station . . . to go on getting the means to search for Earth, they'd given in and allowed the initial personnel and equipment drops.

And two hundred years now from the War of the Landing, what did any human on earth know . . . but this world, and a way of life they'd gotten used to, and neighbors they'd reached at least a hope of understanding at distance?

Damn, he thought, angry, *outraged* at the intrusion over their heads, and he didn't imagine that there was overmuch joy in Mospheira's conversations with the ship, either.

Charges and counter-charges. Charges his office could answer with some authority—but when *Phoenix* asked, Where *is* this interpreter, where *is* the paidhi-aiji, what opinion does *he* hold and why can't we find him? . . . what could Mospheira say? Sorry—we don't know?

Sorry, we've never lost track of him before?

And couldn't the Commission office, knowing what they knew, realize that, with that ship appearing in the skies, they'd better *call* his office in Shejidan? Or realize, if their call didn't go through, that he was in trouble, that atevi knew what was going on, and that he might be undergoing interrogation somewhere?

Damned right, Hanks knew. Deana Nuke-the-Opposition *Hanks* was making decisions in his name on Mospheira, because he was out of touch.

He needed a phone, a radio, anything. "I have to talk to my own security," he said, "about that ship up there. Please, nadiin, can you send someone to bring Jago back, or Banichi . . . *any* one of my staff? I'll talk to Cenedi. Or the dowager."

"I fear not, nand' paidhi. Things are moving very quickly now. Someone's gone for your coat and for heavier clothes. If you'd care for breakfast . . ."

"My coat. Where are we going, nadiin? *When* are we going? I need to get to a phone or a radio. I need to reach my office. It's extremely important they know that I'm all right. Someone could take very stupid, very dangerous actions, nadiin!"

"We can present your request to Cenedi," Giri said. "In the meantime, the water's already hot, nand' paidhi. Tea can be ready in a very small moment. Breakfast is waiting. We would very much advise you to have breakfast now. Please, nand' paidhi. I'll personally take your request to Cenedi."

He couldn't get more than that. The chill was back, a sudden attack of cold and weakness that told him Giri was giving him good advice. He'd gone to see Cenedi last night before supper. His stomach was hollow to the backbone.

And if they'd kept breakfast waiting and water hot since his meeting with Ilisidi, it wasn't that they meant to take the usual gracious forever about bringing it.

"All right," he said. "Breakfast. But tell the dowager!"

Giri disappeared. The other guard stood where he'd been standing, and Bren strayed back to the fireside, with his hair inching loose again, falling about his shoulders. His clothes were smudged with dust from the cellars. His shirt was torn about the front, somewhere in the exchange—most likely in his escape attempt, he thought. It wasn't humanity's finest hour. Atevi around him, no matter the sleep they'd missed, too, looked impervious to dirt and exhaustion, impeccably braided, absolutely ramrod straight in their bearing. He lifted sore arms, both of them, this time, wincing with the effort, and separating his tangled hair, braided three or four turns to keep it out of his face—God knew what had happened to the clip. He'd probably lost it on the stairs outside. If they went out that way he might find it.

A servant carried in a heavy tray with a breakfast of fish, cheese, and stone-ground bread, along with a demi-pot of strong black tea, and set it on a small side table for him. He sat down to it with better appetite than he'd thought he could possibly find, in the savory smell and the recollection of Giri's warning that meals might not be on schedule again . . . which, with the business about getting his coat, meant they were going to take action to get him out, maybe *through* the opposition down in Maidingi . . . on Ilisidi's authority, it might be.

But breaking through a determined mob was a scary prospect. Trust an atevi lord to know how far he or she could push . . . atevi had that down to an art form.

Still, a mob under agitation might not respect the aiji-dowager. He gathered that Ilisidi had been with them and changed her mind last night; and if she tried to lie or threaten her way through a mob who might be perfectly content with assassinating the paidhi, there could well be shooting. A large enough mob could stop the van.

In which case the last night could turn out to be only a taste of what humanity's radical opposition might do to him if it got its hands on him. If things got out of hand, and they couldn't get to a plane—he could end up shot dead before today ended, himself, Ilisidi, God knew who else . . . and that could be a lot better than the alternative.

He ate his breakfast, drank his tea, and argued with himself that Cenedi knew what he was doing, at least. A man in Cenedi's business didn't get that many gray hairs or command the security of someone of Ilisidi's rank without a certain finesse, and without a good sense of what he could get away with—legally and otherwise.

But he wanted Banichi and Jago, dammit, and if some political decision or Cenedi's position with Ilisidi had meant Banichi and Jago had drawn the nasty end of the plan—

If he lost them . . .

"Nand' paidhi."

He turned about in the chair, surprised and heartened by a familiar voice. Djinana had come with his coat and what looked like a change of clothes, his personal kit *and,* thank God, his computer—whether Djinana had thought of it, whether Banichi or Jago had told him, or whoever had thought of it, it wasn't going to lie there with everything it held for atevi to find and interpret out of context, and he wasn't going to have to ask for it and plead for it back from Cenedi's possession.

"Djinana-ji," he said, with the appalled realization that if he was leaving and getting to safety this morning, Malguri's staff wouldn't have that option, not the servants whose *man'chi* belonged to Malguri itself. "They're saying people down in Maidingi are coming up here looking for me. That two aijiin are supporting an attack on Malguri. You surely won't try to deal with this yourselves, nadi. Capable as you may be—"

Djinana laid his load on the table. "The staff has no intention of surrendering Malguri to any ill-advised rabble." Djinana whisked out a comb and brush from his kit, and came to his chair. "Forgive me, nand' paidhi, please continue your breakfast—but they're in some little hurry, and I can fix this."

"You're worth more than stones, Djinana!"

"Please." Djinana pushed him about in the chair, pushed his head forward and brushed with a vengeance, then braided a neat, quick braid, while he ate a piece of bread gone too dry in his mouth and washed it down with bitter tea.

"Nadi-ji, did you know why they brought me here? Did you know about the ship? *Do* you understand, it's not an attack, it's not aimed at you."

"I knew. I knew they suspected that you had the answer to it. —And I knew very soon that you would never be our enemy, paidhi-ji." Djinana had a clip from somewhere—the man was never at a loss. Djinana finished the braid, brushed off his shoulders, and went and took up his coat. "There's no time to change clothes, I fear, and best you wait until you're on the plane. I've packed warm clothing for a change this evening."

He got up from the chair, turned his back to Djinana, and toward the window. "Are they sending a van up?"

"No, paidhi-ji. A number of people are on their way up here now, I hear, on buses. I truly don't think they're the ones to fear. But you're in very good hands. Do as they say." Djinana shoved him about by the shoulder, helped him on with the coat, and straightened his braid over the collar. "There. You look the gentleman, nadi. Perhaps you'll come back to Malguri. Tell the aiji the staff demands it."

"Djinana, —" One couldn't even say *I like.* "I'll certainly tell him that. Please, thank everyone in my name." He went so far as to touch Djinana's arm. "Please see that you're here when I come visiting, or I'll be greatly distressed."

That seemed to please Djinana, who nodded and quietly took his leave past a disturbance in the next room—Ilisidi's voice, insisting, "They won't lay a hand on me!"

And Cenedi's, likewise determined:

" 'Sidi-ji, we're getting *out,* damned if they won't come inside! Shut up and get your coat!"

"Cenedi, it's quite enough to remove him out of range. . . ."

"Giri, get 'Sidi's coat! *Now!*"

The guards' eyes had shifted in that direction. Nothing

of their stance had altered. He gathered up his change of clothes and wrapped it about his computer, waiting with that in his arms and his kit in his hand, listening as Cenedi gave orders for the locking of doors and the extinguishing of fires.

But Djinana's voice, distantly, said that the staff would see to those matters, that they should go, quickly, please, and take the paidhi to safety.

He stood there, the center of everyone's difficulty, the reason for the danger to Malguri. He felt that the absolute least he could do was put himself conveniently where they wanted him. He supposed that they would go out through the hall and down; he ventured as far as the door to the reception room, but Cenedi burst through that door headed in the opposite direction, bringing Ilisidi with him, on a clear course toward the rearmost of Ilisidi's rooms, with a number of guards following.

"Where's Banichi?" he tried to ask as they went through the bedroom, with the guards trailing him, but Cenedi was arguing with Ilisidi, hastening her on through the hallways at the back of the apartments, to a back stairs. A man he thought he recognized from last night stood at the landing, holding a weapon he *didn't* know, shoving shells into the butt from a box on the post of the stairs.

That gun wasn't supposed to exist. He had never seen that man on staff in Malguri. Banichi and Jago, and presumably Tano and Algini, with them, had gone somewhere he didn't know, a mob wanted to turn him over to rebels against Tabini—and they were bound down to the back side of Malguri, down, he realized as Cenedi and Ilisidi opened the doors onto shadowed stone—to a stairway beside the stable, where the hisses and grumbling of mecheiti out in the courtyard told him *how* they were leaving Malguri, unless they were taking this route only to divert pursuit—

This is mad, he thought as they came out onto the landing overlooking the courtyard, seeing that the mecheiti were rigged out in all their gear, with, moreover, saddle packs and other accoutrements they'd never used on their morning rides.

This isn't two hundred years ago. They've planes, they've guns like that one back on the stairs . . .

Something exploded, shaking the stones, a vibration that went straight to his knees and his gut. Someone wasn't waiting for the mob in the buses.

"Come *on!*" Cenedi yelled up at them from the court-yard, and he hurried down the steps, with some of Cenedi's men behind him, and the handlers trying to get the mecheiti sorted out.

It was a crazed plan. Reason told him it was beyond lunacy to take out across the country like this. There was the lake. They might have arranged a boat across to another province.

If the provinces across the lake weren't the ones in rebellion.

A second explosion hammered at the stones. Ilisidi looked back and up, and swore; but Cenedi grabbed her arm and hurried her along where handlers held Babs waiting.

He spotted Nokhada, darted, arms encumbered, among the towering, shifting bodies; and wondered how he was to load the saddle packs with his bundled clothes and the computer, but the handlers took his belongings from him.

"Careful!" he said, wincing as the handler almost dropped the computer, the weight of which he hadn't anticipated. His computer went into one bag, the clothes and the kit went into the other, on the other side of Nokhada's lean and lofty rump, Nokhada fidgeting and fighting the rein. The mecheiti this morning all had a glimmer of brass about the jaw, not blunt caps on the rooting-tusks, but a sharp-pointed fitting he'd seen only in machimi— brass to protect the tusks.

In war.

It was surreal. The fighting-brass was, with Nokhada's head-butting tendencies, not a weapon he wanted to argue

with or even stay on the ground with. He took the rein
one handler gave him, couldn't manage it with the sore
arm, shifted hands and hit Nokhada with his fist, trying to
make the creature drop a shoulder. Riders all around him
were already up. Nokhada objected, fidgeted up again,
and resisted a second order, circling him, wild-eyed in all
the surrounding haste and excitement. *That* was how
things were going to go, he thought, unsure he could restrain the creature in an emergency—scared of its
strength and that jaw as he hadn't been since the first.

"Nadi," a handler said, offering a hand, and atevi
strength snared and held the rein.

He grabbed the mounting-strap, relied on the uncere-
monious shove of the handlers, shoved his foot in the stirrup on the way up and landed, sore-boned, and with a
wrench of his sore shoulders, on the pad, with his heart
pounding. He took a quick fistful of rein to bring
Nokhada under control in the general confusion, as someone opened the outward gate.

Cold morning wind blasted through the court, stinging
his face as all the mecheiti began to move. He looked distractedly for Babs and Ilisidi. He brought Nokhada another circle, and Nokhada found a fix on Babs before he
even saw Ilisidi.

He *couldn't* hold Nokhada, then, with Babs headed for
the gate. Nokhada shouldered other mecheiti and struck a
loping pace in Babs' wake, into the teeth of an incoming
gust that felt like a wall of ice.

The arch passed around him as a blur of shadow and
stone. The vast gray of the lake was a momentary, giddy
nothingness first in front of him and then at his right as
Nokhada veered sharply along the edge and up the mountainside.

Follow Babs to hell, Nokhada would.

XII

It was across the mountainside, and up and up the brushy slope, across the gully, the very course he'd bashed his lip taking, the first time he'd ridden after Ilisidi.

And ten or so of Ilisidi's guard, when he snatched a glance back on the uphill, were right behind him ... along with a half a dozen saddled but riderless mecheiti.

They'd turned out the whole stable to follow, leaving nothing for anyone to use catching them—he knew that trick from the machimi. He found himself *in* a machimi, war-gear and armed riders and all of it. It only wanted the banners and the lances ... no place for a human, he kept thinking. He didn't know how to manage Nokhada if they had to break through a mob, he didn't know whether he could even stay on if they took any harder obstacles.

And ride across a continent to reach Shejidan? Not damned likely.

Jago had said believe Ilisidi. Djinana had said believe Cenedi.

But they were headed to the north and west, cut off, by the sound of the explosions, from the airport—cut off from communications, from his own staff, from everything and everyone of any resource he knew, unless Tabini was sending forces into Maidingi province to get possession of the airport—which the rebels held.

Which meant the rebels could go by air—while they went at whatever pace mecheiti flesh and bone could sustain. The rebels could track them, harass them as they liked, on the ground and from the air.

Only hope they hadn't planes rigged to let them shoot at targets. Damned right they could think of it—no damned *biichi-gi* about it: Mospheira had designed atevi planes to make that modification as difficult as possible—

they'd stuck to fixed-wing and generally faster aircraft, but it couldn't preclude some atevi with a reason putting his mind to it. Finesse, he'd heard it said in the machimi, didn't apply in war—and war was what two rebel aijiin were trying to start here.

Push Tabini to the brink, break up the Western Association and reform it around some other leader—like Ilisidi?

And she, twice passed over by the hasdrawad, was double-crossing the rebels?

Dared he *believe* that?

An explosion echoed off Malguri's walls.

He risked a second glance back and saw a plume of smoke going up until the wind whipped it completely away over the western wall. That was *inside,* he thought with a rising sense of panic, and as he swung his head about, he saw the crest of the ridge ahead of them, looming up with its promise of safety from weapons-fire that might come up at them from Malguri's grounds.

And maybe their disappearance over that ridge would *stop* the attack on Malguri, if the staff could convince a mob and armed professionals they weren't there— God help Djinana and Maighi, who had never asked to be fighters, who had strangers like that man with the gun standing on the stairway, people Ilisidi and Cenedi must have brought in ... people who might not put Malguri's historic walls at such a high premium.

Cold blurred his eyes. The shooting pains in his shoulders took on a steady rhythm in Nokhada's lurching climb. There was one craggy knoll between them and sharpshooters that might be trying to set up outside Malguri's mountainward walls—but Banichi and Jago were seeing to that, he told himself so. Brush and rock came up in front of them, then blue sky. Perspective went crazy for a moment as first Ilisidi and Cenedi went over the edge and then Nokhada nosed down and plunged down the other side, a giddy, intoxicating flurry of strides down a landscape of rough rock and scrub that his subconscious painted snow-white and sanity jerked into browns and earth again. Pain rode the jolts of Nokhada's footfalls—torn joints, sore muscles, hands and legs losing feeling in the cold.

No damned place to take a fall. He suffered a moment of panic, then *felt* the mountain, God save his neck— Nokhada ran with the same logic and the same necessities as he knew, and he clenched the holding strap in his good hand and wrapped the rein into the fingers of the weaker one, beginning to take the wind in his face with an adrenaline rush, hyper-awareness of the slope and *where* Nokhada's feet had to touch, however briefly, to make the next stride.

He was plotting a course down the mountain, drunk on understanding, that was the crazed part, his eye saw the course and his heart was racing. His ears felt the shock an explosion made, but it was distant and he was hellbent for catching the riders ahead of him—not sane. Not responsible. *Enjoying* it. He'd damned near caught up to Ilisidi when Babs gave a whip of the tail and took a course that Nokhada nearly killed them both trying to reach.

" *'Sidi!*" he heard Cenedi yell at their backs behind them.

He suffered a second of sane, cold panic, realizing that he'd maneuvered past Cenedi and Ilisidi *knew* he was at her tail.

A rock exploded near them, just blew up as it sat on the hillside. Babs took the slot beside a narrow waterfall and struck out uphill among stones the size of houses, higher and higher into the mountains.

Sniper, sanity said. They were still in range.

But he followed Ilisidi, slower now, more sheltered among the boulders, and he had time and breath to realize the foolishness he'd just committed, that he'd pushed himself next behind Ilisidi, that Cenedi was at his back, and that Nokhada was sensibly unwilling to slow down now and lose momentum on the uphill climb.

Fool, he thought. He'd lost his good sense on the

mountain. Knowing the responsibility he carried, he'd risked his neck *because* he carried it, and because of the things he couldn't do and didn't have, and he didn't care, didn't damned well care, during those few selfish high-speed minutes that were nothing but *now,* risking his life, damn them all, damn Tabini, damn the atevi, damn his mother, Toby, Barb, and the whole human race.

He could have died. He could easily have died in that crazed course. And he discovered so much bitter, secret anger in him—so much rage he shook with it, while Nokhada's saner, more reasoned strides carried him up and up among the protecting rocks. What sent him down a mountain wasn't, then, the delirious freedom he told himself it was, it was what he'd just experienced: a spiteful, irrational death wish, aiming his own destruction at everyone and everything he served—*that* was what he was courting.

Not damned fair. The only thing in his life he enjoyed with complete abandon. And it was a damned death wish.

He hated the pressures at home on Mospheira, the job-generated pressures and most of all the emotional, human ones. At the moment he hated atevi, at least in the abstract, he hated their passionless violence and the lies and the endless, schizophrenic analysis he had to do, among them, of every conclusion, every emotion, every feeling he owned, just to decide whether it came of human hard-wiring or logical processing.

And most of all he hated hurting for people who didn't hurt back. He didn't trust his feelings any longer. He was drained, he was exhausted, he hurt, and he wasn't dealing with either reality sanely anymore.

It was the second personal truth he'd faced—since that dark moment with the gun at his head. It told him that the paidhi wasn't handling the job stress. That the paidhi was scared as hell and not sure of the people around him, and no longer sure he'd done the right thing in anything he'd done.

You didn't know, you didn't damned well *know* with

atevi, what went on at gut level, on any given point, not because you couldn't translate it, but because you couldn't feel it, couldn't resonate to it, couldn't remotely guess what it felt like inside.

They were on the verge of war, atevi were shooting each other over what to do about humans, and the paidhi was coming apart—they'd taken too much away from him last night. Maybe they hadn't meant to do it, maybe they didn't know they'd done it, and he could reason with himself, he knew all the psychological labels: that there was too much unresolved, that there were even physiological reasons behind the sudden fit of chill and fear and the morbid self-dissection this morning that had their only origins in the business last night.

And, no, they'd *not* been playing games last night. It had never been a false threat they'd posed; Cenedi was damned good at what he did, and Cenedi hadn't weighed his mental condition heavily against the answers Cenedi had to have.

It didn't change the fact they'd shaken things loose inside—ricochets that were still racketing about a psyche that hadn't been all that steady to start with.

He couldn't afford to break. Not now. Ignore the introspection and figure out the minimal things he was going to tell atevi and humans that would silence the guns and discredit the madmen who wanted this war.

That was what he had to do.

At least the gunshots had stopped coming. They'd passed out of earshot of the explosions, whatever might be happening back at Malguri, and struck a slower, saner pace on easier ground, where they might have run—a more level course, interspersed with sometimes a jolting climb, sometimes a jogging diagonal descent—generally much more to the south now, and only occasionally to the west, which seemed to add up to a slant toward Maidingi Airport, where the worst trouble was.

And maybe to a meeting with help from Tabini, if Tabini had any idea what was happening here . . . and trust Banichi that Tabini did know, in specifics, if Banichi could get to a phone, or if the radio could reach someone who could get the word across half a continent.

"We're heading south," he said to Cenedi, when they came close enough together. "Nadi, are we going to Maidingi?"

"We've a rendezvous point on the west road," Cenedi said. "Just past a place called the Spires. We'll pick up your staff there, assuming they make it."

That was a relief. And a negation of some of his suspicions. "And from there?"

"West and north, to a man we think is safe. Watch out, nand' paidhi!"

They'd run out of space. Cenedi's mecheita, Tali, forged ahead, making Nokhada throw up her head and back-step. Nokhada gave a snap at Tali's departing rump, but there was no overtaking her in that narrow space between two room-sized boulders.

Pick up his staff, Cenedi said. He was decidedly relieved on that score. The rest, avoiding the airport, getting to someone who *might* have motorized transport, sounded much more sane than he'd feared Cenedi was up to. Rather than a mapless void, their course began to lie toward points he could guess, toward provinces the other side of the mountains, westward, ultimately—he knew his geography. And firmer than borders could ever be among atevi, where individual towns and houses hazed from one *man'chi* to another, even on the same street—Cenedi knew a definite name, a specific *man'chi* Cenedi said was safe.

Cenedi, in his profession, wasn't going to make that judgment on a guess. Ilisidi might be double-crossing her associates—but aijiin *hadn't* a *man'chi* to anyone higher, that was the nature of what they were: her associates knew it and knew they had to keep her satisfied.

Which they hadn't, evidently. Tabini had made his play, a wide and even a desperate one, sending the paidhi to Malguri, and letting Ilisidi satisfy her curiosity, ask her questions—running the risk that Ilisidi might in fact deliver him to the opposition. Tabini had evidently been sure of something—perhaps (thinking as atevi and not as a human being) knowing that the rebels *couldn't* satisfy Ilisidi, or meant to double-cross her: never count that Ilisidi wouldn't smell it in the wind. The woman was too sharp, too astute to be taken in by the number-counters and the fear-merchants . . . and if he was, personally, the overture Tabini made to her, Ilisidi might have found Tabini's subtle hint that he foreknew her slippage toward the rebels quite disturbing; and found his tacit offer of peace more attractive at her age than a chancier deal with some ambitious cabal of provincial lords who meant to challenge a human power Tabini might deal with.

A deal with conspirators who might well, in the way of atevi lords, end up attacking each other.

He wasn't in a position with Ilisidi or Cenedi to ask those critical questions. Things felt touchy as they were. He tried now to keep the company's hierarchy of importance, always Babs first, Cenedi's mecheita mostly second, and Nokhada politicking with Cenedi's Tali for number two spot every time they took to a run, politics that hadn't anything to do with the motives of their riders, but dangerous if their riders' personal politics got into it, he had sopped that fact up from the machimi, and knew that he shouldn't let Nokhada push into that dual association ahead of him, not with the fighting-brass on the tusks. Cenedi wouldn't thank him, Tali wouldn't tolerate it, and he had enough to do with the bad arm, just to hold on to Nokhada.

He'd recovered from his insanity, at least by the measure he now had some idea where they were going.

But he daren't push. He'd gotten Ilisidi's help, but it was a chancy, conditional support for him and for Tabini that he still daren't be sure of . . . never trust that the woman Tabini called 'Sidi-ji wasn't pursuing some course toward her own advantage, and toward her own power in the Western Association, if not in some other venue.

From one giddy moment to the next, he trusted none of them.

Fourteen words, the language had for betrayal, and one of them doubled for 'taking the obvious course.'

XIII

If Ilisidi was following any established trail at all, Bren couldn't see it even when Nokhada was in Babs' very tracks. He spotted Ilisidi high up among towering boulders, Babs moving like one of Malguri's flitting ghosts past gaps in the rocks.

He didn't see the crest of the hill—he only lost track of Ilisidi and Cenedi at the same moment, and, following them, at the head of their column of twenty-odd riders, came out on a windy, boulder-littered hillside above a shallow brook and a set of brush-impeded wheel-ruts.

The road? he asked himself.

Was *that* track the west road Cenedi had talked about, where they were to meet the rest of their party?

Other riders arrived at the crest of the hill behind him, and Cenedi sent a rider down to, as he heard Cenedi say, see whether they saw any recent tracks.

Machine-tracks, that specific word implied.

A truck could possibly survive that road, given a good suspension and heavy tires.

And if service trucks were all the opposition had at their disposal, and they didn't take a plane out of Maidingi Airport, God, Ilisidi could lead them back over the ridge mecheita-back and outrun any pursuit afoot.

So their means of transport out of Malguri wasn't crazy. This *wasn't* Mospheira's well-developed back country. There wasn't a phone line or a power line or a paved road or a rail track for days.

They sat up on their mountainside and waited, while the man Cenedi had sent rode down, had his look, and rode uphill again, with a hand signal that meant negative.

Bren let go a breath, and his heart sank in suppositions and suspicions too ready to leap up. He was ready to object that, considering the fight back at Malguri, they couldn't hold Banichi to any tight schedule, and they shouldn't go on without waiting.

But Cenedi said, before he had a chance to object, that they should get down and wait.

That bettered his opinion of Cenedi. He felt a hundred-fold happier with present company *and* their priorities, in that light, whatever motivated them. He began to get down, the way Cenedi had said, attempted with kicks to get Nokhada to drop a shoulder, but that wasn't a proposition Nokhada seemed to favor. Nokhada ripped the rein forward with an easy toss of her head, sent pain knifing through his sprained shoulder and circled perversely on the slope until her head was uphill and he *couldn't* get down over the increased height, in the condition his legs were in, damn the creature.

He kicked Nokhada. They made one more embarrassing and vainly contested three-sixty on the hillside.

At which point one of the other riders took pity on him and got down to take Nokhada's rein.

"Nand' paidhi." It was the same man, he realized by the voice, who'd beaten hell out of him in the restroom, who faced Nokhada sideways, with the dismount-side to the upslope of the hill, then stood waiting to steady him as he slid down.

He wasn't damned well ready to forgive anyone who'd helped in that charade last night.

But he wasn't among enemies, either, that was the whole point of what Cenedi had been trying to determine; and the man hadn't in point of fact beaten him unnecessarily, only dissuaded him from further contest.

So he gave up his quarrel and surrendered his grudge

with a quiet, "Thank you, nadi," and slid down and dropped.

He'd thought he could at least stand up. The knees went—he'd have been down the slope *under* Nokhada, except for Cenedi's man keeping him upright, and sensation arrived in his lower body about the same moment his legs straightened.

He managed to take Nokhada's rein into his own hand and, with a mumbled thanks for the rescue, to limp aside to a place to be alone and to sit down. It was a very odd pain, he thought—not quite bad, at one moment, blood getting back where it belonged, or flesh figuring out there was supposed to be more of it over certain previously undiscovered bones in the human anatomy.

But he decided he didn't want to sit down at the moment. His eyes watered in the chill wind, and he wiped them, using the arm he hadn't just wrenched getting down. For a moment he was temporally lost—flashed on the cellar and on remembered anger and went dizzy and uncertain of time-sense as he looked down the slope. He settled for shifting from one foot to the other as a way to rest, holding Nokhada's rein while Nokhada lowered her head and rooted with metal-capped tusks after a small woody shrub until it gave up its grip on the hillside. Nokhada manipulated it in her muscular upper lip and happily destroyed it.

Cold helped the pain. He just wanted to stand there mindlessly and watch Nokhada kill shrubs, but conscious thought kept creeping in—about the road down there, and the chance Banichi and Jago might not have made it away from Malguri.

The chance also that Ilisidi's position *wasn't* a simple or even a settled question. She was absolutely a wild card, dangerous to everyone with the Association trying, as it was, to fragment. It was only the fact that they were waiting for Banichi and waiting with a great deal of patience, for atevi, that persuaded him that he was in safe hands at all. Being atevi, Cenedi could return to his project of last night and peel another layer of truth out of him without a qualm if he needed to, at any moment, because, being atevi, Cenedi held his morality was Ilisidi's welfare—consideration of which could shift any time the wind shifted.

How many people on Mospheira, nand' paidhi?

He earnestly wished he had the gun from his bedroom—but that hadn't been in the kit Djinana gave him, he'd felt the weight of it, and he didn't know where it had ultimately gone.

Back to Banichi, he hoped, before it turned up in evidence in some court case Tabini-aiji couldn't prevent.

A scatter of pebbles came down the slope—a riderless mecheita was rooting after something up above. Nokhada hardly twitched an ear, busy chewing.

Then every mecheita's ears came up, and the heads came up, the whole lot of them looking toward the bottom of the hill, where the curve of the slope hid the farther end of the road.

Men all around him ducked into cover behind the rocks. Cenedi arrived in two fast strides, jerked him away from Nokhada and jerked him down with him behind the shelter of a large lump of stone.

He heard an engine then, in all that silence. At the first intimation of danger, the riderless mecheiti had tended together with Babs, and Ilisidi kept hold of Babs—holding the whole pack together on the slope above them.

The engine grew louder, nearer.

Cenedi signaled a query from another man with a hand motion to stay down.

Something rattled and popped and echoed, over the hills.

What was that? Bren wondered for half a heartbeat.

Then he heard the thump of an explosion. Muscles jerked, and his heart began to beat heavily in fright as Cenedi retreated from the post he had and moved rapidly from cover to cover, directing the company back uphill to the mecheiti.

They were leaving—pulling out. That rattle was gunfire; he knew it when that sound repeated itself. An exchange of fire. Cenedi had signaled him first of all. He felt a tremor in his legs he put down to sheer terror. He read Cenedi's signal in retrospect, but he kept hoping for Banichi and Jago to appear from around the hill.

They couldn't leave now, so close—if people were shooting, they were shooting at enemies, and that meant Banichi and Jago were *there*, just beyond the hill, that close to them....

A veil of black smoke rolled along the road below, carried on a stiff wind. In it, from the edge of the hill, he saw someone running, a single black-uniformed figure—

Not an attack, only a single atevi headed around the rocks and then uphill toward them at a desperate, stumbling run—a lighter someone than the average atevi man.

Jago, he realized in a heartbeat; and sprang up and ran, loosing small landslides of gravel, slipping and sliding and losing skin on his hands. He met her halfway to the bottom, dusty, gasping for breath as she caught herself against a boulder.

"Ambush," she breathed, "at the Spires. Get up there! Tell Cenedi go, get clear! Now!"

"Where's Banichi?"

"*Go*, dammit! The tank's blown, it's afire, he can't walk, he'll *hold* them till you get a start—"

"Hell! What, hold them? *Is he coming?*"

"He can't, dammit. Bren-ji,—"

He didn't listen to atevi logic. He lit out running, down to the brush-choked road, down into the smoke. He heard Jago running behind him, swearing at him and telling him he was a fool, get back, don't risk himself.

Then he heard riders following. He skidded in the pebbles on the last of the slope and ran, catching at a boulder to make the sudden turn onto the road, into the smoke, afraid of the mecheiti running him down, afraid most of all of Cenedi catching him, forcing a retreat and leaving Banichi behind for no damn reason.

He felt heat in the smoke, saw a hot red center in the black, rolling cloud that turned into the burning skeleton of a truck with the doors open. The rattle of gunfire echoed off the surrounding hills, and amid that, he heard the sharp report of gunfire close at hand, from the area around the truck.

"Banichi!" he yelled, rubbing tears and soot, trying to make out detail through the stinging smoke. He saw something dark against the gray of the rocks, off the road, a black figure aiming a pistol up at the hills. Dirt kicked up around him, an explosion of gravel—a shot hitting the ground—and he ran for that figure, with the smoke for his only cover. Chips exploded off the rocks ahead of him. One stung his leg as he ducked behind the rocks where Banichi sheltered.

"You damned *fool!*" Banichi yelled at him as he arrived, but he didn't care. He grabbed Banichi's sleeve and his arm, trying to pull him up, onto his feet. Banichi was clearly in pain, catching at the rocks and waving him off as pieces exploded off the boulders around them.

They weren't alone, then—Jago was beside him, grabbing Banichi on the other side, and, overwhelmed with help, Banichi gave up and cooperated with them, the three of them laboring across the ruts, while gunfire broke out loudly on their left, at ground level. Bullets shattered rock and thudded into the burning wreckage of the truck, the heat of the fire blasting breath away and stinging the skin as they crossed the road, using the smoke for cover.

More shots hit the truck. "That's Cenedi!" Jago gasped. "He's on the road!"

"Along the stream!" Banichi yelled, limping heavily, taking both of them downslope as, just past the truck, they slid down the bank of the stream, among boulders and knee-deep into cold water, all in a haze of smoke.

Lungs burned. Eyes watered. Bren choked back coughs, hanging onto Banichi, trying to cope with the uneven ground and Banichi's lurching steps, Jago's height giving her more leverage on Banichi's other side.

But they were out of the firing. Coughing and stumbling, they came beyond the area where the bullets were hitting. Banichi slipped to his knees on the stony bank, and, coughing, collapsed on the rocks, trying to get his gun back in its holster.

"Nadi, where are you hit?" Bren asked.

"Not hit," Banichi said between coughing fits. "They were ready for us. At the Spires. Explosives. —Dammit, is that Cenedi's lot?"

"Yes," Jago said shortly, and tried to get Banichi up again. Banichi tried, on one knee. Whatever was wrong, his leg on Jago's side couldn't bear his weight, and Bren shoved with all his strength to help Banichi up the bank toward Cenedi's position in the windborne haze of smoke.

Gunfire kicked up the dirt around them. Bren flung himself down with Banichi and Jago, flattened himself as much as he could among the humped rocks at the edge of the road, expecting a bullet to find his back as round after round kicked up the earth and ricochets went in random directions, chipping rock, disturbing the weeds.

Then a moment's quiet. He started to get up, and to pull Banichi up with him, but a man came running out of the smoke, and immediately after, two mecheiti, riderless—one caught the man with its head and threw him completely into the air. He landed and the mecheiti were on him, ripping him with their bronze-capped tusks, trampling him under them.

"Move!" Jago yelled, as Banichi flung himself up and forward, and Bren caught him as best he could on the right side. Banichi lost his footing on Jago's side and cost them more effort to get him up. Mecheiti were coming at them, riderless shapes in the haze. Banichi was yelling something about his gun.

Then another mecheita was into it—Nokhada, ripping with her tusks, spinning and butting and slashing at retreating rumps—it was that fast, and Bren grabbed Banichi by the belt and tried to get him up and out of the road—but another mecheita darted in on Nokhada's flank, raked Nokhada's side with a glancing blow; and then, God, Babs was into it, riderless, laying about him at both combatants, forcing them apart, driving Nokhada off the road downslope, Tali off into the smoke, others scattering, as they struggled to get Banichi toward the rocks—the mecheiti had gone amok—and a barrage of fire came from somewhere in the smoke as they reached the boulders at the foot of the hill. Bren heard someone yelling orders to draw back, not to pursue, get the mecheiti.

Another voice shouted, "They'll be up our backs, nadi!"

"They've already radioed!" Banichi yelled as loudly as he could, resting his arms against a boulder. "Dammit! Get out of here!"

"We were clear!" a man protested, Giri turning up at Bren's elbow, catching at his arm. "Nand' paidhi, *what* were you doing?"

"He lost his wits," Jago said sharply. Giri brushed past Bren, took his place supporting Banichi on that side. Others of their company were arriving out of the smoke, still firing down the road, but nothing seemed to be coming back.

"They're going to try to get behind us, or they've got a van farther back," he heard Jago say to someone, on a gasped breath. "We've got to get out of here—they'll have called our location in. We'll have planes in here faster than we can think about it. Those are no amateurs."

Men were running, sorting out the mecheiti. Bren spotted Nokhada in the milling about and ran and caught Nokhada's trailing reins—Nokhada had a raking wound down her shoulder, and a bleeding puncture from a blow to the neck, and she resisted any signal to lower a shoulder for him, circling on the pivot of the rein and throwing her head. He tried again, holding on to the mounting-straps with his sore arm, trying not to require anyone's help.

Someone grabbed him by the right arm, spun him against Nokhada's shoulder, and hit him in the side of the head—he didn't even see it coming. He came to bruised and on the stony ground with Jago's voice in his ear, arguing with someone.

"Tell me what he's up to!" Cenedi's voice, then. "Tell me where he thinks he's going—when the shooting starts, a man takes his *real* direction—or do they say that in Shejidan?"

His eyes were blurred, his ear was ringing, and he put his hand on a sharp rock, trying to prop himself on the better arm. "He doesn't know better," Jago was saying. "I don't know what he'll do next, nadi! He's not atevi! Isn't that the point of all this?"

"Nadi," Cenedi said coldly, "*inform* him what he'll do next. Next time I'll shoot him in the knee and not discuss the matter. Take me very seriously."

A towering shadow came between them and the sun. Babs, and Ilisidi, only watching, while Bren staggered to his feet.

"Aiji-ma," came Jago's quiet voice from beside him, and Jago's hard grip on his arm, pulling him aside. He stood there with the side of his face burning, with hearing dimmed in one ear, as Ilisidi drifted past and Cenedi stalked off from him. "Damned *fool!*" Jago said with a shake at his arm.

"They'd have left him!"

"Did you hear him?" Another shake at his arm. "He'll cripple you. It's not an idle threat!"

Two of Cenedi's men had caught Nokhada, and brought her, shaking her head and fighting the restraint. He groped after the rein a man offered him, and made a shaken effort to get the stirrup turned to mount—one of them got Nokhada to drop the shoulder, and he got his toe in the stirrup, but he slipped as Nokhada came up, a thorough botch. He hung from the mounting-straps with both feet off the ground, until someone shoved him from below and he landed far enough on to drag himself the rest of the way aboard.

He saw Jago getting onto another of the spares, the last

two men mounting up, as Ilisidi started into motion and Nokhada started to move with the group. His vision grayed out on him in the sudden motion—had been graying out since Jago had lit into him, for reasons doubtless valid to her. His hands shook, and balance faltered.

"You stay *on*," Jago said, drawing near him. "You stay *with* the mecheita, do you hear me, nadi?"

He didn't answer. It made him mad. He could understand Cenedi hitting him, he knew damned well what he'd done in going after Banichi. He'd violated Ilisidi's chain of command—he'd forced them into a fight Cenedi would have avoided, because Cenedi was looking out for the dowager—and possibly, darker suspicion, because Cenedi would all along as soon leave Banichi *and* Jago in the lurch and have him completely to himself and the dowager's politics. Cenedi personally would gladly sell him to the highest bidder, that was the gut-level fear that had sent him down that hill, he thought now, that and the equally gut-level human conviction that the treason he was committing was, humanly speaking, minor and excusable.

It wasn't, for Cenedi. It wasn't, for Jago, and *that* was what he couldn't understand—or accept.

"Do you *hear* me, nadi, do you understand?"

"Where's Algini and Tano?" he challenged her.

"On a boat," Jago snapped, her knee bumping his, as the mecheiti moved next to each other. "Likewise providing your enemies a target, and a direction you could have gone. But we'll be damned lucky now if—"

Jago stopped talking and looked skyward. And said a word he'd never heard from Jago.

He looked. His ears were still ringing. He couldn't hear what she heard.

"Plane," Jago said, "dammit!"

She reined back in the column as Ilisidi put Babs to a fast jog into the stream and across it, close to the mountain. Nokhada took a sudden notion to overtake the leaders, jostled others despite a hard pull on the rein.

He could hear the plane coming now. There wasn't anything they could do but get to the most inconvenient angle for it that they could find against the hills, and that seemed to be their leaders' immediate purpose. It wasn't a casually passing aircraft. It sounded low, and terror began to increase his heartbeat. He wondered whether Ilisidi and Cenedi were doing the right thing, or whether they should let the mecheiti run free and get into the rocks. It wasn't damned fair, being shot at without any weapon, any cover, any way to outrun it—it wasn't anything like *kabiu*, it wasn't the way atevi had waged war in the past—*he* was the object of contention, and it was human tech atevi were aiming at each other, human tactics . . .

They kept their course along the mountainside, Ilisidi and Cenedi holding a lead Nokhada wasn't contesting now, the rest of the column behind, strung out along the streamside. Cenedi was worried. He saw Cenedi turn and look back and up at the sky.

The engine sound came clearer and clearer, illegal use, unapproved use, to fire from the air—they'd designed the stall limits to discourage it, considering that Mospheira was situated as it was, easily within reach of small aircraft. They'd kept the speed up, not transferred anything to do with targeting—no fuses, no bomb sights; it was the paidhi's job to keep a thing like this from happening. . . .

His mind was busy with that train of thought as the plane came down the stream-cut roadway, low, straight at them. Its single engine echoed off the hills. The riders around him drew guns, a couple of them lifted hunting rifles—and he didn't know to that moment whether atevi had figured out how to mount guns on aircraft, or whether it was only a reckless pilot spotting them and trying to scare them.

The plane's skin was thin enough bullets might get to the pilot or hit something vital, like the fuel tanks. He didn't know its design that intimately. It hadn't been on his watch. Wilson's, it had probably been Wilson's tenure . . .

His heart thudded in panic. Their column had stopped entirely now and faced about to the attack. He held Nokhada on a short rein, while gunfire racketed around him, aimed aloft.

The plane roared over them, and explosions went off in midair, over their heads, making the mecheiti jump and all but bolt. Puffs of smoke lingered after the fireballs. Rocks rolled down the mountain, dislodging slides of gravel.

"Dropping explosives," he heard someone say.

Bombs. Grenades. Above all, trust that atevi handled numbers. They wouldn't make that many mistakes. "They haven't got the timing down," he said urgently to Banichi, who'd reined in near him. "It blew above us. They'll figure it. They'll reset those fuses. We can't give them any more tries at us."

"We haven't got a choice," Banichi said. Atevi didn't sweat. Banichi was sweating. His face was a color he'd never seen an atevi achieve, as he methodically shoved in another clip, from the small number remaining on his belt.

The plane was coming around again, and their group moved as Babs started out at a fast pace, descending as the stream-cut road descended. The mecheiti bunched up now, as close as the terrain allowed, trampling shrubs.

Changing the altitude, changing the targeting equation, Bren thought to himself—it was the best thing they could do, besides find cover the land didn't offer them, while that atevi pilot was trying to work out the math of where his bombs had hit. Somebody behind him was yelling something about concentrating fire on the fusilage and the pilot, not the wings, the fuel tanks were closer in.

It was all crazed. He heard the roar of the engine and looked up as the plane came streaking down at them, this time from the side, over the mountain opposite them, and gave them only a brief window of fire.

Explosions pounded the hill above them and showered

them with rock chunks and dirt—Nokhada jumped and threw her head at an enemy she couldn't reach.

"Getting smart, the bastard," someone said, and Ilisidi, in the lead, led them quickly around the shoulder of the hill, off the road now, while they could hear the plane coming back again.

Then came a distant rumble out of the south, the sound of thunder. Weather moving in.

Please God, Bren thought. Clouds and cover. He'd nerved himself for the bombs. The prospect of rescue had his hands trembling and the sweat breaking out under his arms.

Another pass. A bomb hit behind them and set brush burning.

A second plane roared over immediately behind that, and dropped its bombs the other side of the hill.

"There's two of them," Giri cried. "Damn!"

"That one's still figuring it out," Banichi said. The number one plane was coming back again. They were caught on an open hillside, and Banichi and Jago and Cenedi and the rest of them drew calm aim, tracked it as it came—Cenedi said, at the last moment, "Behind the cowling."

They opened up, gunfire echoing off the other hill.

The plane roared over and didn't drop its bombs. It ripped just above the crest of the hill and a second later a loud explosion shook the ground.

Nobody cheered. The second plane was coming in fast and they were on the move again, picking their way over the rocks, traveling as fast as they could. Thunder boomed again. One assumed it was thunder. The second plane came over again and dropped its bombs too soon. They hit the hill crest.

They descended the steep way, then, into a narrow ravine, a smaller window for the plane at its speed than it was for them. They heard a plane coming. Its engine was sputtering as thunder—it had to be thunder—rolled and rumbled in the distance.

That plane's crippled, Bren thought. Something's wrong with it. God, there's hope.

He didn't think it would drop its bombs. He watched it make its pass in the narrow sky above them.

Then an explosion went off right over them, and Nokhada jumped. A sharp impact hit his shoulder, and the rider next to him went down—he didn't see why—brush came at his face and he put up a hand to protect himself as Nokhada ran him up the hill and stopped close to Babs.

He was half-deaf from the blast, but not so he couldn't hear mecheiti screaming in fright or pain. He looked back, saw riders down where he'd been, and tried to turn back. Nokhada had other ideas and fought him on the slope, until other riders went back.

But Banichi was still in sight; he saw Jago among those afoot, heard a single gunshot. The screaming stopped abruptly, leaving the silence and the ringing of his ears; then, after a moment of milling about, and another of Nokhada's unwilling turn-abouts on the slope, he saw people mounting up again, the column reorganizing itself.

A rider came forward in the line, and reported to Cenedi and Ilisidi three men dead, and one of the names was Giri.

He felt—he didn't know what, then. An impact to the gut. The loss of someone he knew, a known quantity when so much was changing around him—he felt it personally; but he was glad at the same time it wasn't Banichi or Jago, and he supposed in a vague, dazed way, that his sense of loss was a selfish judgement, on selfish human standards that had nothing to do with *man'chi*, or what atevi felt or didn't feel.

He didn't know right and wrong any longer. His head ached. His ears were still ringing and there was a stink of smoke and gunpowder in every breath he drew. Dirt had spattered him and Nokhada, even this far up the column, dirt and bits of leaves—he wasn't sure what else had, and he didn't want to know. He only kept remembering the shock of the bomb bursting, a wall of air and fragments that made itself one with the explosions on the road—recalled the shock of something hitting his arm with an impact that still ached. It was a fluke, that single accurate bomb. It might not happen again.

Or it might on the next such strike—he didn't know how much farther they had to ride or how long their enemies could keep putting up planes from Maidingi Airport and hitting at them over and over again, with nothing, nothing they could do about it.

But the second plane didn't come back, whether it had crashed in the mountains or made it back to the airport, and in the meantime the rumbling of thunder grew louder.

In a while more, clouds swept in, bringing cold air, first, then a spatter of rain, a crack of thunder. The riders around him delved into packs without getting down, pulled out black plastic rain-cloaks and began to settle them on as the drops began to fall. He hoped for the same in his gear, and discovered it in the pack beside his knee, someone's providence in this season of cold mountain rains. He sorted it out in the early moments of the rain, settled it over his head and over as much of him and the riding-pad as he could, latching it up about his throat as the chill deluge began, blinding him with its gusts and trickling down his neck.

The plastic kept body heat in, his and Nokhada's, the turbulence and the cloud cover up above the hills was a shield from aircraft, and if he froze where the stiff gusts plastered the plastic against his body or whipped up the edges of it on a shirt and coat beginning to be soaked from the trickle down his neck, any discomfort the storm brought on them was better than being hammered from the air.

For the most part he trusted Nokhada to follow Babs, tucked his hands under his arms and asked himself where Ilisidi's strength possibly came from, because the more he let himself relax, the more his own was giving way, and the more the shivers did get through. Thin bodies chill faster, Giri had said that, he was sure it had been Giri, who was dead, now, spattered all over a hillside.

His brain kept re-hearing the explosions.

Kept falling into black patches, when he shut his eyes, kept being back in that cellar, listening to the thunder, feeling a gun against his head and knowing Cenedi would do it again and for real, because Cenedi's anger with humans was tied up with Ilisidi's ambition and what had and hadn't been possible for atevi to achieve even before that ship appeared in the skies, he read that much. Cenedi's *man'chi* was with Ilisidi, the rebels offered Ilisidi association with them, Ilisidi had told Cenedi find out what the paidhi was, and in Cenedi's eyes, it was his fault he'd convinced her not to take that rebel offer.

Hence Cenedi's anger—at him, at Ilisidi's surrendering her fight for the seat in Shejidan—to age, to time, to God knew what motive. The paidhi had no confidence he could interpret anything, not even himself, lately. He'd become a commodity for trade among atevi factions. He didn't even know who owned him at the moment—didn't know why Cenedi had waited on the hill for Banichi.

Didn't know why Jago had been angry at him, for going after Banichi.

Jago . . . make a deal with Cenedi? Betray Tabini *and* Banichi? He didn't think so.

He refused to think so, for no logical reason, only a human one—which didn't at all apply to her. He knew that, if he knew nothing else, in the confusion of his thoughts. But he didn't change his opinion.

Hill after hill after hill in the blinding rain.

Then another deeply cut ravine, where a tall growth of ironheart sheltered them from the blasts, and the thready leaves streamed and clumped with water, dumping it, when they chanced to brush against them, in small, icy floods that found their way down necks, more often than not.

But that cover of brush was the first relief from the wind they'd found, and Ilisidi called a rest and bunched them up, the twelve of them—only twelve surviving riders, he was dismayed to realize, and six mecheiti on their own, trailing them through brush and along the stony hillsides. He hadn't realized the losses, he hadn't counted . . . he didn't know where they might have lost the others, or whether, at some silent signal he'd missed, the party had divided itself.

He held on to the mounting-straps and slid down Nokhada's wet side, not sure he could get up again unaided, but glad enough to rest. For the first moment he had to stand holding to Nokhada's harness just to keep his feet, his legs were so rubbery from riding. Lightning flickered and the thunder muttered over their heads. He could scarcely walk on the rain-slick hillside without grabbing onto branches and leaning on one rock and the next. He wandered like a drunken man along the steep slope, seeking a warm spot and a place a little more out of the wind. He saw that Banichi had gotten down—and he worked his way in that direction, where four other men had gathered, with Jago, one of them squatting down beside her and holding Banichi's ankle. The water-soaked boot was stretched painfully tight over the joint.

"Is it broken, Jago-ji?" he asked, getting down beside her.

"Probably," she said darkly, not looking at him. By the stablehands' foresight, she and Banichi both had raincloaks, and she huddled in hers, not looking at him, not speaking, not willing to speak; he read that in the shoulder she kept toward him. But it was no place to argue with her, when Banichi was in pain, and everything seemed short-fused.

The man who was dealing with Banichi at least seemed sure of what he was doing—might even be a real medic, Bren thought. Tabini had one in his guard. It made sense the aiji-dowager might take such a precaution, considering her breakneck rides and considering the politics she had a finger in.

"The boot stays *on*," Banichi said, to a suggestion they cut it off. "It's holding it together. I can at least—"

At which the man made a tentative probe that sent Banichi's head back and his breath hissing through his teeth.

"Sorry," the man said, and spoke to another of the guards kneeling by him. "Cut me a couple or three splints."

One more of their company walked up to watch, steps whispering over sodden leaves, disturbing the occasional rock. Jago squatted, blowing on her clasped hands to warm them. Banichi wasn't enjoying being the center of attention. He ebbed backward onto the ground and lay there staring up into the drizzle, ignoring all of it. The ground chill had to come through the plastic rain-cloak. But the staff's providence hadn't extended to blankets, or to tents.

Ilisidi limped over, using her cane, and Cenedi's arm, on the uneven ground. There ensued another discussion between Ilisidi and the perhaps-medic as to whether Banichi's ankle was broken; and Banichi, propping himself glumly on his elbows, entered the argument to say it had gone numb when the truck blew up and he'd finished the job when he'd jumped out under fire and hit a rock.

Which was more detail of what had happened in the ambush than he'd yet heard from Banichi.

"Can you walk on it?" Cenedi asked.

"In an emergency," Banichi said, which proved nothing at all about how bad it was. It *was* broken, Bren thought. The ankle didn't rest straight. "Not what I'd choose, nadi. What walking did you have in mind?"

"Outside Maidingi Airport, which seems unavailable, there are two, remotely three ways we can go from here." Thunder rumbled, and Cenedi waited for it, while the rain fell steadily. "We'd confirmed Wigairiin as reliable, with its airstrip—hence the feints we asked for lakeward and southwest. But our schedule is blown to hell now. The rebels in Maidingi township have no doubt now that our answer to their association is no and that we're going west. They can't be so stupid as to forget our association with Wigairiin."

"North of here," Banichi said.

"North and west. On the edge of the hills. The rebels are bound to move to take Wigairiin's airstrip—or to take it out."

"Foolish to strike at Wigairiin," Ilisidi said, "until they're sure both Malguri *and* Wigairiin aren't going with them. And they won't have known that until we went out the stable gate."

"Not an easy field to take from the air," Cenedi said. "Expensive to take."

"Unless they moved in forces overland, in advance of Malguri's refusal," Banichi said.

"Possible," Cenedi said. "But let me tell you our other choices. There's the border. Fagioni province, just at the foot of Wigairiin height. But it could be a soft border. Damned soft in a matter of hours if Wigairiin falls, and we're left with the same guess where the border into loyal territory firms up after that if Wigairiin falls. There's also the open country, if we ignore both Wigairiin and Fagioni township and head into the reserve there. That's three hundred miles of wilderness, plenty of game. But no cover."

"More air attacks," Ilisidi said.

"We might as well resign the fight if we take that route." Banichi shifted higher, to sit up, winced, and settled on an elbow. "Railhead at Fagioni. They'll have infiltrated, if they've got any sense. Major force is already launched. Rainstorm won't have stopped the trains. They know we didn't take the lake crossing. They know the politics on this side. You were the only question, nand' dowager."

"So it's Wigairiin," Cenedi said.

"There's south," Banichi said. "Maidingi."

"With twelve of us? They'd hunt us out in an hour. We've got this storm until dark, if the weather reports hold. That long we've got cover. We can make Wigairiin. We can get out of there."

"In *what?*" Banichi asked. "Forgive me. A plane that's a low-flying target?"

"A jet," Cenedi said.

Banichi frowned and drew in a slow breath, seeming to think about it then. "But what is it," Banichi asked, "since they took Maidingi? Four, five hours? Tabini has commercial aircraft at his disposal. He might *be* in Maidingi by now. He could have landed a force at the airport."

"And the whole rebellion could be over," Ilisidi said, "but I wouldn't bet our lives on it, nadiin. The Association is hanging together by a thread of public confidence in Tabini's priorities. To answer a rising against him with brutal force instead of negotiation, while the axe hangs over atevi heads, visibly? No. Tabini's made his move, in sending Bren-paidhi to *me*. If that plane goes out of Wigairiin, if I personally, with my known opposition to the Treaty, deliver the paidhi back to him—the wind is out of their sails, then and there. This is a political war, nadiin."

"Explosives falling on our heads, nand' dowager, were not a sudden inspiration. They were made in advance. The preparation to drop them from aircraft was made in advance. Surely they informed you the extent of their preparations."

"Surely my grandson informed you," Ilisidi said, "nadi, the extent of his own."

What are we suddenly talking about? Bren asked himself. What are they asking each other?

About betrayal?

"As happens," Banichi said, "he informed us very little. In case you should ask."

My God.

"We go to Wigairiin," Cenedi said. "I refuse, with 'Sidi's life, to bet on Maidingi, or what Tabini may or may not have done."

"I have to leave it to you," Banichi said with a grimace and a shift on the elbow. "You know this area. You know your people."

"No question, then," Ilisidi said, and punctuated it with a stab of her walking-stick at the sodden ground. "Tonight. If this rain keeps up—it's not an easy airfield in turbulence, Cenedi assures me. Not at all easy when they're shooting at you from the ground. If we get there we can hold the airstrip with two rifles, take the rest of the night off, and radio my lazy grandson to come get us."

"I've flown in there," Cenedi said. "Myself. It's a narrow field, short, single runway, takeoffs and landings right out over a cliff, past a steep rock where snipers can sit. The house is a seventeenth-century villa, with a gravel road down to Fagioni. The previous aiji was too aristocratic to fly over to Maidingi to catch the scheduled flights. She had the airstrip built, knocked down a fourteenth century defense wall to do it."

"Hell of a howl from the Preservation Commission," Ilisidi said. "Her son maintains the jet and uses it. It seats ten. It can easily handle our twelve, Cenedi's rated for it, and it's going to be fueled."

"If," Cenedi said, "if the rebels haven't gotten somebody in there. Or sent them down, as you say, into Fagioni, to come up overland. If we have to scramble to take that field, nadiin, will you be with us? *That's* the walk that could be necessary."

"No question," Banichi said glumly. "I'm with you."

"None," said Jago.

"The paidhi will take orders," Cenedi said.

"I," Bren started to answer, but Jago hit his knee with the back of her hand. "The paidhi," she said coldly, "will do what he's told. Absolutely what he's told."

"I—" He began to object on his own behalf, that he understood that, but Jago said, "Shut the hell up, nadi."

He shut up. Jago embarrassed him. The anger and tension between Banichi and Cenedi was palpable. He looked at the rain-soaked ground and watched the rain-drops settle on last year's fallen leaves and the scattered stones, while they discussed the geography of Wigairiin, and the airstrip, and the aiji of Wigairiin's ties to Il-isidi. Meanwhile the putative medic had brought his splints, three straight sticks, and elastic bandage, and proceeded to wrap Banichi's ankle—"Tightly, nadi," Banichi interrupted the strategy session to say, and the medic said shortly he should deal with what he knew about.

Banichi frowned and leaned back, then, because it seemed to hurt, and was out of the discussion, while Jago asked pointed questions about the lay of the land.

There was an ancient wall on the south that cut off the approach to Wigairiin, with a historic and functional iron gate; but they didn't expect it to be shut against them. Just before that approach, they were going to send the mecheiti with one man, around the wall, north and east, to get them home to Malguri.

Why not stable them at Wigairiin? Bren asked himself. Why not at least have them for a resource for escape if things went wrong there, and they had to get away?

For a woman who seemed to know a lot about assaulting fortresses, and a lot about airstrips and strategy—removing that resource as a fall-back seemed a stupid idea. Cenedi letting her order it seemed more stupid than that, and Banichi and Jago not objecting to it—he didn't understand. He almost said something himself, but Jago had said shut up, and he didn't understand what was going on in the company.

Best ask later, he thought.

The dowager valued Babs probably more than she did any of them. That part was even understandable to him. She was old. If anything happened to Babs, he thought Ilisidi might lose something totally irreplaceable in her life.

Which was a human thing to think. In point of any fact when he was dealing with atevi feelings, he didn't know *what* Ilisidi felt about a mecheiti she'd attacked a man for damaging. Forgetting that for two seconds was a trap, a disturbing, human miscalculation, right at the center of a transaction that was ringing alarm bells up and down his spine, and he couldn't make up his mind what was going on with the signals he was getting from Banichi and Jago. God, what was going on?

But he couldn't put it together without understanding what Ilisidi's motive was, what she valued most, what she was logical about and what she wouldn't be.

On such exaggerated threads his mind was running, chasing down invalid chains of logic, stretching connections between points that weren't connected, trying to remember what specific and mutable points had persuaded him to believe what he believed was true—the hints of motivation and policy in people who'd been lying to him when they told him the most basic facts he'd believed.

Go on instinct? *Worst,* worst thing the paidhi could ever do for a situation. Instinct was human. Feelings were human. Reasonable expectations were definitely human. . . .

Ilisidi said they should get underway, then. It was a good fifty miles, atevi reckoning, and she thought they could get there by midnight.

"Speed's what we can do," she said, "that these city-folk *won't* expect. They don't think in terms of mecheiti crossing hills like this that fast. Damn lot they've forgotten. Damn lot about this land they never learned."

She leaned on her cane, getting up. He wanted to believe in Ilisidi. He wanted to trust the things she said. Emotionally . . . based in human psyche . . . he wanted to think she *loved* the land and wanted to save it.

Intellectually, he wanted answers about sending the mecheiti back to Malguri—where there were, supposedly, rebels having breakfast off the historic china.

He didn't get up with the rest. He waited until the medic packed up and moved off.

"Banichi-ji," he said on his knees and as quietly as he

could. "She's sending the mecheiti away. We might still need them. Is this reasonable, nadi-ji?"

Banichi's yellow eyes remained frustratingly expressionless. He blinked once. The mouth—offered not a thing.

"Banichi. Why?"

"Why—what?"

"*Why* did Tabini do what he did? Why didn't he just damn *ask* me where I stood?"

"Go get on, nadi."

"Why did you get mad when I came to help you? Cenedi would have left you, with no help, no—"

"I said, Get on. We're leaving."

"Am I that totally *wrong,* Banichi? Just answer me. Why is she sending the mecheiti back, before we know we're safe?"

"Get me up," Banichi said, and reached for Jago's hand. Bren caught the other arm, and Banichi made it up, wobbly, testing the splinted ankle. It didn't work. Banichi gasped, and used their combined help to hobble over to his mecheita and grab the mounting-straps.

"Banichi-ji." It was the last privacy he and Banichi and Jago might have for hours, and he was desperate. "Banichi, these people are *lying* to us. Why?"

Banichi looked at him, and for one dreadful moment, he had the feeling what it must be to face Banichi . . . professionally.

But Banichi turned then, grasped the highest of the straps on the riding-pad, and with a jump that belied his size and weight, managed to get most of the way up without even needing the mecheita to drop the shoulder. Jago gave him the extra shove that put him across the pad and Banichi caught up the rein, letting the splinted leg dangle.

Banichi didn't need his help. Atevi didn't have friends, atevi left each other to die. The paidhi was supposed to reason through that fact of life and death and find a rationale other humans could accept to explain it all.

But at the moment, with bruises wherever atevi had

laid hands on him, the paidhi didn't understand, couldn't understand, *refused* to understand why Banichi should have died back there, for no damned reason, or why Banichi was lying to him, too.

Men were getting up, ready to move out. If he wasn't on Nokhada, Nokhada would leave him, he had no doubt of it, they'd have to come back to get the reason—he still supposed—of this whole exercise, and nobody was going to be damned happy with him. He quickened his pace, limped across the slant of the hill and caught Nokhada.

Then he heard the tread of someone leading a mecheita in his tracks across the sodden leaves. He faced around.

It was Jago. A very angry Jago. "Nadi," she said. "You don't have the only valid ideas in the world. Tabini-ji told you where to be, what to do. You do those things."

He shoved up the rain-cloak plastic and the sleeve of his coat, showing the livid marks still on his wrist. "That, for their hospitality last night, that, for the dowager's questions—which I've answered, Jago-ji, answered well enough that *they* believe me. It's not my damn fault, whatever's going on. I don't know what I've done since the dowager's apartment, that you look at me like that."

Jago slapped him across the face, so hard he rocked back against Nokhada's ribs.

"Do as you're told!" Jago said. "Do I hear more questions, nadi?"

"No," he said, tasting blood. His eyes were watering. Jago walked off from him in his blurred vision and got on her mecheita, her back to him the while.

He hit Nokhada harder than his wont. Nokhada dropped her shoulder and stayed down until he had his foot in the stirrup and landed astride. He kicked blindly, angrily, after the stirrup, fought the rain-cloak out of his way as he felt Nokhada jolt into motion. A low vine raked his head and defensive arm.

Jago hadn't hit with all her force—left the burn of her hand on his face, but that was nothing. It was the anger—

hers and his, that found a vital, painful spot and dug in deep.

He didn't know what he'd said—or done. He didn't know how he'd come to deserve her temper or her calculated spite, except Jago didn't like the questions he'd asked Banichi. He'd trod on something, a saner voice tried to say to him. He might have vital keys if he shut down any personal feeling, remembered exactly what he'd asked, or exactly what anyone had said. It was his job to do that. Even if atevi didn't want him doing it. Even if he wasn't going to get where they promised him he was going.

He lost the hillside a moment. He was on Ilisidi's balcony, in the biting wind, in the dark, where Ilisidi challenged him with facts, and the truth that he couldn't trust now to be the truth, the way he couldn't pull the pieces of recent argument out of his memory.

He was on the mountain, alone, seeing only the snow—

On the rain-drenched hillside, with Jago deserting Banichi, cursing him for going after her own partner—and in the smoke, with the ricocheting bullets left and right of him.

The cellar swallowed him, a moment of dark, of helpless terror—he didn't know why the images tumbled one over the other, flashed up, replacing the rainy thicket and the sight of Ilisidi and Cenedi ahead of him.

The shock of last night had set in—a natural reaction, he told himself, like the details of an accident coming back, replaying themselves over what was going on around him—only he wasn't doing it in safety. There wasn't any safety anywhere around him. There might never be again, only the bombs had stopped falling, and he had to focus and deal with what was ringing alarm bells through the here and now.

Banichi had challenged Ilisidi on the preparation of those bombs for a reason.

Banichi wasn't a reckless man. He'd been probing for something, and he'd gotten it: Ilisidi had come back on him with a What do you know? and Banichi had claimed to know nothing of Tabini's plans, implicitly challenging Ilisidi again to take *him* to that cellar and see what they could get.

Where was Banichi's motive in the confrontation? Where was Ilisidi's in the question, with so much tottering uncertain?

Putting Tabini's intentions in question. . . .

God, the mind was going. He was losing the threads. They were multiplying on him, his thoughts darting this way and that way . . . not making sense and then making him terribly, irrationally afraid he still hadn't figured the people he was with.

Jago hadn't backed Banichi, anywhere in the argument. Jago had attacked *him,* told him to shut up, followed him across the hill to say exactly what she'd already told him and then hit him in the face. Hard.

Nobody had objected to Jago hitting him. Ilisidi hadn't. Banichi hadn't. They'd surely seen it. And nobody stopped her. Nobody objected. Nobody cared, because the human in the party didn't read the signals and maybe everybody else knew why Jago had done it.

The threads kept running, proliferating, tangling. The dark was all around him for a moment, and he lost his balance—caught himself, heart thumping, with a hand on Nokhada's rain-wet shoulder.

It was the cellar again. He heard footsteps, but they were an illusion, he knew they were. He'd taken a knock on the head and it hurt like hell, shooting pains through his brain. The footsteps went away when he insisted to see the storm-gray of the hills, to feel the cold drops off the branches above him trickling down his neck. Nokhada's jarring gait scarcely hurt him now.

But Banichi was alive. He'd made that choice, whatever atevi understood. He couldn't have gone off and left him and Jago, to go off with Ilisidi—he didn't know what part of a human brain had made that decision, the way atevi didn't consciously know why they, like mecheiti, darted after the leader, come hell come havoc—he hadn't thought, hadn't damned well *thought* about the transaction, that the paidhi's life was what aijiin were shooting each other for. It hadn't mattered to him, in that moment, running down that slope, and he still didn't know that it mattered—not to Tabini, who could get a replacement for him in an hour, who wasn't going to listen to him in anyone else's hands, and who wasn't going to pay a damn thing to get him back, so the joke was on the people who thought he would. He didn't know anything. It was all too technical—so that joke was on them, too.

The only thing he had of value was in the computer— which he ought to drop into the nearest deep ravine, or slam onto a rock, except it wouldn't take out the storage—and if they collected it, it wasn't saying atevi experts couldn't get those pieces to work. And experts weren't the people he wanted to have their hands on it.

He *should* have done a security erase. *If* he'd had the power to turn it on.

God, do what to save that situation, tip them off it was valuable? Make an issue, then botch getting rid of it?

Just leave it in the bag, let Nokhada carry it back to Malguri?

The rebels were sitting in Malguri.

Dark. The steps coming and going.

The beast on the wall. Lonely after all these centuries.

He couldn't talk to Banichi. Banichi couldn't walk, couldn't fight them—he couldn't believe Banichi lying back like that, resigning the argument and all their lives to Cenedi.

But Cenedi was a professional. Like Banichi. Maybe together they understood things he couldn't.

Jago crossed the width of the hill to blame him and hit him in the face.

Cold and dark. Footsteps in the hall. Voices discussing having a drink, fading away up the steps.

A gun was against his skull and he thought of snow,

snow all around him. And not a living soul. Like Banichi.
Just shut it out.

Give it up.

He didn't understand. Giri was dead. Bombs just
dropped and spattered pieces all over hill, and he
didn't know why, it didn't make any sense why a bomb
fell on one man and not another. Bombs didn't care. Killing him must be as good as having him, in the minds of
their enemies.

Which wasn't what Cenedi had said.

There began to be a sea-echo in his skull, the ache
where Cenedi had hit him and the one where Jago had,
both gone to one pain, that kept him aware where he was.

In his own apartment, before Cenedi's message had
come, before she'd left, Jago had said ... I'll never betray you, nadi Bren.

I'll never betray you ...

XIV

Not doing well, he wasn't—with one pain shooting
through his eyes and another running through his elbow to the pit of his stomach, while two or three other
point-sources contested for his attention. The rain had
whipped up to momentary thunder and a fit of deluge,
then subsided to wind-borne drizzles, a cold mist so thick
one breathed it. The sky was a boiling gray, while the
mecheiti struck a steady, long-striding pace one behind
the other, Babs leading the way up and down the rain-
shadowed narrows, along brushy stretches of streamside,
where frondy ironheart trailed into their path and dripped
water on their heads and down their necks.

But there wasn't the same jostling for the lead, now,
among the foremost mecheiti. It seemed it wasn't just

Nokhada, after all. None of them were fighting, whether Ilisidi had somehow communicated that through Babs, or whether somehow, after the bombs, and in the misery of the cold rain, even the mecheiti understood a common urgency. The established order of going had Nokhada fourth in line behind another of Ilisidi's guards.

One, two, three, four, regular as a heartbeat, pace, pace, pace, pace.

Never betray you. Hell.

More tea? Cenedi asked him.

And sent him to the cellar.

His eyes watered with the throbbing in his skull and with the wind blasting into his face, and the desire to beat Cenedi's head against a rock grew totally absorbing for a while. But it didn't answer the questions, and it didn't get him back to Mospheira.

Just to some damned place where Ilisidi had friends.

Another alarm bell, he thought. Friends. Atevi didn't have friends. Atevi had *man'chi,* and hadn't someone said—he thought it was Cenedi himself—that Ilisidi hadn't *man'chi* to anyone?

They crossed no roads—with not a phone line, not a tilled field, not the remote sound of a motor, only the regular thump of the mecheiti's gait on wet ground, the creak of harness, even, harsh breathing—it hypnotized, mile after rain-drenched and indistinguishable mile. The dwindling day had a lucent, gray sameness. Sunlight spread through the clouds no matter what the sun's angle with the hills.

Ilisidi reined back finally in a flat space and with a grimace and a resettling on Babs' back, ordered the four heavier men to trade off to the unridden mecheiti.

That included Cenedi; and Banichi, who complained and elected to do it by leaning from one mecheita to the other, as only one of the other men did—as if Banichi and mecheiti weren't at all unacquainted.

Didn't hurt himself. Expecting that event, Bren

watched with his lip between his teeth until Banichi had straightened himself around.

He caught Jago's eye then and saw a biding coldness, total lack of expression—directed at him.

Because human and atevi hormones were running the machinery, now, he told himself, and the lump he had in his throat and the thump of emotion he had when he reacted to Jago's cold disdain composed the surest prescription for disaster he could think of.

Shut it down, he told himself. Do the job. Think it through.

Jago didn't come closer. The whole column sorted itself out in the prior order, and Nokhada's first jerking steps carried him out of view.

When he looked back, Banichi was riding as he had been, hands braced against the mecheita's shoulders, head bowed—Banichi was suffering, acutely, and he didn't know whether the one of their company who seemed to be a medic, and who'd had a first aid kit, had also had a pain-killer, or whether Banichi had taken one or not, but a broken ankle, splinted or not, had to be swelling, dangling as it was, out of the stirrup on that side.

Banichi's condition persuaded him that his own aches and pains were ignorable. And it frightened him, what they might run into and what, with Banichi crippled, and with Ilisidi willing to leave him once, they *could* do if they met trouble at the end of the ride—if Wigairiin wasn't in allied hands.

Or if Ilisidi hadn't told the truth about her intentions—because it occurred to him she'd said no to the rebels in Maidingi, but she'd equally well been conspiring with Wigairiin, evidently, as he picked it up, as an old associate only apt to come in with the rebels if Ilisidi did.

That meant queasy relationships and queasy alliances, fragile ties that could do anything under stress.

In the cellar, they'd recorded his answers to their questions—they *said* it was all machimi, all play-acting, no validity.

But that tape still existed, if Ilisidi hadn't destroyed it. She'd not have left it behind in Malguri, for the people that were supposedly her jilted allies.

If Ilisidi hadn't destroyed it—they had that tape, and they had it with them.

He reined back, disturbing the column. He feigned a difficulty with the stirrup, and stayed bent over as rider after rider passed him at that rapid, single-minded pace.

He let up on the rein when Banichi passed him, and the hindmost guards had pulled back, too, moving in on him. "Banichi, there's a tape recording," he said. "Of me. Interrogation about the gun."

At which point he gave Nokhada a thump of his heel and slipped past the guards, as Nokhada quickened pace.

Nokhada butted the fourth mecheita in the rump as she arrived, not gently, with the war-brass, and the other man had to pull in hard to prevent a fight.

"Forgive me, nadi," Bren said breathlessly, heart thumping. "I had my stirrup twisted."

It was still a near fight. It helped Nokhada's flagging spirits immensely, even if she didn't get the spot in line.

It didn't at all help his headache, or the hurt in his arm, half of it now, he thought, from Nokhada's war for the rein.

The gray daylight slid subtly into night, a gradual dimming to a twilight of wind-driven rain, a ghostly half-light that slipped by eye-tricking degrees into blackest, starless night. He had thought they would have to slow down when night fell—but atevi eyes could deal with the dark, and maybe mecheiti could: Babs kept that steady, ground-devouring pace, laboring only when they had to climb, never breaking into exuberance or lagging on the lower places; and Nokhada made occasional sallies forward, complaining with tosses of her head and jolts in her gait when the third-rank mecheita cut her off, one constant, nightmare battle just to keep control of the creature, to keep his ears attuned for the whisper of leaves ahead that forewarned him to duck some branch the first riders had ducked beneath in the dark.

The rain must have stopped for some while before he even noticed, there was so much water dripping and blowing from the leaves generally above them.

But when they broke out into the clear, the clouds had gone from overhead, affording a panorama of stars and shadowy hills that should have relieved his sense of claustrophobic dark—but all he could think of was the ship presence that threatened the world and the fact that, if they didn't reach this airstrip by dawn, they'd be naked to attack from Maidingi Airport.

By midnight, Ilisidi had said, they'd reach Wigairiin, and that hour was long since past, if he could still read the pole stars.

Only let me die, he began to think, exhausted and in pain, when they began to climb again, and climb, and climb the stony hill. Ilisidi called a halt, and he supposed that they were going to trade off again, and that it meant they'd as long to go as they'd already ridden.

But he saw the ragged edge of ironheart against the night sky above them on the hill, and Ilisidi said they should all get down, they'd gone as far as the mecheiti would take them.

Then he wished they had a deal more of riding to go, because it suddenly dawned on him that all bets were called. They were committing themselves, now, to a course in which neither Banichi nor Jago was going to object, not after Banichi had argued vainly against it at the outset. God, he was scared of this next part.

Banichi didn't have any help but him—not even Jago, so far as he could tell. He had the computer to manage ... his last chance to send it away with Nokhada and hope, *hope* the handlers, loyal to Ilisidi, would keep it from rebel attention.

But if rebels did hold Malguri now, they'd be very interested when the mecheiti came in—granted anything had gone wrong and they didn't get a fast flight out of

here, the computer was guaranteed close attention. And
things could go wrong, very wrong.

Baji-naji. Leaving it for anyone else was asking too
much of Fortune and relying far too much on Chance. He
jerked the ties that held the bags on behind the riding-pad,
gathered them up as the most ordinary, the most casual
thing in the world, his hands trembling the while, and slid
off, gripping the mounting-straps to steady his shaking
knees.

Breath came short. He leaned on Nokhada's hard,
warm shoulder and blacked out a moment, felt the chill of
the cellar about him, the cords holding him. Heard the
footsteps—

He tried to lift the bags to his shoulder.

A hand met his and took them away from him. "It's no
weight for me," the man said, and he stood there stupidly,
locked between believing in a compassion atevi didn't
have and fearing the canniness that might well have
Cenedi behind it—he didn't know, he couldn't think, he
didn't want to make an issue about it, when it was even
remotely possible they didn't even realize he had the machine with him. Djinana had brought it. The handlers had
loaded it.

The man walked off. Nokhada brushed him aside and
wandered off across the hill in a general movement of the
mecheiti: a man among Ilisidi's guard had gotten onto
Babs and started away as the whole company began to
move out, afoot now, presumably toward the wall Ilisidi
had foretold, where, please God, the gate would be open,
the way Ilisidi had said, nothing would be complicated
and they could all board the plane that would carry them
straight to Shejidan.

The man who'd taken the bags outpaced him with long,
sure strides up the hill in the dark, up where Cenedi and
Ilisidi were walking, which only confirmed his worst suspicions, and he needed to keep that man in sight—he
needed to advise Banichi what was going on, but Banichi

was leaning on Jago and on another man, further down the slope, falling behind.

He didn't know which to go to, then—he couldn't get a private word with Banichi, he couldn't keep up with both. He settled for limping along halfway between the two groups, damning himself for not being quicker with an answer that would have stopped the man from taking the saddlebags and not coming up with anything now that would advise Banichi what was in that bag without advising the guard with him—as good as shout it aloud, as say anything to Banichi now.

Claim he needed something from his personal kit?

It might work. He worked forward, out of breath, the hill going indistinct on him by turns.

"Nadi," he began to say.

But as he came up on the man, he saw the promised wall in front of them, at the very crest of the hill. The ancient gate was open on a starlit, weed-grown road.

They were already *at* Wigairiin.

XV

The wall was a darkness, the gate looked as if it could never again move on its hinges.

The shadows of Ilisidi and Cenedi went among the first into an area of weeds and ancient cobblestones, of old buildings, a road like the ceremonial road of the Bu-javid, maybe of the same pre-Ragi origin—the mind came up with the most irrational, fantastical wanderings, Bren thought, desperately tagging the one of Ilisidi's guards who had his baggage, and his computer.

Banichi and Jago were behind him somewhere. The ones in front were going in as much haste as Ilisidi could manage, using her cane and Cenedi's assistance, which could be quite brisk when Ilisidi decided to move, and she had.

"I can take it now, nadi," Bren said, trying to liberate the strap of his baggage from the man's shoulder much as the man had gotten it away from him. "It's no great difficulty. I need something from the kit."

"No time now to look for anything, nand' paidhi," the man said. "Just stay up with us. Please."

It was damned ridiculous. He lost a step, totally off his balance, and then grew angry and desperate, which didn't at all inform him what was reasonable to do. Stick close to the man, raise no more issue about the bags until they stopped, try to claim there was medication he had to have as soon as they got to the plane and then stow the thing under his seat, out of view ... that was the only plan he could come up with, trudging along with aches in every bone he owned and a headache that wasn't improving with exertion.

They met stairs, open-air, overgrown with weeds, where the walk began to pass between evidently abandoned buildings. That went more slowly—Ilisidi didn't deal well with steps; and one of the younger guards simply picked her up after a few steps and carried her in his arms.

Which with Banichi wasn't an option. Bren looked back, lagged behind, and one of the guards near him took his arm and pulled him along, saying,

"Keep with us, nand' paidhi, do you need help?"

"No," he said, and started to say, Banichi does.

Something banged. A shot hit the man he was talking to, who staggered against the wall. Shots kept coming, racketing and ricocheting off the walls beside the walk, as the man, holding his side, jerked him into cover in a doorway and shoved his head down as gunfire broke out from every quarter.

"We've got to get out of here," Bren gasped, but the guard with him slumped down and the fire kept up. He tried in the dark and by touch to find where the man was hit—he felt a bloody spot, and tried for a pulse, and couldn't find it. The man had a limpness he'd never felt in a body—dead, he told himself, shaking, while the fire bounced off walls and he couldn't tell where it was coming from, or even which side of it was his.

Banichi and Jago had been coming up the steps. The man lying inert against his knee had pulled him into a protected nook that seemed to go back among the weeds, and he thought it might be a way around and down the hill that didn't involve going out onto the walk again.

He let the man slide as he got up, made a foolish attempt to cushion the man's head as he slid down, and in agitation got up into a crouch and felt his way along the wall, scared, not knowing where Ilisidi and Cenedi had gone or whether it was Tabini's men or the rebels or what.

He kept going as far as the wall did, and it turned a corner and went downhill a good fifty or so feet before it met another wall, in a pile of old leaves. He retreated, and met still another when he tried in the other direction.

The gunfire stopped, then. Everything stopped. He sank down with his shoulders against the wall of the cul de sac and listened, trying to still his own ragged breaths and stop shaking.

It grew so still he could hear the wind moving the leaves about in the ruins.

What *is* this place? he asked himself, seeing nothing when he looked back down the alleyway but a lucent slice of night sky, starlight on old brick and weeds, and a section of the walk. He listened and listened, and asked himself what kind of place Ilisidi had directed them into, and why Banichi and Jago didn't realize the place was an ancient ruin. It felt as if he'd fallen into a hole in time—a personal one, in which he couldn't hear the movements he thought he should hear, just his own occasional gasps for breath and a leaf skittering down the pavings.

No sound of a plane.

No sound of anyone moving.

They couldn't all be dead. They had to be hiding, the way he was. If he went on moving in this quiet, somebody might hear him, and he couldn't reason out who'd laid the ambush—only it seemed likeliest that if they'd just opened fire, they didn't care if they killed the paidhi, and *that* sounded like the people out of Maidingi Airport who'd lately been dropping bombs.

So Ilisidi and Cenedi were wrong, and Banichi was right, and their enemies had gotten into the airport here, if there truly was an airport here at all.

Nobody was moving anywhere right now. Which could mean a lot of casualties, or it could mean that everybody was sitting still and waiting for the other side to move first, so they could hear where they were.

Atevi saw in the dark better than humans. To atevi eyes, there was a lot of light in the alley, if somebody looked down this way.

He rolled onto his hands and a knee, got up and went as quietly as he could back into the dead end of the alley, sat down again and tried to think—because if he could get to Banichi, or Cenedi, or any of the guards, granted these were Ilisidi's enemies no less than his—there was a chance of somebody knowing where he was going, which he didn't; and having a gun, which he didn't; and having the military skills to get them out of this, which he didn't.

If he tried downhill, to go back into the woods—but they were fools if they weren't watching the gate.

If he could possibly escape out into the countryside . . . there was the township they'd mentioned, Fagioni— but there was no way he could pass for atevi, and Cenedi or Ilisidi, one or the other, had said Fagioni wouldn't be safe if the rebels had Wigairiin.

He could try to live off the land and just go until he got to a politically solid border—but it had been no few years since botany, and he gave himself two to three samples before he mistook something and poisoned himself.

Still, if there wasn't a better chance, it was a chance—a man could live without food, as long as there was water to drink, a chance he was prepared to take, but—atevi night-vision being that much better, and atevi hearing being quite acute—a move now seemed extremely risky.

More, Banichi must have seen him ahead of him on the steps, and if Banichi and Jago were still alive ... there was a remote hope of them locating him. He was, he had to suppose, a priority for everyone, the ones he wanted to find him and the ones he most assuredly didn't.

His own priority ... unfortunately ... no one served. He'd lost the computer. He had no idea where the man with his baggage had gone, or whether he was alive or dead; and he couldn't go searching out there. Damned mess, he said to himself, and hugged his arms about him beneath the heat-retaining rain-cloak, which didn't help much at all where his body met the rain-chilled bricks and paving.

Damned mess, and at no point had the paidhi been anything but a liability to Ilisidi, and to Tabini.

The paidhi was sitting freezing his rump in a dead-end alley, where he had no way to maneuver if he heard a search coming, no place to hide, and a systematic search was certainly going to find him, if he didn't do something like work back down the hill where he'd last seen Banichi and Jago, and where the gate was surely guarded by one side or the other.

He couldn't fight an ateva hand to hand. Maybe he might find a loose brick.

If—

He heard someone moving. He sat and breathed quietly, until after several seconds the sound stopped.

He wrapped the cloak about him to prevent the plastic rustling. Then, one hand braced on the wall to avoid a scuff of cold-numbed feet, he gathered himself up and went as quickly and quietly as his stiff legs would carry him, in the only direction the alley afforded him.

He reached the guard's body, where it lay at the entry to the alley, touched him to be sure beyond a doubt he hadn't left a wounded man, and the man was already cold.

That was the company he had, there in the entry where old masonry made a nook where a human could squeeze in and hide, and a crack through which he could see the walk outside, through a scraggle of weeds.

Came the least small sound of movement somewhere, up or down the hill, he wasn't sure. He found himself short of breath, tried to keep absolutely still.

He saw a man then, through the crack, a man with a gun, searching the sides and the length of the walk—a man without a rain-cloak, in a different jacket than anyone in Cenedi's company.

One of the opposition, for certain. Looking down every alley. And coming to his.

He drew a deep, deep breath, leaned his head back against the masonry and turned his face into the shadow, tucked his pale hands under his arms. He heard the steps come very close, stop, almost within the reach of his arm. He guessed that the searcher was examining the guard's body.

God, the guard was armed. He hadn't even thought about it. He heard a soft movement, a click, from where the searcher was examining the body. He daren't risk turning his head. He stayed utterly still, until finally the searcher went all the way down the alley. A flashlight flared on the walls down at the dead end, where he had recently hidden. He stayed still and tried not to shiver in his narrow concealment while the man walked back again, this time using the flashlight.

The beam stopped short of him. The searcher cut the flashlight off again, perhaps fearing snipers, and, stepping over the guard's body, went his way down the hill.

Mopping up, he thought, drawing ragged breaths. When he was as sure as he could make himself that the search had passed him, he got down and searched the dead guard for weapons.

The holster was empty. There was no gun in either hand, nor under the body.

Damn, he thought. He didn't naturally *think* in terms of weapons, they weren't his ordinary resort, and he'd made a foolish and perhaps a fatal mistake—he was up against professionals, and he was probably still making mistakes, like in being in this dead end alley and not thinking about the gun before the searcher picked it up; they were doing everything right and he was doing everything wrong, so far, except they hadn't caught him.

He didn't know where to go, had no concept of the place, just of where he'd been, but he'd be wise, he decided, at least to get out of the cul de sac; and following the search seemed better than being in front of it.

He got up, wrapped the cloak about him to be as dark as he could, and started out.

But the same instant he heard voices down the street and ducked back into his nook, heart pounding.

He didn't know where the solitary searcher had gone. He grew uncertain what was going on out there now— whether the search might have turned back, or changed objectives. He didn't know what a professional like Banichi might know or expect: having no skill at stealth, he decided the only possible advantage he could make for himself was patience, simply outlasting them in staying still in a concealment one close search hadn't penetrated. They hadn't night-scopes, none of the technology humans had known without question atevi would immediately apply to weaponry. They didn't use any tracking animals, except mecheiti, and he hoped there were no mecheiti on the other side. He'd seen one man ripped up.

He stood in shadow while the searchers passed, also bound downhill, and while they, too, checked over the dead man almost at his feet, and likewise sent a man down to look through the alley to the end. They talked together in low voices, some of it too faint to hear, but they talked about a count on their enemies, and agreed that this was the third sure kill.

They went away, then, down the hill, toward the gate.

A long while later he heard a commotion from that quarter, a calling out of instructions, by the tone of it. The voices stopped; the movements went on for some time, and eventually he saw other men, not their own, walking down toward the gate.

That way of escape was shut, then. There *wasn't* a way out the gate. If any of their party was alive, they weren't going to linger down there, he could reason that. The force was concentrating behind him for a sweep forward, and he visualized what he in his untrained and native intelligence would do—hold that gate shut until morning and scour the area inside the gate by daylight.

He took a breath, looked through the screen of weeds growing in the chinks in the wall near his head, and ducked out again onto the walk, wrapped in his plastic cloak and aiming immediately for the next best cover, a nook further on.

He found another alley. He took it, trying to find somewhere in it a small dark hole that a searcher might not automatically think to look into even in a daylight search. He could fit where adult atevi wouldn't fit. He could squeeze into places searchers couldn't follow and might not realize a human could fit.

He followed the alley around two turns, feared it might dead-end like the other one, then saw open space ahead— saw flat ground, blue lights, and a hill, and a great house sprawling up and up that hill, with its own wall, and white lights showing.

Wigairiin, he said to himself, and saw the jet down at the end of the runway, sitting in shadow, its windows dark, its engines silent.

Ilisidi hadn't lied, then. Cenedi hadn't. There was a plane and it had waited for them. But something had gone terribly wrong, the enemy had moved in, taken Wigairiin the way Banichi had warned them they might. Banichi had been right and no one had listened, and he was here, in the mess he was in.

Banichi had said Tabini would move against the rebels—but there was that ship up in the heavens, and Tabini couldn't talk to Mospheira unless they'd sent Hanks, and, damn the woman, Hanks wasn't going to be helpful to an aiji fighting to solidify his support, to a population dissolving uneasy associations and lesser aijiin trying to position themselves to survive the fall of the aiji in Shejidan. Hanks had outright *said* to him that the country assocations didn't matter, he'd argued otherwise, and Hanks had refused to understand why he adamantly took the position that they did.

All around him was the evidence that they did.

And Ilisidi and Cenedi *hadn't* lied to him. The plane existed—no one had lied, after all, not their fault the rebels had figured their plan. It got to his gut that, at least that far, the atevi he was with hadn't betrayed him. Ilisidi had possibly meant all along to go to Shejidan—until something had gone mortally wrong. He leaned against the wall with a knot in his throat, light-headed, and trying to reason, all the same, it didn't mean they didn't mean to go somewhere else, but after hours convinced they were being dragged into a trap, knowing at least that the trap closing around him was not the doing of people he'd felt friendly . . .

Felt friendly, *felt, friendly* . . . Two words the paidhi didn't use, but the paidhi was clearly over the edge of personal *and* professional judgment. He wiped at his eyes with a shaking hand, ventured as carefully as he knew along the frontage of abandoned buildings, among weeds and past old machinery, still looking for that place to hide, with no idea how long he might have to hold out, not knowing how long he could hold out, against the hope of Tabini taking Maidingi and moving forces in to Wigairiin along the same route they'd come.

Give or take a few days, a few weeks, it might happen, if he could stay free. Rainy season. He wouldn't die of thirst, hiding out in the ruins. A man could go unfed for a week or so, just not move much. He just needed a place—any place, but best one where he might have some view of what came and went.

He saw old tanks of some kind ahead, facing the field, oil or jet fuel or something, he wasn't sure, but the ground was grown up with weeds and they didn't look used. They offered a place, maybe, to hide in the shadows where they met the wall—his enemies might expect him down closer to the gate, not on the edge of the field, watching them, right up in an area where they probably worked. . . .

Another, irrational flash on the cellar. He didn't see where he was, saw that dusty basement instead and knew he was doing it. He reached out and put his hand on the wall to steady himself—retained presence of mind enough at least to know he should watch his feet, there'd been other kinds of debris around, in a disorder not ordinary for atevi. Old machine parts, old scrap lumber, old building stone, in an area Wigairiin clearly didn't keep up.

Knocked down an ancient wall to build the airstrip, Ilisidi had said that. Didn't care much for the old times.

Ilisidi did. Didn't agree with the aijiin of Wigairiin on that point.

They'd talked about dragonettes, and preserving a national treasure. And the treasure was being blasted with explosives and atevi were killing each other—for fear of humans, in the name of Tabini-aiji, sitting where Ilisidi had worked all her life to be—

Dragonettes soaring down the cliffs.

Atevi antiquities, leveled to build a runway, so a progressive local aiji didn't have to take a train to Maidingi.

He reached the tanks, felt the rusted metal flake on his hands—blind in the dark, he slid down and squirmed his way into the nook they made with the wall—lay down, then, in the wet weeds underneath the braces.

Wasn't sure where he was for a moment. He didn't hurt as much. Couldn't see that conveniently out of the hole he'd found, just weeds in front of his face. His heart beat so heavily it jarred the bones of his chest. He'd never felt it do that. Didn't hurt, exactly, nothing did, more than the rest of him. Cold on one side, not on the other, thanks to the rain-cloak.

He'd found cover. He didn't have to move from here. He could shut his eyes.

He didn't have to think, either, just rest, let the aches go numb.

He wished he'd done better than he'd done.

Didn't know how he could have. He was alive and they hadn't found him. Better than some of the professionals had scored. Better luck than poor Giri, who'd been a decent man.

Better luck than the man who'd dragged him to cover before he died—the man hadn't thought about it, he supposed; he'd just done, just moved. He supposed it made most difference what a man was primed to do. Call it love. Call it duty. Call it—whatever mecheiti did, when the bombs fell around them and they still followed the mecheit'-aiji.

Man'chi. Didn't mean duty. That was the translation on the books. But what had made the man grab him with the last thought he had—that was *man'chi,* too. The compulsion. The drive that held the company together.

They said Ilisidi hadn't any. That aijiin didn't. Cosmic loneliness. Absolute freedom. Babs. Ilisidi. Tabini.

I send you a man, 'Sidi-ji. . . .

Wasn't anything Tabini wouldn't do, wasn't anything or anyone Tabini wouldn't spend. Human-wise, he still *liked* the bastard.

He still *liked* Banichi.

If anybody was alive, Banichi was. And Banichi would have done what that man had done with the last breath in him—but Banichi wouldn't make dying his first choice: the bastards would pay for Banichi's life, and Jago's.

Damn well bet they were free. They were Tabini's, and Tabini wasn't here to worry about.

Just him.

They'd have found him if they could.

Tears gathered in the corners of his eyes. One ran down and puddled on the side of his nose. One ran down his cheek to drip off into the weeds. Atevi didn't cry. One more cosmic indignity nature spared the atevi.

But, over all, decent folk, like the old couple with the grandkids, impulses that didn't add up to love, but they felt something profound that humans couldn't feel, either. Something maybe he'd come closer to than any paidhi before him had come—

Don't wait for the atevi to feel love. The paidhi trained himself to bridge the gap. Give up on words. Try feeling *man'chi.*

Try feeling why Cenedi'd knocked hell out of him for going after Banichi on that shell-riddled road, try feeling what Cenedi had thought, plain as shouting it: identical *man'chi,* options pre-chosen. The old question, the burning house, what a man would save . . .

Tabini's people, with their own *man'chi,* together, in Ilisidi's company.

Jago, violate *man'chi?*

Not Banichi's partner.

I won't betray you, Bren-ji, . . .

Shut up, *nadi Bren.*

Believe in Jago, even when you didn't understand her. Feel the warm feeling, call it whatever you wanted; she was on your side, same as Banichi.

Warm feeling. That was all.

There was early daylight bouncing off the pavings. And someone running. Someone shouting. Bren tried to move—his neck was stiff. He couldn't move his left arm from under him, and his right arm and his legs and his back were their own kind of misery. He'd slept, didn't remember picking the position, and he couldn't damned move.

"Hold it!" came from somewhere outside.

He reached out and cautiously flattened the weeds in

front of his nose, with the vast shadow of the tank over his head and the wall cramping his ankle and his knee at an angle.

Couldn't see anything but a succession of buildings along the runway. Modern buildings. He didn't know how he'd gotten from ruins to here last night. But it was cheap modern, concrete prefab—two buildings, a windsock. Electric power for the landing lights, he guessed; maybe a waiting area or a machine shop. The wall next to the tank above him was modern, he discovered, sinking down again to ease the strain on his back.

Left arm hurt, dammit. Good and stiff. The legs weren't much better. Couldn't quite straighten the one and couldn't, with the one shoulder stiff, conveniently turn over and get more room.

Gunshots. Several.

Someone of their company, still alive out there. He listened to the silence after, trying to tell himself it wasn't his affair, and wondering who'd be the last caught, the last killed—he couldn't but think it could well be Banichi or Jago, while he hid, shivering, and knowing there wasn't a damned thing he could do.

He felt—he didn't know what. Guilty for hiding. Angry for atevi having to die for him. For other atevi being willing to kill, for mistaken, stupid reasons, and humans doing things that had nothing to do with atevi—in human minds.

Someone shouted—he couldn't hear what. He wriggled up on the elbow again, used the back of his hand to flatten the weeds on the view he had of the space between his building and the other frontages.

He saw Cenedi, and Ilisidi, the dowager leaning on Cenedi's arm, limping badly, the two of them under guard of four rough-looking men in leather jackets, a braid with a blue and red ribbon on the one of them with his back to him—

Blue and red. Blue and red. *Brominandi's* province.

Damn him, he thought, and saw them shove Cenedi

against the wall of the building as they jerked Ilisidi by the arm and made her drop her cane. Cenedi came away from the wall bent on stopping them, and they stopped him with a rifle butt.

A second blow, when Cenedi tried to stand up. Cenedi wasn't a young man.

"Where's the paidhi?" they asked. "Where is he?"

"Shejidan, by now," he heard Ilisidi say.

They didn't swallow it. They *hit* Ilisidi, and Cenedi swung at the bastards, kicked one in the head before he took a blow from a rifle butt full in the back and another one on the other side, which knocked him to one knee.

They had a gun to Ilisidi's head, then, and told him stop.

Cenedi did stop, and they hit him again and once more.

"Where's the paidhi?" they kept asking, and hauled Cenedi up by the collar. "We'll shoot her," they said.

But Cenedi didn't know. Couldn't betray him, even to save Ilisidi, because Cenedi didn't know.

"Hear us?" they asked, and slapped Cenedi in the face, slamming his head back into the wall.

They'd do it. They were *going* to do it. Bren moved, bashed his head on the tank over him, hard enough to bring tears to his eyes, and, finding a rock among the weeds, he flung it.

That upset the opposition. They shoved Cenedi and Ilisidi back and went casting about for who'd done it, talking on their radio to their associates.

He really had hoped Cenedi could have taken advantage of that break, but they'd had their guns on Ilisidi, and Cenedi wasn't leaving her or taking any chances with her life—while the search went up and down the frontage and back into the alley.

Boots came near. Bren flattened himself, heart pounding, breaths not giving him air enough.

Boots went away, and a second pair came near.

"Here!" someone shouted.

Oh, damn, he thought.

"You!" the voice bellowed, and he looked up into the barrel of a rifle poking through the weeds, and a man lying flat, the other side of that curtain, staring at him down that rifle barrel, with a certain shock on his face.

Hadn't seen a human close up, Bren thought—it always jarred his nerves, to see that moment of shock. More so to know there was a finger on the trigger.

"Come out of there," the man ordered him.

He began to wiggle out of his hole, not noble, nothing gallant about the gesture or the situation. Damned stupid, he said to himself. Probably there was something a lot smarter to have done, but his gut couldn't take watching a man beaten to death or a brave old woman shot through the head: he wasn't built that way.

He reached the daylight, crawling on his belly. The rifle barrel pressed against his neck while they gathered around him and searched him all over for weapons.

Besides, he said to himself, the paidhi wasn't a fighter. The paidhi was a translator, a mediator—*words* were his skill, and if he was with Ilisidi, he might even have a chance to negotiate. Ilisidi had some kind of previous tie to the rebels. There might be a way out of this. . . .

They jerked the rain-cloak off him. The snap resisted, the collar ripped across his neck. He tried to get a knee under him, and two men caught him by the arms and jerked him to his feet.

"He's no more than a kid," one said in dismay.

"They come that way," red-and-blue said. "I saw the last one. Bring him!"

He tried to walk. Wasn't doing well at it. The left arm shot blinding pain, and he didn't think they'd listen to argument, he only wanted to get wherever they were going—and hoped they'd bring Cenedi and Ilisidi with him. He needed Ilisidi, needed someone to negotiate *for*, himself and his loyalties being the bargaining chip. . . .

Claim *man'chi* to Ilisidi: they'd read his actions that way—they could, at least, if he lied convincingly.

They hauled him into the next building, and Cenedi

and Ilisidi *were* behind him, held at gunpoint, shoved up against the wall, while they said someone's neck was broken—the man Cenedi had kicked, Bren thought dazedly, and tried to make eye contact with Ilisidi, staring at her in a way atevi thought rude.

She looked straight at him. Gave a tightening of her mouth he didn't immediately read, but maybe she caught his offer—

Someone grabbed him by the shirt and spun him around and back against the furniture—red-and-blue, it was. A blow exploded across his face, his sight went out, he wasn't standing under his own power, and he heard Cenedi calmly advising the man humans were fragile and if he hit him like that again he'd kill him.

Nice, he thought. Thanks, Cenedi. You talk to him. Son of a bitch. Tears gathered in his eyes. Dripped. His nose ran, he wasn't sure with what. The room was a blur when they jerked him upright and somebody held his head up by a fist in his hair.

"Is this yours?" red-and-blue asked, and he made out a tan something on the table where red-and-blue was pointing.

His heart gave a double beat. The computer. The bag beside it on the table.

They had it on recharge, the wire strung across the table.

"Mine," he said.

"We want the access."

He tasted blood, felt something running down his chin that swallowing didn't stop. Lip was cut.

"*Tell* us the access code," red-and-blue said, and gave a jerk on his shirt.

His brain started functioning, then. He knew he wasn't going to get his hands on the computer. Had to make them axe the system themselves. Had to remember the axe codes. Make them *want* the answer, make them believe it was all-important to them.

"Access code!" red-and-blue yelled into his face.

Oh, God, he didn't like this part of the plan.

"Fuck off," he said.

They didn't know him. Set himself right on their level with that answer, he did—he had barely time to think that before red-and-blue hit him across the face.

Blind and deaf for a moment. Not feeling much. Except they still had hold of him, and voices were shouting, and red-and-blue was giving orders about hanging him up. He didn't entirely follow it, until somebody grabbed his coat by the collar and ripped it and the shirt off him. Somebody else grabbed his hands in front of him and tied them with a stiff leather belt.

He figured it wasn't good, then. It might be time he should start talking, only they might not believe him. He stood there while they got a piece of electrical cable and flung it over the pipes that ran across the ceiling, using it for a rope. They ran the end through his joined arms and jerked them abruptly over his head.

The shoulder shot fire. He screamed. Couldn't get his breath.

A belt caught him in the ribs. Once, twice, three times, with all the force of an atevi arm. He couldn't get his feet under him, couldn't get a breath, couldn't organize a thought.

"Access code," red-and-blue said.

He couldn't talk. Couldn't get the wind. There was pain, and his mind went white-out.

"You'll kill him!" someone screamed. Lungs wouldn't work. He was going out.

An arm caught him around the ribs. Hauled him up, took his weight off the arms.

"Access," the voice said. He fought to get a breath.

"Give it to him again," someone said, and his mind whited out with panic. He was still gasping for air when they let him swing, and somebody was shouting, screaming that he couldn't breathe.

Arm caught him again. Wood scraped, chair hit the

floor. Something else did. Squeezed him hard around the chest and eased up. He got a breath.

Who gave you the gun, nand' paidhi?

Say it was Tabini.

"Access," the relentless voice said.

He fought for air against the arm crushing his chest. The shoulder was a dull, bone-deep pain. He didn't remember what they wanted. "No," he said, universal answer. No to everything.

They shoved him off and hit him while he swung free, two and three times. He convulsed, tore the shoulder, couldn't stop it, couldn't breathe.

"Access," someone said, and someone held him so air could get to his lungs, while the shoulder grated and sent pain through his ribs and through his gut.

The gun, he thought. Shouldn't have had it.

"Access," the man said. And hit him in the face. A hand came under his chin, then, and an atevi face wavered in his swimming vision. "Give me the access code."

"Access," he repeated stupidly. Couldn't think where he was. Couldn't think if this was the one he was going to answer or the one he wasn't.

Second blow across the face.

"The code, paidhi!"

"Code . . ." Please, God, the code. He was going to be sick with the pain. He couldn't think how to explain to a fool. "At the prompt . . ."

"The prompt's up," the voice said. "Now what?"

"Type . . ." He remembered the real access. Kept seeing white when he shut his eyes, and if he drifted off into that blizzard they'd go on hitting him. "Code . . ." The code for meddlers. For thieves. "Input date."

"Which?"

"Today's." Fool. He heard the rattle of the keyboard. Red-and-blue was still with him, someone else holding his head up, by a fist in his hair.

"It says 'Time,' " someone said.

"Don't. Don't give it. Type numeric keys ... 1024."

"What's that?"

"That's the code, dammit!"

Red-and-blue looked away. "Do it."

Keys rattled.

"What have you got?" red-and-blue asked.

"The prompt's back again."

"Is that it?" red-and-blue asked.

"You're in," he said, and just breathed, listening to the keys, the operator, skillful typist, at least, querying the computer.

Which was going to lie, now. The overlay was engaged. It would lie about its memory, its file names, its configuration ... it'd tell anyone who asked that things existed, tell you their file sizes and then bring up various machine code and gibberish, that said, to a computer expert, that the files did exist, protected under separate passcodes.

The level of their questions said it would get him out of Wigairiin. Red-and-blue was out of his depth.

"What's this garbage?" red-and-blue demanded, and Bren caught a breath, eyes shut, and asked, in crazed delight:

"Strange symbols?"

"Yes."

"You're into addressing. What did you *do* to it?"

They hit him again.

"I asked the damned file names!"

"Human language."

Long silence, then. He didn't like the silence. Red-and-blue was a fool. A fool might do something else foolish, like beat him to death trying to learn computer programming. He hung there, fighting for his breaths, trying to get his feet under him, while red-and-blue thought about his options.

"We've got what we need," red-and-blue said. "Let's pack them up. Take them down to Negiran."

Rebel city. Provincial capital. Rebel territory. It was the

answer he wanted. He was going somewhere, out of the cold and the mud and the rain, where he could deal with someone of more intelligence, somebody of ambition, somebody with strings the paidhi might figure how to pull, on the paidhi's own agenda . . .

"Bring them, too?"

He wasn't sure who they meant. He turned his head while they were getting him loose from the pipes, and saw Cenedi's bloodied face. Cenedi didn't have any expression. Ilisidi didn't.

Mad, he said to himself. He hoped Cenedi didn't try any heroics at this point. He hoped they'd just tie Cenedi up and keep him alive until he could do something—had to think of a way to keep Cenedi alive, like ask for Ilisidi.

Make them *want* Ilisidi's cooperation. She'd been one of theirs. Betrayed them. But atevi didn't take that so personally, from aijiin.

He couldn't walk at first. He yelled when they grabbed the bad arm, and somebody hit him in the head, but a more reasonable voice grabbed him, said his arm was broken, he could just walk if he wanted to.

"I'll walk," he said, and tried to, not steadily, held by the good arm. He tried to keep his feet under him. He heard red-and-blue talking to his pocket-com as they went out the door into the cold wind and the sunlight.

He heard the jet engines start up. He looked at the plane sitting on the runway, kicking up dust from its exhaust, and tried to look back to be sure Cenedi and Ilisidi were still with them, but the man holding his arm jerked him back into step and bid fair to break that arm, too.

Long walk, in the wind and the cold. Forever, until the ramp was in front of them, the jet engines at the tail screaming into their ears and kicking up an icy wind against his bare skin. The man holding him let go his arm and he climbed, holding the thin metal handrail with his good hand, a man in front of him, others behind.

He almost fainted on the steps. He entered the sheltered, shadowed interior, and somebody caught his right arm, pulled him aside to clear the doorway. There were seats, empty, men standing back to let them board— Cenedi helped Ilisidi up the steps, and the other men came up after Cenedi.

A jerk on his arm spun him away. He hit a seat and missed sitting in it, trying to recover himself from the moveable seat-arm as a fight broke out in the doorway, flesh meeting bone, and blood spattering all around him. He turned all the way over on the seat arm, saw Banichi standing by the door with a metal pipe in his hand.

The fight was over, that fast. Men were dead or half-dead. Ilisidi and Cenedi were on their feet, Jago and three men of their own company were in the exit aisle, and another was standing up at the cockpit, with a gun.

"Nand' paidhi," Banichi gasped, and sketched a bow. "Nand' dowager. Have a seat. Cenedi, up front."

Bren caught a breath and slumped, bloody as he was, into the airplane seat, with Banichi and Cenedi in eye-to-eye confrontation and everyone on the plane but him and Jago in Ilisidi's *man'chi*.

Ilisidi laid a hand on Cenedi's arm. "We'll go with them," the dowager said.

Cenedi sketched a bow, then, and helped the aiji-dowager to a seat, picking his way and hers over bodies the younger men were dragging out of the way.

"Don't anybody step on my computer," Bren said, holding his side. "There's a bag somewhere . . . don't step on it."

"Find the paidhi's bag," Banichi told the men, and one of the men said, in perfect solemnity, "Nadi Banichi, there's fourteen aboard. We're supposed to be ten and two crew—"

"*Up* to ten and crew," somebody else called out, and a third man, "Dead ones don't count!"

On Mospheira, they'd be crazy.

"So how many are dead?" the argument went, and Cenedi shouted from up front, "The pilot's leaving! He's *from* Wigairiin, he wants to see to the household."

"That's one," a man said.

"Let that one go," Bren said hoarsely, with the back of his hand toward the one who'd said his arm was broken, the only grace they'd done him. They were tying up the living, stacking up the dead in the aisle. But Banichi said throw out a dead one instead.

So they dragged red-and-blue to the door and tossed him, and the live one, the one who'd resigned as their pilot, scrambled after him.

Banichi hit the door switch. The door started up. The engines whined louder, the brake still on.

Bren shut his eyes, remembering that height Ilisidi had said rose beside the runway. That snipers could stop a landing.

They could stop a takeoff, then, too.

The door had shut. Engine-sound built and built. Cenedi let off the brakes and gunned it down the runway.

Banichi dropped into the seat next the window, splinted leg stiff. Bren gripped his seat arm, fit to rip the fabric, as rock whipped past the windows on one side, buildings on the other. Then blue-white sky on the left, still rock on the right.

Sky on both sides, then, and the wheels coming up.

"Refuel, probably at Mogaru, then fly on to Shejidan," Banichi said.

Then, then, he believed it.

XVI

He hadn't thought of Barb when he'd thought he was dying, and that was the bitter truth. Barb, in his mind and in his feelings, went off and on like a light switch . . .

No, *off* was damned easy. *On* took a fantasy he flogged

to desperate, dutiful life whenever the atevi world closed
in on him or whenever he knew he was going back to
Mospheira for a few days' vacation.

'Seeing Barb' was an excuse to keep his family at
arms' length.

'Seeing Barb,' was the lie he told his mother when he
just wanted to get up on to the mountain where his family
wasn't, and Barb wasn't.

That was the truth, though he'd never added it up.

That was his life, his whole humanly-speaking emotional *life,* such of it as wasn't connected to his work, to
Tabini and to the intellectual exercise of equivalencies,
numbers, and tank baffles. He'd known, once, what to do
and feel around human beings.

Only lately—he just wanted the mountain and the wind
and the snow.

Lately he'd been happy with atevi, and successful with
Tabini, and all of it had been a house of cards. The things
he'd thought had made him the most successful of the
paidhiin had blinded him to all the dangers. The people
he'd thought he trusted . . .

Something rough and wet attacked his face, a strong
hand tilted his head back, something roared in his ears,
familiar sound. Didn't know what, until he opened his
eyes on blood-stained white and felt the seat arm under
his right hand.

The bloody towel went away. Jago's dark face hovered
over him. The engine drone kept going.

"Bren-ji," Jago said, and mopped at a spot under his
nose. Jago made a face. "Cenedi calls you immensely
brave. And very stupid."

"Saved his damn—" Wasn't a nice word in Ragi. He
looked beside him, saw Banichi wasn't there. "Skin."

"Cenedi knows, nadi-ji." Another few blots at his face,
which fairly well prevented conversation. Then Jago hung
the towel over the seat-back ahead of him, on the other
side of the exit aisle, and sat down on his arm rest.

"You were mad at me," he said.

"No," Jago said, in Jago-fashion.

"God."

"What is 'God?' " Jago asked.

Sometimes, with Jago, one didn't even know where to begin.

"So you're not mad at me."

"Bren-ji, you were being a fool. I would have gone with you. You would have been all right."

"Banichi couldn't!"

"True," Jago said.

Anger. Confusion. Frustration, or pain. He wasn't sure what got the better of him.

Jago reached out and wiped his cheek with her fingers. Business-like. Saner than he was.

"Tears," he said.

"What's 'tears'?"

"God."

" 'God' is 'tears'?"

He had to laugh. And wiped his own eyes, with the heel of the hand that worked. "Among other elusive concepts, Jago-ji."

"Are you all right?"

"Sometimes I think I've failed. I don't even know. I'm supposed to understand you. And most of the time I don't know, nadi Jago. Is that failure?"

Jago blinked, that was all for a moment. Then:

"No."

"I can't make *you* understand me. How can I make others?"

"But I do understand, nadi Bren."

"*What* do you understand?" He was suddenly, irrationally desperate, and the jet was carrying him where he had no control, with a cargo of dead and wounded.

"That there is great good will in you, nadi Bren." Jago reached out and wiped his face with her fingers, brushed back his hair. "Banichi and I won over ten others to go with you. All would have gone. —Are you all right, nadi Bren?"

His eyes filled. He couldn't help it. Jago wiped his face repeatedly.

"I'm fine. Where's my computer, Jago? Have you got it?"

"Yes," Jago said. "It's perfectly safe."

"I need a communications patch. I've got the cord, if they brought my whole kit."

"For what, Bren-ji?"

"To talk to Mospheira," he said, all at once fearing Jago and Banichi might not have the authority. "For Tabini, nadi. Please."

"I'll speak to Banichi," she said.

They'd charged the computer for him. The bastards had done that much of a favor to the world at large. Jago had gotten him a blanket, so he wasn't freezing. They'd passed the border and the two prisoners at the rear of the plane were in the restroom together with the door wedged shut, the electrical fuse pulled, and the guns of two of Ilisidi's highly motivated guards trained on the door. Everybody declared they could wait until Moghara Airport.

Reboot, mode 3, m-for-mask, then depress, mode-4, simultaneously, SAFE.

Fine, easy, if the left hand worked. He managed it with the right.

The prompt came up, with, in Mosphei': *Input date.*

He typed, instead, in Mosphei': *To be or not to be.*

System came up.

He let go a long breath and started typing, five-fingered, calling up files, getting access and communications codes for Mospheira's network, pasting them in as hidden characters that would trigger response-exchanges between his computer and the Mospheira system.

The rebels, if they'd gotten into system level, could have flown a plane right through Mospheira's defense line.

Could have brought down Mospheira's whole network. Fouled up everything from the subway system to the earth station dish—unless Mospheira, being sane, had long since realized he was in trouble and changed those codes.

But that didn't mean they were totally out of commission. They'd just get a different routing until he got clearance.

He hunted and pecked, key at a time, through the initial text.

Sorry I've been out of touch. . . .

Banichi had been forward in the plane, standing up, talking to Ilisidi and one of her men, who was sitting at the front. Now he came down the aisle, leaning on seatbacks, favoring the splinted ankle.

"Get off your feet, damn it!" Bren said, and muttered, politely, "Nadi."

Banichi worked his way to the seat beside him, in the exit aisle, and fell into it with a profound sigh, his face beaded with sweat. But he didn't look at all unhappy, for a man in excruciating pain.

"I just got hold of Tabini," Banichi said. "He says he's glad you're all right, he had every confidence you'd settle the rebels single-handed."

He had to laugh. It hurt.

"He's sending his private plane," Banichi said. "We're re-routed to Alujisan. Longer runway. Cenedi's doing fine, but he says he's getting wobbly and he's not sorry to have a relief coming up. We'll hand the prisoners over to the local guard, board a nice clean plane and have someone feed us lunch. Meanwhile Tabini's moving forces in by air as far as Bairi-magi, three-hour train ride from Maidingi, two hours from Fagioni and Wigairiin. Watch him offer amnesty next—*if,* he says, you can come up with a reason to tell the hasdrawad, about this ship, that can calm the situation. He wants you in the court. Tonight."

"With an answer." He no longer felt like laughing. "Banichi-ji, atevi have all the rights with these strangers on the ship. We on Mospheira don't. You know our presence in this solar system was an accident . . . but our landing wasn't. We were passengers on that ship. The crew took the ship and left us here. They said they were going to locate a place to build. We weren't damned happy about their leaving, and they weren't happy about our threat to land here. Two hundred years may not have improved our relationship with these people."

"Are they here to take you away?"

"That would make some atevi happy, wouldn't it?"

"Not Tabini."

Damned sure not Tabini. Not the pillar of the Western Association. That was why there were dead men on the plane with them: fear of humans was only part of it.

"There are considerable strains on the Association," Banichi said somberly. "The conservative forces. The jealous. The ambitious. Five administrations have kept the peace, under the aijiin of Shejidan and the dictates of the paidhiin. . . ."

"We don't dictate."

"The iron-fisted suggestions of the paidhiin. Backed by a space station and technology we don't dream of."

"A space station that sweeps down from orbit and rains fire on provincial capitals at least once a month—we've had this conversation before, Banichi. I had it with Ilisidi's men in the basement. I just had it, abbreviated version, with the gentlemen in the back of the plane, who broke my arm, thank you very much, nadi, but we don't have any intention of taking over the planet this month." He was raving, losing his threads. He leaned his head back against the seat. "You're safe from them, Banichi. At least as far as them coming down here. They don't like planets to live on. They want us to come up there and maintain their station for them, free of charge, so they can go wherever they like and we fix what breaks and supply their ship."

"So they will make you go back to the station?" Banichi asked.

"Can't get at us, I'm thinking. No landing craft. At least they didn't have one. They'll have to wait for *our* lift capacity." He began to see the pieces, then, in a crazed sort of way, while the arm hurt like bloody hell. "Damned right they will. The Pilots' Guild will negotiate. They're scared as hell of you."

"Of *us?*" Banichi asked.

"Of the potential for enemies." He turned his head on the head rest. "Time works differently for space travelers. Don't ask me how. But they think in the long term. The very long term. You're not *like* them, and they can't keep you at the bottom of a gravity slope forever." He gave a dry, short laugh. "That was the feud between us from the outset, that some of us said we had to deal with atevi. And the Pilots' Guild said no, let's slip away, they'll never notice us."

"You're joking, nadi."

"Not quite," he said. "Get some sleep, Banichi-ji. I'm going to do some computer work."

"On what?"

"Long-distance communications. Extreme long distance."

Ilisidi was on her feet, hovering over Cenedi's shoulder, Banichi and Jago were leaning over his. He had the co-pilot's seat. It was a short patch cord.

"So what do you do?" Ilisidi asked.

"I hit the enter key, nand' dowager. Just now. It's talking."

"In numbers."

"Essentially."

"How are these numbers chosen?"

"According to an ancient table, nand' dowager. They don't vary from that model—which I assure you we long ago gave to atevi." He watched the incoming light, waiting, waiting. The yellow light flickered and his heart jumped. "Hello, Mospheira."

"Can they hear us?" Ilisidi asked.

"Not what we say, at the moment. Only what we input."

"Dreadful changes to the language."

" 'Put in,' then, nand' dowager." Lights flashed in alternation. *ID,* came up. The plane was on autopilot, and Cenedi diverted his attention to watch the crawl of letters and numbers on a small screen, all of which ended in:

—the further content of the lines wasn't available to the screen.

Humans had, at least in design, set up the atevi system. It answered very well when a human transmission wanted through. The systems were talking to each other, thank God, thank God.

The plane hit bumpy air. Pain jolted through the nerve ends in the shoulder. Things went gray and red, and for a moment he had to lean back, lost to here and now.

"Nand' paidhi?" Jago's hand was on his cheek.

He opened his eyes. Saw a message on the screen.

The Foreign Office wanted to talk on the radio. He'd a headset within reach. He raked it up and fumbled with it, one-handed. Jago helped him. He told Cenedi the frequency, heard the hail sputtering with static.

"Yeah," he said to the voice that reached him, "it's Cameron. A little bent but functioning on my own. Where's Hanks?"

There was a delay—probably for consultation. They hadn't, the report was, finally, heard from Hanks. She'd gone into Shejidan and dropped into a black hole four days ago.

"Probably all right. The atevi have noticed we've got company upstairs. Ours, I take it?"

The Foreign Office said:

"That's Phoenix, *in a high-handed mood."*

"What's the situation with it?" he asked, and got back: *"Touchy."*

"You want atevi cooperation? You want an invitation to *be* here?"

Are you under duress? the code phrase came back at him.

He laughed. It hurt, and brought tears to his eyes. "Priority, priority, priority, FO One. Just bust Hanks' codes back to number two and give me the dish on Adams, tonight, in Shejidan. I am *not* under duress."

The Foreign Office alone couldn't authorize it—so the officer in charge claimed.

"FO, I'm sitting here talking in Mosphei' with a half a dozen extremely high-ranking atevi providing me this link on their equipment. I'd say that's a fair amount of trust, FO, please relay to the appropriate levels."

Atevi didn't have a word for trust. The Foreign Office said so.

"They've got words we don't have either, FO. Go with Hanks or go with me. This is a judgement call I'm required to make. We *need* the aiji's permission to be on this planet, FO. Then where's *Phoenix'* complaint?"

The Foreign Office thought they'd talk to the President.

"Do that," he said. "Much nicer if my call to *Phoenix* goes out through the dish on Adams. But the intersat dish on Mogari-nai is the aiji's alternative, and I think he'll use it, directly. Atevi could deal without me in the loop. If they wanted to. Do you understand? Tabini's government is under pressure. That's the disturbance in Maidingi Province. That's where I've been. Tabini has to make a response to this ship. He'll offer Mospheira a chance for input in that response. United front, FO. I think I can get that arrangement."

Three hours, the Foreign Office said. They'd have to talk to the President. Assemble the council.

"Three hours max, FO. We're *in* the Western Association, let me remind you. Tabini will act ultimately in the best interests of the Association. I earnestly suggest we join them."

The Foreign Office signed off. The computer exchange tailed off. He shut his eyes, felt a little twinge of human responsibility. Not much. He'd be human after the hasdrawad met. After he'd talked to Tabini. He'd get a plane to Mospheira . . . trust the hospitals there to know where to put the pieces.

"Nand' paidhi," Banichi said after a moment.

They couldn't have followed that exchange. Banichi might have followed every third word of it, but none of the rest of them. Damned patient, they were. And very reasonably anxious.

"Tell Tabini," he said, "prime the dish on Mogari-nai to talk to that ship up there, tonight. I think we'll get the one on Allan Thomas, but when you're dealing with Mospheira, nadiin, you always assure them you have other choices."

"What other choices," Ilisidi said, "do we tell that ship up there we have?"

Sharp woman, Ilisidi.

"What choice? The future of relations between atevi and humans. Cooperation and association and trade. The word is 'treaty,' nand' dowager. They'll listen. They have to listen."

"Rest," Jago said, behind him, and brushed his hair back from his forehead. "Bren-ji."

Didn't want to move for the moment. It hurt enough getting up here to the cockpit.

Figure that Tabini probably knew everything they'd just said—give or take the computer codes; and don't bet heavily on that, once the experts got after it. Anything you used, numerically speaking, to get past atevi, you couldn't go on using.

But peace was in everyone's interests. Certainly it was in Tabini's. And in the interest of humans, ship's crew and planet-bound colonists a long, long way from the homeworld.

He'd told Djinana they might walk on the moon. Lay bets on it, now, he would. Granted Malguri was still standing.

He made an effort to fold up the computer. Jago shut the case for him, and disconnected the cord. After that—the necessity of getting up.

He made it that far. Ended up with Banichi's arm around him, Banichi standing on one leg. The dowager-aiji said something rude about young men falling at her feet, and go sit down, *she* was in command of the plane.

"Let me," Jago said, and got an arm about his middle, which stabilized the aisle considerably.

Banichi limped after them. Sat down beside him.

"Long distance, is it?" Banichi said. "If you go up there, we go, nadi."

He couldn't say he understood Jago *or* Banichi, *or* Tabini.

Couldn't say they understood him.

Scary thought, Banichi had. But he suddenly saw it as possible, even likely, when negotiations happened, when Mospheira got that lift vehicle, or the ship up there built one in order to deal with them. Atevi were going into space. No question. In his lifetime.

Baji-naji. The lots came down, Fortune and Chance made their pick. You weren't born with your associates. You found *man'chi* somewhere, and you entered into something humans didn't quite fathom with an altogether atevi understanding.

But in the way of such things, maybe atevi hadn't found the exact words for it, either.

Pronunciation

A=ah after most sounds; =ay after j; e=eh or =ay; i varies between ee(hh) (nearly a hiss) if final, and ee if not; o=oh and u=oo. Choose what sounds best.

-J is a sound between ch and zh; -ch=tch as in itch; -t should be almost indistinguishable from -d and vice versa. G as in *go*. -H after a consonant is a palatal (tongue on roof of mouth). as: paidhi=pait'-(h)ee.

The symbol ' indicates a stop: a'e is thus two separate syllables, ah-ay; but ai is not; ai=English long i; ei=ay.

The word accent falls on the second syllable from the last if the vowel in that syllable is long or is followed by two consonants; third from end if otherwise: Ba'nichi (ch is a single letter in atevi script and does not count as two consonants); Tabi'ni (long by nature)--all words ending in -ini are -i'ni; Brominan'di (-nd=two consonants); mechei'ti (because two vowels sounded as one vowel) count as a long vowel. If confused, do what sounds best: you have a better than fifty percent chance of being right by that method, and the difference between an accented and unaccented syllable should be very slight, anyway.

Also, a foreign accent if at least intelligible can sound quite sexy.

Plurality: There are pluralities more specific than simply singular and more-than-one, such as a set of three, a thing taken by tens, and so on, which are indicated by endings on a word. The imprecise more-than-one is particularly chosen when dealing in diplomacy, speaking to children, or, for whichever reason, to the paidhi. In the non-specific plural, words ending in -a usually go to -i; words ending in -i usually go to -iin. Ateva is, for instance, the singular, atevi the plural, and the adjectival or descriptive form.

Suffixes: -ji indicates intimacy when added to a name or good will when added to a title; -mai or -ma is far more reverential, with the same distinctions.

Terms of respect: nadi (sir/madam) attaches to a statement or request to be sure politeness is understood at all moments; nandi is added to a title to show respect for the dignity of the office. Respectful terms such as *nadi* or the title or personal name with *-ji* should be inserted at each separate address or request of a person unless there is an established intimacy or unless continued respect is clear within the conversation. *Nadi* or its equivalent should always be injected in any but the mildest objection; otherwise the statement should be taken as, at the least, brusque or abrupt, and possibly insulting. Pronunciation varies between nah'-dee (statement) and nah-dee'? (as the final word in a question.)

There are pronouns that show gender. They are used for nouns which show gender, such as mother, father; or in situations of intimacy. The paidhi is advised to use the genderless pronouns as a general precaution.

Declension of sample noun

Singular	Non-specific plural
aiji Nominative	aijiin Nom pl. Subject The aiji
aijiia Genitive	aijiian Gen pl. Possession's, The aiji's
aiji Accusative	aijiin Acc. Pl. Object of action (to/against) the aiji
aijiu Ablative	aijiiu Abl. Pl. From, origins, specific preposition often omitted: (emanating from, by) the aiji

Glossary

Adjaiwaio	a remote atevi population
Algini	glum servant's name, security agent
Alujis	river Brominani disputes re water rights
agingi'ai	felicitous numerical harmony
aiji	lord of central association
aijiia	aiji's
ateva, pl. atevi	name of species
Babsidi	"Lethal"; a mecheita
Banichi	security agent
Barjida	aiji of Shejidan during the War
Bergid	mountain range visible from Shejidan
Brominandi	provincial governor, long-winded
baji	Fortune
bihawa	impulse to test newcomers
biichi-gi	finesse in removing obstacles
bloodfeud	principal means of social adjustment
bowing	done, if deep, with hands on knees
Dajoshu	township of Banichi's origin
dahemidei	a believer in the midei heresy
Didaini	a province visible from Malguri
Dimagi	an intoxicant
dajdi	an alkaloid stimulant
haronniin	systems under stress, needing adjustment
hasdrawad	lower house of atevi legislature
hei	of course
Ilisidi	grandmother of Tabini
insheibi	indiscreet, provoking attention

Intent, filing of	legal notification to the victim of Feud
Jago	security agent
kabiu	'in the spirit of good traditional example'
Maidingi	Lake Maidingi
Maiguri	estate at Lake Maidingi
Matiawa	breed of Ilisidi's horse
Moni	servant of Bren
Mospheira	human enclave on island; also name of island
Mosphei'	human language
machimi	historical drama with humor and revenge
man'chi	primary loyalty to association or leader
man'china	grammatical form of man'chi
man'chini	grammatical form of man'chi
mecheita	riding animal
midarga	an alkaloid stimulant, noxious to humans
midedeni	a supporter of the midei heresy
midei	a heresy regarding association
mishidi	awkward, regarding others' position
Nisebi	province that allows processed meat
nadi	mister
nadi-ji	honored mister
nai'aijiin	provincial lords, pl. form
nai'am	I am
nai'danei	you two are
na'itada	refusing to be shaken
nai-ji	respected person
naji	Chance
nand', nandi	honorable
Nokhada	"Feisty"; a mecheita

o'oi-ana	nocturnal quasi-lizard, likes vines
paidhi	interpreter
paidhi-ji	sir interpreter
Ragi	culture to which Tabini belongs; eats game only
Ragi Association	Tabini's area, also known as the Western Assc'n
ribbons, document	important in culture, on braids, documents
ribbons, braid	status, class
ribbon, color	says who's in what class
rings, finger	ornamental and official: used as seals
Shejidan	City of the Ragi Association
Shigi	township in weather report
sigils, document	marks on documents, seals
somai	together
Tabini	aiji of the Ragi
Tachi	herding community once on Mospheira
tadiiri	sister
Tadiiri	The Sister, fortress near Malguri
Taigi	previous servant of Bren
Taimani	province visible from Malguri
Talidi	Province of Banichi
Tano	more cheerful partner of Algini
Toby	Bren's brother
Transmontane	crossmountain Highway
tashrid	upper house of the legislature
Valasi	Tabini's father
Weinathi Bridge	bridge in the city, site of air crash
wi'itkiti	dragonette
Wilson	Bren's predecessor
Wingin	city mentioned in weather report
-ji	sir; miss; ma'am
-ma	honored sir, honored lady

C.J. CHERRYH
THE ALLIANCE-UNION UNIVERSE

DAW

More Top-Flight Science Fiction and Fantasy from
C.J. CHERRYH

SCIENCE FICTION
- [ ] HESTIA   UE2208—$2.95
- [ ] WAVE WITHOUT A SHORE   UE2101—$2.95

THE MORGAINE CYCLE
- [ ] GATE OF IVREL (BOOK 1)   UE2321—$3.95
- [ ] WELLS OF SHIUAN (BOOK 2)   UE2322—$3.95
- [ ] FIRES OF AZEROTH (BOOK 3)   UE2323—$3.95
- [ ] EXILE'S GATE (BOOK 4)   UE2254—$3.95

COLLECTION
- [ ] VISIBLE LIGHT   UE2129—$3.50

FANTASY
The Ealdwood Novels
- [ ] THE DREAMSTONE   UE2013—$2.95
- [ ] THE TREE OF SWORDS AND JEWELS   UE1850—$2.95

S. Andrew Swann

☐ **FORESTS OF THE NIGHT**   UE2565—$3.99

When Nohar Rajasthan, a private eye descended from genetically manipulated tiger stock, is hired to look into a human's
murder, he finds himself caught up in a conspiracy that in-
cludes federal agents, drug runners, and a deadly canine assassin. And he hasn't even met the real enemy yet!

☐ **EMPERORS OF THE TWILIGHT**   UE2589—$4.50

She was the ultimate agent. Her name: Evi Isham, her species:
frankenstein, her physiology bioengineered to make her the
best in the business. Evi has suddenly found herself on the
run from an unidentified enemy, and even the Agency might
not be able to save her from those who sought her life!

☐ **SPECTERS OF THE DAWN**   UE2589—$4.50

This is the story of Angelica Lopez, a moreau descended from
rabbit stock. When Byron the fox comes into her life, Angel
finds herself dragged into the deadly underground of information peddling, and exposed to a series of confrontations that
could blow the whole country wide open!

C.S. Friedman

☐ **IN CONQUEST BORN**　　　　　　　　　　　UE2198—$5.99

Braxi and Azea—two super-races fighting an endless war. The Braxaná—created to become the ultimate warriors. The Azeans, raised to master the powers of the mind. Now the final phase of their war is approaching, spearheaded by two opposing generals, lifetime enemies— and whole worlds will be set ablaze by the force of their hatred.

☐ **THE MADNESS SEASON**　　　　　　　　　　UE2444—$5.99

For 300 years, the alien Tyr had ruled Earth, imprisoning the true individualists, the geniuses, and forcing them to work on projects which the Tyr hoped would reveal humankind's secrets. But Daetrin's secret was one no one had ever uncovered. Taken into custody by the Tyr, he would have to confront the truth about himself at last—and if he failed, all humans would pay the price. . . .

The Coldfire Trilogy

☐ **BLACK SUN RISING (Book 1)**　　　　　　　　UE2527—$5.99
　　　　　　　　　　　　　　　　Hardcover Edition:　UE2485—$18.95

Centuries after being stranded on the planet Erna, humans have achieved an uneasy stalemate with the *fae*, a terrifying natural force with the power to prey upon people's minds. Now, as the hordes of the dark *fae* multiply, four people— Priest, Adept, Apprentice, and Sorcerer—are drawn inexorably together to confront an evil beyond imagining.

☐ **WHEN TRUE NIGHT FALLS (Book 2)**
　　　　　　　　　　　　　　　　Hardcover Edition:　UE2569—$22.00

Determined to seek out and destroy the source of the *fae*'s ever-strengthening evil, Damien Vryce, the warrior priest, and Gerald Tarrant, the immortal sorcerer known as the Hunter, dare the treacherous crossing of the planet's greatest ocean to confront a power that threatens the very essence of the human spirit.
